Drifting Together

A Bethany Beach Summer Romance

Robin Paul

Lakewood Ranch, Florida

monday, may 16

BETHANY BEACH.

The welcome sign greeted visitors along Coastal Highway like it had been since Austin McGinnis was a kid. He blew the horn of his Mustang, his way of saying hello to his home for the next three months. Sunny days and sandy beaches. The crash of waves and the squawk of gulls. Late nights and later mornings.

And Savannah.

He peered into the rearview mirror to make sure she hadn't gotten lost at the last intersection. She caught his eye and stuck her tongue out. He stuck his out too, then returned his attention to the road just in time to see something large and yellow entering the crosswalk a few yards ahead. He jammed on the brakes and felt the seat belt grab as the car screeched to a stop six feet short of the crosswalk.

A woman on a yellow cruiser bike glared at him from under a white floppy hat as she pedaled through the crosswalk. "Bikes have the right of way," she shouted as she adjusted her oversized sunglasses. Austin didn't argue. His legs were shaking, and he was sweating through his shirt.

"Sorry," he said feebly.

The woman turned and motioned behind her, to where another cyclist labored to catch up. She smiled and waved as she passed, too far behind to have seen Austin nearly run down her friend. He waved back, then double-checked the crosswalk before moving on. He was still shaky several blocks later when he came upon a skateboarder waiting patiently for traffic to clear. Not wanting to take a chance, Austin stopped and motioned for the kid to cross.

"Cool car, mister!" he called out.

Mister? When had he become a mister? Didn't a guy at least have to be out of college to be addressed as mister?

Austin gave him a thumbs up, but the kid's attention had shifted to Savannah's red BMW convertible. Or perhaps he was checking out Savannah. He might be a kid, but he was still a guy, and Savannah was definitely worth checking out.

Austin took a left onto Parkwood Street and glimpsed the dunes leading to the Atlantic Ocean. He lowered his window and breathed the salt air as he pulled into the driveway of the raised two-story that would be their home away from home for the next few weeks. He jumped out of the car and met Savannah as she parked beside him.

"That woman in the big ugly hat shouldn't have yelled at you like that," she complained as she unbuckled her seat belt. "You weren't that close to hitting her."

Austin smiled and hoped she didn't notice how much he was sweating as he opened her door. She squealed with delight as she looked past him to the house. "I can't believe we're spending the whole summer here!"

"Well..." Austin pulled her close and kissed her forehead. "Not the whole summer, but at least until the Fourth of July."

Savannah turned to get a better look at the house that had been one of Austin's family rental properties for the past five years. "Can I invite some friends down?"

"Sure. The place has four bedrooms."

She squealed again. She was beautiful when she was happy. Jaw-droppingly beautiful. Beautiful enough to turn heads wherever they went. Austin's University of Pennsylvania frat brothers often kidded him about dating above his pay grade. One of them, an upperclassman on the Penn wrestling team, had put the moves on Savannah soon after she and Austin started dating sophomore year. She had rebuffed the guy's advances, then told Austin. Since the guy outweighed him by sixty pounds and was used to throwing other guys around for sport, Austin let it slide.

"Want the grand tour?" he asked as he pulled up the door code on his phone.

Savannah purred as she took his hand and led him up the steps. "Only after I show you how much I appreciate getting to spend the summer with you."

KATHRYN SHEA STOPPED her bike on the sidewalk and waited for her friend Jane to catch up.

"How inconsiderate was that?" she grumbled.

"What?" Jane asked, red-faced and panting from the minimal effort of pedaling the bicycle. She had been oblivious to the squeal of brakes and Kathryn's shouted warning. It was just one more sign that her hearing was failing. Jane, at fifty-seven, twenty years older than Kathryn, was the least healthy of their small group of friends. The twice-weekly bicycle rides had been Kathryn's idea, but over the past two months Jane had bowed out of most of them.

"Oh nothing. We'll have to stay on the streets near my house when summer season starts." The near miss with the guy in the white car was a reminder that, in two weeks, she and Jane would risk their lives if they dared bike along Coastal Highway. They kept the pace leisurely as they chatted on the way to Kathryn's house on Sea Turtle Court, three blocks from the beach. Kathryn dismounted in front of what used to be her grandfather's workshop and pulled open the creaky door. The old shed was musty, and pinholes of sunlight found their way through the tin roof. She still picked up the faint smells of sawdust and motor oil, despite there having been none of either in the shed since her grandfather's passing three decades ago.

"Are you ready for a fun summer?" Jane asked as she pushed her bicycle to its usual spot. Jane had moved into a condo years earlier after her husband's death. Space was tight, so she kept her bike next to Kathryn's in the workshop.

"I will be when I finish summer semester in July." There was always summer semester. Kathryn disliked all the time it took, but loved the extra income; money she set aside to pay the house's exorbitant winter heating bills. The walls weren't insulated enough to stand up to the worst of Delaware winters, but it was a fair tradeoff for being within walking distance of the sand and surf.

She walked her friend to her car, then returned to the house. It was three in the afternoon, and she suspected Jane would stop at Dairy Queen on her way back to her condo. She saw she had a voice message on her phone but put off checking it after glancing at her laptop on the kitchen counter. She gasped when she spotted a heart on the dating app she had left open. After filling a glass with water, she clicked on the app and saw the latest message from *Rodney-SellsRehoboth*.

To kshea:

Kathryn had been clueless when she selected the screen name. Since joining the internet dating site, she'd read news stories about internet stalkers who hung out on dating sites, just waiting for people like her who chose screen names that made it easier to figure out who they were. Her only solace came from the fact that she was, according to one of those people-finder sites, one of sixty-some females in the state of Delaware with the surname Shea. If a stalker was going to hunt her down, he would have to work his way through the list.

Kathryn, I enjoyed meeting for coffee last week and was hoping we might have dinner this weekend. How about Saturday night? I can pick you up or we can meet somewhere. Good wishes, Rodney.

An online dating service was entirely out of character for her.

But darn it, she wanted more from life.

Hitting the button to sign up had nearly caused her to hyperventilate. Going three weeks with no response had cut deeper than she'd wanted to admit. Wasn't there someone for everyone?

But then came Rodney's message. *Meet for coffee?*

She'd accepted, then nearly backed out a dozen times. They met—*rendezvoused,* as they said in the movies—at a coffee shop in Ocean View. *RodneySellsRehoboth* was a local realtor. He talked about himself too much, but Kathryn figured that once he ran out of stuff to say about himself, he might ask about her life. It had been several years since she'd last been on a date, so she was willing to wait.

I would love it. Please pick me up at my home. 111 Sea Turtle Court in Bethany Beach.

She hit send and took a deep breath. She had a date. An actual date. Dinner. With a man.

What should she wear?

She got up from the table and was headed upstairs to figure that out when she remembered the voicemail. She returned to her phone and played the message.

"Kathryn, it's Casper. I need to visit with you this week. My schedule is open tomorrow morning at 10:15. If that works for you, I'll see you then. If not, please return this call. Thank you."

Casper was Casper Fillmore. Dean of Humanities at Lower Delaware Community College. He determined who taught what. He had only been at the college for a year, and word was he was already interviewing at larger colleges. A few of Kathryn's colleagues didn't trust him, but he had always been fair in his dealings with her. And she admired him for his drive and ambition. In some ways Casper *was* her, albeit five years younger. And male.

No. That wasn't right. Casper wasn't her at all. At least not as she was now. He was, she realized, who she *used* to be, back when she aspired to be more than an English instructor at a tiny junior college no one had heard of.

She jotted down the next day's appointment, then tapped her lip with the pen and tried to figure out when she had lost the ambition she admired in Casper Fillmore.

Was there a point when good became good enough? When her hope to fast track to important jobs at prestigious universities became a slow track? Or even a dead end?

She couldn't come up with the answers she sought, and that made her sad.

‖‖‖‖‖

AUSTIN'S PHONE BUZZED. It was probably his sister, Holly, back home in Philadelphia. She had a knack for calling at the most inopportune moments.

But it wasn't Holly this time. It was Dad.

"Did you get to Bethany okay, son?"

"I just got here."

"Have you checked our rentals? Does everything seem okay?"

"I've only seen the house on Parkwood. Everything looks okay there."

He wouldn't mention that he was speaking from the Parkwood's master suite. Or that Savanah was lying beside him. Dad was unaware that the family who had rented the house for six weeks canceled at the last minute, despite not being able to get their money back. Holly had taken over that side of the business since graduating from Penn three years earlier, and she'd said the renters didn't even put up a fuss when she told them there would be no refund. It sucked for them, but Austin was ecstatic. It was his ticket out of that awful efficiency apartment in the Windermere Building, a decrepit firetrap that was a summer home to carnies and concession stand vendors.

Things were great. And they would stay great as long as Dad didn't find out that his son and his son's girlfriend were occupying the Parkwood house.

"Now don't forget why you're there," Dad continued. "We fired the management company, so you're responsible for cleaning up after guests leave and getting everything shipshape for new arrivals."

Austin tried to hide his impatience as Dad went

7

through the same spiel he had given three times before. Clean up, address complaints, mow lawns, trim shrubs. Keeping up with the seven rental properties would be easy. The minimum rental was for three weeks, and the only time he had to clean up was when renters left on the last day. Complaints weren't an issue. It was the beach. No one complained when they were at the beach. The summer was going to be easy peasy.

"And don't forget your classes."

Geesh. Enough already.

"I won't, Dad."

"You should have never put yourself in this situation, Austin. It's up to you to get yourself out of it."

"I'll take care of it."

The *it* was Austin's grades. They weren't good. In fact, they were so bad that he was close to being placed on academic probation. The only way to avoid it was to get Bs in two courses he had flunked sophomore year. He would take them remotely, which at Penn meant virtual classes and online assignments.

Austin relaxed into the soft mattress as Dad went on about his tenuous standing at college. Savannah rubbed his shoulders for a few moments before pressing herself against him from behind. Austin had to strain to keep his mind on Dad's words until he finally took a breath.

"Dad, I know I didn't work as hard as I should have. I can do better, and I'll try not to let you down."

The line was quiet for a moment before Dad said, "You know how proud your mother and I are of you. We just want to make sure you keep your eye on the prize, son. You graduated from high school at the top of your class, and you've done pretty well at a tough university. But getting into law school is hard enough without the burden of having to repeat two classes."

And there it was. The issue at the center of everything.

Law school.

Mom and Dad wanted it—expected it—for him.

Austin, not so much.

"You enjoy the rest of the day, son, and be sure to stay on top of things, okay?"

"Yes, sir. I love you guys. Tell Mom I said hey."

Austin laid the phone on the nightstand. That ache in his gut was back, the one that came whenever his parents brought up the future. Savannah wrapped her arms around him from behind.

"You'll pass those classes and everything will be fine,"

But it won't, he wanted to tell her. *Yeah, I'll graduate next year, but then what?*

Law school. The bar exam. Then he would assume his spot as attorney for the family business. Just like it was supposed to be.

The thought of it made him feel as if he was backed into a corner.

He probably should tell Savannah. Share his feelings and all that stuff. She knew he wasn't enthused about three more years of college, but did she have any idea how much?

And besides, it wasn't something he wanted to think about at the moment. Savannah's hands were making him crazy.

tuesday, may 17

FOUR OF THE rental properties Austin's family owned were in Bethany Beach. The one on Parkwood was the largest. The others were two-bedroom cottages within walking distance of the beach. There were also a pair of bungalows and a condo six miles south, in Fenwick.

By 9:30, Austin had made stops at all seven. He inspected the yards and exteriors to make sure all was well, then took quick looks inside those that weren't yet occupied. The interiors were strikingly similar. Nautical decor was a big thing on the Delaware shore, and it was Mom's idea that all the McGinnis properties feature plenty of driftwood lamps and towels with anchors and seashells. Furnishings could be moved from one property to another without throwing off the theme.

Finding everything in place and ready for tourist season, Austin drove back to Bethany Beach. At a small market on the edge of town, he picked up a few necessities, including that crappy plain yogurt that Savannah mixed with berries and called a meal. His next stop was a fast food place for a bag of sausage biscuits. Savannah wouldn't touch them, which meant he would have the rest of the morning to devour the entire bag himself before they headed to the beach for some afternoon sun. After pulling away from the drive-through, he punched Savannah's number on his phone.

"Hello, sexy." Her voice was husky with sleep.

"I'm bringing food. I have one quick stop to make, so I should be there in about fifteen minutes."

"Did you get my—"

"Your Greek yogurt. Yeah, I got it."

He heard her take a deep, sleepy breath. "I'll be right where you left me. Hurry back."

The thought of where he'd left her and how she had snuggled against him caused Austin to press the accelerator a little firmer. He wouldn't break any speed limits, but he wouldn't waste any time, either.

But he had that one quick stop, at a cottage on Cedar-wood Street, just a few blocks from Parkwood. It was the first property his parents had purchased, way back when Austin was in elementary school, and he remembered wonderful summer weeks spent there, before they decided that income was more important than family vacations. He checked his list; the Ramsey family from Baltimore was staying there. They were in the second of a three-week rental.

Austin knocked on the door and waited until a short, balding man his dad's age answered.

"Yeah?" the man asked.

"Hi, Mr. Ramsey. I'm Austin McGinnis. Our family owns this property, and I just wanted to stop by and—"

"What are you talking about? Your family *what*?"

"We own this home, and I—"

Ramsey scowled at him and took a step back inside.

"This place is owned by some outfit called Cornerstone Properties. Now I don't know what your angle is, but if you're trying to scam me, you've come to the wrong place."

"No, sir. Our family is Cornerstone Properties. And I'm not here to scam you. My parents just wanted me to stop by and make sure that everything is okay."

"What did you say your name is?"

"Austin McGinnis."

"Well..." Ramsey glanced down the hallway. "Since you're here, we're having trouble with the downstairs toilet."

Oh, crap. Toilets were the worst.

"Yeah, there's something keeping it from flushing. I'm not sure what, but we've had to use the other bathroom since day before yesterday."

"It's probably just clogged, sir. There should be a plunger in the hallway closet. You can use it to—"

Ramsey's face puckered. "Are you nuts? I'm on vacation here, bud. I'm not sticking my hands in a john that ain't mine."

Austin forced a smile. "I'll have a look, sir."

WHAT WAS it about guys who preferred bow ties? Did they think they made them appear smarter? More academic? Casper Fillmore was the third humanities dean in the last seven years, and the second who wore bow ties. The ties, his thick round glasses, and an unfortunate overbite made him look like the lovechild of Teddy Roosevelt and Donald Duck.

"Good to see you, Kathryn," he said, getting to his feet as she entered his office. His light blue eyes looked like fishbowls behind the thick glasses. His handshake was soft. "Please have a seat."

The office was only slightly larger than Kathryn's, which was only slightly larger than a closet. Two chairs and a medium-sized desk left little room for much else. Casper had done an admirable job arranging his diplomas and awards on the wall behind him. They had the same number of diplomas—three—but Casper's awards and commendations easily outdistanced hers. Most prominent was a photo of him with a former United States vice president. Casper was barely into his thirties but was already on his way.

She sat down and smoothed the wrinkles in her clothes. She had selected her outfit, a pale yellow blouse and dark slacks, to communicate professionalism. When he had arrived, a couple of Kathryn's colleagues had suggested that maybe she and Casper would be a good romantic pairing, but Casper didn't seem the dating type. And besides, he was her boss. And kind of ugly.

"Do you have big summer plans?" he asked as he straightened a couple of knickknacks on the corner of his desk.

"Just my remedial English courses. You?"

"A quick getaway to my parents' place in Michigan, but mostly I'll be preparing for the fall semester." Casper eyed a folder on the corner of his desk, looked at her, then glanced away. He took a deep breath.

Okay. So there *was* something substantial he wanted to talk about.

"Kathryn, have you looked at the spring semester faculty evaluations?" he blurted.

"Are you referring to the evaluation you performed back in January? When you came into my composition course?"

Casper shook his head and took another deep breath.

"No, I'm referring to the evaluations that students complete at the end of each semester."

"I haven't. Honestly, Casper, we've never taken those seriously."

"Well... yes, I understand what you're saying, but they do have some value."

Kathryn stiffened. The previous deans, even the other bow tie wearer, had viewed student evaluations as meaningless. But one thing she had noticed about Casper Fillmore was that he gave student opinions more than just lip-service. He had upgraded student lounges, boosted Wi-Fi reception in classrooms, and, toward the end of spring semester, convened a student advisory panel.

"I'm not sure I see the value," Kathryn said. "A-students usually give good evaluations, and students with lower grades usually give lower evaluations."

"Maybe, but..." Casper blinked several times as he pulled off his glasses and wiped them with a tissue. Without them, he looked less like Donald Duck and more like Porky Pig. Regardless, this wasn't shaping up to be a cartoon type of moment. "Kathryn, your evaluations of the past two semesters have not followed that trend."

What was he saying? What did he mean by her evaluations didn't follow the trend? Kathryn felt her stomach tighten, but did her best to push it away. There was no way the college was giving credence to student evaluations. Was there?

Casper opened the file and picked up a chart with lines going in different directions. He placed it on the desk between them so she could see it. "Kathryn, the evaluation system we use accounts for your assertion that critical reviews only come from poor students. If you look right here..." He pointed to a blue line that ran nearly straight across the graph. "This represents evaluations adjusted for bias."

She had no idea what he was talking about. Bias?

"D and F students who give low assessments count for less of the total, as do A and B students who give high assessments. Does it make sense?"

Not really, but she wasn't going to appear stupid. "I suppose so."

"What we're learning, Kathryn, is that B and C students are some of your harshest critics." He moved his finger to another part of the graph where lines skewed up and down. "Even your best students say your class isn't particularly interesting or stimulating."

Her mind raced. How should she address what sounded like an insult of her teaching capabilities? Suzanne would know what to say. She had regaled Kathryn and their friends with stories of confrontations she'd had with the college administration while on the faculty senate. Yes, Suzanne faced things head-on. The only problem was, she wasn't Suzanne. She wasn't confrontational. That had never been her way.

But she couldn't just sit there and allow Casper Fillmore to disparage her. She was the longest-tenured instructor in the English department. In fact, she had applied for the very job Casper currently held. She hadn't gotten it, but she had applied. And she might apply again, once Casper moved on. "Casper, with all due respect, interesting and stimulating don't always apply to courses in the English department. I mean, some students just aren't turned on by Shakespeare or Chaucer."

There. She sat back. Satisfied that she had let him know how she felt.

Little good it did.

"But Kathryn, shouldn't more of your students, the ones who excel in your class, shouldn't they find the course material stimulating?"

"I believe that many find it stimulating. Perhaps they don't know how to express it on the evaluations."

Rather than respond, Casper picked up the chart. He turned to the next page. "These are student comments. I'll read a few."

"Seriously, Casper?" Kathryn tried to sound forceful, but the words came out squeaky and pleading.

"'Dr. Shea doesn't know who I am,'" he read. "'She seems indifferent to my situation. Assignments are boring and don't help me understand the topic. I asked for help and she couldn't remember my name. I learned more from reading on my own.'"

"Wow." Kathryn laughed. "I guess there's always one in every class, but do we want to allow that one person to—"

"Kathryn, that's not one student. Those are the comments of five students."

Kathryn's insides churned. Her lip quivered, and she was suddenly afraid of bursting into tears in front of Casper Fillmore. She bit her lip. "Five students? I teach a hundred and thirty students each semester."

"There are more like this, Kathryn, but I don't want to pile on." He slid the file to her. "Take a look."

▓▓▓▓

"THERE'S a tennis ball stuck in here," Austin said as he pulled it from the toilet.

"I don't know anything about that," Mr. Ramsey snapped. "You must have had some careless guests in the past."

Yeah, right. *A previous guest.* Austin did his best to ignore the tennis equipment next to the front door. And act like he didn't notice how Ramsey's ten-year-old son made himself scarce when he saw Austin rooting around in the toilet. The little putz.

When he held the ball up, Mr. Ramsey took a step back. "Dispose of it on your way out," he snipped. No thank you. No conversation. No offer of a glass of water or a cup of coffee. Austin went to the bathroom sink to wash his hands, but realized he would only soil them again when he picked up the tennis ball. He carried it outside and slam-dunked it in a bin next to the house, then leaned over the outdoor spigot to wash his hands.

A pretty brown-haired girl came up behind him. "My dumbass brother did it."

Austin turned and looked at her. "I know."

"Sorry that my dad is such a jerk."

"It's okay."

"And sorry you had to go fishing in our toilet."

Austin smiled. "Try to keep your brother from dumping any more tennis balls."

She laughed. "No promises. I'm Carly."

"Austin."

"Do you live here, Austin?"

"For the summer. I go to Penn."

"An Ivy League guy. That's cool. I go to West Virginia. Not as prestigious as Penn, but we're ranked as one of the ten best party schools, so there's that. Do you frat?"

"Yeah. I'm a Kappa."

"Wow! That's crazy. I'm a Kappa little sis."

Austin stood up and dried his hands on his shorts. Carly was nearly as tall as him, at least five-ten. Slender, with an athletic build.

17

She held his gaze.

"My family will be here clogging your toilets for the next ten days. Want to hang out?"

"It would be nice, but my girlfriend might not like it."

Carly pushed a strand of hair from her face. "She won't have to know. I mean, I've got a boyfriend in Ohio, but he's in Ohio."

"Savannah isn't in Ohio, though. She's about six blocks from here. Waiting for me to get back."

"Damn. And you're really good-looking. I was kinda hoping that we might... oh well, good meeting you, Austin."

Carly returned to the house. Austin headed to his car. Would it be too much to hope that Savannah's yogurt hadn't spoiled after nearly an hour in the morning sun? Or that his sausage biscuits were still edible?

Maybe the summer was going to be a bit more complicated than he had thought.

WHEN SHE GOT BACK HOME, Kathryn sat on the sofa and read through the list of student comments Casper had shared. It was like a bad movie that she couldn't stop watching. A really bad movie. Like, the worst ever.

I always got good grades until Dr. Shea's class.

"Maybe try working harder?" she mumbled.

We spent two weeks on the rules of good creative writing. If there are so many rules, why is it called CREATIVE writing?

"I explained it over and over again. Rules make you a better writer."

We read stuff by some guy named Tolkien. I have no idea what any of it was about.

"Perhaps you should have dug deeper or read a

commentary."

European Literature was a snore. I'm not even sure the teacher liked it.

"Shows what you know."

Instructor was impersonal.

"I'm not your mother. Or your best friend. We will not pal around after class, so grow up."

Dr. Shea is aloof.

"Where did you learn that word?"

"It's not that you're a weak teacher, Kathryn," Casper had said. "You're just not... *inspirational.*" He smiled with pride at his word choice. "You don't inspire excellence in your students."

They're the sons and daughters of farmers and fishermen, she'd wanted to say. *Good kids, but not exactly Ivy League material. They come to our school because they can't afford or don't have the grades to get into the local four-year schools like Salisbury or Delaware State.*

Didn't Casper understand that?

Obviously not, because he explained how students of any background deserved the very best the college could provide. His points were valid. He said little that Kathryn disagreed with. But after twelve years of facing row after row of blank stares and heavy eyelids, how much more could he expect?

Apparently much more.

He gave it to her in writing. Her first ever Professional Improvement Plan, or PIP.

Her? A PIP?

Kathryn had never known anyone who got a PIP. She'd heard stories about a sociology professor who got one for swearing in class, but that was it.

Now she knew someone.

She picked it up from the coffee table. It felt as if it weighed fifty pounds, though it was only four pages long. She started reading, but the tears returned before she made it past the first paragraph. She'd already had a good cry on the drive home. Didn't Casper understand she had tenure? In her twelve years at the college, she had chaired a half-dozen committees ranging from equal access to the President's Tea. She had been part of the delegation that welcomed Delaware's governor and a pair of state representatives to campus two years earlier. Her suggestion of *Excelling at Meeting Lower Delaware's Learning Needs!* had been a finalist for the college's new slogan. She was seventh among all faculty in terms of years of service.

Didn't Casper see those things were much more important than what a handful of kids wrote on some silly evaluation?

Obviously not, because on the last page of the PIP, Casper stated that unless her performance improved over the next two semesters, she would not have the option of teaching summer classes.

To some, that might be a reason to celebrate. Many of her colleagues stuck around because they had summers off. In a community where the beach was minutes away, a summer free of lesson planning and term papers was more than enough to counterbalance so-so salaries and terrible health insurance. Kathryn was different. When she had arrived at the college, summer classes were viewed as recognition for hard work and longevity. When the offer came to teach her department's summer remedial classes, she had jumped at it. Sure, it was a lot of work. And she was starting to miss having summers to do what she liked. But she craved the prestige and recognition. Casper's attempts to snatch that away cut deep.

She was supposed to sign the PIP and return it to Casper's office. She wiped her eyes and pulled up the faculty handbook to see what her rights were. Perhaps she could appeal his assessment. She had always gotten along well with Dr. Rosa Cuellar, the college's president. Rosa would agree that student evaluations shouldn't be held against her, wouldn't she? Kathryn scanned the handbook section on appeals. As a tenured faculty member, she had to go first to the faculty senate, who would review her situation and determine if she had a case.

She had friends on the faculty senate. They would certainly side with her.

But did she want them reading those dreadful student comments?

Instructor was impersonal.

Dr. Shea is aloof.

Even if they came from disgruntled students, the comments hurt. Were other faculty members rated low? Were their jobs on the line? Was there any way to find out?

Should she talk to Suzanne, her longtime friend and colleague? Suzanne taught in the econ department and was up on college politics.

But the thought of Suzanne seeing the comments made her stomach hurt worse.

A few years ago, she would have sought her mother's advice. Mom never worked in academia, but she had been a tenacious attorney and community leader in West Virginia. How many times over the past few years had Kathryn grabbed the phone to call her for advice, only to be hit by the reminder that she had passed away from breast cancer?

Nope, with Mom gone and her unwillingness to share her misery with Suzanne, there wasn't anyone left.

And that thought made her cry again.

21

THREE
saturday, may 21

KATHRYN WOKE to Ocean 95's morning weather and traffic report blasting through her grandparents' old clock radio.

Seventy-six and sunny with a gentle southerly breeze.

Perfect.

Ocean temperatures reaching seventy-two degrees.

Still chilly, but good for May. Perfect for long walks along the beach.

And traffic? Light, with no delays. Also perfect.

If everything was so darn perfect, why did she feel so perfectly miserable?

Oh yeah. The PIP. She still didn't know what to do about that.

"It's a beautiful day to be in Bethany Beach, folks," the deejay said as the opening notes to an old Fleetwood Mac song played in the background. "Enjoy it while you can, because *they* will be here before you know it."

They were tourists. The sun worshippers, beachgoers, anglers, boaters, and partiers who flocked to Bethany Beach from Memorial Day through Labor Day. Kathryn had heard estimates ranging from fifteen to fifty thousand of them each week, all hoping for a slice of heaven.

And she had to admit it was heavenly. At least until Casper Fillmore came along with his stupid PIP.

She hit the button to turn off the radio, but it didn't work, so she smacked it and pretended it was Casper Fillmore's head. That did the trick. How much did a new alarm clock cost anyway? Twenty bucks? She had no idea and didn't intend to find out. The old General Electric was a remnant from her childhood summers in Bethany Beach. It belonged there as much as she did.

Kathryn showered, then put on green capris and a white long-sleeve T-shirt, then added a jacket just in case she became chilly. She made her bed, checked herself in the mirror, and opened the shades. East side first, toward the beach. The sun was already climbing the sky, and if Kathryn peered past the Hungry Pelican and over the roof of that kitschy souvenir shop, she could see a sliver of the Atlantic. *Ocean view*, the rental agencies called it. From what she had seen in the real estate ads, a few properties claimed ocean views even when they were six blocks or more from the beach. Hers was a tiny view from one upstairs window, but a view, nonetheless.

She checked the time as she quickly pulled the shades on the west side. She glanced out, started to turn away, and did a double take.

Trash was strewn across the yard. Not as much as on the other side of the picket fence that separated her property from the place next door, but still a lot of trash. Beer cans, paper plates, and crumpled newspaper rustled in the breeze. It wasn't yet the official start of tourist season, but a few eager beavers always showed up early. And a few of those didn't care if their merriment infringed on her.

It wasn't the first time Kathryn had issues with renters. She kept the management company's phone number on a dry erase board for just such occasions. It was seven-forty. Their office didn't open until nine, but someone was always on call.

"Seahorse Property Management. This is Bruce."

"This is Dr. Kathryn Shea. I live at 111 Sea Turtle Court."

"How can I help you?" His voice took on a guarded edge. The people at Seahorse knew her. This wasn't the first time she'd had issues with the place next door.

"Your renters at 113 Sea Turtle Court have left trash and debris in the yard. A lot of it is on my side of the fence."

"Hold on a minute." Bruce put her on hold for a few moments before returning. "Dr. Shea, that property is no longer part of our portfolio. We can't help you."

"What do you mean?"

"The owners are managing it themselves. You'll have to call them."

"Who are they?"

"I can't help you with that. Sorry."

"So who do I call?"

"Can't help you with that, either."

Kathryn took a deep breath. "You have no additional information? No forwarding information? No phone number? Nothing?"

"Look, lady, I'm just the weekend guy. Call on Monday and speak to Mitch or one of the other reps."

"Should I also tell them how rude you were? Will they like hearing that, Bruce?"

She heard him sigh, then swear under his breath. "Give me a minute."

Bruce's minute stretched to five before he came back on

the line. "Okay, here's what I have. The owners are an outfit in Philly. Cornerstone Properties."

"What's the number?"

"I can't help you with that. You can probably find it on the internet. You know about the internet, right?" Bruce didn't stay on the line to hear her reply.

She went to her office in the back of the house and woke her laptop. A search for Cornerstone Properties provided a number that she dialed and fully expected to go to voice-mail, but a pleasant woman named Holly took Kathryn's information and promised that someone would address the issue that morning. Kathryn put on her jacket, rolled her bicycle from the shed, and pedaled off toward the boardwalk.

"I THINK YOU'RE GETTING A CALL."

Austin rolled over and pulled Savannah close. The pleasing fragrance of perfume lingered on her skin, mingling with less pleasant remnants of beer and cigarettes from a party they'd stumbled upon the night before. He hated the smell of cigarettes, but not enough to be turned off by the sight of Savannah's bare shoulder. He lightly kissed that shoulder, then her neck.

She groaned with pleasure.

His phone rang again.

He knew who was calling, so he ignored it. It was after three when he and Savannah had Ubered back to the house, and he was beat.

But he also knew what was expected of him. How could he forget? Dad had reminded him a dozen times.

He searched through the jumble of sheets until he

located his phone, then moaned when he saw his sister's name. He cleared his throat and answered.

"Hey."

"Austin, where are you?"

"Where do you think I am at this time of the morning?"

Savannah snuggled closer and murmured.

"Who's there with you? Is that Savannah?"

"None of your beeswax," he answered, repeating the line Holly always used when they were kids.

"The renters on Sea Turtle Court trashed the yard last night. The neighbor called to complain. You need to go clean it up."

"I didn't make the mess. Call the renters and tell them to clean it up."

"You know how that goes. They may clean up. They may not. I promised the neighbor that we would get right on it, so get right on it."

"You're not the boss of me, Holly." Another line they used to throw at one another.

"Yeah, this summer I kind of am. And I'm telling you to get over to Sea Turtle Court. And take a couple trash bags."

"Fine." He hung up and tossed his phone onto the nightstand.

"Who was it?" Savannah mumbled.

"My bossy sister. I have to go clean up somebody else's trash. Want to go with me?"

"Not a chance." Savannah turned toward him, put her arms around him, and drew him close. "I'm comfy right where I am."

Everything in him wanted to delay his departure. Or not go at all. Savannah was warm and ready. And she was right about the bed. It was incredible. Nothing like the brick of a mattress at the loft he shared with his brilliant nerdy friend, Derek, at the edge of the Penn campus.

Sea Turtle Court could wait a little longer. He kissed Savannah. She kissed him back.

His phone buzzed with a text message. He reached behind him and picked it up.

GET GOING!

"She really is bossy," Savannah complained as he got dressed. "My sister would never talk to me that way."

"Your sister isn't the property manager for your family business. Technically, I'm working for Holly this summer."

"My sister still wouldn't talk to me like that. What are we doing today?"

"I'm going to pick up trash. You're probably going back to sleep. Later we'll go to the beach, then tonight we'll drive down to that bar in Ocean City that we liked so much last year."

"That sounds fun. Don't be long," she said, pulling the covers over her head.

▥

THRILL SEEKERS WERE SOMETIMES disappointed by their first glimpse of the Bethany Beach boardwalk, but Kathryn thought it was perfect. The half-mile length and twelve-foot width made it ideal for casual strolls. Ocean City and Rehoboth Beach could keep their expansive boardwalks overrun with bicycles, rollerblades, and trams.

Milo's had, according to legend, served the same breakfast in the same location for half a century. There were a few locals who claimed to remember when it wasn't around, but they became scarcer by the year. It was one of the few boardwalk locations that unapologetically catered to locals, which seemed to make it even more popular with tourists. Sure, they grumbled every time a year-round resident was seated ahead of them, but they kept coming back.

There was never any question about Kathryn and her friends' standing at Milo's. Harvey Bodenschatz, the grizzled owner, made sure their table was waiting for them every Saturday at eight, even if it required he displace dawdling Philadelphia or Baltimore sunbirds. Harvey's rule for tourists was simple: one drink refill was fine. The second came in a to-go cup. If you didn't get the message, Harvey would call you out in front of everyone.

Her friends were sipping coffee when she arrived. Suzanne always showed up first. Hillary sat on her left, Jane across from her. Kathryn's usual seat was open. Hillary checked her watch as Kathryn pulled out her chair. It wouldn't be beyond her to comment that Kathryn was running fifteen minutes late. Or twelve minutes, because Hillary was like that. She was an accountant with an eye for minutiae. Instead, she said, "Glad you made it."

They shook their heads disapprovingly while Kathryn described the scene in her yard. Tourists were a common topic of conversation. They clogged the streets, disrespected traditions, and caused food and gas prices to skyrocket. What was usually left unsaid was that they infused the tiny community with revenue that provided jobs.

"What will you do?" Hillary asked.

"I called the management company. Hopefully someone shows up today."

"Don't hold your breath," Jane said.

They placed their breakfast orders. French toast for Kathryn and Hillary. Oatmeal for Suzanne, who always watched her weight. Bacon, eggs, and a blueberry waffle for Jane, who should be watching hers. Hillary asked their opinion of a movie that she and Stuart, her longtime boyfriend, were contemplating. Jane had heard it was quite good and might even win an Oscar, but Kathryn knew that wouldn't matter. Hillary and Stuart contemplated all kinds of things, from Mississippi River cruises to Las Vegas junkets. In the end, they always settled for Saturday night TV and a carryout sausage and pepperoni from Grotto Pizza. After all, Stuart had to be up early Sunday morning to teach his empty nesters class at the Methodist church.

Suzanne would spend her weekend completing a journal article about trends in economic education at community colleges, an article that likely wouldn't be read by anyone other than Suzanne. Jane was going to crochet a blanket for her niece's new baby. And Kathryn?

For the first time in forever, Kathryn had plans.

Her date with *RodneySellsRehoboth*.

Kathryn shared the details.

"Oh my gosh, Kathryn." Hillary said, her hand going to her heart. "What possessed you to do *that*?"

It was a fair question. The truth was, Kathryn was starting to feel she was growing old before her time. Suzanne, at forty-three, was six years older. The others were in their fifties. Jane was retired. They were further along in their lives, and Kathryn sometimes felt she was being pulled along with them. She was only thirty-seven. Not ready to throw in the towel yet, or settle for weekends of pizza and TV like Hillary and Stuart.

She wanted more.

She wanted romance.

But she wanted it on her terms.

Not like before, with Troy. It needed to be different this time. More about her, at least sometimes.

Kathryn noticed they were looking at her, waiting for her response. "I guess... it seemed like something worth trying. Men aren't exactly knocking down my door."

"Yes," Jane said, "but online dating? The internet?" She lowered her voice. "What if he's a stalker?"

"What if he has some weird shoe fetish?" Hillary asked.

"Then I'll send him to your house."

They laughed at Kathryn's reply. Hillary had twice as many shoes as the rest of them combined.

"He's not a stalker. He's a realtor in Rehoboth Beach."

"How old?" Jane asked.

"Forty-four."

"Kids?"

"Three. Two in college, the other living with his ex in Ohio."

"Oh, that's not good," Hillary said. "He doesn't see his children."

"Stop it, Hillary," Suzanne chided. "Any available middle-aged man is going to come with baggage." She turned to Kathryn. "Where is he taking you?"

"The Claypool in Ocean City."

"Oooh," Jane bubbled. "Roger used to take me there for our anniversary."

"Fancy, fancy," Hillary chimed in. "Just don't let him stick you with the bill."

"How about we meet back here tomorrow morning?" Suzanne suggested.

"On a Sunday?" Hillary asked. "What about church? I always go to Stuart's Sunday School class."

"We need to make sure Kathryn makes it home safely," Suzanne said, waving off Hillary. "Church has been around for two thousand years. They'll get by without you for a week."

"Actually, there has been church since way before that. Probably—"

"Save us the history lesson, Hillary," Suzanne said, cutting her off. "Jane?"

"I can be here. I'll record that handsome TV preacher I like."

"Good. Kathryn? How about it? Are you up to sharing the details?"

"I'll be here." She assumed a tone she hoped came across as breezy. "I've been meaning to ask you, Suzanne. Do you ever look at those evaluations the students complete at the end of every semester?"

"Never. But I heard someone say that Casper Fillmore might use them to get some of the faculty to step up their performance. Probably just rumor. If there's one thing I know about people at the college, it's that they love their rumors."

"Hmm," Kathryn said, pretending interest in something across the restaurant.

"Why do you ask?"

"I've heard the same rumors, and I was wondering what I would do if Casper tried something like that with me."

"I can tell you what I would do." Suzanne sipped her coffee, then leveled her gaze at Kathryn. "I would tell him to stick those evaluations where the sun don't shine. I'm tenured, and I'll be damned if some snotty-nosed burger flipper in a freshman econ class is going to dictate how I do my job."

Kathryn had no doubt that Suzanne would do just that. And get away with it. The economics department was just four instructors. Each had their specialty, and none had an interest in extra duties or assignments. Nor did they care to engage in school politics. That made Suzanne bulletproof. Kathryn envied her that. With eleven instructors, the English department offered an ambitious dean like Casper Fillmore the opportunity to hold prime teaching assignments as incentives, doling them out to faculty members he liked best.

It was tempting to spill the details about what she'd been through that week, but she knew Suzanne would tell her to fight with everything she had.

Kathryn wasn't a fighter, though. She never had been.

She just wanted the problem to go away.

⫟⫟⫟⫟⫟

AUSTIN GROANED when he caught a glimpse of the yard. The renters had obviously grilled out the previous evening. Aluminum foil, still partially tethered to the grill grates, flapped in the breeze. Greasy paper plates, plastic utensils, and empty cans of cheap beer were scattered about.

Some people could be total pigs.

Austin had warned Holly about doing a better job of vetting prospective renters. This appeared to be another example of adults renting the place in their name, then turning it over to their kids without supervision. It violated the rental agreement, but was often ignored by landlords trying to make money.

The shades were drawn and there was no sign of activity, so Austin grabbed the trash bags and headed for the carnage. He stooped to pick up a jar of spoiled mayonnaise and gagged when the smell hit him.

Twenty minutes later, he was pulling an impaled potato chip bag from the shabby picket fence that separated the property from the neighbor when his phone buzzed. If it was Holly, he would give her hell for not doing her job better.

It wasn't Holly, though. It was Dad.

"Did you enroll in your summer classes?"

Well hello to you too, Dad.

"I'm doing it this afternoon."

"Don't miss the deadline. You know what missing the deadline means."

"I won't miss the deadline." It wasn't for another week, but that was the way Jay McGinnis did things.

"What is Savannah doing down there?"

That was another thing his father did. Change the direction of the conversation without notice, keeping Austin perpetually off-balance.

"She's down for the weekend."

And next week. And the week after that. Truth was, Savannah had no summer obligations other than helping her favorite professor supervise a two-week high school civics camp back at Penn. Her rich parents never expected her to do anything in the summer.

"It sounds like she's getting in the way of you getting your work done."

"She's not, Dad. I'm keeping up with the properties just like you wanted."

"If you were keeping up with the properties, your sister wouldn't have to call and let you know about the trash on Sea Turtle Court. Have you been over there yet?"

Damn that Holly. It was like having a third parent.

"I'm there now. Just finishing up."

"Well, I have a couple of things you need to know. First,

we've rented out the place on Parkwood for the next two months."

Austin nearly dropped the phone. "Dad, that's where I'm staying. You can't rent it out from under me. Besides, the people who were supposed to be there already paid in full."

Dad chuckled. "You didn't think I'd find out they were no-shows, did you? Well, I did, and I've decided to give them back part of their rent. Some folks called this morning and offered to pay in advance. And they didn't even try to negotiate the price."

"Where am I supposed to go?"

"Are you forgetting the efficiency apartment we bought at the Windermere?"

He should have known. "Dad, have you seen that place?"

No, he hadn't. Otherwise, he wouldn't expect Austin to stay there.

"I'm sure it's fine, Austin. Holly talked to the agent before we bought it. She thinks it was a good investment that will pay for itself many times over."

"It's one room, Dad. A bed, a microwave, a mini-fridge, and a lawn chair. The walls haven't been painted since they built the place."

"I'll spring for the paint and brush. You provide the manpower."

"The place stinks of cigarettes. I can't do it, Dad."

"It's one summer. We'll rent it out to one of the life-guards next year."

"Dad, the lifeguards won't step foot in the place. Did you know a guy was killed in the boiler room two summers ago?"

"It was an isolated incident. And how much time will

you really spend there? Between cleaning up the rental units during the day and studying at the library at night, you'll be too busy to notice."

Austin could have argued that maintaining the rental units took less than a couple hours a day, and that nobody studied at the library anymore. What he couldn't mention, but knew his dad was aware of, was that Savannah would never agree to stay at the Windermere, where the bathroom was down the hall and you shared a communal kitchen with carnies, drifters, and vagrants. Nope, arguing wouldn't do any good. When Dad made up his mind about something, there was no room for argument. And besides, hadn't he said there were *a couple* of things he needed to tell Austin?

"What else, Dad?"

"Oh, yeah, I nearly forgot. We bought that bungalow on Riley Street."

"After I told you not to?"

Uh-oh. There was a way to talk to Dad and a way not to. That was the way not to. Austin braced himself.

"You didn't *tell* me anything, Austin. You recommended we not buy it. We overruled you. Mom and I have that prerogative, you know?"

"Dad, it's a mess. The place will need to be gutted and rebuilt."

"I agree. And I told the realtor the same thing when I looked at it Thursday. He—"

"Wait a minute. You were here Thursday?"

"Just for the afternoon to look at that place."

"And you didn't call me?"

"I had a meeting back here in Philly that night. There wasn't time."

What was the bigger gut punch—being relegated to the

Windermere or Dad skipping a chance to stop by and say hey? Neither really. They were more like a one-two combination that hurt like hell. Why was everyone so busy anymore?

"Your mom and I are going to be monitoring your grades, Austin. We don't need to remind you how important they are, do we?"

Gut punch number three. "No, sir. I'll work hard."

"Good to hear. Now, I want you to get in touch with that home remodel guy we used in Fenwick. Tell him we're ready to begin the demo on that Riley Street property. We'll pay him fifteen percent above his regular rate, provided he gets started right away."

KATHRYN SPOTTED him as she wheeled her bicycle into the driveway. Young. Early twenties, probably. The handyman for the owners of the place next door. He was leaning against the house, talking on his phone without a care in the world while trash blew around her yard. After a few minutes, he put the phone in his pocket, picked up a bag of trash, and carried it to the curb.

"Trash day isn't until Tuesday," Kathryn called out.

He looked at her, shrugged, and dropped the bag next to the street.

"Raccoons and seagulls will get it if you leave it there," she said.

Another look. Another shrug. But at least he grabbed the bag and carried it to a car parked out front. A white car that looked familiar, but from where she wasn't sure.

"There's still a lot of trash in my yard. You need to pick it up, too."

"I'm getting to it, lady," he snapped. "Give me a break, okay?"

Kathryn leveled him with the same stare she gave students who talked during her lectures. It was a withering look that did the trick in class, but the handyman seemed unaffected. He returned to his car, pulled out an empty trash bag, took a long drink from a water bottle, and sauntered over to her yard, taking his own sweet time.

"Thank you," Kathryn called out. He didn't respond, and she didn't have time to worry about it. *RodneySellsRehoboth* was due at five. Before then, she had to clean the house, do some laundry, and figure out what to wear. The prospect of an evening out with a man was both scary and exhilarating. The handyman could clean up the yard just fine without her supervision.

IT TOOK Savannah forty-two seconds in the Windermere to announce she would head back to her parents' place in Hershey.

That was forty-one seconds longer than Austin had expected. He was doomed from the moment they entered the building's musty stairwell and encountered a middle-aged couple making out on the landing. The guy had two full sleeves of vulgar tattoos and a work shirt with the name *Benny* embroidered on one side and *Castle Amusements* on the other. She had wild hair and the crazy eyes of a meth addict.

"I think I can get Daddy to spring for a room at the Sheraton on weekends, but there's no way he'll let me stay all the time." Savannah giggled. "He thinks I'm with Mandy and Ashley."

"What about tonight? Can you stay?"

Savannah looked over Austin's shoulder at the Windermere, turned up her nose, and shook her head. "Sorry, babe. I love you and all, but I can't do this place. Did you see that girl in the hallway? She doesn't even shave her legs. I'm going back to Hershey and see what's going on there."

It was four-fifteen. Austin had to get his stuff out of the Parkwood house and get the place cleaned up in time for the new tenants' arrival at eight. He considered asking—begging—Savannah to stay long enough to help, but that would be the last thing she wanted to do. And who could blame her?

It was going to be a hell of a night.

▓▓▓▓▓

"I HOPE you're ready for a hell of a night."

Kathryn smiled and tried to ignore the expletive. His name was Rodney Sells, and he had been quick to inform her during their meeting over coffee that everyone along the Delaware shore knew him as *RodneySellsRehoboth*, thus the nickname on the dating app.

"I was fourteenth in annual sales for all of Delaware last year," he proclaimed as he walked her to his black sports car. "And that includes the big corporate realtors up in Wilmington."

Perhaps he was full of himself, or maybe it was just nerves. Kathryn couldn't tell. What she could tell was that he was good-looking and had a full head of hair. He was tall and broad shouldered and well dressed in navy slacks and a tan blazer. He opened her door and waited for her to get situated. Had he tried to sneak a peek at her legs as she got in? If so, he would see that she had shaved *and* lotioned, not things she regularly did between semesters.

"I hope the car's not too flashy for you," he said as he backed from her driveway. "Some people see a Porsche and get the idea you're trying to impress them."

"Not at all. I don't know one car from another."

He appeared disappointed, but recovered quickly. "So, have you eaten at The Claypool?"

"No, but my friends were telling me how nice it is."

"Best place in the area, hands down. Their crab soup was featured on one of those gourmet food shows. I eat there at least once a month."

Kathryn flashed a smile that she hoped looked excited and appreciative. And maybe a little sexy. "I can't wait."

Coastal Highway was busy for early in the summer, but Rodney diced through traffic, changing lanes frequently and speeding up or slowing down as the situation dictated. His car—the Porsche—rumbled with power that Kathryn could feel through the seat.

"This certainly is a lot more fun than my Camry," she said.

"It's a blast to drive. Maybe I'll let you try it out sometime."

How much did a Porsche cost? Probably more than a garage full of Camrys. She flashed that smile again. "I'll take you up on that."

Ocean City was long and skinny. Four or five streets wide in many areas and well over a hundred blocks long. The Claypool was on Third Street, a stone's throw from the Ocean City Inlet where sun worshippers gathered by the tens of thousands each summer.

"Don't you love beach life?" Rodney asked as he

scanned the side streets for a parking spot. "Did your family vacation here when you were growing up?"

"We usually stayed pretty close to Bethany Beach. The house I live in was built by my grandfather in the late forties. We came down every summer."

"You're one of the lucky ones. That place of yours could easily fetch a million-two if you were to put it on the market."

"That's what I've been told."

"Yeah, a million-two easy. So would you?"

"Would I what?"

"Consider putting it on the market?"

"I don't think so. Where would I live?"

"A million-two would get you a damn nice condo a few miles inland with plenty left over."

"Hmm. I guess it's something to think about."

"I could probably sell it for you in a day or two."

"Yeah... no. I'm not ready."

"But you'll think about it?"

"Maybe in a few years."

Rodney spotted an open parking space in a hotel lot and rolled in like he owned the place.

"Aren't you worried about your car being towed?"

"Excuse me?"

"Your car? There's a sign over there that says unauthorized vehicles are subject to tow."

"They won't tow it."

"My friend Suzanne and I went to a sand sculpture exhibition. It was Sunday, and the only parking we could find was at a County Farm and Merchant Bank. The bank was closed, so I pulled in. We came back and my car was gone."

"That's terrible."

"It cost me three hundred dollars and four hours of my time to get it back. If it came down to burying my life savings in a sock in the backyard or depositing it at County Farm and Merchant Bank, I go with the sock."

Rodney laughed. "Maybe I should sneak over some night and start digging around your yard."

"No use. I don't have much, but what I have is in a bank that isn't County Farm and Merchant."

Two other couples were entering The Claypool at the same time. Rodney said hello to one of the men and received an icy stare in return.

"Long story about a deal that went south," he whispered as they waited to be seated.

The place was ritzier than Kathryn had expected, with white tablecloths, sedate lighting, and tuxedoed servers moving efficiently between tables. One of the women who had entered ahead of them was wearing a cocktail dress, the other a tea-length gown. Kathryn felt underdressed in her off-the-rack floral print, but Rodney didn't seem to notice.

Their table was in the center of the restaurant. Two more people acknowledged Rodney as they passed. Theirs were friendlier greetings, obviously bigger fans of *Rodney Sells Rehoboth* than the guy at the entrance.

"You know a lot of people," Kathryn noted.

"In my business, it pays to be known," he said as the waiter arrived to take their drink order. White wine for her and a vodka tonic for him.

The menu was one page with a handful of appetizers and just six main courses. The crab soup was a no-brainer.

"What do you recommend?" she asked him.

"The crab cakes are always good. The beef medallions are too." He perused the menu, then added, "The beer and onion porkchop is my personal favorite, but maybe you should consider something else tonight."

"Why?"

"Well," he said slowly, "it's a bit... robust, if you know what I mean. And if we... you know... later, I wouldn't want things to get sidetracked by a case of onion breath."

Uh-oh. Hold the phone. Was *RodneySellsRehoboth* thinking they were going to... him and her? That night?

She leaned closer. "You mean if we... kiss?"

He grinned. "Yeah. Kiss... for starters."

Kathryn nodded slowly, then grinned back. "Kiss... for starters?"

"Yeah."

"Before we move on to... *other things*?"

"Exactly." Rodney knocked back a gulp of his vodka tonic and smiled at her. No. Not smiled. More like leered. That's what it was. Definitely a leer.

"Because... it's safe to assume that things will quickly escalate beyond kissing?" Kathryn teased each word, drawing them out.

A hint of worry flittered across Rodney's face. Just a flitter, though.

"Listen, Kathryn... do you ever go by anything other than Kathryn? Kathy, maybe? Or Kate?"

"Just Kathryn."

He nodded. "I assumed that with you being a schoolteacher... and still unattached at your age, that you would just naturally..."

Schoolteacher?

At your age?

Okay, that was it.

"Ah," Kathryn said. "The old maid schoolteacher out for a romp in the hay?"

A sheen of sweat appeared on Rodney's pink face.

Kathryn continued, "The lonely spinster, sitting at home, waiting for Mr. Right to come along?"

Their waiter, a somber man in his sixties, approached. "Are you ready to order?"

"Uh... yeah," Rodney stammered. "I'll have the crab cakes... and another vodka tonic. And the lady...?"

It was too good a moment to pass up, at a time that wasn't exactly overflowing with good moments. So, Kathryn jumped in with both feet. "I'll have the beer and onion porkchop, please."

"Certainly, madam." The waiter jotted down the order. Rodney opened his big ugly mouth but couldn't come up with anything to say. That was okay, because Kathryn wasn't quite finished. She winked seductively at Rodney, then turned to the waiter.

"And will you tell the chef to include plenty of beer and onion?"

<hr>

THE LAST PLACE Austin wanted to spend Saturday night was the Windermere, so after getting the Parkwood house ready for the new arrivals, he stopped at a little out of the way bar on the outskirts of Bethany. It was a place where locals hung out, with two pool tables and a jukebox that alternated between Garth Brooks and Eminem.

He never had trouble fitting in at locals' places, and when he took a seat at a table near the restrooms, no one paid him much attention other than a pink-haired girl named Felicity who was the odd-person out in a couples-only dart tournament. Felicity made it known that she needed a partner and could be amenable to whatever might happen after, but Austin wasn't feeling it. The girl he had wanted to spend the night with was already back in Hershey, Pennsylvania, and the thought of taking a woman back to the thin-walled Windermere made his stomach sour. So, after downing a beer and buying one for Felicity, he feigned an emergency and took off.

He was at a traffic light a few blocks from the Windermere when a late model Porsche rumbled by, barely beating the traffic signal's change from yellow to red. A man was slumped against the passenger-side window. A woman was at the wheel, and judging by the whining protest of the motor, she was driving in low gear.

Austin fell in behind them.

Three blocks north, the car turned onto a side road with a bit more speed than necessary. Austin winced when the Porsche jumped the curb. That was going to leave a mark. He followed, more out of curiosity than anything else. Watching someone trash a Porsche was preferable to returning to the Windermere.

The lady took a left and a right without shifting out of low gear. Then, in the middle of the block, she signaled and pulled to the curb.

Austin slowed as he passed and was about to continue on when he caught a glimpse of the driver. It was the uptight neighbor from Sea Turtle Court. Was she okay? Was she drunk? She was certainly driving like it. He pulled in ahead of her and watched through his rearview mirror as she opened the door and got out.

KATHRYN SHUT THE CAR OFF, stuck the key fob in the pocket of *RodneySellsRehoboth's* jacket, and got out. She had planned to leave him at the municipal parking lot near the beach, but the sound of the Porsche's wheels scraping the curb had scared her.

She was reaching in to lock the car when she spied his phone on the console. She picked it up and, after seeing it didn't have a lock screen, scrolled through until she found the dating app. It turned out that she was one of eleven women Rodney had been conversing with. After a few clicks, that number was ten. Rodney was oblivious as he continued to snore. His gaping mouth had left a string of saliva on the window. One of the fancy after-dinner mints from The Claypool was on the console. Kathryn had already eaten hers, so she took his. She popped it into her mouth and jammed the wrapper into his pocket with the key.

"Not quite the sexy hunk you think you are," Kathryn muttered. "But you certainly were right about the beer and onion pork chop. Very robust."

She closed the door and looked up the street.

Fifty yards ahead, a car idled at the curb. Kathryn tensed, then tried to get back into Rodney's car.

Locked.

It was Bethany Beach. This was a perfectly safe neighborhood. And she was only four blocks from home.

Even if it was dark... with no one else around —

The driver's door of the other car opened.

Was someone getting out?

Holy crap! Was this where it ended?

Someone was getting out. A guy. Medium build, dark-haired. The streetlights were dim, so they were no help. Kathryn threw back her shoulders, clutched her purse against her, and started walking in the other direction, hopeful he didn't see how badly her legs were shaking.

"I know you," he said.

The voice was familiar. Or maybe it wasn't familiar at all. Maybe he just sounded like someone she knew. Maybe it was all a ploy to get closer to her. Kathryn kept walking.

"It's me... the guy who cleaned up your yard this morning."

Kathryn stopped and turned.

It *was* him. "Oh, hi!" she said, sudden relief making her sound much too cheery for a Saturday night chat with a stranger on a dark street.

He approached and inspected the Porsche.

"Nice car."

"Yeah. It's not mine."

The guy nodded slowly. "Did you... steal it?"

Kathryn laughed and pointed at *RodneySellsRehoboth*. "It belongs to him. Long story."

"I'm sure. Can I give you a ride home?"

"No, I don't live far from here."

He chuckled. "I know where you live, remember?"

"Oh, yeah. I'll still walk. I mean, I don't really know you."

"Sure, you do. I'm that guy who tried to leave a bag of trash at the curb three days before pickup. The guy whose ass you chewed for nothing more than doing his job."

Kathryn eyed him carefully. It was a good half-mile to Sea Turtle Court. And the shoes she was wearing pinched her feet, especially the left one.

"You're not going to take me to some deserted part of town and strangle me, are you?"

The guy looked up and down the street. "It looks like you're already in a deserted part of town."

He had a point. "Okay, I accept your ride. What is your name?"

"Austin McGinnis. And you're Mrs. Shea, right?"

"Good memory. Except it's not Mrs."

Kathryn followed him back to his car where he even opened the door for her. If he was a strangler or serial killer, at least he was a well-mannered one. She slid in and, as he walked in front of the car, checked for bulges in his clothes that might be a gun or knife. The interior of the car smelled faintly of lemon and cologne. Other than a suitcase on the backseat, it was clean and neat. Not what she would have expected from a guy about the same age as her students.

"You really did a number on the wheels of that Porsche," he said as he drove toward Sea Turtle Court. "By the way, how did you like the seven-speed transmission?"

"Seven? Really? I only found one."

"Yeah," Austin laughed. "I was afraid of that. The poor guy's scuffed wheels might be the least of his worries. New transmissions cost a lot of money."

"He deserved it."

"Is he... someone that you..." He paused as if he wasn't sure if he should ask. Then changing course, "We're almost at your house."

"I know that," Kathryn replied. "Remember, I'm the one who lives there."

"Yes, you are," he said as he turned onto her street.

░░░░░

SHE WAS AN UNUSUAL WOMAN. Austin guessed her to be in her forties, maybe younger. Her clothes and the way she did her hair made her look older than she probably was. Career wise? Probably accountant or librarian. Some job where she spent most of her time alone. Her responses seemed forced at times, but there was also a wittiness lurking somewhere underneath, like when she asked if he planned to strangle her.

He pulled to a stop in front of her house and was about to come around and open the door for her, but she beat him to it. "Thank you for the ride," she said coolly. "And if the police ask, you didn't get a look at the woman driving the Porsche."

There was that wittiness. He chuckled. "I saw nothing."

He watched her walk to her house, unlock the door, and go inside. Yes, she was definitely unusual, but it might be fun to get to know the part of her who joked about him being a strangler or swore him to secrecy about the Porsche. But that would mean having to get to know the part of her that had been so rude to him earlier that morning.

Worth it? Nah.

Too unusual.

Unusual indeed.

FOUR

sunday, may 22

"HE ACTUALLY CALLED you an old maid schoolteacher?"

Milo's was subdued for a Sunday, and Hillary's question seemed to reverberate off the walls. Several diners turned to check out the old maid schoolteacher.

"Geesh, Hillary, can you talk a little louder?" Suzanne snapped. Then, to Kathryn, "Old maid schoolteacher? Really?"

"Not exactly in those words, but yeah," Kathryn answered.

"Was that before or after he got drunk?"

"Before, though the way he knocked back those vodka tonics, it wasn't much before."

"Oh, honey, I'm so sorry," Suzanne said.

Hillary shook her head. "Can't say I'm surprised. You're not the kind to be hanging out on computer dating programs."

"They're called apps, not programs." Kathryn sipped her coffee, smiled, and said, "Hey, at least it made for an interesting story to share with my friends."

"Yeah," Suzanne said. "Jane's going to kick herself for going to church instead of joining us for breakfast."

"And I got to drive a Porsche."

"What was that like?" Hillary asked. "Stuart has a sports car, but he never lets me drive it."

"Stuart's car is a fifteen-year-old Kia," Suzanne said.

"It's two doors instead of four," Hillary insisted. "Doesn't that make it a sports car?" She turned back to Kathryn. "Did you go fast?"

"No. It's a stick shift, and I've never driven one before, but I finally got it to go. It was so loud, though. Nothing like when Rodney was driving."

"How did you know when to shift the gears?"

"I stayed with the one I found. Why tempt fate?" As she spoke, Kathryn remembered Austin asking how she liked the Porsche's seven-speed transmission. The memory made her smile.

Suzanne nearly choked on her orange juice. "You drove from Ocean City back to Bethany in first gear?"

"I did. But I slowed down after I scraped one of the hubcaps. It made a terrible noise, but Rodney was asleep. When I got a few blocks from home, I gave up and parked at the curb. I left the keys in his pocket."

Suzanne grinned. "He had it coming. Besides, he'll never remember how he got there."

"Do you expect he'll ask you out again?" Hillary asked.

"Nope. I removed my number from his phone. While I was in there, I also deleted my profile from his dating app."

Hillary nodded her approval. "That was good thinking. I still can't believe he called you an old maid schoolteacher. Doesn't he know you're a tenured college professor?"

"The conversation never got that far." Kathryn shook her head. "We never really talked about me at all."

Suzanne shook her head slowly. "Ladies, I think it's just better if we all stick to dating the old-fashioned way."

They were quiet for a moment as the server refilled their drinks. Kathryn glanced around at the surrounding tables. There were a few single men, mostly working types wearing caps advertising seed corn and poultry plants. Nice enough, but none came close to being the kind of man Kathryn saw herself settling down with. Suzanne might know a lot about a lot of things, but when it came to dating, she was way off base.

The old-fashioned way of dating wasn't such a good idea. And it sure as heck wasn't working.

⫟⫟⫟⫟

"WHAT THE HELL? Get out of here, asshole!"

Austin yanked the bathroom door shut, leaned against the wall, and took a deep breath. Why hadn't she locked it when she went in? He considered running away to avoid seeing her when she came out, but he needed the bathroom. Bad. The closest gas station was blocks away. He'd just have to wait until she came out.

Five minutes passed.

Ten.

The pain was becoming nearly unbearable when she finally stepped out of the bathroom trailing steam and a whiff of dollar store perfume. She wore a tie-dyed bathrobe that barely covered her butt. Her hair was wet and limp and stringy. If it weren't for her eyes, he wouldn't have recognized her as the woman he and Savannah had seen making out with Benny from Castle Amusements.

"Do you always barge in like that, moron?" she asked.

"Lock the door next time."

She paused and sized him up. "You're new."

Austin nodded.

"Ain't no lock." She pointed to a coat hanger on a nail next to the door. "If the hanger is on the nail, someone's using the john. If it's on the floor, it's open. I'm Charlene."

"Austin."

She sized him up again, then pulled the towel off her shoulder, causing the top of her bath robe to gape open at the chest. "Do you tweak?"

"What?"

"Tweak? Do meth?"

"Nope. Sorry."

Charlene rolled her eyes. "Too bad. You're kinda cute. Great ass, too. You'd be fun to party with."

She sauntered off before Austin could figure out how to respond.

KATHRYN JAMMED on her bicycle's brakes in the middle of the street and nearly launched herself over the handlebars.

More trash, and it was worse than the day before. This time there was nothing to stop it from blowing into her yard because an eight-foot section of the picket fence her grandfather had erected a half-century before—the very picket fence she'd watched him lovingly maintain—was knocked to the ground. How could people care so little about the work of others?

She pulled out her phone and called the number in Philly. It rang several times before the same woman as yesterday answered. Kathryn gave her an earful. Then, without waiting for a reply, exclaimed, "You need to send Austin the handyman back here immediately."

AUSTIN'S PHONE was buzzing when he returned to his room.

"What?"

"You need to go back to Sea Turtle Court. They trashed the yard again, and this time they knocked down the neighbor's fence."

"Screw you, Holly. Do you have any idea where I spent the night?"

"The Ritz? Four Seasons?"

She wasn't laughing out loud, but she was definitely enjoying his misery. "You know exactly where I am. You let Dad lease the Parkwood property out from under me."

"You know better than that, little brother. Dad and Mom do what Dad and Mom want to do."

"And you're right there with them. You'll be happy to know that I had to wait fifteen minutes to take a dump this morning so some meth head could finish her shower."

"Wait a minute. You don't have your own bathroom?" Again the laughing without laughing. Holly knew everything, including how squalid the Windermere was.

Austin didn't respond, instead choosing to dig through his suitcase full of wrinkled shorts and T-shirts until he found something that was at least presentable. Sunday would have been laundry day at the Parkwood property. Now he would be hunting for a laundromat.

"Well, get on over to Sea Turtle Court this morning. The neighbor is pretty mad about the fence. She went on and on about how her grandfather built it and she helped fix it and a bunch of other stuff I didn't catch."

"Holly, did you ever tweak?"

"Never. Or smoke, or shoot up, or snort. Did you?"

"How did you know what it meant?"

"I majored in business, little brother. Do you know how many low-level dealers enroll in business school with aspirations of becoming drug kingpins?"

"I would guess... none."

"Guess again. Now get your ass over to Sea Turtle Court."

KATHRYN MET him on the sidewalk as he was getting out of his car. She had been staring at the mess in her yard for half an hour. It had been kind of him to give her a ride the night before, but enough was enough.

"You need to do something about this. I won't put up with it all summer. Do I have to call the city council?"

Austin looked as if he was recovering from a rough night, but it wasn't enough to convince her to go easy. Tourist season was difficult enough without having to deal with trashy neighbors.

"I'll clean it up. I promise."

"And what about the fence?"

"It's in pretty bad shape. You ever consider getting rid of it?"

Get rid of it? "My grandfather built that fence with his own two hands. It's as much a part of this property as the house itself."

He rubbed his face and squinted as he surveyed the

situation. "I'll pick up the trash first, then I'll get to the fence."

"Well, I'm going to be away until late this afternoon. I expect this to be taken care of by the time I return."

SUNDAYS BACK at Penn usually meant late mornings sleeping off the effects of the previous night. Then maybe a midafternoon stop at one of those twenty-four-hour breakfast places for chocolate-chip pancakes, eggs, and sausage, followed by a Phillies or Sixers game on TV. Perhaps a bit of homework before bed, but more likely not.

Which was why his grades sucked so bad he needed to enroll in summer semester.

He was as far away from those glorious Sundays at Penn as he could possibly be. Living at the Windermere, the beach ghetto. Propositioned by a fellow resident who actually scared him a little. And, as if it couldn't get any worse, that crabby Shea woman on Sea Turtle Court had jumped down his throat because of the neighbors. And now he was facing the greasy, smelly remains of another drunken barbeque.

It was nearly eleven, but like yesterday there was no sign of life inside the house. Enough was enough, though, so he went to the front door, rang the bell, and waited.

And waited.

Finally, a girl pulled open the door. Mascara was smeared around her eyes, lipstick around her mouth. Her hair jutted out in every direction. She wore shorts and a bikini top with barbeque sauce on the left cup. She looked at him, looking at her, then said, "What?"

"I'm the owner of this place."

"O-kay," she said slowly.

"Are you the renter?"

"I'm just here. I think the guy staying here is named Terry, but I'm not sure. He and the others left an hour ago."

"Where did they go?"

She shrugged. "I was puking in that big-ass bathtub upstairs."

Austin groaned. "Please tell me you didn't puke in the jacuzzi."

"Uh... yeah."

"Somebody needs to clean up that mess in the yard. The neighbor complained."

"I guess I can tell Terry when he comes back. I might not be here, though. I need to get back to my parents' place before one."

"You're local?"

"No, my parents rented a place for the week. I have to get back to school tomorrow. It's finals week."

"Really? I go to Penn. Where do you go?"

"Towson High School. I'm a junior."

"And you're here? Instead of with your parents?"

She tried to make eye contact but couldn't stop hers from crossing. She held the door for support as she said, "Are you a cop or something? One of those undercover cops that sneaks into high schools? Like in the movie?"

"No, I'm just—"

"I gotta go, man. I think I'm going to puke again."

She slammed the door and was gone before Austin could warn her about puking in the jacuzzi. He tried the door, but it was locked.

It was cleanup time. Again.

THE AFTERNOON SUN was low on the horizon when Kathryn pulled into her driveway. The trash was gone, but the fence was still on the ground.

Austin ambled out of the shed carrying her grandfather's wooden toolbox. Looking for all the world like he owned the place. *Who did he think he was?*

She scrambled out of her car and marched to meet him. "What are you doing in there? That door was closed and locked. You have no right to break in and—"

He set the toolbox on the ground and stepped back. "It wasn't locked, and—"

She pulled out her phone. "I'm calling the police. You broke in and now you're stealing my grandfather's toolkit."

"I'm not stealing anything. I'm trying to fix the fence."

Kathryn paused. "Why are you in my shed?"

"I was hoping you might have some pickets to replace the broken ones. I took a couple to the hardware store, but it turns out they're not a standard size."

"What do you mean?"

"Your grandfather made them by hand. He didn't buy them from a store. I was hoping there might still be some in your shed."

"Were there?"

"Three." He pointed to an area of the yard where the fence was still intact. "I used them over there to replace some that were missing. I'm going to have to make the rest by hand, like your grandfather did."

Kathryn's gaze followed his. Three fresh slats filled the space where a neighbor's dog came through sometimes to do his business in her yard. It looked pretty good.

"Do you even know how to make–what did you call them?"

"Slats. Or pickets. That's why it's called a picket fence. Your grandfather did a good job, but like I said this morning, it's not been kept up. And yes, I know how to make them. They're pretty easy, really, provided I have the right tools."

"Do you?"

"Do I what?"

"Have the right tools?"

"Sort of. I usually have power tools, but there are some old hand tools in your shed that I can work with if you're okay with me using them."

Was he serious? "Hand tools?"

"There's a hand saw, a scroll saw, and hand plane. I've used those before, but it was a long time ago. There's another tool called a brace and bit. I've never used one, but I found a video online." He tried to hold back a smile. "I'm kind of excited to try it."

There was no mistaking the change that came over him as he described the process of repairing the fence. Kathryn found herself warming to him, much as she had the evening before.

There was only one thing. She wasn't sure she liked the idea of having him around. What if he broke in after she left for school? What if he pawned her jewelry to buy beer? What if he turned out to be a pervert who put secret cameras in her bedroom?

Oh yeah, those would put him to sleep. Not much to see there.

"I don't need you to do all that. Just stand the fence back up."

"It'll fall down again."

"Not if you pick better renters."

That made him smile. "Tell my sister that the next time you call to complain."

"That's your sister?"

"Holly. She's the property manager."

"She's quite good."

He shrugged. "A real chip off the old block, I guess."

"You mean she's like your parents?"

"Exactly."

"What about you? Another chip off the old block?"

"More like the rock that sank to the bottom of the lake. If it's okay with you, I'll start on the fence tomorrow. I can be back around ten."

"Like I said, you don't have to fix the fence. Just stand it up."

He sighed, obviously growing weary of their back and forth. "It really needs to be fixed. Or taken down. It's not going to last long in the condition it's in."

What was his angle? Could she trust him? He had given her a ride home, but...

"I'm not sure I want to pay for that. Your tenants knocked it down."

"Will you buy the materials? I'll bring receipts."

"Why would you do that?"

"I enjoy it." He paused and looked toward the setting sun. "A lot more than... never mind. Do you want the fence fixed or not?"

She considered his proposal—and him—for a few moments. She liked the idea of the fence looking nice again. Her grandfather would have liked that, too.

"Yes, I would like it fixed. But I'll pay for the materials and your time."

Kathryn stuck out her hand. Austin shook, then turned to leave.

"Hey," Kathryn called out as he was getting in his car. "How do you know so much about woodworking?"

He paused, then glanced toward her shed. "I have a grandfather who is very special to me, too. He taught me."

FIVE

monday, may 23

"WELCOME TO REMEDIAL FRESHMAN ENGLISH."

There were twenty-four of them. Another class would follow next period. Most were just days removed from the excitement and celebration of high school graduation. A few were older; one appeared to be in her fifties. They wore short shorts, board shorts, tight shorts, and baggy shorts. A hulking farm boy in a sky-blue *Got Jesus?* T-shirt was chatting up a petite blonde in an expletive-laden anti-government sweatshirt. *She probably doesn't* Got Jesus, Kathryn thought as she looked the class over.

The only things they had in common were sleepy eyes and scowls of indifference that were impervious to her cheery welcome. "I know you would rather be at the beach," she said.

That got her a few nods of agreement. "Or still in bed," one guy groused.

Had he tried harder in high school English, maybe he would still be in bed. Or at the beach. "Lower Delaware

Community College requires a C average in high school English to enroll as a full-time student. I'm Dr. Shea, and my job over the next few weeks is to help you get there."

"I suck at English," a red-haired girl said from the second row. A half-dozen others echoed her sentiment.

Kathryn smiled and handed out the syllabus. Most teachers had switched to posting it online, but Kathryn preferred that students show up to receive it. It was her sixth summer of teaching the course since taking over for Clarence Brohawn, who was pushed out for failing too many students and being a general pain in the ass to everyone, from colleagues to the college president. Kathryn knew her job. Make the course challenging, but passable. When in doubt, err toward passable. Money was always tight at the college. More students meant more revenue. Sometimes it also meant faculty pay raises, but not often enough.

Kathryn recited from memory. "Your grade will be based upon a research paper, weekly writing projects, and class participation."

"Does that mean we have to come every day?" *Got Jesus?* asked.

"I'll have to miss at least three classes," a girl with purple hair called out. Kathryn remembered her from the previous summer, and how she had dropped the course after the first week.

"You need to be here to participate," Kathryn said as she returned to the podium. "This isn't one of those classes where—"

The door opened, and Casper Fillmore entered in all his bow-tied glory. Student eyes shifted from Kathryn to Casper, then back. Her hands became clammy, and her stomach churned. She nodded, but he didn't respond as he made his way to a seat in the rear.

His intent was obvious. He was observing her.

Evaluating.

Assessing.

Confirming that what her students had written about her was true.

Her hands began to shake. She gripped the podium. Where had she left off?

Oh, yeah. She was answering questions about class. She pointed to a girl in the back, one seat from Casper, who still had her hand raised.

"How long is it?" the girl asked.

"How long is what?"

The girl huffed and rolled her eyes. "The research paper. How long is it?"

"It's explained in the syllabus."

"Can we use any size font we want?"

It was a trick as old as the personal computer. The larger the font, the fewer words needed to fill the page quota. "Twelve-point or smaller."

"Can the creative writing projects be on any topic we want?" another student called out.

"There are limits, but you have latitude about what you choose."

Was it okay that she put limits on students? Would Casper Fillmore think she was being excessively demanding? There weren't limits until a few students wrote stuff that was so dark and depressing that Kathryn had trouble sleeping at night. No devil worship, no murder-suicides, no swearing for the sake of swearing. It had seemed like a good idea at the time, but now she wasn't so sure.

"There will be reading assignments for each class, mostly short stories, but some longer. You will come to class prepared to discuss the readings. If you can do that and finish the papers, you'll do fine."

Did Casper know the numbers? Ninety percent of the students in front of her would pass the course. A couple would fail and be ineligible to enroll for the fall semester. None would enjoy the course. What was there to enjoy? She was one of two gatekeepers, along with Felicia Torres, who was teaching remedial freshman math across campus to an equally disinterested group of prospective freshmen.

Had Felicia Torres gotten a *PIP*? Were her student comments as heartless as Kathryn's?

And was Casper going to come to class every day? Once a week? More? Would his presence unsettle her so much every time?

It was going to be a long six weeks.

THE HOME REMODEL guy from Fenwick was named Duke Brumley. Austin caught him at his shop.

But Brumley wasn't interested in taking on the Riley Street job. "Maybe August, but no promises."

Austin tossed out his father's offer of fifteen percent above whatever Brumley was making on his current project. He raised an eyebrow, but quickly shook his head.

"I'm finally on the inside with Zander and that bunch. It took me six years to get in with them, and I'm not gonna fudge that up for some side gig."

Zander was one of the largest developers in the area. Hotels and restaurants. Big stuff that allowed contractors like Brumley to hire full-time crews and take winter vacations in the Bahamas.

"Do you know anybody else?"

"Nah. Everybody's busy... but... wait a minute." He pulled out his phone and scrolled through his contacts before reading off a number. "His name is Pettibone, but everybody calls him Joker. He finished a rehab in Bethany two weeks ago. Probably been on a bender since then, so he'll need the money." Brumley mimicked taking a drink. "He lives in a shack near Millsboro. Does good enough work and shows up pretty regular, but drinks most of what he makes."

"I can trust him?"

"He stays busy." Brumley jotted down an address on a notepad and handed it over. "If he doesn't answer your call, try going to his place. He might be your only option."

KATHRYN'S HEART skipped a beat when she arrived home to sawhorses and worktables set up in the backyard. The scene took her back three decades. She was on summer vacation from grade school, returning from the beach with her parents. Her grandfather was working on another of his many projects. His tools were carefully arranged in the bright sunshine on those same tables. She looked toward the door of the shed, hopeful he would emerge with a smile and a wave.

And then there he was.

Except he wasn't.

It was the handyman. Austin. And while he smiled and waved, the sweet memories of her grandfather made her heart ache a little.

She got out of the car and walked across the yard.

Austin grabbed two pickets and held them up. "The first one took me an hour, but I'm getting faster. The hand tools are fun, but I wouldn't want to rely on them every day."

Kathryn took a picket and turned it over in her hands. She knew nothing about woodworking, but he certainly seemed proud.

"Want to see how they're made?"

She really didn't. She was drained from two sections of remedial English and wanted nothing more than a quick bite of lunch and a nap. Perhaps a stroll on the beach later.

But he was so enthused about his work. She hadn't seen his kind of passion from her students. "I would love to see how they're made, but I'm famished. Have you eaten?"

He hadn't.

"Would you like a ham and cheese sandwich?"

He would.

Kathryn considered inviting him into the house but thought better of it. He seemed a nice enough young man, but people thought the same of Ted Bundy. "I'll run inside and get everything ready. Meet me on the front porch in ten minutes."

"WHAT DO YOU WANT?" The voice on the other end of the line was gruff. And maybe hungover.

"Is this Joker Pettibone?"

"Who wants to know?"

"My name is Austin McGinnis, Joker. My family has investment properties in Bethany and we're looking for someone to do some rehab. Duke Brumley gave me your name."

"Duke, huh? Why did he pass on the job?"

"He's busy with other projects."

"What makes you think I'm not?"

"He thought you just finished a project." Austin didn't mention Duke's suspicions about what Joker might have been up to since then. Joker hemmed and hawed, then agreed to meet him at the Riley Street property later that afternoon.

With that out of the way, Austin walked to the front porch and took a seat on the steps. He had five minutes to burn, so he opened the Penn website and accessed his account. A banner of red letters screamed at him from the top of the page.

YOU ARE IN JEOPARDY OF BEING PLACED ON ACADEMIC PROBATION.

He flinched, then clicked on the registration page. The courses he needed were Organizational Theory and Introduction to Southern Literature. He searched until he found them, enrolled, then used his father's credit card to pay the bill.

He was finishing up when Ms. Shea appeared with two plates. She'd made him two sandwiches, both thick with ham, cheese, and mayonnaise. He didn't care for mayo, but since she'd already slathered it on, he wouldn't mention it. She returned to the house and reappeared with two bottles of water. She handed him one, then took a seat in a pink metal chair about six feet away.

"Wouldn't you prefer to sit up here in the shade?" she asked, motioning to a matching chair.

Austin joined her on the porch. The temperature was a few degrees cooler in the shade, a welcome relief.

"You've been busy this morning," she said.

"Not much to show for it yet," he said between bites. "Now that I've figured out the tool situation, I should be able to turn out a dozen more pickets this afternoon."

"How many do we need?"

"Probably three dozen. That will be enough to replace the broken ones."

A lull emerged as they ate their sandwiches. While she was being considerably kinder than the previous day, there was still an expanse between them. Probably the age difference. He glanced at her while she ate and tried to guess her backstory. Black hair, cut short in one of those mom hairstyles. She wore a tan dress and sandals. Her nails were cut short and painted dark red. Not much makeup. She looked like someone he might pass in the supermarket, someone with whom he had nothing in common.

"Would you like another bottle of water?" she asked.

"Yes, please, but you can refill it. Don't get a new one."

She took his bottle, got up, and went back inside. She considered refilling it before choosing to get a cold one from the fridge. When she returned, he had polished off the first sandwich and was into the second.

"Thank you," he said as she handed him the bottle. "I don't think I caught your first name."

"I'm..." Where to go? Kathryn? That seemed personal for a young man who appeared to be about the same age as her students. Ms. Shea? She had never liked Ms., even if it was the accepted title for a single woman. Dr. Shea? That was pretentious. He would probably misunderstand and think she was a medical doctor. "It's Kathryn."

He stood up and placed his plate on the small wicker table between their chairs. "Thank you for lunch, Kathryn. Now, would you like to see how they made pickets in the old days, before power tools?"

"Yes, I would like that."

He motioned for her to go ahead of him, quite a show of manners for someone his age. She put her plate on his and led the way to the shed. He picked up a piece of wood, took some measurements, and got to work. Fifteen minutes later, he handed her the finished product.

She turned it over in her hand, admiring his handiwork. "Very nice, but it seems like a lot of work for something so unimportant."

"You can buy pickets at any hardware store, but these were specially made."

"By my grandfather, but why wouldn't he just take the easy way out and buy them?"

Austin gazed at the fence and smiled. "He cared about his work. Anyone can throw together a fence. He built something special."

Kathryn nodded and struggled to keep her eyes from welling up. "That's how I remember him." She ran her fingers along a splintered picket. "He took good care of it when he was alive. I feel guilty for letting it get so run down."

Austin smiled. "He would understand. Not everyone is interested in the same things." He picked up another piece of wood and started measuring. "You probably have your own interests that your grandfather didn't share."

"He never cared for reading like I do."

"There you go."

Kathryn watched for a few moments. Austin seemed to disappear into his work. Measuring and measuring again, examining the wood, placing it on the table, positioning the saw.

"How about you?" she finally said.

"How about me, what?"

"What are your interests?"

He held up the piece of wood. "I like doing this."

"Because of your grandfather?"

He nodded.

"Did he have a workshop?"

"He built houses. My family still operates the company he started, but it's a lot bigger."

"I'll bet your grandfather would be proud to see how it's grown."

"Oh, he's seen it. He's still alive. He never cared as much for the business side as he did for building houses, though. Grandpa gave me my first set of hand tools when I was nine. I still have them. I'm going to pass them on to my kids."

"You have children?"

"No," he laughed. "Not yet. But someday. And I want them to appreciate working with their hands."

Kathryn watched him for a few moments as he crafted two more pickets. She was intrigued by his attention to detail, using a plane to shave away a tiny sliver of wood so each picket exactly matched the others, and how he held each one up and slowly turned it in his hands before smiling and setting it aside. She sensed his satisfaction, his understated delight at doing a good job. It was so different from the forty-five students who had largely zoned out on her earlier in the day, suffering through another step in the process of getting to wherever they hoped to go in life. When they eventually arrived there, would it be a place that brought them joy? The same type of joy she saw on Austin's face as he crafted chunks of wood into a new fence?

Had she ever arrived at that spot? Had she ever found joy?

That thought sent her back to the house to prepare the next day's lessons.

JOKER PETTIBONE SHOWED UP DRUNK.

Okay, maybe drunk was too strong a word. Maybe buzzed fit better. He walked straight enough and seemed to comprehend what needed to be done to restore the property to rentable condition. He slurred his words, though, and needed a few extra moments to take measurements that were second nature to any experienced carpenter.

After taking a look around, he returned to his battered truck to work up an estimate. Austin wandered through the house while he waited, pulling away wall boards and tossing them to the floor, beginning the demolition that Joker would hopefully complete over the next couple weeks. The place wasn't as bad as he'd initially thought. While not much was salvageable, the old girl seemed to have good bones.

Austin tried to imagine it as it would look when the work was complete. Kitchen, dining area, and living room on the first floor. A small half-bath to cut down on traffic going up and down the stairs. A gas fireplace in the living room? Maybe, but rentals dropped in the winter, and the offsetting insurance costs might dictate the money be spent on something more useful.

There would be three bedrooms upstairs. A bathroom would be added to the master that would cut the size of the room by a third, but an en suite bath was a big deal to renters. There'd be larger windows on the south side to take advantage of natural light and summer breezes. The heating system was a mess, and the place still had window air conditioners that were noisy and took away from the charm. Those would have to go.

He was considering the possibility of adding a back porch when Joker returned, handed him a folded paper with his estimate, and left.

Austin sat down on the front steps and unfolded the page. His breath caught at the final figure—and caught again at Joker's timeframe.

Four months.

Joker wasn't planning on being done until the first of October. Tourist season at Bethany dwindled to almost nothing after Labor Day, and the few who came during the colder months were lured by rock-bottom rental rates that allowed the owner to break even at best. Joker was looking for a money grab. The project should take a small crew no longer than six weeks. Even factoring in labor and materials, the bid was a third higher than Austin expected.

"Sorry, Joker," he mumbled. "You're not getting this job."

But would he?

Would Mom, Dad, and Holly bite the bullet to get the job done? Dad might come down and meet with Joker, maybe lean on him a little and get him to agree to move up the deadline. He might even sweeten the pot, throw in some upfront money to kick Joker into gear.

Or maybe Mom would come down. She would lay on the charm like he'd seen her do to contractors in the past. Whichever one it was, they were going to pay too much for too little, and based upon what Austin had heard and seen of Joker, he probably wasn't a good risk.

While he grappled with his thoughts, he went back inside and continued to pry away the living room drywall, exposing the studs. His efforts were limited to what he could do with the tiny crowbar and claw hammer he kept in his car, but it was therapeutic, nonetheless. His thoughts drifted to his summer classes and how he had to earn Bs. Organizational Theory he could handle. He would have made a B in that one the first time around if he hadn't gone home with Savannah the week before final exams. The sixty-three dropped his grade to a D.

But Introduction to Southern Literature? He had enrolled in that one sophomore year because it met at two in the afternoon. He was a fraternity pledge at the time and wanted to avoid early morning classes at all costs. Big mistake. The professor back then was a fat windbag who cleared his throat every two minutes while lecturing on how quality Southern literature died with William Faulkner in the 1960s. They were required to read *Gone with the Wind*, hailed by many as a classic, but turning out to be a thousand-page sleeping pill for Austin.

This time around the class was taught by someone named Professor Vihaan Chakraborty, whose Penn profile identified as a scholar of classical Greek literature from the first century. Not exactly an ideal match, but at least they wouldn't be required to read *Gone with the Wind* again. Austin had taken a quick look at the syllabus and discovered that Professor Chakraborty allowed them to choose three books classified as Southern literature. That was encouraging.

The sun was setting through the kitchen windows at the rear of the house when Austin came up for air. It was after eight and, without realizing it, he had ripped apart most of the living room and kitchen. Piles of drywall and chunks of stucco were everywhere, and the air was thick with dust.

Austin coughed several times before opening the front door for fresh air. He took one last look around. Demo was the easy part, the unskilled part. The little bit he did might allow Joker Pettibone to shave a few days from his completion date, assuming he got the job. Austin grabbed his tool belt and backpack, wiped the dust from his face, and contemplated his return to the Windermere.

It was depressing.

SIX

friday, may 27

BORED FACES and blank expressions stared at Kathryn as she did the math in her head.

Six weeks, five days a week.

Thirty days.

Oh yeah, Memorial Day was the coming Monday. No school on Memorial Day. Twenty-nine days.

Four days done, the fifth almost done.

Twenty-four days to go.

Two classes a day, seventy-five minutes each. A hundred and fifty minutes a day. A hundred and fifty multiplied by twenty-four days. Three thousand and—*holy guacamole*—was it really three thousand minutes? Or was it more?

She suddenly craved wine. And it wasn't even noon.

Class discussions were proving to be a disaster. Worse than any previous summer. Students weren't reading the material. She had already spotted several copies of those skinny paperback summaries that promised to provide the main idea but always fell short. Essays were brief and uninspired. She'd overheard a group of students saying the class was a snooze fest. That was bad enough, but then one referred to her as Dr. Snore.

Dr. Snore!

Ouch.

Was there perhaps a bottle of wine in her office? Maybe. Hadn't she stuck a bottle in her bottom drawer? Behind her old copies of *Literature Professor Monthly*? Yes! She was sure she had. That partial bottle left over from the farewell celebration for the department secretary three years before. She could step out for a moment. It wouldn't take long to chug some down. Finish the bottle and hide it in the wastebasket.

Geesh, Kathryn, what are you thinking?

Is it really that bad? Drinking on the job?

She glanced at the clock, which hadn't moved since the last time she'd glanced at it. Students were supposed to be completing extemporaneous writing assignments about an incident that made them laugh out loud. A few were writing. Some were doing the assignment on laptops. Others stared into space. One boy was picking his nose. A girl two rows away observed him with more interest than she had ever paid to Kathryn's lectures.

Three thousand minutes?

🏛

PROFESSOR CHAKRABORTY WAS a funny and sensitive man who admittedly knew little about Southern literature. The professor who was supposed to teach the class had flown the coop, departing Penn for a dean's gig at Cornell.

"We will learn together," Professor Chakraborty exclaimed two minutes into the course, his head and shoulders filling the screen. As students introduced themselves, Austin came to the uneasy conclusion that he was the only non-lit major. Two-thirds had already dived into the first required reading. Some were into the second. Austin listened to the names of the authors they tossed about. Harper Lee, Steinbeck, Fitzgerald. Old stuff like that sleep-inducing *Gone with the Wind* from sophomore year. Wasn't there any new Southern literature? He considered asking, but didn't want the others figuring out he was the lone outsider, so he kept his mouth shut.

Someone had overdosed in a broom closet overnight at the Windermere. It was at the far end of the hall from Austin's room, but the police hadn't seemed to understand that others were trying to sleep, clomping by constantly between two and five, gabbing among themselves and into their radios. It would have been enough to drive Austin nuts had he not come up with a solution that just might get him out of there.

When class was over, he went to work on his Windermere exit strategy, alternating his time between the internet and a spreadsheet. A few of the figures he guessed at; the rest he pulled from wholesale websites. By noon, he was done, except for one final but very important detail. He grabbed his phone and placed the call.

"Hello?"

Was Grandpa the only person on earth who answered his cellphone with *hello*? "Grandpa, it's me."

"Hey, Austin. How are things down at the beach?"

"Busy. I started one of my classes this morning. The other starts Monday."

"Good luck with that, boy. I remember when summer meant not worrying about school. When are you coming up to Coatesville again?"

"Maybe this weekend. I have a favor to ask. It's a big one."

"How much do you need, son?"

"No, sir, it's not money. I'm taking on a project and need power tools. I looked into renting them, but it was going to cost way too much."

Grandpa Staley's basement shop had always been one of his favorite places. He was constantly building or repairing something. His neighbors in Coatesville called on him for anything from mending the cane bottom of a chair to enlarging a living room window. Austin couldn't be sure if he would be willing to loan out his tools.

"What do you need?"

Austin went down the list. It was extensive.

But Grandpa didn't hesitate. "Come and get 'em."

"Are you sure you won't need them for a couple months, Grandpa?"

"I'll need them if they're here, but if you got 'em, I won't. You know how much I like you working with your hands, Austin."

"I'll be there tomorrow with a rental truck."

"Don't waste your money. Just ride the bus up and take Calvin back with you."

The possibility of borrowing Calvin, the name his grandfather had given his 1963 International pickup, hadn't occurred to Austin. "Are you sure? Won't you need Calvin?"

Grandpa laughed. "For what? You're taking all my tools."

The mirth in his voice said it all. He was happy to loan the tools.

KATHRYN REFILLED her glass and corked the bottle of red wine. After gulping the first two glasses, she sipped her third and gazed out the kitchen window at the nearly completed fence.

Only one section remained to be repaired and painted. She wanted to tell Austin how marvelous a job he was doing, but their paths hadn't crossed since earlier in the week. The lovely fence was the only evidence of his coming and going, as he was meticulous about putting away the tools and cleaning up.

A handful of people had stopped by to admire his work, including Mr. Malone, a longtime neighbor and friend of Kathryn's grandfather who shared stories of their Bethany Beach neighborhood as it was in the fifties and sixties. She found his stories both enjoyable and comforting, reflecting on a time when Bethany Beach was little more than a strip of sand and a few clapboard houses and shanties. His stories brought her peace and a sense of belonging, as if she were part of the local history rather than just another late-comer. She'd have to share those stories with Austin when she saw him.

What was she thinking? A guy his age wouldn't care about local history. Especially if he was hearing it from *freaking Dr. Snore*. She couldn't even get a bunch of summer semester kids to appreciate the importance of language and literature.

The thought of returning to class made her stomach hurt. Or maybe it was the wine. Suzanne was right. She didn't need the aggravation of remedial college English. She would email Casper at the end of the semester and let him know she would willingly give up the summer courses. Maybe that would appease him enough to stop dropping by.

✟✟✟✟✟

AT THE RILEY STREET HOUSE, Austin constructed a makeshift workbench from some of the demo materials, then sat down. He had his numbers ready. It was time to kick off his Windermere exit plan.

He called the office in Philadelphia, hopeful Dad would answer. He asked fewer questions. It was late on Friday afternoon, about the time Mom usually left the office to get her hair done.

But not that week. Mom answered, her voice cheerful. "Hi, honey."

"Mom. I'm surprised to get you."

"Why? I work here too, you know."

"Yeah, but you usually... Dad asked me to line up someone to renovate the Riley Street property. I was calling back to let him know that we're set to go."

"He's in Pittsburgh. I know all about that property, though. Who do you think it was who convinced your father to buy it?"

Of course it was Mom. She pulled the strings in the company. Theirs was an interesting dynamic. None of Austin's friends' parents were in business together, other than Jared Clough's. Jared's father ran a plumbing business; his mother answered the phone and did the books. The situation at Cornerstone Properties was much different. Dad scouted building sites, and Mom did marketing. Grandpa built houses until he retired. Holly was heir apparent to lead the company. The plan for Austin was that he would go to law school and join his sister.

"Were you able to get the man we used before?" Mom asked.

"He was tied up. He recommended another local, but he showed up drunk."

"Oh, dear."

"I found someone else, though, Mom."

"Really, who?"

Let the subterfuge begin! No lying, though. Stretch the truth, don't break it.

"He knows the area. And I've seen some of his work. He can start right away and finish in six weeks."

"Have we used him before?"

"I don't think so. He may have done some work for us, but not as lead."

"There are so many subcontractors down there. What's his company name?"

Ack! He hadn't seen that one coming.

"Austin?"

"I'm here."

"What's the company name, honey?"

"It's... Picket Fence Construction."

He could hear keystrokes on the other end of the line.

"Nope. It doesn't show up in our records."

"I think it used to be something else. He knows all about you guys and said he has worked on your houses before."

"Did he give you an estimate?"

Austin told her the number.

"That's within what we budgeted." Mom paused for a moment. "What do you think, Austin?"

It was a question she'd never asked him before. They probably asked Holly's opinion all the time. Austin's? Nope. Mom's sudden faith in him warmed his insides, then made him feel guilty for misleading her. "I think he's our best option. He seems reliable, and I believe him when he says he'll get the job done."

"That's good enough for me. Send me the estimate for our records and tell him to get started. Does he need a deposit?"

Another question he hadn't considered.

"Yeah... he asked for twenty-five-hundred."

"That's not bad. I'll cut a check and send it to you. Now, you'll be checking on his work, right?"

"Yes, Mom. Every day."

"How about your classes? Did you get signed up?"

"We started this morning."

"And you're going to make your grades this time, right?"

"Yes, Mom."

"How are things at the Windermere?"

"Not great at first, but getting better."

"Good to hear, honey. Have a great weekend. Study hard."

Austin put his phone away and turned to look at the old house.

"Goodbye, Windermere," he muttered as he stepped inside. The back bedroom upstairs was the most habitable space. He would move his stuff in there and get the hell out of the Windermere before the place went up in a fiery, crack-fed blaze. It would be dusty and hot, but at least he would have a bathroom to himself.

Things were looking up.

SEVEN

saturday, may 28

AUSTIN PULLED through a McDonald's drive-through in Rehoboth Beach and bought six sausage biscuits before setting out on Route 1 toward Pennsylvania. Grandpa was expecting him the next day at noon. He would spend Saturday with Savannah at her family home in Hershey. They would eat dinner with her parents before finding an excuse to break away for some alone time. After much thought, he had passed on taking the bus in favor of driving. He would leave the Mustang in Coatesville and drive Grandpa's truck instead. Calvin was over fifty years old and had a half-million miles on the odometer but would work fine for Austin's short commutes between the Riley Street house and the area lumber yards.

He hadn't realized how hungry he was until he bit into the first biscuit. Sleep had been fitful on his last night at the Windermere, but at least there were no police in the hallway. He hoped that Grandpa would let him borrow that old army cot he kept in the attic. It would serve just fine as his bed at the Riley Street house.

Between biscuits, he called Savannah to let her know

when he would be arriving. "Any chance we can take a dip in your parents' hot tub?" he asked.

"Sure," she said, then lowered her voice. "But we'll have to keep our swimsuits on."

That was the least of his worries. His arms and shoulders were throbbing from the hours he'd spent working on the fence. He'd finished up an hour earlier, hoping to say farewell to Kathryn before leaving, but she hadn't been home. He made a mental note to run by the following week and get the money he was owed for materials. With the Riley Street project beginning Monday, he would need it.

THE FENCE WAS DONE. And it was magnificent! Each picket in perfect alignment to the one beside it. All painted the same brilliant white. No varying shades of gray like before.

Austin was an amazing craftsman. Kathryn wanted to let him know how thrilled she was, but there was no sign of him. He had come and gone while she was at Milo's with her friends. Somehow she would track him down, and she would start by calling the number she kept on the dry erase board.

"Cornerstone Properties. This is Holly."

"Hello, this is Kathryn Shea. I live on Sea Turtle Court in Bethany Beach. I spoke to you last week."

"Of course, Ms. Shea. I hope you're not having trouble with the people next door again."

"Not at all. Actually, I was hoping you could give me Austin's number. He repaired my fence and I need to pay him."

"Ms. Shea, you don't owe Austin anything. Our renters broke the fence. We'll cover the damages."

When Kathryn explained that Austin had not just repaired the damaged section, but the entire fence, Holly seemed surprised.

"All the way around your house?"

"Yes. He finished it this morning while I was away, and it's perfect. It hasn't looked this good since my grandfather was still alive. I really want to get in touch with Austin and pay him for his time."

"I'll see if I can locate him, Ms. Shea."

🏠

SEEING Savannah again after a week was wonderful.

Reclining in her parents' hot tub while the jets went to work on his shoulders was otherworldly.

They were the master and mistress of decorum, donning their swimsuits and remaining a few inches apart, until Savannah's mother came out to inform them she and Savannah's father were leaving for a cookout at the house of some friends a few blocks away. Savannah shrugged off her bikini top as soon as they heard the garage door close. Austin offered no complaints as she moved closer and kissed him.

When his phone rang, he reached for it, but Savannah slapped his hand away. "No, no. Fun now. Phone later."

"I need to check, just in case it's something for work. I'm waiting on a quote for cabinets."

Savannah reluctantly moved aside, but remained where he could gaze at her while he took his call.

"Austin? It's Kathryn Shea."

"Oh. Hey Kathryn."

Savannah arched her eyebrows. Truth was, he still felt a little strange referring to Kathryn by her first name. And now Savannah was wondering if he was talking to someone he shouldn't.

"The fence is beautiful. You did a marvelous job."

"Thank you. Sorry it took so long, but with the hand tools and all."

"The fact that you crafted it by hand makes it even more special. I want to pay you for your work. Are you in Bethany?"

"No, not now. I'm actually in..." Austin glanced at Savannah, who was hanging on every word. "I'm in Pennsylvania. I came up to see... my grandfather."

Savannah frowned, then reached for her bikini top.

"Will you be back next week?"

"I'll be back tomorrow."

"Would you like to come for supper tomorrow evening?"

Had Savannah heard Kathryn's question? Austin glanced her way. She'd put her top back on and was already immersed in something on her phone.

"I don't know if..." He paused, then glanced at Savannah. She was glaring at him. "Sure. I can do that."

"Seven?"

"Seven is great."

He laid the phone aside and scooched to Savannah's side of the tub. He could tell by the look she gave him that he had some explaining to do before the bikini top came off again, so he got busy.

sunday, may 29

GRANDPA WAS PERCHED on a stepladder when Austin pulled into his driveway. His weight was on one leg as he reached far to his right to trim an already nicely shaped boxwood. Grandpa and ladders had an unfortunate history, but Austin bit his tongue rather than say anything.

Miss Leona Robinson, Grandpa's renter and neighbor, kept an eye on him from her side of the duplex. Her outfit was typical Miss Leona. Bright floral stretch pants and a James Brown T-shirt from the seventies. She started in the moment Austin stepped out of the car.

"I keep telling him not to be climbing up and down that ladder," Miss Leona called out. "He always was a hard-headed man, but it's worse since Marlene went home to the Lord."

Grandpa climbed off the stepladder. "Marlene never nagged me like you do, Leona." He met Austin and pulled him into an embrace that made Austin feel seven years old again. "Good to see you, boy."

"He ain't eating as well as he should neither," Miss

Leona said. "Tuna fish for lunch about every day. Soup and sandwiches for supper."

Grandpa waved her off. "Leona, if I eat like you want me to, I'll weigh three hundred pounds."

They remained in the yard for a few minutes while Miss Leona described her latest medical maladies and a few of Grandpa's. She had rented the right side of the duplex for as long as Austin could remember and was as much a part of a trip to Coatesville as Grandpa's workshop and a burger from Willy's Family Restaurant.

Eventually Grandpa was able to get them away from Miss Leona and into the house. Everything about the place —the furniture, the color of the walls, the smells of coffee and hair tonic—was as it always was. The only thing missing was the scent of Grandma's White Shoulders perfume. After she died, Grandpa had regularly sprayed it about the house until the bottle ran out.

"You want a grilled cheese sandwich, or do you want to go see what we can get at Willy's?" Grandpa asked.

"Grilled cheese sounds great."

Grandpa opened a cabinet and lifted out a cast-iron frying pan. "Remember when Sunday lunch was a big deal around here?"

Austin remembered. The four of them—Mom, Dad, Holly, and him—used to come to Coatesville two Sundays a month for lunch. Dad grumbled sometimes. For that matter, so did Holly and Austin, but Mom was unrelenting.

"I told you when we moved to the city that we would come back often," she would scold Dad. That did the trick. They usually arrived a little before noon. Grandma would be busy in the kitchen; Grandpa would be in front of the TV or in his basement wood shop. Austin always hoped for the latter.

"Marlene would never have served grilled cheese, that's for sure," Grandpa said. He placed American cheese on white buttered bread and dropped it into the frying pan. The room filled with the warm sweet aroma of grilling cheese.

Austin watched him as he moved about the kitchen. He was doing well. Grandpa had always been a busy man, and Grandma's passing pushed him to become busier. If he wasn't fixing a toilet or hanging a closet door somewhere on the block, he was hauling day-old bread from local grocery stores to a food pantry in West Chester. It wasn't that Grandpa was particularly civic-minded as much as he enjoyed having things to do.

"There was another break-in a few blocks up the street last week," he said, placing a hot, toasty sandwich in front of Austin. "Broad daylight. Family named Rockwell. He works at the steel plant and she's a teacher's aide at the elementary school."

Grandpa mentioned crime in the area more frequently than when Grandma had been alive. Coatesville had its share of problems, as did other communities in the area. Mom used to pester him about finding a place closer to the city, but Grandpa would never leave Coatesville. And so far, his home had remained untouched. He said it was because the neighbors looked out for one another. "None of them are the same people who lived here when we bought the place," he'd told Austin many times, "but they're good people who want to live in a safe neighborhood."

The conversation meandered from break-ins to the weather and the Philadelphia Phillies' lack of hitting. "What are you working on that requires so many tools?" he asked as they finished their grilled cheese.

Austin wiped his hands on his napkin. He couldn't say

too much about his plans for the Riley Street property in case Grandpa slipped and mentioned it to Mom. "Just a few jobs we couldn't get locals to take on."

"I like when you get in there and do the work yourself. You got that from me, you know?"

Austin knew. His earliest memories were of the two of them building things together after church while the rest of the family watched football or napped. Grandpa taught him the best and safest ways to use his tools, then gave him space when he wanted to create.

"What will you do while your shop tools are gone?" Austin asked.

"Pete Proctor needs someone to do inventory at his lumber yard. I'll help with that. I might go see your Uncle Raymond in New Jersey. He's been pestering me to come up and see Skyler's baseball team."

"Are you doing any work for Mom and Dad, Grandpa?"

"They don't ask much anymore. They have those crews they hire for the construction work. I don't have a union card, so the job foremen don't much like seeing me show up." Grandpa chewed the last bite of his sandwich, then said, "It's not like it used to be, Austin. Back when I was building houses, I could make a run into the city and round up a dozen good men for any job. No contracts other than a handshake." Grandpa shook his head sadly. "I miss those days."

Austin ached for the emptiness Grandpa was feeling. His parents had unintentionally pushed him to the sideline following a fall a few years before. Perhaps if things worked out in Bethany he could invite him down to help. The thought of working side-by-side on a big project made him smile. He considered telling Grandpa Staley but kept it to himself. At least for the time being.

THE SUBJECT *of my creative writing assignment is my dog.*

Ugh. Another dog paper. The fourth of the afternoon. Kathryn massaged her temples and prayed that this one might actually be creative.

He is a terrier mix, and his name is Dog.

A dog named Dog. Oh, boy. Not much creativity there.

Dog likes to play fetch and bark at the neighbors.

No! Please, save me.

Dog was just seven months old when he had his first beer.

Wait! Kathryn read that sentence again, just to make sure she hadn't read wrong. Maybe it said *his first beef.*

Nope. It said beer. Dog the terrier liked beer. On command, he would scamper to the fridge and pull out a beer for his master and another for himself.

"At least it's creative," Kathryn mumbled as she reached the end. She gave the paper a B for effort, and because it held her attention much longer than rambling accounts of muskrat hunts and bachelorette parties.

Three more papers and she'd had enough. Kathryn decided to clean the house. It wasn't needed, but she wanted to freshen it up anyway. Was it the dust motes floating in the early afternoon sunlight that made her decide to clean or the lackluster student papers? Both? Neither?

Maybe it was because Austin was coming for dinner. She didn't have many guests other than her small circle of friends. Suzanne dropped by every so often, usually to share college gossip. Hillary did too, but less frequently. Mostly, they met at Milo's or the movie theater. Sometimes they would ride into Ocean City or Rehoboth for shopping or outdoor concerts. She used to like to shop with her friends, but not so much anymore. It seemed so unnecessary. She had a closet full of clothes but migrated to the same few things. She really needed to take some stuff to Goodwill, but what if she needed it later?

As she pushed her grandfather's Electrolux over the living room carpet, she debated what to make for dinner. She enjoyed preparing fresh seafood, and crab cakes were a particular favorite. But would a guy Austin's age like them or would he prefer something more filling? She still had her mother's meatloaf recipe. She could also whip up a pretty mean cheesesteak.

Hmm. What to make?

<hr />

BACK WHEN HE WAS A KID, Austin had always assumed that his grandpa's pickup was named for President Calvin Coolidge. He hadn't learned until he was in high school that the namesake was actually a long-ago neighbor named Calvin Turner, a bricklayer who worked with Grandpa in the sixties. Calvin bought the International truck from a dealer, then decided he didn't like the way it drove or its flat black color. He and Grandpa bartered back and forth before swinging a deal. The 1963 International became Grandpa's, and Grandpa's sky-blue 1961 Ford F-150 and a wet saw went to Calvin.

"That Ford made it until Calvin left it idling in gear and it ran into Brandywine Creek in sixty-seven." Grandpa used to laugh as he reminisced. "He traded the wet saw for a pit bull named Homer who went everywhere with Calvin until that dog died at the ripe old age of seventeen."

So even though he'd never met Calvin Turner, Austin felt as if he knew him.

"Calvin has his scars, same as me," Grandpa said as they loaded the power tools into the truck. "He ain't the prettiest truck around, but he'll get you where you're going and never complain about it." Calvin's exterior had a few dings and scrapes, many inflicted by careless loading and unloading, but the motor purred and the tires had less than eight-thousand miles on them.

When the power equipment was strapped down, Austin handed Grandpa the keys to his Mustang. "Drive it as much as you need."

"Nah, I'll park it in the garage until you get back. Your grandmother's car needs some airing out, so I'll use it." Grandpa Staley placed his large strong hands upon Austin's shoulders and squeezed. "I know you have a lot going on with college and all, son, but make sure you have some fun while you're down there at the beach."

"I promise, Grandpa. And thank you for everything. I love you."

"I love you, too, Austin."

CRAB CAKES IT WAS.

Made with Miss Eleanor's special recipe.

Only a few people, all locals, would know Miss Eleanor if they passed her on the street.

And only a few of those who knew Miss Eleanor, again locals except for one enterprising Washington, D.C. restaurateur, knew her crab cake recipe. Kathryn's grandmother had been one of the lucky ones. She had wisely written it down and placed it in her wooden recipe box where

Kathryn still kept it. Kathryn assembled the ingredients on the counter, then got to work forming the cakes and setting them aside. Fresh-cut french fries and locally grown pickled cucumbers would round out a true Eastern Shore meal.

And if Austin didn't like crab cakes? If he was one of those guys who preferred a burger and a beer? Well, too bad about the burger, but Kathryn had picked up a six-pack of Dogfish Head beer.

When everything was ready, she showered and dug through her closet before settling on a yellow sundress. She was pulling it over her head when her phone buzzed. Could it be Austin? Canceling? He was about that age where plans changed suddenly. Maybe a date? A girl he met while out on the town? If so, Kathryn could always freeze half the crab cakes. The cucumbers would keep just fine. The fries would be a loss, though.

It was Suzanne.

"I saw Malinka Callaway at the produce stand today," she said, in place of a greeting. "You won't believe what the science department found out this past Friday."

Kathryn checked the time. Six thirty. She needed a few minutes to finish getting ready, but Suzanne wasn't one to be put off. She was still talking twenty minutes later. Campus politics and rumors, but nothing that couldn't have waited. Kathryn tried to listen while she fixed her hair but missed much of what was said. When Suzanne finally came up for air, she jumped in.

"Suzanne, I really have to go."

"What is it? Something on TV?"

"No, I have a... someone coming for dinner."

"Oh really? Don't tell me it's that real estate guy from last weekend."

"No, it's... the handyman. The kid who fixed my fence. He's coming to get paid, and I offered to fix dinner."

"Are you certain that's a good idea, Kathryn?"

Kathryn reached for her curling iron and nearly grabbed it at the wrong end, pulling back just in time. "It'll be fine."

"You said he's a kid? How old is he?"

"I didn't mean a kid... exactly. He's young, but he works for a living. It's hard to say. Twenty-five? Twenty-something?"

"What are you making?"

"Crab cakes."

"For a kid who builds fences?"

"He's not a kid, Suzanne."

"A handyman who builds fences?"

"Handymen like seafood too."

"Yeah, but I've seen how much crabmeat costs this summer. You kind of went overboard for a handyman, didn't you?"

"Maybe, but I felt like having crab cakes. Listen, Suzanne, I really have to go. Can I talk to you this week sometime?"

"You better, and good luck with your... handyman."

There was a lewdness in the way she said the word that stuck in Kathryn's mind as she finished getting ready. Austin, the handyman, wasn't expecting anything more than dinner. Or was he? Had she led him on somehow? Made him think that...

Oh, for goodness' sake. The thought made her laugh out loud. Suzanne was teasing her, and she had allowed her imagination to run away a bit. Austin had been considerably more interested in her grandfather's tools than in her. Their conversations had been short and pretty boring, really.

Nope. This was dinner between a grateful homeowner and the... handyman who'd repaired her fence.

Nothing else.

#

BARNEY'S TOW TRUCK, with Austin in the passenger seat, pulled up in front of Ms. Shea—Kathryn's—house at ten past seven. Austin grabbed his duffel bag from beside his feet and pushed the door open. "Thanks for the ride, Barney. And for helping me unload the equipment."

"You bet," Barney said, straightening his stained John Deere cap. "Just don't tell my boss when you come to pick up your truck. I'm not supposed to be a taxi service."

"Not a word. And I'll be at your house Tuesday night to put those blinds up."

Barney drove away with Calvin in tow.

So much for dependability.

Calvin had overheated before Austin reached the Delaware state line. His car repair skills lagged far behind his woodworking skills, but he knew enough to pull over and allow the truck to cool down before continuing. That happened four times before he figured out there was a leak in the radiator. He limped into Rehoboth Beach before giving up and calling a tow truck. Barney hemmed and hawed before agreeing to help unload the power equipment on the condition that Austin would hang six window blinds his wife had been nagging him about since last fall. Bartering was alive and well in lower Delaware.

He was hot and dirty from crawling around under Calvin. His favorite shirt, a sky-blue plaid button-down, a Christmas gift from his sister the year before, had grease splotches on the left sleeve and collar. His shorts were black, so at least they hid the dirt.

He considered bailing on dinner, but his options weren't appealing. The water was off at the Riley Street house. He had meant to call and get it turned on, but forgot. There was still the Windermere, but he was already depressed enough with how the day was winding down. One more encounter with Charlene the tweaker might be enough to send him home to Philly, begging Mom and Dad to relieve him of his summer duties.

Nope. That wouldn't be happening. And it wasn't like Kathryn was expecting anything from him. She knew him as the guy who fixed the fence. Some handyman who was there one day, gone the next. Dinner would probably be pizza and lemonade along with a check for materials and a promise to recommend him to her friends. With any luck, he would be out of there by eight.

But where would he go?

He stepped onto the front porch and rang the bell. An odor similar to spoiled food came at him from some place. He sniffed around, then realized the foul smell wasn't coming at him, but *from* him. He checked his overnight bag before remembering he had left his deodorant on the back seat of the Mustang. Kathryn Shea might take one look at him, get a whiff, and call the cops.

Yes, Officer, there's a homeless man on my front step. Can you come get him? He smells like motor oil and antifreeze.

And perhaps grilled cheese.

He was considering making a run for it when she opened the door. She wore a bright sundress free of grease or sweat stains. She smelled wonderful. She looked at him, then did a double take.

"AUSTIN? ARE YOU..."

Oh, my. What had she been about to say?

Are you okay?

Is this how you dress for dinner?

He looked as if he had been rolling around in the street. Maybe he had. Perhaps he had fallen off a skateboard. His shirt had something black on the sleeve and collar. His dark brown hair kind of went one way, then another.

And his neck? What was going on with his neck? There were beads of something, like dirt maybe, that circled it.

He was, it turned out, just a handyman. The poor guy probably didn't own any clothes that were free of spots and stains.

He dropped a scuffed duffel bag next to the door. "Sorry I'm late."

He sounded different. Forlorn? Whipped? Kathryn offered her best smile, stepped back, and held the door open.

"I'm delighted you came. Follow me to the kitchen."

He followed her through a cozy living room with clean, but dated furniture. Sturdy stuff built to last for decades, with nary a trace of beachy decor. The kitchen was larger than he expected, with a drop-leaf table that could open to seat six or eight, a large gas range, and newer appliances.

"Have a seat at the island. Would you like something to drink? I have water and lemonade. And beer. Would you like a beer?"

"Beer sounds great. Thank you."

She pulled one from the fridge and handed it to him. He

twisted off the top and downed half of it. She stifled a laugh when he smacked his lips.

"I'm sorry for the way I look," he said.

"There's nothing wrong with your appearance. This is Bethany Beach. Anything goes."

Austin took another swig and shook his head. "I ran into a little trouble on my way back from Pennsylvania."

She pulled another beer from the fridge, slid it across to him, then took a seat. "Goodness, did you get mugged?"

The words were spoken before she considered how they might come out. He looked up from his beer, then burst into laughter. "Is that what it looks like?"

His reaction flustered her. "No... it's just that you look like you were knocked down... or something."

He glanced at his shirt. "Nothing that bad, and I don't usually show up looking like this," He sniffed at his shirt and waved his hands in front of his face in disgust. "My deodorant is melting on the back seat of my car in Pennsylvania. Maybe I should go sit on the porch and you can hand my dinner out through the window."

She laughed. "I've smelled sweaty guys before. Listen, it's going to take me a few minutes to pull dinner together." She considered what was about to come out of her mouth. Was she really about to invite him to take a shower? Right there, in her house? "How old are you, Austin? If you don't mind me asking."

He looked at her curiously, then glanced at the beer in his hand. "Twenty-two, so don't worry. You aren't serving alcohol to a minor."

Twenty-two. So young. So, so young. "No, that wasn't it." Kathryn's face grew hot. She laughed to conceal it, but knew she couldn't. "I was just curious. But what I was about to say was, it will be another half hour before dinner is ready. Would you like to take a shower?"

He appeared confused, and maybe suspicious. Kathryn exhaled sharply when she realized how that must have sounded.

Would you like to take a shower?

He's twenty-two, for crying out loud. He has probably seen plenty of movies with couples showering together, so he has to think that... oh, God, no.

"Because if you do, I can show you where the upstairs bathroom is. Then I can come back down here. While you shower... alone... upstairs... while I'm finishing dinner."

Get a grip, Kathryn.

Austin glanced toward the stairs, then nodded. "I would appreciate that. I have a change of clothes in my bag, so yes. If you don't mind."

Kathryn led the way up the stairs. He was two steps behind her. Close. Too close? What was he looking at while they climbed the stairs? That was a stupid question. What would any twenty-two-year-old guy be looking at? She suddenly felt self-conscious in the thin sundress and tried to climb the steps in a way that caused her to... sway less, maybe?

IT WAS KIND OF her to offer the use of her bathroom, but why was she acting strangely? And what was with the way she climbed the stairs? About halfway up, her legs tightened, and she started moving as if she'd had a stroke. At the top step, her foot banged against the wall, and for a moment it looked like she might fall. He reached out to steady her, but she kept her footing.

Was she older than she looked? Was there a medical condition? Something that made stair-climbing difficult?

At the landing, she went to the first door on the right, opened it, and turned on a light. "The towels are fresh," she said. "You should find everything you need under the sink."

He dropped his duffel bag to the floor just outside the bathroom, and she jumped, then stepped around him toward the door. "The hot water takes a couple minutes to warm up," she blurted. "I'll get dinner ready." She made a beeline for the stairwell and nearly stumbled. Austin could see she was anxious about something.

Was it him? If so, he needed to let her know he was harmless.

"Kathryn?"

She turned around.

"Thank you."

She smiled and started down the stairs. Austin pulled his shirt over his head as he stepped into the bathroom, not bothering to unbutton it. He should probably throw it away. Grease never came out. He closed the door and pulled off his shorts. They were salvageable, at least. His socks too

—

Wait. He scanned the bathroom floor. Where was his bag?

In the hallway, where he'd left it of course. He opened the door —

Kathryn stood at the top of the stairs. Their eyes met.

And just as quickly, she looked away, then down at the floor. "I forgot to ask if you like crab cakes," she said.

Austin grabbed his bag from the floor and held it in front of him. "Uh, yeah, I like them a lot."

That was awkward.

He stepped back inside and closed the door. He took a

deep breath and started the water. While it warmed, he took a quick look into the hall, just to make sure she hadn't returned. The hallway was empty. He heard the clatter of pots and pans downstairs.

HE RETURNED to the kitchen in white board shorts and a gray T-shirt that fit snugly across his chest. Kathryn had set their places across from each other at the kitchen table and poured herself a glass of wine. "Another beer?" she asked.

"No, thank you. I will take a glass of whatever you're having, though."

"It's Moscato. Have you tried it?"

"I don't think so. What's it like?"

"Sweet. And kind of bubbly. It's not something that a wine connoisseur would recommend with crab cakes and fries, but—"

"Are you a wine connoisseur?"

Kathryn's laugh came out as more of a snort. "Gosh, no. I just know what I like, and I like Moscato."

"It sounds great."

She retrieved a glass from the cabinet and filled it. Austin sipped it thoughtfully, then smiled. "I like it."

She handed him a serving plate containing six crab cakes. "I hope you can say the same for dinner."

He took one, reconsidered, and added a second. "Lunch was a long time ago," he said with a grin as he reached for the cucumbers and fries. She liked the way he dug in.

They were quiet for a few moments while they ate. Austin made his crab cakes disappear in short order. Kathryn saw him eyeing the remaining three and encouraged him to take them. "One is all I want," she said. She would have eaten two or three, but watching him enjoy the meal was better.

"What do you do besides fixing fences?" she asked.

"My family has rental properties in the area. I keep an eye on things, clean up after renters leave, respond to complaints."

"Like mine?"

He nodded. "Most renters are pretty good, but a few get crazy. Those guys who made a mess of your yard won't be able to rent from us again."

"Well, you went above and beyond, Austin, and I appreciate it." She wiped her hands as she stood up, then went to the kitchen counter for her checkbook.

"How much were the materials?" she asked after sitting back down.

"I have the receipts in my backpack. Let me go get them."

"That's not necessary. I'm sure you know how much everything costs."

"The materials and hardware were three hundred, but you don't have to pay. Our company can cover it."

She smiled, then started filling out the check. She ripped it from the checkbook and handed it to him. His eyes widened when he saw the amount.

"This is too much."

"I insist. I was pretty harsh with you that first morning, and you've been a gentleman. I love my new fence and want you to have it."

He looked at the check once more, then folded it and stuck it in his shorts pocket. "Thank you. Really. You don't know how much this will come in handy."

⊞

HE HAD CONSIDERED INFLATING the material costs by ten or twenty percent. It was a common practice. Some called it handling charges. Others didn't bother calling it anything. In the end, he'd quoted her the actual cost of the materials. A little less, actually, as the bill was closer to three-fifty. Kathryn's check would cover materials, Calvin's radiator repairs, and leave some spending money for the next couple of weeks. The deposit his mother was sending for renovation at the Riley Street place would arrive by midweek.

Things were looking up.

"What else do you do?" Kathryn asked after refilling their wineglasses.

"What do you mean?"

"You manage your family's investment properties. Is there anything else?"

"I'm a college student."

⊞

Uh-oh. A student?

Had he been in one of her classes? Perhaps a couple of years earlier? She usually remembered faces, but a few classes were quite large, and some students were content to blend into the crowd.

If he had been one of her former students, what was she to do? The college had strict rules about teacher-student fraternization. There had been a handful of instances when teachers were found to be in violation of the policy. The most egregious was a biology instructor who got a coed pregnant. His contract was not renewed. Could that happen to her? Could they fire her for cooking dinner for a student who fixed her fence? Could Casper use it as a reason to get rid of her? Suzanne would know. She kept up on stuff like that. But did she want Suzanne knowing she had dated a student? Was it best to keep it quiet and hope no one found out?

Or maybe it wasn't even a thing.

Please don't let him be a student at my college. "So, you're a student? Really?"

He nodded. "I go to Penn."

Phew.

"Or I used to go to Penn. If I don't get Bs in my summer courses, I won't be able to go back."

"I'm sorry to hear that. Penn is very rigorous. What year are you?"

"I should be starting my senior year."

"What's your major?"

"Pre-law."

There was something in the way he said it that caught Kathryn's attention. She regarded him across the table but said nothing.

"I'll go to law school, then work in the family business. It's all planned out. Mom handles marketing, Dad develops construction sites, and my sister manages things."

"When did you decide to pursue law?"

He shrugged. "I'm not sure I did. We always knew that one of us, Holly or me, would go into law. I did better on the SATs so it fell to me."

"What did you score?"

Kathryn nearly fell out of her chair when he answered.

"Goodness, Austin. That's amazing."

He shrugged.

"No wonder you got into Penn. Did you apply to other universities?"

He named off five colleges, including two other Ivy League schools.

"How many accepted you?"

"All of them."

Her handyman was a genius. A freaking genius. Yet there he was, on academic probation. Why? "What classes are you taking this summer?"

"Organizational Theory."

Kathryn nodded. "I've heard of it. Business, right?"

Austin smiled. "So I'm told. I'll do okay in that one. It's the other one that's got me worried. Don't laugh when I tell you, okay?"

"Never."

"Southern Literature."

Kathryn's face lit up when he said it.

"Why are you in Southern Lit? It's not typically an elective that non-lit majors take."

"I took it sophomore year. It was a crazy time. Do you think I should drop it and take something else?"

"Do you like to read?"

Austin shrugged. "I don't mind reading if I like something. So far I haven't found anything I like."

"What was the last book you read?"

"All the way through?"

Kathryn nodded.

Austin tried to remember. "I read all the *Hank the Cowdog* books."

"I'm not familiar with those. Who's the author?"

"I have no idea. It was fourth grade."

Her eyes grew large. "You're kidding me."

He grinned. "Yeah, I am. I read *Holes* in fifth grade. I did a book report on it. Sixth grade too."

"Same book for both years?"

"Different schools."

"Oh my goodness, Austin. You really don't read much, do you?"

"Not novels. I read stuff online, though."

"What kinds of stuff?"

"I like civil rights. My parents took us to the National Civil Rights Museum when I was in junior high. I thought it was interesting, so I look at stuff about that sometimes. Dr. King, sit-ins and marches. That kind of stuff."

"Have you heard of *To Kill a Mockingbird*?"

"I started it but didn't get into it."

"How about *The Help*?"

"Is that the book about the maids?"

"Yes."

"Half of our class is reading that one. If I read it too, they'll bury me. I'm the only person in the class who doesn't live and breathe Southern lit."

"You want something that no one else will choose?"

"Yes. And doesn't put me to sleep."

Kathryn took a sip of wine, sat back in her chair, and considered the possibilities.

"How do you know so much about southern literature?" he asked.

"I teach in the English department at the local college."

"Seriously?"

She nodded.

"You don't seem like a college professor."

"I teach junior college. We're called instructors, not professors, but yes, that's what I do. My PhD is in literature."

"You're a doctor?"

"I am."

"What was your dissertation project? Don't all doctors have to do those?"

"Yes, and you don't want to know."

"Sure, I do."

"No, you don't. It would put you to sleep, but suffice it to say it's not Southern literature. I do have some ideas for books you might enjoy, though. I might even have a couple in my office."

"I don't want to put you out, Kathryn..." Austin grinned. "*Doctor* Shea."

She laughed. "Too late for that. It's Dr. Shea to my students. My fence artist calls me Kathryn."

"Fence artist?" He smiled as he considered the title. "I like that. Maybe I'll have cards printed up." He looked at her across the table, seeing more of the witty and intelligent woman he had picked up on the roadside, and less of the frumpy woman who complained about the neighbors. She wasn't like the professors he'd had at Penn, but then he'd never known them outside the classroom. Perhaps over crab cakes and Moscato they might be pretty nice too.

Conversation continued. When he glanced at his phone, it was after nine. They'd spent over an hour chatting and enjoying good food.

"I should be going," he said, getting to his feet. "Dinner was great."

"I'm glad you came." She dipped her head, glancing away as she said, "It's been fun. I don't do this often enough."

He picked up his plate and was carrying it to the sink when she said, "Leave it. I'll walk you out and do those later."

She opened the front door and followed him onto the porch. It was a beautiful starlit night.

"Do you hear that?" She asked.

Austin listened. A cricket was chirping close by. From somewhere down the street, he could just make out the end of a Justin Bieber song he used to like. A streetlight hummed in front of the house.

"The ocean," she whispered. "If you listen closely and try to block out everything else, you can hear it."

The Bieber song ended. Austin concentrated, pushing his senses past crickets and other ambient noise.

And there it was.

"Our family has been coming here for years, and I've never noticed that."

She smiled and came a step closer. She kept her voice low, as if she didn't want to interrupt the moment. "Now that you hear the surf, try to smell it."

He raised his head and gazed in the direction of the ocean. It wasn't visible beyond the buildings, but as he focused, he detected the trace of salt in the air, as if it was being pushed their way by a southerly breeze. He took a deep breath, then another.

"It's... how did I miss it before?"

She laughed. "You weren't open to it. Me neither until a few years ago. Now I come out here almost every night and breathe the air and listen to the ocean. It reminds me why I love Bethany so much."

They didn't speak for a bit. Austin appreciated that Kathryn didn't feel the need to fill every moment with chatter.

"Where is your car?"

He told her about the breakdown.

"I'll give you a ride."

"You've already done enough. The place I'm staying isn't far."

"Nonsense. Besides, I owe you from when you rescued me from the side of the road the other night. Let me grab my keys."

🏚

KATHRYN OCCASIONALLY GLANCED at him while following the directions he gave. It was considerably different from the week before when she had driven a drunk *RodneySellsRehoboth* back from dinner in his Porsche. Austin, though buzzed from the beer and Moscato, was in full control of his senses. He chatted freely about his family and his life at Penn. His girlfriend's name was Savannah. His summer plans included rehabbing a house his parents had just purchased. "They would go nuts if they knew I wasn't spending every minute in the library," he said.

That reminded Kathryn of her offer to find him a book. "I never gave you a book to read. I can bring it by your house if you'd like."

"Would it be okay if I came to your office? I have errands to run during the day."

She was giving him her summer office hours when he pointed to a frame house with debris piled on the porch and yard. The upstairs windows were open, and the place had a gloomy quality in the darkness. She pulled to the curb and put the car into park. "Oh, my," she said before she caught herself.

"It will look better soon."

He sounded confident. "You're doing the work yourself?"

"Most of it. I'll hire subs for some things, but I'm excited to get started."

"More excited than you are about Southern Lit?"

He laughed. "Way more excited." He turned in his seat and observed her in the dim light. "But maybe you can change my mind about that."

They remained there for several moments, parked at the curb in front of the dark, dilapidated house. She should be going, but she was enjoying the moment. Even at such a young age, he had more going for him than *RodneySellsRehoboth* and most of the handful of other men she had known over the past decade. He readily admitted his shortcomings, but also held out hope for what was ahead. Being with him had brightened her day.

"Thank you again for dinner, Kathryn. And the check."

"Thank you, Austin. Take care."

He got out of the car and gently closed the door behind him. Kathryn watched as he picked his way through piles of broken drywall that had been tossed outside. Before going inside, he turned and motioned for her to lower the window.

"Is it okay if I get that book sometime this week?"

"Of course. We're off for Memorial Day tomorrow, and I have an appointment Tuesday afternoon. How about Wednesday?"

"Is one o'clock okay? After your classes?"

It was.

He waved farewell, turned on a flashlight, and stepped inside.

She waited until the door was closed before driving away. Finally she had something that week to look forward to.

NINE

wednesday, june 1

THE COMPLAINTS CAME from every corner of the classroom. Kathryn had grown to expect them in summer semester. It was the first assignment, and some students had trouble adapting to the jump in expectations from high school to college. A few didn't try. She kept her snarky replies to herself.

"I worked hard on this."

Sure, you did.

"I'm dropping this course."

Good, but you won't get accepted for the fall.

"Are you curving the grades?"

No, sorry. Four students earned solid As. There is no curve.

"Isn't this supposed to be an easy course?"

The only way I can make it easier is if I write the papers for you.

A pretty girl with a cheerleader's smile, one of the four As, raised her hand. "That's a pretty dress, Dr. Shea. Where did you get it?"

Okay, that one deserved a spoken reply. "Thank you,

Emma. I don't remember where I found it. Nice job on the paper, by the way."

"It wasn't hard."

Exactly.

A skinny boy seated behind Emma spoke up. "I think it's a pretty dress too, Dr. Shea."

"Thank you, Ernesto."

"Would you be willing to take another look at my paper? I thought it was better than a D-plus."

"Sorry, Ernesto. Work harder next time."

Kathryn's step was a bit lighter as she announced the next assignment. She had only worn the pale-green sleeveless dress twice before retiring it to the back of her closet, feeling it just wasn't right for her. The hemline was a couple inches shorter than most of her dresses, and it fit her shape a bit more closely. She usually wore pants and a comfortable long-sleeve shirt that kept her warm since the air conditioning never strayed from a chilly sixty-eight degrees.

The class came to a merciful end, and Kathryn watched the students surge for the door as if the place were on fire. How was it that movies and TV shows always showed students hanging out with the professor after class to discuss life and academics? The only way that might happen was if Kathryn brought cookies, which she had done several times back when she was a new instructor. There just wasn't time for cookies anymore, though.

She gathered her notes, jammed them into her briefcase, and headed for the door. A gaggle of female students clustered in the hallway.

Odd. Students never hung around after class.

Farther up the hall, Austin leaned against the wall, engrossed in his phone. Completely unaware of the girls' attention or the comments they whispered among themselves.

"Who is *he*?"

"Look at those shoulders."

"And his biceps. He must work out."

Brianna, a surly brunette who'd gotten a D on her paper, flipped her hair over her shoulder, and told her friends, "I'm going over there." She threw back her shoulders and walked confidently to where Austin was waiting. His eyes met Brianna's for a second before he spotted Kathryn.

And waved.

Brianna turned to see who he was waving at. The other girls did too.

Kathryn waved back and motioned for him to follow her.

"Is he her brother or something?" one girl asked, unworried that someone might overhear her.

"He seems to know her pretty well."

"He might be a student, but I've never seen him around."

"They find you fascinating," Kathryn said quietly as they walked toward her office.

"Who?"

"Brianna, Chloe, Natalie, and Anna."

Austin looked back and spotted them checking him out. Brianna waved.

"Oh. I didn't notice."

"Sure, you didn't," Kathryn teased. "How is your day?"

"I'm still doing demo work. The downstairs walls are mostly gone, but I need a better crowbar. I'm going to get that after I leave here. I need a dumpster too."

"Any word on your grandfather's truck?"

"It's fixed. Hey, would you like to go for a ride?"

The day was already planned out. There were papers to grade and a long to-do list back at the house. Jane had mentioned that she might come by to borrow a stepladder.

"Where?"

"Lunch? And then to the hardware store and the dumpster place."

Dumpster place?

"I've never been dumpster shopping before."

"You won't be able to say that after today."

"I really shouldn't... Jane is supposed to..." *Dumpster shopping? Why should she go dumpster shopping?* "Sure. Why not?"

Any uneasiness between them was gone, likely washed away by dinner and Moscato. Austin moved through the hallway with a confidence that wasn't evident in the male students they passed. He had a few years of college under his belt, Kathryn reminded herself. Life at Penn had to be considerably different from a tiny commuter college, which she suspected was not all that different from high school.

"My office is right down here," Kathryn said, pointing to a small hallway.

"You look nice," he replied. "Your dress. It looks good on you."

Kathryn blushed. "This old thing," she said quickly, not bothering to mention that she had tried five other outfits before choosing it.

▓▓▓▓

HE TOOK a seat in her cramped office and watched as she looked through the shelves of books that filled the wall behind her desk. The place was cluttered, but smelled nice

115

and had a homey feel to it. Her green dress really looked nice. It made her look younger. Her bare arms were tan and firm, probably from working in the yard. She didn't seem like the type to have a gym membership.

"Aha," she said as she pointed to an upper shelf, then stretched to pull down a book. She turned, smiled, and held it out to him.

"It's thick," Austin joked as he took it and skimmed the cover. "*Chiefs*?"

"It reads fast. Are you familiar with Stuart Woods?"

"Nope."

"This was one of his first books, when he still wrote Southern literature. It's a story about how three small-town police chiefs from the 1920s through the sixties work to solve a series of murders. You might ask your professor if it's acceptable."

"I'm sure it will be. I'll start reading tonight."

"If you like it, I can come up with others."

"Same author?"

"Probably not. He wrote a few more in the genre but has moved on to contemporary literature. I have some ideas, though."

Austin flipped through the book while Kathryn tidied her desk and packed her laptop. "Were you serious about taking me for a ride in your pickup?"

He nodded. "And lunch. What would you like?"

"Surprise me."

IF SHE FELT self-conscious getting into the cab of a dusty half-century old truck, she didn't let it show. Austin had parked in a thirty-minute loading zone, figuring no one would question a work truck. They hadn't. He held the passenger door open as she stepped in, trying not to notice her legs and the slightest glimpse of thigh as she got situated.

"The mechanic had it fixed early yesterday morning," Austin said as she looked it over.

"Your grandfather has taken great care of his truck."

"Calvin."

"Excuse me?"

"Its name is Calvin. That's what Grandpa calls it."

They chatted as Austin drove north on Coastal Highway through the seaside community of Fenwick and into Rehoboth Beach. He continued onto King Charles Avenue and across Silver Lake until coming to Rehoboth Avenue.

"Does the sun bother you?" he asked as he searched for a parking spot close to the beach.

"Not at all."

He pulled into a spot, helped her out of the truck, and fed the meter. "I was thinking about pizza on the boardwalk."

"It sounds perfect."

They passed small shops and ice cream stands on their walk to Rehoboth's historic boardwalk bandstand. Unlike Bethany Beach, Rehoboth's boardwalk was expansive. Austin pointed to a pizza joint next to a candy shop. They stepped to the counter and ordered. Two slices of pepperoni for him, a sausage slice for her. Bottled water for both. Kathryn reached for her purse, but he stopped her and picked up the tab.

The day was ideal. Upper seventies, a cloudless sky. Two hundred feet of brown sand separated the boardwalk from the Atlantic surf. A few people were braving the chilly water temperatures. Many more stretched out on beach towels and played on the shore.

Austin found a bench on the boardwalk and turned it so they faced the surf. They sat down and placed their food between them. Sea gulls clustered a few feet away, their begging caws mixing with the sounds of crashing waves, playing children, and other noises that formed a sound-track of summer.

Austin took a bite and chewed slowly as he looked around. "It's perfect, isn't it?"

"I love their pizza," Kathryn replied.

"No, I mean..." He motioned to their surroundings. "All of this. You're lucky to live here year round."

She smiled and turned her gaze toward the ocean. "I take it for granted sometimes. It's a vacation destination, but when you live here, you have the same problems vaca-tioners come here to get away from. Bills to pay, taxes, stress. I need to remind myself to enjoy it more often. Just sitting like this takes away all the stress of the day."

"Your day was stressful?"

Kathryn told him about her students' lack of interest.

"That's too bad," he said. Then, smiling, "I'm in the same boat they are this summer. Pass or kiss school goodbye."

"Their situation and yours aren't quite the same. You attend an Ivy League school. My summer semester students don't even have the grades to get into community college."

"But you help them, right?"

|||||||

WAS he questioning her commitment to teaching?

Easy, girl. He's not Casper Fillmore. He's just a young guy trying to keep the conversation moving. "What do you mean by help them?"

Austin shrugged. "Nothing really. Just... help them make the grades."

"I make the material as easy as I can without giving them the answers. I show up every day. I keep regular office hours. How much more can I do?" She sounded defensive, but what did he expect? It was college. Not kindergarten.

Austin picked up on her tone. "I understand. I do."

"But?"

"But... nothing. I really understand. See that sailboat?"

She looked to where he was pointing, at a spot along the horizon. He had clumsily but effectively changed the subject. Probably just as well. They kept things light for the next twenty minutes as they finished their slices. Austin took the used paper plates and napkins to a nearby trash can, then returned and held out his hand.

"Are you ready to go dumpster shopping?"

"Can I pick out the color?"

"As long as it's red."

They window-shopped on the way back to his truck. After leaving the beach, they stopped at one of those big-box hardware stores and walked the aisles in search of a crowbar, then checked out and continued inland. The dumpster place was in Georgetown, a twenty-minute drive from Rehoboth. Austin asked if she minded if he opened the windows to allow in the breeze. She said she didn't and enjoyed the wind and salt air that flowed in.

"What about you?" he asked as they entered George-town. "You asked me last night what I did besides fixing fences. What do you like to do other than teach?"

The truth was, she sometimes didn't much like the

teaching, but that was something to keep to herself. "Well, as you can tell from my office, I like to read."

"Yes. And?"

"I enjoy getting together with my friends on Saturday mornings. We meet at a breakfast place in Bethany."

He nodded, but kept his eyes on the road. Even to Kathryn's ears, hers sounded like the life of a little old woman. *Reading? Breakfast with friends?* Geesh, shoot me now.

"I go clubbing on the weekends."

His eyes grew wide.

"I'm teasing. I haven't been clubbing since... since... I'm not really sure what clubbing even is. I saw it in a TV show."

Austin grinned. "Clubbing is fun. Want to go sometime?"

"I don't think that's a good idea. I would probably run into some of my students and end up bloodied in a back alley."

"I suspect you can handle yourself." He turned off the main road into a small parking lot with a bunch of dumpsters off to the side. "Here we are."

They were only inside for a few minutes. Austin chatted with the owner, signed some papers, and left a check. They were back in Calvin when Kathryn asked, "Aren't we taking it with us?"

"They deliver."

"Darn. I was hoping we could ride by my friend Jane's house and show her our dumpster."

"Jane?"

"Yeah, she's one of my three best friends, along with Suzanne and Hillary."

"The friends who have breakfast every Saturday morning?"

"That's them."

God, did she sound boring. She wracked her brain for something interesting to toss out but came up empty.

"Are all of you single?"

"My friends? Yes. Hillary is divorced. Jane is a widow. Suzanne has never been married. And I'm single too."

"I picked up on that," Austin said with a laugh. "Your bathroom is like the powder room at a teahouse."

"How many teahouses have you been to?"

"None, but I bet their bathrooms look like yours. Are you seeing someone?"

"That's kind of personal, isn't it?"

"I told you about Savannah."

True. He had. "As a matter of fact, I had a date just last weekend. A very successful realtor."

"Ah, the owner of the abandoned Porsche. And look at you now. Slumming around in a beat-up old truck."

"It's been a lot more fun than the realtor. I got to drive his car, though."

They both laughed at that.

"Did you ever hear from him?"

"I erased my phone number from his phone. If he stopped by, it was while I was gone."

"You sound like a fun date," Austin said as they got back on the highway. "Nobody special at the moment, though?"

"Nope."

There was more, but Kathryn didn't want to go there. She was enjoying herself too much to talk about past relationships, particularly when it involved a failed marriage. She did as Austin had earlier and changed the subject to more generic topics. A half hour later, they arrived back at campus. She directed him to the lot where her car was parked.

"Thanks for the book and for going dumpster shopping with me."

"My pleasure. Thank you for the pizza. Let me know what you think of the book."

"I will. For sure."

They remained there for a few moments. Kathryn wasn't sure why she lingered, other than she had enjoyed his company.

"Well," he said slowly. "Thanks again."

That was his way of telling her he was ready to leave. She had never been very good at picking up signals. She opened the door, said a last goodbye, and watched as he drove away.

TEN

saturday, june 4

"AGAIN?"

"Really, Kathryn? Wasn't one attempt at online dating enough?"

They were relentless. Kathryn was starting to wish she'd passed on the Saturday morning get-together at Milo's.

"He called you an old maid, then got drunk and passed out."

"A different man," Kathryn said as she flagged down their server. "I'm not stupid."

The conversation paused as coffee mugs were refilled and plates removed. The way her friends were looking at her made her reconsider her decision to take another stab at online dating. Suzanne appeared horrified. There was pity on Jane's face.

Hillary's eyes bored in on Kathryn's as she snapped her fingers and said, "I have an idea."

"Tell us," Kathryn answered, uncertain she wanted to know.

"Stuart and I will go with you. We can record our Saturday night shows and join you. It'll be fun!"

"That's a perfect idea," Jane said. "He's not as likely to mug you at gunpoint if Stuart's in the car."

"Yeah," Suzanne added. "Take Stuart and Hillary with you."

It was a terrible idea. Stuart had a personality like sugar-free vanilla ice cream. And Hillary wouldn't shut up. Besides, who wanted their friend along for a first date? "I'll be fine. Really. We're meeting this afternoon."

"Don't let this one know where you live," Jane cautioned. "I've worried for the last two weeks that the real estate guy might show up at your house in the middle of the night demanding restitution for wrecking his car."

Kathryn took a deep breath. "I didn't wreck his car. I just banged the curb. A little." She recalled what Austin had said about how much Porsche wheels cost and hoped Rodney wouldn't show up on her doorstep as Jane fore-warned. She had thought about him a lot, actually. Austin, not Rodney.

"We're meeting at the bandstand in Rehoboth," Kathryn continued. "We'll decide after we get there what to do next."

"Be sure to park someplace where there's plenty of light," Jane warned. "And don't walk too close to the build-ings. You don't want him pushing you into an alley."

"Jane, for goodness' sakes, it's Rehoboth," Kathryn snapped.

Jane glanced away, but not before Kathryn saw the hurt. "I'm sorry, honey," Kathryn said. "I just wish you guys were happy that I'm trying. I'm tired of spending every weekend alone."

"What do you mean, alone?" Suzanne said. "We're here for you. All you have to do is call."

Suzanne didn't get it. That wasn't surprising. She had always put her career ahead of dating and romance. And where had that gotten her? She talked a good game about scholarly writing and attending conventions with academic bigwigs, but in the end she and Kathryn were both stuck at the same little community college. Suzanne might want to continue searching for her career pot of gold, but Kathryn was ready for more. Life *had* to be about more than work.

"Well, if you change your mind, give me a call," Hillary said cheerily. "Stuart and I are planning on staying close to home tonight, so we'll be around."

SHEA.

Austin hit enter and watched the results pile up.

A small tropical island tree.

Society for Healthcare Epidemiology in America.

What the heck was that?

Shea butter.

Shea Stadium.

He sighed and chastised himself for not using better search terms. He had just a few minutes of down time. Getting to the public library had taken most of it. And now he was wasting the rest with too broad a search.

Kathryn Shea.

More results. Different results.

A CEO somewhere down south.

An attorney somewhere out west.

A realtor somewhere up north.

Then, pay dirt. Kathryn's profile from the community college website.

BS from James Madison.

Masters from the University of Richmond.

PhD from the University of Virginia.

And a list of publications. Only one from the present decade, though. The picture appeared to be dated, too. Kathryn with longer hair. A smile that seemed happier. Eyes that were less guarded.

What happened to that Kathryn?

It wasn't that she looked completely different. Just a little, but enough for Austin to notice. It wasn't an age thing, either. The Kathryn who went dumpster shopping with him the previous Wednesday didn't have wrinkles or anything like that. The old Kathryn, the one in the photo, just appeared to be enjoying herself more.

What would that Kathryn be like?

Austin cleared the search box and entered *Kathryn Shea dissertation*.

And there it was. He read the title and wasn't sure he completely understood it, so he read it again. And right below the title, an abstract. And below the abstract, the opportunity to purchase the dissertation from some clearing house in Poughkeepsie, New York. Austin clicked, saw the price, and started to close the box when he had an idea. He printed the page and went looking for a librarian, finally locating one, a kindly older man straightening magazine stacks.

"Yes, we can send for a copy through our interlibrary loan program," he said after Austin explained what he was looking for. "It will take a few days to arrive." Austin provided his contact information, then headed back to work. Savannah would arrive early in the afternoon, and he wanted to surprise her with how much he had gotten done on the house.

⁂

THE PARKING SPACES along Rehoboth Avenue were full. Kathryn drove the side streets until coming across a spot in front of a house on Maryland Avenue. By the time she had walked seven blocks back to the bandstand, she was hot and sweaty and wishing she had opted for a sleeveless blouse and shorts instead of jeans and a T-shirt.

They'd agreed to meet on the west side of the bandstand, a landmark as much a part of Rehoboth Beach as the ocean itself. Kathryn found a shady seat and sat down to wait, smiling when she spotted the pizza place where she and Austin had eaten three days before and wondered if he liked *Chiefs*. She could have called to find out but had stupidly mistaken his number with that of *RodneySellsRehoboth* and erased it from her call history. A couple times she'd driven by the house he was renovating on her way home from the market and the library. Lights had been on in the back of the house, but there was no sign of him. Probably reading. Good for him.

She glanced around, hoping to spot her date as he arrived. His name was Scott Delaney. If everything he said in his bio was true, they could be a good match. Forty years old, a sociology professor at Delaware State University in Dover. Divorced, no kids. Enjoyed reading, movies, and travel. His photo was up-to-date and matched one Kathryn found on the university website. Dark hair, dark features. Nice eyes.

She was hopeful. Even a little excited.

||||||

AUSTIN LAID the book aside when his phone buzzed. He had started reading *Chiefs* the day before and was already two-thirds through. He could hardly put it down.

It was Savannah. "Hey," she said. "I'm passing through Dover. I'll be in Rehoboth in an hour. Want to meet me at the hotel?"

"I want you to see the house first."

She was quiet for a moment. "Okay, I guess we can. I thought that since I'm running late, we could see it another time."

"Oh..." *Darn it.* "Okay."

"I really want to see it, Austin. But I want to see you more."

"I know. Me too. You can see it next time."

"I'll bet you're excited to spend the night in a comfy bed instead of that old army cot."

"It will be great. I can't wait." The army cot really wasn't bad at all, and there was something about waking up surrounded by his work that energized him. But waking up next to Savannah was pretty special too.

They disconnected, and he went back to the book. Kathryn was right about *Chiefs*. The story moved along at a quick pace and the characters were interesting. He decided to read for another half hour, then head to Savannah's hotel.

||||||

SCOTT ARRIVED at three on the dot and looked good doing it. Muted red shorts. White button-down shirt. Boat shoes. Very nice. He paused about twenty feet away and glanced around until his gaze settled on Kathryn. She waved. He smiled and came over. Introductions were easy. His eyes were as nice as they looked in his photo.

"Shall we go someplace and chat?" he asked.

"That would be good. Are you hungry?"

"Famished. What sounds good?"

Kathryn told him to pick. He surveyed the nearby businesses, then said, "I love beach pizza. How does that sound?"

His eyes were on the same pizza stand where she had eaten with Austin. "That'll be great."

They walked over and were waited on by the same kid from before. He recognized her and grinned. "Sausage slice?" he asked.

Kathryn nodded.

"Wow, you must eat here a lot," Scott laughed.

"I was here last week. He has a good memory."

Scott ordered a slice of anchovy and green pepper, then changed his mind and made it two slices. And a beer.

"Water for me," Kathryn said.

"I hope you're okay with me enjoying a beer. It just goes so well with pizza."

She waved him off. "Don't give it a second thought."

When their slices were ready, they walked toward the boardwalk, taking the same route she and Austin had taken. There were two benches open.

"This okay?" Scott pointed to the bench where she and Austin sat a few days before. It should have been fine, but...

Don't be silly, Kathryn.

It's not like you and Austin had your own bench.

Hundreds of people have sat there since Wednesday. A bunch of seagulls, too.

"How about over there?" Kathryn said, motioning to one a few yards away.

But there was spilled soda and seagull poop on that bench, so they returned to the other one. Without thinking about it, Kathryn took a seat on the right, just as before. Scott sat down and placed the slices between them. Déjà vu. She took a bite of her slice, looked out at the ocean, and said, "It's perfect, isn't it?" It was what Austin had said, and it seemed the perfect sentiment.

"I don't do this enough," Scott replied as he wiped away an anchovy that had fallen on his chin. "I've been in Delaware long enough to start taking the beach for granted."

It was a strange reenactment of Wednesday, with Kathryn taking Austin's role and Scott taking hers. She liked his role better.

"You should never take this for granted," Kathryn said, because she couldn't think of anything else to say. And because it was probably what Austin would have said.

WHEN HIS PHONE BUZZED AGAIN, Austin jumped.

Four-fifteen. Three pages to go and he would finish *Chiefs*. Wow. What a book. He closed the book around his finger to hold his place. Savannah was probably wondering where he was and what he was doing.

"I'm sorry," he said. "I was doing some homework and... you know."

She handled it well, and thirty minutes later he was standing in front of Room 414 at the Rehoboth Beach Sheraton. He knocked. Savannah opened the door. She was wearing a towel.

†††††††

DINNER WAS light after the pizza a few hours earlier. They shared appetizers with drinks at a bar near the board-walk, then played Skee-Ball at a beachfront arcade. Skee-Ball was Kathryn's idea. She'd never played, but thought it would be fun to try something different. Scott hadn't either. They blew through three rolls of quarters, eventually earning enough tickets to win a Mickey Mouse keychain worth about fifty cents.

The boardwalk at dusk was crowded, but the pace was slower than during the day. Neon signs gave everything an old-timey feel. Young couples strolled hand-in-hand, while older ones watched from benches.

"That was fun," Scott said as they walked along the boards. "I like how you're so spontaneous."

Kathryn thanked him and smiled. No one had ever called her spontaneous before.

When he reached for her hand, she didn't pull it away. "So, what's next?" he asked.

There was something in his tone, a huskiness, that made her wonder if he was already thinking of other things. She wasn't, but maybe she should. "How about ice cream? Have you ever had an orange twist?"

He hadn't. Kathryn hadn't either, at least not since she was ten years old. She pointed to a stand further up the boardwalk. They got two cones and returned to the bench where they had eaten earlier.

"I guess this is supposed to be our spot," Scott remarked as he licked his cone.

"I guess so."

Kathryn was watching a seagull tear into a french fry when she heard a familiar voice speak. "Hey, Kathryn."

She looked up.

Austin.

With a girl.

A very pretty girl. A beautiful girl.

"Hi, Austin." Kathryn paused, disoriented for a moment. "Austin, this is..."

Oh, crap. She'd forgotten his name.

"Scott." He stood and held out his hand.

Austin shook it, then gestured to the girl. "This is Savannah."

They filled the next few moments with awkward small talk.

"Isn't the beach beautiful in the evening?"

"What plans do you have tonight?"

Austin glanced at Kathryn when Scott told of eating pizza on the boardwalk. She looked away, feeling strangely guilty for taking someone else to *their* spot. Which was dumb. It wasn't their spot, but it was how she felt.

"We're going to a place a couple blocks up that plays hip-hop," Savannah said. "Want to join us?"

Scott appeared as if he was about to say yes.

"No," Austin and Kathryn blurted simultaneously. Kathryn mumbled something about being tired while Austin mumbled something about the place being crowded. Their eyes searched one another's while they stood there awkwardly, each waiting for the other to move on. It was Austin who finally made the break.

"Good to meet you," Savannah said cheerily as Austin led her away. Kathryn watched as they moved down the boardwalk, glancing away quickly when Austin looked back over his shoulder.

"Nice kids," Scott said as he took the last bite of his cone.

"Austin isn't a kid," Kathryn said as she tossed her cone in the trash.

"SHE'S the woman who called you last week, right? When we were in my parents' hot tub?"

"Yeah. I fixed her fence."

"She doesn't seem like a bitch."

"Who said she was?"

"I figured, you know, how she bitched to your sister about the renters and everything."

"The renters were idiots. She had a right to complain."

As they continued down the boardwalk, Austin's mind kept going back to Kathryn and the guy she was with. She had mentioned that she dated occasionally, but seeing her out like that was a jolt.

Why?

Why had it affected him? And why had she returned to the same place—the same bench—they had shared earlier in the week?

It had to be a coincidence.

Didn't it?

THEY BROWSED through a couple of art studios along Rehoboth Avenue, where prints of sand dunes and beach grass vied for wall space with images of the area from bygone years. It was a favorite pastime for Kathryn, but she remained unsettled after running into Austin and Savannah.

"Do you like this one?" Scott asked from behind her. Kathryn turned. He was holding up a large colorful print of fifties-era cars converging on the bandstand.

She hated it. It was kitschy and not at all representative of the way things really looked during that time period.

"It's nice. Are you thinking about buying it?"

He checked the price, then replaced it on a stack with others just like it. "I'll probably come back at the end of the season when they go on sale. What do you want to do next?"

"Let's walk on the beach."

"It's dark. Are you sure you feel comfortable doing that?"

Kathryn nodded. "It's fun. I love the feeling of not knowing when the water is going to rush over my feet."

"Like I said, you are certainly spontaneous. Would you mind if I run my wallet and phone back to my car first? I don't want them to get wet."

Scott had lucked into a metered spot a block away. His car was an older Volvo station wagon, gray or dark blue.

"Is this a stick shift?" Kathryn asked as he jammed his phone and wallet under the seat.

"No. Why do you ask?"

"Oh, no reason. I drove a stick shift for the first time a couple weeks ago."

The sidewalks were teeming as they returned to the beach. The bar crowd was making its appearance. It was a younger, more enthused, and more inebriated bunch than earlier, as families and older folks had retreated to the food buffets and motel pools for the evening. The line at Thrasher's French Fry stand was fifty deep. Kathryn led the way past, shouldering her way around a dozen or so people before taking to the street where the line was thickest. As she stepped off the curb, she smiled when she spotted Austin's pickup parked in a spot reserved for city vehicles.

"Hey, Calvin," she whispered as they moved past.

"Did you say something?" Scott said as he caught up.

"Just saying hello to a friend."

Scott came along beside her and took her hand like he had earlier. "I was surprised you didn't want to go to the hip-hop place with your friends," he said as they stepped off the boardwalk onto the cool sand.

"Why would I do something like that?"

"You just seem like the type."

"I'm more the type who prefers moonlit walks on the beach."

"You do this a lot?"

"Enough."

Scott would never know that it had been years since she had ventured onto the beach after dark. Let him think she was crazy, spontaneous, Kathryn. It was better than being pegged as an old maid schoolteacher, right?

And it was enjoyable. Crashing waves and a stout breeze off the Atlantic muted the sound of bar bands and boardwalk revelers, allowing Kathryn and Scott the time to chat. Career challenges, rewards, personal likes and dislikes. He was a baseball fan, Cincinnati Reds because of his Ohio roots; the only baseball players' names she could remember were Babe Ruth and Cal Ripken, Jr., and she wasn't sure if either played for the Cincinnati Reds. He attended church regularly; she less often. He read a lot; she did too. Historical literature for him. She liked that as well, along with other genres.

He was lonely.

She was too.

The conversation slowed as they turned and started back toward the bandstand. The air was growing cool, and Kathryn felt a chill, but there was nothing she could do about it. She always kept a sweatshirt in her car but hadn't thought she would need it. Her arm brushed Scott's. He felt its coolness and wrapped his arm around her. She snuggled closer and took a deep breath of satisfaction.

Or was it a sigh of disappointment?

It was, she concluded as they continued their walk, disappointment.

Why? Scott was a good match for her. Smart, successful, respected. Well-spoken and kind.

And peculiar.

And kind of timid.

And boring.

It was almost as if she was looking in the mirror. At a male version of herself.

Except he saw her as spontaneous. And fun.

Suzanne would laugh at that. And she would be right to laugh. No one from her past would ever describe her as spontaneous. She was, like Scott, smart, successful, and respected. She was well-spoken and tried to be kind to others.

But spontaneous?

Not by a mile.

She liked that he considered her that way though.

Austin? He would never say she was spontaneous.

Speaking of Austin, what were he and Savannah up to?

Dancing?

Swaying to the beats of some hip-hop deejay?

Did people sway to hip-hop? Or did they jump up and down? It was, after all, called hip-hop.

Whatever Austin and Savannah were doing, Kathryn suspected she knew what they would be doing later that evening.

Not hip-hopping.

And it made her feel lonely again.

"Kathryn?"

And sad for what her life had become.

"Kathryn?"

And disappointed that she had not —

"Kathryn, are you okay?"

She turned suddenly. Scott had been speaking to her. She had heard him, but he seemed far away. It wasn't Scott that was far away, though. It was her. "I'm sorry. What were you saying?"

He smiled. She could see his smile in the semi-darkness. It was a handsome smile. He smelled good, and his arm felt wonderful wrapped around her.

"I was asking if you were ready to call it a night?"

"Yes, I suppose I am."

They were silent for a few moments as they returned to the bandstand, then Scott said, "Thank you for a pleasant evening. I've had a wonderful time."

They stopped at the bench where they had met several hours earlier. Kathryn turned, so they were looking at one another. She ran her arms around his waist and pulled him close.

"Follow me home."

ELEVEN

sunday, june 5

AUSTIN AWAKENED with a feeling of being suffocated, but it was only Savannah's arm over his face. He moved it, but she didn't stir.

It wasn't yet seven o'clock. She would probably sleep for two more hours. He normally would have too. The Sheraton's bed was soft, and the air conditioning was doing its job.

But the Riley Street house was calling.

The electrician was scheduled to begin the next day. Ductwork for the new HVAC system was being installed later in the week. Austin wanted to get things cleaned up for them to do what they needed to do, plus there were a bunch of other little tasks that he could complete before Savannah knew he was gone.

He hurriedly dressed and left the hotel. They charged twenty dollars a night for parking, so he had left Calvin on a side street between two dumpsters. A doughnut shop on the edge of Rehoboth wasn't busy, so he pulled in for a dozen glazed and a large chocolate milk, then continued toward Bethany Beach. Coastal Highway traffic was light, and his mind drifted to *Chiefs*. If he had known of books like it back when he took Southern Lit the first time, he wouldn't be repeating the course two years later. He owed Kathryn a big thank-you for pointing him in the right direction.

On Bethany Beach's main drag, he passed a small grocery store where a worker was setting up a sidewalk display of potted plants. He backed Calvin into one of several open spots and walked a block back to the place. Plants weren't his specialty any more than truck repair, but he picked one he liked, then stepped inside and purchased it along with a thank-you card.

"Jade," the clerk said as he rang up the sale.

"Excuse me?"

He pointed at the plant. "It's a jade plant. A succulent."

"What's that mean?"

"Succulents store moisture in their leaves. You don't have to water them as often as other plants. Perfect for people who are away from home a lot."

When he got back to Calvin, he pulled a pen from his pocket, opened the card, and started writing.

An amazing book! I can't wait to talk about it with you.

He paused and considered the blank space that remained at the bottom of the card. He tapped the pen against his chin while he thought about how to fill it. More than anything, he wanted Kathryn to know how much her kindness meant to him. He had enjoyed dinner at her house and spending the afternoon with her the previous week, too.

Dinner, maybe?

She probably didn't have time. As he had seen the previous night, she had more of a social life than she let on. It made sense. She was smart and pretty. That guy, Scott?

He seemed like a good match for her. They would probably be spending a lot of time together. The thought made his stomach feel heavy.

He still needed to finish the card, though.

And he would enjoy seeing her again, if only to chat about school and life. And get another book for class.

He reread what he had written, then added, *The plant is a succulent. You don't have to water it much. I can explain when I see you again. Dinner? This week maybe?* Then he sealed the envelope and pointed Calvin toward 111 Sea Turtle Court.

KATHRYN UNTANGLED herself from the sheets, pulled on her robe, and tiptoed out of the bedroom. She'd shower in the hall bathroom, and maybe Scott would be gone by the time she finished.

She opened the bathroom door—was there still a trace of Austin's cologne in the air? Not that it had been anything special; probably whatever scent of the month young guys were wearing. More likely, it wasn't really his scent. It had been a week since he was there, after all. Her mind was playing tricks on her.

But then she thought of him standing in the upstairs hallway, stripped out of his clothes, when she'd returned to ask if he liked crab cakes. She'd had only the briefest glimpse before she'd turned away, and she really hadn't seen anything from her vantage point in the stairwell. What she saw was still enough to cause her mind to take flight.

Was that wrong?

Not at all. He was a man. A young man, but a man, nonetheless.

And speaking of men, there was still the matter of Scott. Snoring noisily as he dozed in her bed.

Why had she done that?

Scott wasn't right for her at all. Maybe at one time, but no more.

She closed and locked the bathroom door, turned on the water to allow it to warm up, and prayed a brief prayer that he might be gone after she finished taking the longest shower of her life.

▓▓▓▓

THE FIRST THING Austin noticed as he pulled onto Sea Turtle Court was the fence. It commanded his gaze.

The second thing was the clean yard at the rental house. The current renters were in town for three weeks and were proving to be perfect tenants.

The thing that caused him to tighten his grip on the steering wheel was the car in Kathryn's driveway. An older Volvo station wagon.

Scott?

Nah, Austin, decided. Not Scott. Probably one of Kathryn's friends stopping by to catch up. He pulled Calvin to the curb behind the Volvo, grabbed the book, and stuck the thank-you card inside. He got out and was reaching back to retrieve the houseplant when he caught sight of a parking tag on the Volvo's rear window.

Delaware State University Faculty.

Scott had mentioned being from Dover. That was where Delaware State was located.

Had he spent the night?

Kathryn didn't seem the type to... What was he thinking? Why wasn't she the type to have a man stay over? She

141

was an attractive single woman, still young. He knew as well as anyone how lonely it could get being alone.

So why did he feel so weird about it?

He had spent many nights with Savannah.

But that was different.

That was just... He and Savannah were...

What were they, exactly?

Was there a future there? Or were they just two young people who were together until something better came along?

They had never talked much about the future. About where they might wind up, or even if they would stay together. They just kept on doing what they did. Parties and bars. Late nights and late mornings. Doing what kids did when they were without other obligations.

But there was the rub.

They weren't really kids anymore, were they?

Austin had friends who were already earning paychecks. A few were married. They were making their way in life. Like adults.

Perhaps that was part of why he enjoyed spending time with Kathryn. She treated him like an adult, even when she was mad about trash in her yard.

He stood next to Calvin for a few moments, book in hand, considering what to do next. Several cars passed by. He overheard voices from the backyard of the house across the street. The neighborhood was coming to life.

It was time to go.

He carried the book and plant to the front door and set them on the side table where he and Kathryn had eaten sandwiches. He turned to walk away but wondered if the plant and card were too much. Probably so. How awkward could it get if Kathryn and Scott came outside and spotted his gift?

Scott might say, *Look, Kathryn. Someone left you a card and a plant.*

Oh, she would reply, *it's just Austin. The guy we saw at the beach. The one who fixed my fence.*

He removed the card before returning the book to the table, grabbed the plant, and left.

KATHRYN EMERGED from the bathroom fully dressed and tiptoed back to her bedroom.

Scott was still there. Still sleeping. Still snoring.

She stood in the doorway a few moments, watching as his chest rose and fell with each snore, wondering what to do next.

Wake him?

Run away until she knew he was gone?

Make breakfast for him?

She heard a sound outside. A car door, perhaps, followed by a vehicle driving away. It was probably across the street. They were early risers, even on Sunday.

She settled on making coffee, as much for herself as for Scott. She turned away from the bedroom and padded downstairs in bare feet. The pot was brewing a half hour later when Scott made his appearance. The walk of shame, Kathryn had heard it called when a girl left a guy's place the next morning wearing the same clothes she had shown up in. Did guys have a walk of shame? Probably more a walk of triumph, given how they saw the world.

Did Austin see the world that way? He was probably still snuggled up next to cute little Savannah wherever they'd spent the night, which probably wasn't his fixer upper. Savannah didn't seem the type who chose unfinished houses over luxury hotels.

But Savannah wasn't Kathryn's concern. Hers was Scott, and he had a smile on his face as he came toward her with his arms outstretched for a good morning hug. Kathryn raised her hands in front of her to slow him down.

Scott's smile disappeared. "Kathryn, I—"

"I'm sorry, Scott, but last night was a mistake."

He appeared confused. Of course he was. What guy wouldn't be?

"Bringing home a man isn't something I normally do, especially when I don't have strong feelings for him."

"I thought you... we..."

"We're not right for each other, and I prefer to end things now, Scott. I'm sorry if I gave you the wrong idea, but I'm not... I think you should leave."

He started to speak several times, but nothing came until finally he uttered, "Can I call you? In a few weeks, maybe?"

"Maybe another time, when..."

When what?

When there is no one else?

When I'm ready to settle for less than I deserve?

That's not fair to Scott.

"I would prefer you not."

He stood for a few moments, as if trying to grasp what had just happened, then shrugged and walked to the door. She was tempted to follow and apologize one more time. She stayed where she was though and peeked out the window as his car started. After he disappeared at the top of the street, she walked outside for a much-needed breath of fresh air. She lowered herself onto a chair. Something caught her eye. It was *Chiefs* on the side table.

Austin.

He had come by. Had that been him she'd heard earlier?

If it was, he'd seen Scott's car.

And if he'd seen Scott's car, he knew.

She picked up the book and opened it, hoping he'd left a note inside. There was none. She sighed as she set it aside and noticed a small plant clipping. She picked it up and examined it, smiling when she recognized what it was.

Jade.

She loved jade, and always admired the jade plants she came across at local greenhouses. She raised it to her nose and breathed in its light sweet fragrance. Still fresh. How had it gotten to her porch?

And then, a thought. Perhaps the same way *Chiefs* got to her porch?

But the book was still there.

She slowly turned it over in her hands as she considered its presence, then opened the book and placed the clipping inside.

Had Austin also dropped off a plant? Had he brought a gift, but reconsidered when he saw Scott's car?

She closed her eyes and tried to imagine what might be about to play out. What did he think of her? Would she even see him again? And why did it matter?

⚏

AUSTIN AND SAVANNAH checked out of the Sheraton at noon, left Calvin in a supermarket parking lot, and drove her car to the beach. The day was brilliantly sunny, and the sand was a patchwork of bodies stretched out on towels and blankets.

After a brisk dip in the ocean, Savannah became engrossed in one of those paranormal romance novels she was always reading. Austin caught up on what his college buddies were doing on social media, then started planning what he would get done on the Riley Street house that week.

He had been putting in plenty of hours, but it seemed like he'd underestimated how much time it would take to get everything done. Plumbing was a big reason for the delay. Old pipes needed replacing, and Austin's plumber of choice was a couple weeks out. He could work around the man's schedule, but it wasn't ideal.

With his week planned, he pulled up the assignment list for Organizational Theory and slogged through two mind-numbing journal articles about managing innovation. How could innovation be so boring?

Staying on track was even harder when his mind wandered back to the sight of Scott's Volvo in Kathryn's driveway. Was he her boyfriend now? Did people Kathryn's age call them boyfriends? It sounded sort of juvenile. Savannah was his girlfriend. That was okay. But how about when you reached thirty or whatever milestone birthday Kathryn had passed?

The jade plant was still in the back of the truck. Would the plant still be there when he returned? Would the sun cause it to wither? Did it even matter? He'd considered giving it to Savannah, but she would think it strange that he bought her a plant. She loved flowers and gushed when he gave her roses for Valentine's Day. But a plant? Nope, that would be weird.

But not for Kathryn. She would understand that the gift

of a plant was special. A plant didn't have to be tossed out after a few days. It grew and became part of your life.

He should have left it with the book.

It was midafternoon when Austin interrupted Savannah's reading. "When are you starting for home?" he asked.

She looked up from her book and lifted her sunglasses. "I hadn't thought about it. Do you want me to go?"

"Of course not. I was just wondering."

"Do you have a big date tonight?" she teased. "Some local girl you met while I was home?"

Austin chuckled. "You know me better than that."

Savannah picked her book back up and read for a couple minutes before she spoke again. "What do you make of the fence lady and her guy?"

"What do you mean?"

"Were they, like, on a date yesterday? A real date?"

Austin shrugged. "It looked like it."

"It did to me, too. Kind of sad, really."

"How is it sad?" he asked.

"That they're still going on dates and stuff when they're that old."

Austin rolled over on his side and looked down at her. "They're not old."

"Sure, they are. Forty, maybe? I can never tell with old people. Probably my parents' age, though."

"Maybe they didn't find the right match when they were younger. Maybe they put their careers first."

Savannah smirked. "Seriously, Austin. If they put their careers first, would they be here?"

"What's wrong with here?" Austin motioned to the surroundings. "What could be better than living near the beach?"

"She's a college professor, right?"

Austin nodded. "Her name is Kathryn."

"Kathryn, then. A professor at some little college in the middle of nowhere. Not exactly what I would call a dream job."

"To each his own. What would be your dream job?"

It was a fair question. Both of them had been raised in privilege. Private schools, new cars when they got their drivers' licenses, family vacations in exotic locales, Ivy League educations.

The difference was that Savannah's parents asked for almost nothing in return. From the time he was in junior high, Austin had responsibilities around the house or within the company. He had spent many weekends cleaning up construction sites as new homeowners pushed to gain occupancy. Mom and Dad were perfectly happy to pay the tuition at Penn, but when Austin moved into a fraternity house, the extra expense had been his to cover. They were generous, but there were limits.

Now, at age twenty-two, he felt he had a pretty good idea about life in the real world.

Savannah? Not so much.

"My dream job," she said after a few moments, "is a cabinet post in the White House."

"How do you plan to get there? I don't think the president hires right out of college."

Austin meant to sound as if he was teasing, but as the words flew out of his mouth, he realized he sounded like a smartass.

"Do you think I'm stupid?" she snapped. "You didn't ask about my *first* job. You said dream job."

"Sorry. What about your first job?"

"Daddy knows people in Harrisburg. He thinks I can get

an internship in the governor's office for starters. Once they see what I can do, I'll be on my way."

Austin didn't doubt it. Savannah's father was well connected. And Savannah was smart and talented. Sure, she was spoiled, but she knew when to turn it up a notch. Her near perfect grades at Penn were testament to that.

"I'll be in Harrisburg. You'll be working with your parents in Philly. That's a couple hours, right?"

It was.

"We can see each other all the time." She flashed a dazzling smile. "Or we could live someplace in the middle, assuming... you know?" She wiggled the fingers of her left hand.

If he popped the question, she'd say yes. Austin was certain of it. Two of her sorority sisters were getting married later in the summer, and she had mentioned countless times how much she looked forward to planning her own wedding.

"You're assuming I even make it to law school. Shoot, I might not make the grades I need to return in the fall."

"You'll pull it out." She pushed herself up and kissed his cheek. "You always do. Have you started your classes yet?"

"I told you yesterday that I just finished my first book for Southern Lit."

Savannah blinked several times. "I guess it slipped my mind. Sorry."

It wasn't a matter of slipping her mind. He had mentioned it on the drive to the beach, but Savannah had been texting her friends. She never heard him.

Her phone buzzed with a text message. She read it, then scrambled into a sitting position. "Can you come up to Hershey next weekend? Mom and Dad are going to New York City with the Higdons. They'll be gone all weekend."

"I don't know yet. I'll have to see how things are going at the house."

"They can't make you work twenty-four seven. You must get time off for good behavior, right?" She leaned into him and this time kissed him on the lips. "I'll make it worth your time."

"I'll try. I really will."

※※※

IT WAS ALMOST eight when Kathryn pulled into the driveway on Riley Street and parked behind Calvin. The front yard was cloaked in shadows, and sounds of power equipment drifted from the house's open windows.

She checked her reflection in her rearview mirror before stepping out of the car, canvas bag in hand. Lipstick on Sunday night wasn't a regular occurrence. The shorts she'd chosen weren't in her usual rotation, either. Tan, cuffed, a bit tighter than the baggy ones she usually wore. The top was sleeveless, white, and buttoned up the front.

She picked her way toward the front door, stepping around debris still cluttering the yard. On the porch, she peered through an open window.

Austin was sawing a board. His back was to her—and he was shirtless. His muscles tensed and relaxed as he worked. Kathryn's mind flashed back to the week before when he'd walked out of her bathroom. She licked her lips and tried to remember why she had come over in the first place.

Oh, yeah. The book.

She banged on the door, but he didn't hear her over the roar of the saw.

She could probably just walk in.

But what if she startled him? And he hurt himself on the saw?

Nope. Better to wait until he stopped.

She watched as he fed one board into the saw, then grabbed another. And another. He was sweating heavily. She didn't like sweat, but it looked good on him. Really good.

She'd have been content to watch through the window for an hour or so, but he eventually turned the saw off. When she knocked again, he turned to see who it was.

And smiled.

He came to the door and opened it. "Hey."

"Hey, Austin."

And then silence.

She glanced around and smiled nervously. Why hadn't she considered what she would say next?

Austin gestured behind him. "Want to see what I've been doing?"

She did.

He started in the sawdust-covered living room. Walls were laid bare to where she could see the wiring and insulation. Austin took her from room to room, pointing out what he had done and the work that remained. She enjoyed walking along, absorbing his knowledge of a field that was as foreign to her as Sanskrit. The house was little more than bones, but as they continued the tour he pointed as he explained what each room would become. A new bathroom. A larger closet. Windows in what used to be a solid wall.

The last space they entered was a small upstairs room, the only one that still had a door. Inside was a lumpy cot, a desk formed from plywood and sawhorses, and a laptop.

Shirts hung from nails. Shorts spilled out of a suitcase on the floor.

"Sorry it's a mess," he said, grinning. "If I'd known you were coming, I would have cleaned up."

Kathryn giggled. It sounded strange to her and must have to Austin too, because he laughed.

Then it was quiet again.

She still didn't know what she came there to say. It was different from before. He had been to her house to drop off the book. He must know that Scott had spent the night. Did that change the way he thought about her?

"So... Savannah has returned home?"

"Yeah. About five. I just got back here a half hour ago. Your timing was perfect."

"Well," Kathryn answered slowly. "Or maybe not so perfect." She felt her face and neck become warm. "It was the third time I've been by."

He did a double take. "Really? Three times, huh? Is something wrong?"

"No... yes... well, I wanted to let you know I got the book."

"You came by three times just to tell me you got the book?" The way he looked at her, the tilt of his head, indicated he was doubtful that was all she wanted.

"I wish I would have known you came by this morning. I would have... No, I mean..."

She couldn't think of what to say.

I would have left Scott sleeping in bed to make you breakfast.

You're probably wondering why there was a car in my driveway.

I'm not the kind of girl who sleeps with a guy on the first date, but I did just this once.

"It's okay," Austin said. "I had to get back."

More awkward silence passed before her brain finally slipped into gear. She pulled a book from her canvas bag and handed it to him.

He wiped his hands on his shorts, took it, and examined the cover. "Pat Conroy?"

"Are you familiar with him?"

Austin wasn't.

Kathryn rattled off several of his books that had been made into movies. *The Great Santini, The Prince of Tides, Conrack.* None of them rang a bell.

"He writes with a lot of flourishes. He loves to describe everything in detail. People, settings, feelings." She pointed to the book. "*The Lords of Discipline* is about a southern military academy. Conroy based it on his experiences at the Citadel."

"It's a biography?"

"No, it's fiction, but it's close enough to reality that his college blackballed him for many years."

As he had with *Chiefs*, Austin flipped through the book and scanned the back cover. "I'll start it this week."

"His writing is heavier than Stuart Woods'. Stick with it, though. I think you'll enjoy it."

He laid it on his sawhorse table and turned to face her. They were just a few feet apart, and the heat of the day and the heat of his proximity made Kathryn woozy.

"Maybe we should go back outside where it's cooler," he said. He led the way, stepping carefully past lumber, tools, and rubble. "Did you and Scott have a good time last night?"

Her stomach lurched before she realized he wasn't referring to... "The beach was very pleasant. Scott is a nice man."

Who I'll never see again.

They walked onto the porch. Night had fallen. The streetlights were on. Traffic on Coastal Highway rumbled in the distance as tourists headed back to their workaday lives. The air was a few degrees cooler, thanks to a southerly breeze full of the combined scents of salt water and marshland.

"Thank you for the book. For both books," Austin said when they reached her car.

She eased into the car and placed her bag on the seat next to her. Austin closed the door. She started the car and rolled down the window. "Thank you for showing me your work," she said. "I admire your skill."

There was so much more she wanted to say, about Scott, about last night. About her feelings for Austin. The words escaped her, though.

"Chicken," she mumbled after rolling up her window and putting the car into reverse.

⁜

HE WATCHED as she backed out of his driveway. There was something in the way she said it. *I admire your skill.*

Her words made him feel something, something good. About himself.

But also about Kathryn.

It would have been great if she'd stayed a while longer. They could sit on the porch and enjoy the breeze. And each other's company.

But the porch was filthy. And the only chair was in his bedroom. The cot was there too, but... no.

He thought of the card. And the plant. And knew then that he wanted her to have both. "Kathryn!" He waved his hands to get her attention. She slowed at the end of the driveway. "Don't leave yet!"

He retrieved the card from Calvin, then grabbed the jade plant from the back. It was a bit tattered from the wind, but still presentable.

"I got you this," he said, handing the plant to her through the window. "It's called jade."

She smiled as she took it. "One of my favorites." She studied it in the dim light of the street. "I'll treasure it, Austin."

He smiled, took a deep breath, and thrust out the card. "I got you this too."

She opened it, read it, and looked up into his eyes. "Is the dinner invitation still open?"

"Yes."

"I would love to. What night?"

Yes! Austin didn't try to hide the grin that was spreading across his face.

"Thursday?"

She nodded. Her smile was pretty big, too. "See you then."

thursday, june 9

WAS it possible to sleep with your eyes open? Kathryn would not have thought so, but a guy in the third row appeared to be doing just that. The girl seated next to him waved her hands in front of his face, but he didn't even flinch. Moments later, eyes still open, he began to snore.

The guy who'd worn the *Got Jesus?* shirt the first day of class had become romantically involved with a classmate who learned makeup application from Alice Cooper and had ear gauges large enough to push a tube of lipstick through. The two passed notes back and forth while pretending to be immersed in the day's impromptu writing assignment.

At least they were writing something. Others stared at their phones or doodled. A girl to Kathryn's left was an excellent doodler, having progressed from Mickey Mouse to Justin Bieber and a darn good image of the pope. A caricature she'd done of Kathryn during the previous day's quiz was spot-on, except for the frown.

Did she really frown all the time?

In class? Yep. She probably frowned all the time.

Except today.

Her students probably wondered what was going on. She'd overheard one girl tell her friends that it looked like Dr. Shea had taken happy pills.

"Maybe she got laid," a male student whispered.

They giggled at his vulgarity, unaware that Dr. Shea's hearing was off the charts.

But she kept smiling.

She had good reason to smile.

"MAN, Austin, you don't know how much this means to me." The electrician, a short, thin man, tucked the check into his shirt pocket. "So many contractors leave us hanging for weeks before we see any money."

"Your men did good work, Ralphie."

Ralphie smiled. "Let me know when you have more. I can always squeeze you in."

Austin watched Ralphie and his men load up their equipment and take off, happy that another of Grandpa's life lessons had taken hold.

Treat your subcontractors like family. Pay 'em good and pay 'em quick.

Mom had resisted when he'd asked her to release the check and then agreed when he'd explained that good electricians were hard to come by and that the guy from Picket Fence Construction didn't want to risk losing the one he had. Austin had danced around the truth a bit, but it was worth it in the end. Ralphie had his check, and the electrical work was done.

Next up was HVAC. The sub had been scheduled for the day before but never showed. That happened sometimes during peak construction season, so Austin bit his tongue and left a message that he was ready for him. He hadn't shown that morning either, but called and promised to have two guys there the next day.

All in a day's work. Home building and renovation could be a strange and fickle field. Little victories, like Ralphie completing the electrical work early, could be wiped out by an HVAC sub who no-showed. Austin maintained a smile and an open mind, just like he'd seen Grandpa do.

Which made returning to his little upstairs room to study Organizational Theory even more difficult.

He pulled out his phone, and after checking the time, typed a text message to Kathryn. *Are we still on?* He hit send, then had another thought. Did she text? Was she one of those people who preferred speaking to a human voice?

The answer came within seconds. A smiley emoji— followed by a call. Austin answered with a cheerful hello, expecting her voice.

"Mr. McGinnis? This is Joanne from the Bethany Beach Library. The dissertation you ordered has arrived. We can hold it for three days."

▓▓▓▓▓

KATHRYN BOUNDED out the front door before Austin could get out of the truck. She was beaming and looked different. Younger. She wore a pink summer blouse and a white skirt that ended just above her knees. And sandals.

She stopped a few feet away, put her hands on her hips, and looked the truck over from front to back. "It looks like Calvin had a bath."

"I ran him through a car wash. It might be his first bath, other than rain."

"He looks quite handsome." She looked up at him. "And so do you."

Austin glanced away to hide the color spreading across his cheeks. "How is the plant?"

"Thriving. It's in my kitchen window, but I may move it outside this weekend. I look at it often. It was such a thoughtful gift."

A thoughtful gift. That sounded nice.

"So," she said, "where are we going?"

"I've narrowed it down to two places. I'll let you choose."

The first place he suggested was a seafood place on Fenwick Island, a place where Kathryn occasionally dined with her friends. The food was good; the atmosphere was nautical. A bit touristy, but every restaurant was at that time of year.

"The second is a little off the beaten path."

"That sounds interesting. Tell me more."

"The menu is sort of limited."

"How limited?" She asked.

"Do you like clams?"

"Very much."

"How about oysters?"

"Raw?"

"And steamed. Smoked too, but they run out of those early. First come, first served."

"Hmm," she said. "What else?"

Austin grinned. "That's it. I think they have burgers, but I've never seen anybody order one."

Kathryn glanced up and down the street while she considered her decision.

"Clams and oysters, huh? How about beverages? Wine?"

"Nope. Beer. Longnecks. Nothing fancy. The place has a reputation for getting rough sometimes, but I've never run into trouble there. The food makes it worth the risk."

"And if we do run into trouble? Do you promise you'll look out for me?"

"I promise to grab your hand and run as fast as we can."

She laughed. "In that case, count me in."

They left Bethany Beach heading west, passing through the tiny communities of Ocean View and Clarksville.

"It's about twenty minutes from here," Austin said. "And four back roads."

She settled back into the seat, smoothed her skirt, and said, "Have you started reading *The Lords of Discipline?*"

"I plan to get started this weekend. Work is keeping me pretty busy. By the way, my professor loved my report on *Chiefs*. He had me share it with the class."

Kathryn applauded. "Were you intimidated by all those English and literature majors?"

"A little. One guy commented that *Chiefs* wasn't true Southern literature because the author also turns out pulp fiction."

"Lit majors can be such snobs."

"That's kind of what our professor said. He asked the guy to explain what he meant, then chopped his arguments into little pieces."

"Bravo for your professor. You're going to get an A in that class."

Austin turned south along Route 113 to a narrow road just outside of Selbyville. The sun was setting in their faces as he made two more turns and pulled into a crowded gravel parking lot fronting a pole barn with Christmas lights strung from end to end. A lighted sign on a post advertised a beer brand that Kathryn had thought was extinct. Another sign displayed the name of the place.

Elijah's.

"Like in the Bible," she said.

"There's nothing biblical about the place," Austin said. "Except the food. It's heavenly."

He jumped out of the truck and came around to open her door. He took her hand and helped her from her seat. She loved that he did that. Few guys bothered.

They strolled past row after row of cars and pickups. Mostly pickups. Elijah's backed up to a thick pine forest. Dusk-to-dawn lights on each end of the building were the only outside illumination other than the beer sign. Two men were in a deep conversation on one side of the entrance. Both had cigarettes in their mouths and long-necks in their hands. They nodded at Austin and ogled Kathryn but said nothing.

"They'll be asking you to dance before the night's over," Austin whispered as he held the door for her.

"You didn't say there was dancing."

"I forgot."

Kathryn paused in the doorway. "I don't dance."

"What do you mean you don't dance? Everybody dances."

They stepped through a vestibule, and the interior came into view. She had expected to be knocked over by the foul odors of smoke and stale beer, but the air smelled like seafood. Fresh seafood. Like just-caught-that-day seafood. And after twelve years in Bethany Beach, she knew the difference. Her mouth was watering before they found a corner table beneath a neon sign touting Pabst Blue Ribbon.

"What do you think?" Austin asked with a grin.

Kathryn nodded and smiled. She found it both exciting and very different from anything she had experienced. The other tables were taken by people of all sizes and colors. Conversations in English and Spanish filled the air, along with those intoxicating smells of clams and oysters. She was suddenly very hungry.

"Where's the menu? I'm ready to eat."

"There isn't a menu. They don't need one."

"Okay. So what are we having?"

"Fried clams. Or oysters."

"What side items?"

"More clams or oysters."

"I'll have smoked oysters."

"And a beer?"

"And a beer."

Austin headed to the bar to order their food.

Kathryn took a good look around. She would never have felt comfortable in such a place, but with Austin it seemed not just safe, but fun. In the farthest corner from their table, a deejay was setting up his equipment on a raised platform while he cut up with nearby customers. It seemed like everyone was a regular.

"How did you find this place?" she asked Austin when he returned with their beers.

"The owners are parents of a girl I know at Penn. She brought Savannah and me here two summers ago. Savannah didn't care for it, but I've been back by myself a few times."

"It doesn't seem like the kind of place you come to alone. Do you have other friends in Bethany?"

Austin shook his head. "Just you." He raised his long-neck and held it out toward her. "Here's to good friends."

Kathryn tapped her beer against his and took a drink. It

was cold enough to give her a headache. She squinted to fight off the sting, and when she opened her eyes, Austin was watching her. She met his gaze and held it. His eyes were dark brown, with a brooding quality that brought Christian Bale and a young Richard Gere to mind.

"What are you looking at?" she teased.

He smiled but didn't respond. He didn't have to. His eyes were on her, and she liked it.

"Which one of you ordered the arsters?"

The guy carrying their plates was a mountain of a man, late twenties perhaps, with a mullet. His thick accent gave him away as a local.

"I'm having the oysters," Kathryn said.

When he set them down in front of her, there was sweat on his arms. His tank top was drenched. He nearly dropped Austin's clams. "You want vinegar?" he asked Austin.

"Yeah, please."

The server reached across the two people seated at the adjoining table and grabbed a bottle of malt vinegar from between them.

"I'm not done with that," the man said sharply.

"Hell you ain't," the server growled as he set the bottle in front of Austin, who sprinkled the vinegar liberally on his clam strips.

"Need anything else? More beers?"

"Yeah, bring us a couple more." Austin said.

"Sure. Sure." He pointed at Kathryn. "You work out to the college, don'tcha?"

"Yes."

"You teach writing and stuff, right?"

"English, yes."

"I was in your class."

Kathryn looked up at him, studying his face. Wouldn't she remember someone so large and imposing?

"Yeah," he said. "It musta been about eight years ago. I got laid off at the fish packing house, and my girlfriend thought I should try college."

"Good for you," Kathryn said.

"Not good for me. I needed to pass your class to get accepted. You flunked me, and I couldn't go back. Killed that dream."

Kathryn shifted in her seat. It was probably a good thing he had already served her food. And no way was she going to drink that second beer. Just in case he was the vindictive type. "That's too bad. I'm sorry to hear it didn't work out for you."

He smiled for the first time. "Ain't no big thing. The family that owns this place hired me right after that. I'm saving my money so I can buy into the place someday. If you'd a passed me, I'd probably be a lawyer or doctor or something. Talk about miserable."

He nodded and left.

Kathryn looked at Austin, trying her best not to laugh.

But Austin's expression was subdued. "I know how he feels," he said quietly.

"Austin—"

An old Merle Haggard song boomed from the speakers, and immediately the atmosphere changed. Diners clapped. A few stomped their feet and shouted. Two couples, one in their twenties, the other well past retirement age, hustled out to a ten-by-ten dance floor in front of the bar. Austin had been about to say something, and Kathryn wanted to hear his thoughts, but that might have to wait. They dug into their food. Kathryn moaned with pleasure as she took her first taste.

"That good, huh?" Austin said, grinning at her.

"Mm-hmm," she exclaimed, her mouth full of the delicious delicacy. It was a perfect combination of sweet, salty, and smoky. She giggled when Austin reached across with his fork and snagged one from the edge of her plate.

"Help yourself," she teased.

THE MUSIC MADE CONVERSATION DIFFICULT, so Austin moved his chair and half-eaten plate of clam strips to Kathryn's side of the table. Four tables separated them from the dance floor. He watched as she took it all in. Was she having a good time? Or was she just being a good sport? He hadn't considered what he would do if she hated it. As Merle Haggard faded into George Strait, she downed the last of her beer, turned to him, and said, "No time better than the present."

Oh no. What happened? He thought she was enjoying herself. "You're ready to go? I'll get the check."

She laughed. "Not on your life. You came here to dance. Let's dance."

"I thought you didn't dance."

Their server appeared and plunked down two more longnecks.

"I don't dance," Kathryn said as she picked up the bottle and took a long pull. "But this will help."

There was no way that two beers would give her that much courage, but he wasn't about to complain. George Strait was into his second verse when Kathryn popped up from her chair and motioned for him to follow.

The dance floor was packed. Kathryn weaved her way toward a small opening. Austin tried to keep up. They claimed their space and started moving with the music. While he liked to dance, Austin didn't consider himself any good at it. He just moved around, but in Elijah's on a Thursday night, moving around was good enough. A couple or two were showing off their moves, but the rest of the crowd just sweated and swayed.

Kathryn's moves were awkward at first, bringing back memories of the night two weeks before when Austin had followed her upstairs. She found the rhythm in short order, though, and her expression morphed into a big grin.

She was having fun.

There was no need to try to talk. The music drowned out everything. The bass made the walls shake. All they could do was dance. So they danced.

FOURTEEN YEARS.

That's how long it had been since Kathryn was on a dance floor.

It was with Troy, at a wedding reception for one of his college buddies. Troy was a groomsman, and Kathryn still remembered how handsome he looked in his black tux. They had been married only ten months. She had just finished her master's degree and was about to start her PhD, and Troy was making good money at an architectural firm in Richmond.

They were on their way up and planned to go higher. He would become a partner at a large firm. She would teach at a major university. There would be children—three—with a house close to their jobs but far enough out of town for the kids to spend time outdoors. It sounded idyllic in a 1950s kind of way, but they had believed it completely.

Two years later, they were divorced.

And as she danced for the first time since that reception, Kathryn felt something inside her letting go, a melancholy that had lingered so deep and for so long that she had accepted it as part of who she was. The feeling of it ebbing away was transforming in its joy and made her wonder what else was lurking inside her. What remnants of her past were waiting to be released?

There was no better time than the present.

And she owed it to her handyman.

The thought that she had considered him as little more than a handyman made her laugh out loud. He looked at her curiously, but she didn't care. She swayed and danced a little freer, winked at him, and laughed some more. He probably thought it was the beer. That was okay too.

The upbeat George Strait tune faded out. The lights dimmed. And while Kathryn hadn't been on a dance floor in years, she knew what it meant when they turned the lights down.

Slow dance time.

Shania Twain.

Kathryn had never been a fan of country music, but she knew the song and how it celebrated the beginning of a new love. Pretty heavy stuff for slow dancing with the handyman.

But he wasn't just the handyman anymore, was he?

They had moved far past that first morning when Kathryn had shown her obstinate side in the front yard.

The handyman was now her friend.

As the song began to play, he looked at her, speaking without words. *Do you want to?*

She answered with a slight tip of her head. *I do want to. Very much.*

He pulled her close.

She let him.

She could just see over his shoulder as they danced. He smelled nice despite a sheen of perspiration. His chest was firm, his shoulder solid. He placed his arms around her waist at just the right spot. Not too low, though Kathryn knew that if he had placed his hands lower, she wouldn't have objected. Not with the way his touch made her skin tingle.

They swayed together as Shania sang.

It was perfect.

Until his phone rang.

AUSTIN TRIED TO IGNORE IT.

Why hadn't he left it at the table?

Or in the truck?

That would have been the smart thing.

But no. It was in his back pocket. It would have gone unnoticed when the music was louder and faster, but Shania's song was soft and contemplative enough to allow the shrill ring of his phone to come through. People nearby gave him the stink eye. He reluctantly removed one arm from around Kathryn's waist, reached into his back pocket, and silenced the phone.

But it was too late. The mood was broken.

And my goodness, what a mood it had been.

"Do you need to take it?" she asked.

"No."

"What if it's one of your subcontractors?"

She had a point. "I'll have to go outside to hear

anything. Want to walk out with me and get a breath of fresh air?"

She did.

He led her through the crowd. He considered grabbing his beer but wanted to make sure their table was still open when they returned, so he left it.

There was another thing he should have done. He should have checked who was calling.

He waited until they were outside to do that.

Savannah.

He considered letting it go to voicemail.

But she would call back.

And call back again.

That was the way things were. They answered when the other called. It was an unspoken promise. Always there, always available.

A promise that meant Austin was about to have a phone call with his girlfriend in front of Kathryn. Right after they had finished slow dancing at an off-the-grid redneck joint.

Right after feeling things for someone who wasn't Savannah.

"Hello."

"Hi, babe," she said cheerfully. "What are you doing?"

Kathryn stood a few feet away, staring at the sky and enjoying the night air. As far as she knew, it was someone calling about the renovation.

"Hey, I'm at Elijah's."

"Oh, Lord. That place."

"Yeah."

"Did you have clams?"

"Yeah."

"Were they good?"

If he answered *yeah* again, she would ask why he wasn't talking much. Her radar worked pretty good that way. "Delicious. I left my plate on our table to come out and talk."

Had he really said *our* table? He smacked his forehead, angry at the slip of tongue.

"Oh, no — Wait a minute. You're there with someone? Who did you talk into going to that awful place?"

"I... Uh, do you remember the lady whose fence got knocked down?"

Kathryn grimaced and pointed back inside. Austin nodded, and she slipped away.

Why was it suddenly hotter outside than it had been inside?

"The professor?" Savannah asked. "Why would she go to a place like that?"

He wiped his forehead. Things were going from bad to worse. "I suggested it."

"So, what do she and... what was his name? Scott? What do she and Scott think of Elijah's?"

"Scott... didn't come."

"It's just her? And you?"

Austin's laughed sounded forced. Savannah would pick up on that. "Well, us and a hundred other people. I wanted clam strips, and there's no place better to get them."

"Who asked who?"

Uh-oh.

"Kathryn... she asked... no, I think I asked her."

"You think?"

IT WAS twenty minutes before Austin returned.

He looked whipped.

"Not a subcontractor, huh?" Kathryn tried to joke, but it fell flat.

He sat down and took a long draw from his lukewarm beer.

"Do we need to go?"

He shrugged. "Savannah's not happy that I went out."

"I understand."

"But I wanted to. It's hard being down here alone."

"I understand that too."

He took another drink. "She has her friends in Hershey. They shop and go to movies and stuff. Down here it's just me and that house. Sometimes I need to get out and enjoy myself."

Kathryn knew she should tread lightly. But the most enjoyable evening she'd had in ages was about to be cut short. "How serious are you two?" she asked.

He pursed his lips and waited a moment before answering. "We started dating sophomore year. We haven't gone out with anyone else since, but it's not like we're engaged or anything."

Things between Austin and Savannah were more serious than she had thought. Kathryn picked up her purse. "I think we better go."

"We don't have to."

"Yeah," she said as she got to her feet. "Savannah assumes you're in a committed relationship. She's two hours away. She calls and learns that you're out with someone else. She's jealous and she's hurt."

"It's not like that, Kathryn. You and I aren't like..." He shrugged. "I think of us as friends, and I have a right to have friends."

"Female friends?"

"Male and female."

"Perhaps you need to let Savannah know that, because she's struggling."

Austin took a deep breath and blew it out through his lips. "I'm going up to see her this weekend. We'll talk about it."

████

THE RIDE back to Bethany Beach was quiet at first. Clearly Austin was sorting through his relationship with Savannah. Part of it was their age. It was harder at twenty-one or twenty-two to realize that relationships sometimes needed space to grow. Another part seemed to be that Savannah was more committed than Austin, and she probably hadn't seen the signs that things were changing between them.

But Kathryn's mind kept going back to something Austin had said when their food arrived. "Austin, can I ask you something?"

He paused, then nodded. "Sure."

"Back when the server was talking about how flunking my class was a good thing, he said that if he had passed, he might have become a doctor or lawyer. Remember that?"

"Mm-hmm."

"And he said how miserable he would have been."

"Right."

"After he left, you said, 'I know how he feels.' What did you mean?"

Austin rubbed his neck, then cracked his window to let in some fresh air. "I guess I meant... I know what it's like to be stuck doing something you don't want to do."

"You're not referring to the rehab work, are you?"

He shook his head. "I love that. I've always wanted to work with my hands."

"It's college, isn't it?"

"Yeah... no. I don't mind college." He grinned. "I really like my fraternity and the parties and stuff."

"That's only part of it."

"Yeah, and some classes are cool. I took a cartography course as an elective last year. If we ever get lost in the wilderness, I can get us out."

"But back to my question. Why were you so quick to agree with him?"

"I don't want to be a lawyer, really. I kind of like the idea of trying cases and putting bad guys away, but I won't be able to do that when I'm working for my parents."

"Then don't become a lawyer."

"It's not that easy, Kathryn. Hey, does anyone ever call you anything other than Kathryn?"

"One of my students called me Dr. Snore."

He chuckled. "You know what I mean. Kathryn is so formal. And kind of long too."

"Not much longer than Austin."

"But Kathryn sounds like a professor."

She laughed. "It's my name."

"I know, but I was wondering if you'd be okay if I called you something different. Like friends have nicknames for one another."

"Sure. How about Rizzo?"

Even in the dim light of the dashboard she could see he didn't get it. "Didn't you see *Grease*?" she asked.

"Never."

"Then Rizzo is out. What do you have in mind?"

"How about... Kate?"

"Like Hepburn?" she replied.

"No, like Perry."

"Doesn't she go by Katie?"

"Yeah, how about Katie?"

"I prefer Kate."

He shrugged. "Okay, Kate it is." He held out his hand to seal the deal. She took it. He didn't let go.

"I hope your weekend goes well," Kathryn said after a few moments of silence.

He stayed silent and caressed her hand.

The sensation caused her stomach to flip-flop.

They reached her house a little after ten. She wanted to invite him in, but knew it would be a mistake. He had a lot on his mind, a lot to figure out. Still, she couldn't resist temptation. She lifted his hand and kissed it gently. "Thank you for a great night."

"Kathryn... Kate?"

She turned toward him. He leaned closer. He appeared nervous.

"Thanks for everything. You've been..."

He paused and looked away. Then, after a deep breath, "Good night."

THIRTEEN

saturday, june 11

WHAT HAD AUSTIN MEANT?

You've been...

What else had he been about to say?

Was that his way of putting distance between them?

It was understandable. Savannah was insecure. If that relationship was going to grow, she needed to feel confident of Austin's commitment to her.

Many couples went through it early on. She and Troy certainly had. She remembered how disappointed she'd been her senior year when she discovered that his guys-only camping trip to the Poconos included several girls. Among them were the girlfriends of two of his buddies. Troy swore he hadn't known they were coming, then told her she had nothing to worry about. His reassurances had assuaged her jealousy, and it would be several years before she learned that she should have worried more.

But that was her. Austin was Austin and Savannah was Savannah. They had to work things out in their own way and in their own time.

That didn't stop her from worrying about him, though.

She woke early, earlier than she usually did on Saturday, and drove by his place on Riley Street on her way to meet the girls at Milo's.

He was gone.

Would he and Savannah work things out?

Harvey Bodenschatz was ringing up a customer when she entered Milo's. "You're early," he said. "There's people at your table."

"It's not a problem, Harvey. I'll wait out front."

"Nah, just give me a minute. They're a bunch of North Jersey loudmouths who've been here long enough. I'll run them out and get your table ready."

Harvey was a man of his word. Five minutes later, two New Jersey couples were cursing him as they stalked out, swearing they would never return.

Harvey grinned as he closed the cash register drawer. "They say that every damned time they come in."

Kathryn was into her second cup of coffee when Suzanne and Jane arrived together. Jane walked with a limp and looked perfectly miserable. Kathryn jumped to her feet and pulled out Jane's chair. "What happened?"

Jane's account of tripping over a tree root in her back-yard was long and detailed and served as a reminder of the twenty-year age gap between them. Jane needed more activity and variety in her life. She was allowing age to get the best of her.

Hillary joined them just as Jane was winding down her story, so she went back to the beginning. Their empathy seemed to bring poor Jane out of her forlorn state, and by the time their breakfast plates arrived, they had moved on to town gossip. It wasn't until they were nearly done eating that Hillary said, "Kathryn, I completely forgot to ask about your date."

"Oh my goodness, how could we have forgotten?" Suzanne exclaimed.

"I was going to call you to find out," Jane said. "Before I hurt my foot."

"Spill the details," Hillary said. "Stuart and I sat around until seven thirty, just in case you called. But you didn't, so we ordered pizza and watched *Antiques Roadshow.*"

"I saw that one," Jane said. "Could you believe that cat litter salesman's curio cabinet was worth so much?"

"And did you see the way his wife's eyes lit up when she heard the price?" Hillary asked. "Stuart thinks she's going to leave him and take the curio cabinet."

"Back to Kathryn," Suzanne cut in. "Was he better than *RodneySellsRehoboth*?"

"He was a very nice man."

Hillary asked, "What did you do?"

Kathryn gave an abridged account of pizza, Skee-Ball, and ice cream. Their eyes grew large when she got to their walk on the beach.

Hillary pressed her hand to her heart. "That's incredibly romantic. Stuart has trouble walking on the beach because of his gout." Then, lowering her voice, she said, "Did he try anything?"

"Hillary," Jane hissed.

"I want to know too," Suzanne said. "We have to live vicariously through you, Kathryn, so spill it."

"We held hands." Their heads might explode if she dished more. "He was nice, but—"

Suzanne cut in. "You're holding back. I can see it in your face."

"Me too," Hillary said.

She couldn't think about what had happened later. Her face would —

177

"You're blushing." Suzanne pointed at her face. "She's blushing."

"You *are* blushing," Jane said.

Hillary's expression was a combination of shock and awe. "Did you... No! Not on the first... Oh, my goodness, Kathryn! You didn't..."

"You slept with him."

Leave it to Suzanne to get to the heart of the matter.

They leaned in close. Jane knocked over a water glass, but it was nearly empty already. Kathryn scanned their faces. Evidently they were expecting the full story. Even Suzanne, who usually was blasé about discussions of romance, waited for more.

"He did spend the night, but—"

They gasped, then started babbling at once.

"I'm happy for you!" Jane exclaimed.

"Thought so," Suzanne chimed in.

Hillary appeared stunned. "You... you... I'm shocked that you... Stuart and I don't even..."

There was silence as the others gawked at Hillary.

"No way," Jane said. "You guys have been together how long?"

Hillary blinked several times. "Nine years."

"And in nine years," Suzanne said, "in *nine years* you have never... *ever*?"

"Stuart is a gentleman."

"Are you sure that Stuart likes women, Hillary?"

"Of course, I'm sure that... Stuart and I are... A girl doesn't kiss and tell."

Suzanne was shaking her head. "Oh, my goodness, Stuart is a virgin."

Kathryn was relieved that the focus of the conversation had shifted, even if it put Hillary on the spot. She watched silently as Suzanne tried to convince Hillary that something was wrong with a fifty-year-old man who had never made a move on his girlfriend of nine years. By the time the argument ended, Hillary was hellbent on skipping that week's episode of *Antiques Roadshow* to prove to all that Stuart was a red-blooded, heterosexual American man.

And if he wasn't? Who cared? He and Hillary enjoyed each other's company and kept each other from being lonely. "I'm with Hillary," Kathryn said. "A girl doesn't kiss and tell."

"At least you've got something to tell if you decide to," Suzanne said, casting a sideways glance at Hillary. "Some people just watch TV every Saturday night."

"I'll have a story to tell soon enough," Hillary snapped.

FOURTEEN

sunday, june 12

KATHRYN FINISHED her schoolwork about nine-fifteen and was settling in for a bit of television before bed when her phone rang. She smiled when she saw the Pennsylvania area code. "Hello, Austin."

"Hey, Kate. Are you okay? Your voice sounds raspy."

"I'm fine. It gets that way when I haven't spoken to anyone all day."

"You haven't said a single word the entire day?"

It must sound strange to a young guy like Austin how someone could go an entire day without human interaction. She felt a pang of embarrassment. "It happens occasionally. Usually on Sundays, when I spend the day at home. Had you not called I might have gone the entire day without opening my mouth."

"That's interesting. There are days I would be smart to keep my mouth shut."

They shared a laugh, then the line was silent until Austin said, "You're probably getting ready for bed."

"Soon. Why do you ask?"

"No reason. I just wanted to say hi."

"Are you back in Bethany Beach?"

"No. I'm in Frederica. Calvin broke down again."

"Oh, no, Austin. Do you need a ride back to town?"

"I could stay here tonight, but I have a window installer coming tomorrow, so I need to... No, I'll be fine."

He was trying to put a good spin on the situation, but she could hear defeat in his voice. "I'm coming to get you."

"Really, Kate. It's almost ten o'clock and you've got class in the morning. I'll hitch a ride into Milford. It'll be fine."

"I'm on my way. When I get close, I'll call. You can drop me at work in the morning and use my car to meet your window people." She cut him off when he started to raise another protest. "I'll be there within an hour."

AUSTIN STUCK a note in Calvin's front window, explaining his dilemma and promising to return. The spot he had chosen was in the far corner of a Methodist church just off Frederica's main road. Calvin had barely made it that far.

Headlights came from the direction of Route 1, and he watched as Kathryn slowed before pulling into the lot. He locked the truck and hid the key in back, then opened the passenger door and practically fell into Kathryn's front seat.

"You look exhausted," Kathryn said as she pulled out of the lot.

"I left Hershey at two so I could be back by six. Calvin overheated the first time outside of Strasburg. I had to stop four more times to let the motor cool. The last time was here. Calvin wouldn't start even after cooling down."

"Is it the radiator again?"

"Yeah, but I think the starter is going too. I'll call a

181

couple of garages in the area tomorrow and see if someone can look at it."

"I'm so sorry. Can you afford all these repairs?"

"I'm okay. It's just discouraging, coming at the same time that I need the truck." He laid his head against the back of the seat. "I'm just ready to be back in Bethany."

They rode in silence for several minutes, and Kathryn wondered if he had fallen asleep. His shirt was covered with grease again, like when he'd shown up for dinner two weeks earlier. It appeared he had tried to clean his hands, and, while they were cleaner than his shirt, they were still discolored with grease and dirt stains.

He opened his eyes and looked at her across the seat. She could see the trace of a smile.

"Did you and Scott have a nice weekend?" he asked.

"I can't speak for Scott, but mine was sort of boring."

He nodded and gazed out the window.

"I'm not seeing Scott anymore."

He turned back to her. "Why?"

"No good reason. I just don't want to."

He considered her response, probably wondering why she would sleep with a guy then dump him. Or maybe he was wondering if Scott dumped her. Whatever he was thinking, he kept to himself.

"How about you?" she asked. "Good weekend with Savannah?"

This got a smile, albeit a melancholy one. "You were right about her feeling insecure. I think I helped her get over it, though."

"That's good. I knew you would handle it well."

He shrugged. Austin was a shrugger. He used them to convey a range of thoughts, from *I don't care* to *I have no idea what I'm doing*. But what did this shrug mean?

"She's coming down next weekend."

"Good. That will give you guys more time to... talk."

"Yeah. Talk. She asked me if I was still committed to our relationship."

Kathryn didn't respond. If he wanted to share his reply, he would.

"I told her I was as committed as I'd ever been."

What did that mean?

Probably that there would not be any more slow dancing at Elijah's. The prospect made her sad.

She took a deep breath. "I think you and I need to put some distance between us," she said, not meaning a word of it.

"I don't want that," he said.

"Savannah probably does, though."

He shrugged again. "She asked what there was between you and me."

"What did you say?"

"That you are a friend. My only friend in Bethany."

"Come on, Austin. You can meet as many people and make as many friends as you want here."

"Sure, I can meet lots of people. But friends? Not like the friendship we have."

When he spoke, there was an urgency in his tone. "Don't you feel it, Kathryn?"

"If you feel what you say you feel, Austin, why did you tell Savannah that you're as committed as ever?"

"Probably for the same reason that you let Scott spend the night."

Should she be offended? Or thankful that he was so candid? It didn't matter—they'd reached a point where all cards were on the table. The problem was, she wasn't sure what cards she held.

Silence prevailed for the next few minutes. What should she say? What *could* she say? Austin was just twenty-two years old. A man, sure, but a young man with fewer life experiences than her.

But what classified some life experiences as valuable and others not? Which ones brought personal growth? Was being a college professor any more a life experience than rebuilding a house? Was Saturday breakfast with her friends more valuable than Saturday night at a hip-hop club? Was a failed marriage any more a life experience than... Yeah, on that one she had him. Marriage was hard. Divorce was damned hard. Nothing in Austin's past compared to that.

"So what will you and Savannah do when she comes down next week?"

He took a deep breath, rubbed the back of his neck, and said, "I don't know. I guess I have five days to figure it out."

WHAT WAS SHE THINKING ABOUT?

What was she feeling?

Austin glanced at Kathryn a couple of hundred times on the drive back. They had been so close to having a real conversation until he couldn't answer her question about his plans with Savannah. He needed to stop beating around the bush. The truth, if she asked again, was that his plans depended upon her. Did she have the same feelings he had? Did she feel the electricity when they held hands? Did she experience the same warmness? And if so, did she wonder where it might lead? How far it might go?

Or was he an idiot?

Because, after all, she was in her thirties. Fifteen years

separated them. She had been in college when he was in kindergarten. Holy crap. That was weird.

What wasn't weird was the way his heart felt. He couldn't describe it, other than to say it seemed to be telling him to do everything he could to get closer to her. Savannah didn't make his heart feel that way. They had a good time together, and she satisfied him physically, but there was an incompleteness that he had never realized until he started spending time with Kathryn. Was it her maturity? Would he feel the same things for Savannah when they were a few years older?

Nope. He wouldn't. He had realized that weekend that Savannah wasn't *the one*. She was at best a placeholder until *the one* showed up. And as they neared the Bethany Beach city limits, he kept asking himself over and over, *Could Kathryn be the one?*

She turned onto Riley Street and pulled to the curb. The house looked dark and cold despite evening temperatures in the upper sixties. It depressed him just to look at it, especially when he knew there was another place he would rather be.

"Thanks for coming to get me."

Kathryn put the car in park and turned to face him. "Stay at my house tonight."

Had she really just said... She had. *She had!*

"I really shouldn't. After everything with Savannah, it would be..."

"If Savannah cares for you, she'll understand. And it's not like we'll be... you know... sleeping together. I have a spare room. With a real bed. And air conditioning. And a hot shower." She smiled, and even in the dark he could see the color rising in her cheeks. "Of course, you already know about the shower."

‖‖‖‖‖

KATHRYN FELT her face flush as she mentioned the shower and was glad it was dark inside the car. He gazed back at her for a couple awkward seconds, then said, "I'd like that."

She didn't wait for him to do something silly, like change his mind. And she didn't reach out for his hand again. Best to lay the ground rules now and hope she was strong enough to enforce them later. She put the car into gear and drove toward home.

After ten minutes of chitchat about nothing in particular, they were home. She led the way inside. It was late. She had class at eight in the morning. And he had work. But before they went any further, she needed to say what she had been holding inside. She waited until they were in her living room with good light so she could see his face. Then she took a deep breath and faced him. "Austin, I hope I'm not being too forward, but I have feelings for you."

He didn't speak. He didn't shrug, either, so there was that. His expression was blank at first and scared her that she was making a fool of herself by expressing such deep sentiment to a guy who was in diapers when she was in high school.

But she wasn't in high school anymore. She was a mature woman. And he was a man. A sensitive, caring, handsome, and sexy man.

A man who wasn't responding after she'd poured out her heart.

She shouldn't have said anything. What was she thinking?

His hand reached out. Touched hers. Stroked her arm.

Gentle strokes, like whispers with his fingers. His voice was gentle, too. "I feel the same."

She wanted more than anything to fall into his arms and have him take her upstairs. But there was so much else to consider. Would making love with him short-circuit everything? Would it be like Scott? Would she make love to him at night and send him packing at first light?

Austin wasn't Scott, though. He was everything Scott wasn't. And he was everything Kathryn wasn't. Their worlds were far apart. Could their feelings for one another bridge those worlds?

"Would you like to explore those feelings?" she asked, then playfully punched him in the arm. "And if you shrug instead of giving me a proper answer, I'll send you back to Riley Street."

He grinned for a moment, then grew serious again. "I want to explore those feelings..."

He was about to say more. She was certain of it.

She barely saw his arms snake around her waist. He pulled her close, and they leaned into one another.

The first kiss was beyond description. Her legs turned soft, but she knew she'd be okay because his arms would hold her up. He pulled back far enough to place his lips on her neck, just below her ear. He kissed her there and gave her chills. He whispered in her ear. "I want to explore what we're feeling, but slowly, if it's okay with you."

"Me too," she croaked, turning her head so she could kiss his neck and earlobe. She breathed in his muskiness, a working man's scent, and found it intoxicating. She tried to imagine how it would be to make love with him and suspected it might be both hard and soft. And wonderful.

"I'm a little scared," he said simply. "I need to set things straight with Savannah. She thinks our relationship is going places that it's not."

She leaned back a bit. "I don't want to be the cause of your breakup."

"Kate, you can send me away right now, and I'll still have an honest talk with Savannah. She's getting serious and I'm not ready for that. At least not with her."

Kathryn pulled away. Reluctantly. She looked up at him and smiled. "We had better slow down then. You have unfinished business to attend to next weekend."

He sighed and closed his eyes. "Savannah and I have been together for a couple years. There was another girl freshman year, and I dated a little in high school, too. But I've never felt the kind of connection that made me want to go deeper. Until now."

He got it. It was a relief knowing he recognized what was happening between them was different from his previous relationships. Recognizing it and doing something about it, though? Could he go that far? Time would tell. She motioned for him to follow her upstairs. He reached for her hand, but she pulled it away, certain that if she gave him her hand, she would likely give him much more. It wasn't time for that. Yet.

At the top of the stairs, she pointed to the guest room. "You can stay there tonight, but maybe you should stay at your house the rest of the week."

"I understand. And I'm really exhausted. It's been a heck of a day."

She grinned at him. "That might be the understatement of the century."

"Are you going to bed too?"

"Not quite yet. I still have work to do. It's not easy to

bore college students." She pecked him on the cheek. "Good night, Austin."

She left him and headed for her bedroom. She was closing the door when he called out. "Kate?"

She opened the door and looked back.

"Cape Henlopen."

"What about it?"

"Take your classes there."

"I don't teach science, Austin. This is remedial freshman English, remember?"

He grinned. "I had a fine arts class sophomore year. The professor took us on a field trip to a nature park. He had assignments and everything. Before that trip, I never understood that art could be found anywhere. In art galleries and museums, sure, but also in nature. I aced that class because he did things different than other professors. You can too."

"But why Cape Henlopen?"

"Why not? It's close, it's cheap, and they have something for everyone. I go there a couple times every summer. It's peaceful and uncrowded. A great place to get away and think."

"What? You get away to think?"

Austin laughed. "Sure. I'm a lot deeper than you think, Kate."

"I know you are, but I guess I never thought about you needing to get away."

He shrugged.

"What should we do there?" she asked.

He winked. "You'll figure that out."

friday, june 17

THE RULES WERE SIMPLE. Students would come to Cape Henlopen State Park for three hours on Friday, and Kathryn would cancel three class periods the following week. They had interrogated her from every angle when she first mentioned it, trying to figure out why she was offering such a sweet alternative.

"Cape Henlopen? Really, Dr. Shea?"

"The college will cover the park entrance fee. You just have to get there."

"They have a beach?"

"Yes. That's where you'll find me if you have questions."

"And fishing?"

"Fishing too."

"I know some guys who play disc golf there. Can we do that?"

"Of course."

"I'm going to bring a six-pack and chill."

"Alcohol is not permitted in the park, and aren't you nineteen?"

Her question got a laugh. The first of the semester.

Things then turned serious when a handful of students tried another ploy.

"What if we don't want to go?"

"What if we can't go? I have to be at work right after class."

"I'll be here next week at our regular class time. You come as always."

The classroom grew quiet while everyone considered the alternative. Then Robert, a guy who hadn't spoken all semester, broke the silence. "What kind of moron would want to be stuck in here when we can be at the beach?"

Another student, a brassy redhead named Carmen, said, "I'll be there. And all we have to do is write a paper?"

"You can choose to write about your day at the park or about an event from your past that the trip brings to mind."

"That's easy enough," she said.

Others nodded in agreement.

Word spread from Kathryn's first class to her second, and their interrogation had been considerably less intense. The excitement had grown all week and, when they showed up Friday morning, only two had opted out.

She sat on the beach in a rented chair under a rented umbrella, sipping concession stand lemonade and keeping tabs on what her students were doing.

Several braved the seventy-two-degree water to frolic in the surf.

Four guys and two girls were fishing. They'd come by to display their catch, a pretty sweet-looking bluefish.

A hastily arranged disc golf tourney was in full swing.

And Robert, the silent guy who'd spoken up in class? She suspected he and Alexis were smoking weed beyond the dunes, but she didn't have the inclination to check. They weren't high schoolers. If they were caught doing something they shouldn't, they would face the consequences.

With a half hour left, most students migrated to Kathryn's spot on the beach. Some opened laptops and started writing. Others sat and visited. A few chatted with Kathryn, asking questions that were both academic and personal.

The iciness was melting away.

When she told them they were free to go, most left. A few remained, enjoying the sun and conversation. The last two peeled off thirty minutes later.

Kathryn was still savoring the moment when Austin appeared over the sand dunes. The sight of him in khaki cutoffs and a sleeveless T-shirt made her insides tingle. They hadn't seen each other since she had dropped him off Monday morning.

"Hello, stranger," she called out.

He smiled and waved, and the tingling intensified. "How did you know I was here?" she asked.

"I didn't. I just hoped you would be. I've come up every day since Tuesday." He held up a paper sack. "I bring my lunch. After the third day the guy at the gate sold me a season pass."

Kathryn was tempted to ask why he hadn't called or texted to find out if she'd be there, but deep down she knew. She'd said they needed to give each other space until he decided how to deal with his relationship with Savannah. "Here," she said, handing him her beach towel.

He spread it out on the sand and sat down.

While he gazed at the ocean, Kathryn gazed at him. He was close enough for her to reach out and stroke his hair. She wanted to, very much, but resisted.

After a few moments, she spoke. "Your idea was spot-on."

"What idea?"

She waved at the surrounding terrain. "You know which idea. This idea."

A mischievous smile crossed his lips. "I don't know what you're talking about. I'm just a dumb handyman."

"My students loved it. They asked if we can do another trip before the semester ends."

"What did you say?"

"I said I would think about it. Want to know the best thing about this day?"

"Me showing up?"

She laughed. "That too. But the best thing was the connection we had. They kept coming by to check in and say hi. Some asked me about myself. It was completely different than in class."

"I have a feeling it will be different in class, too."

"Why?"

"They got to know you as a person. They connected with you. Now it will be up to you to keep that connection alive."

Kathryn sat forward in her chair. "How do you know so much?"

"Lots of bad professors. And a very few great ones. The great ones always connect."

"Are you saying I'm a bad professor?"

His face turned serious as he realized what he'd insinuated. Kathryn laughed. "I'm kidding." Without thinking, she touched his cheek.

He didn't pull away. Instead, he met her gaze, then reached up and stroked her hand.

It was dreamy and surreal, and Kathryn didn't want it

to end. But it had to. She gently pulled her hand away and sat back. "When does Savannah arrive?"

"This evening."

Did he know what he planned to say? Or have any idea about how things might go? Would he tell Savannah about them? Or would he be seduced by her youth and beauty, two things Kathryn could not give him? Were she and Austin having their last moments together? Or was something special about to bloom?

Why did everything have to be so uncertain? So complicated?

It would be unfair to ask, so she said nothing.

He offered her half of his turkey and Swiss. She took it and they ate in silence as they watched the rise and fall of the waves and listened to the roar of the surf. Kathryn took everything in. If these were their last moments together, she wanted to remember every detail.

"How about you?" he asked. "Big weekend plans?"

I would love to spend it with you.

"Nothing exciting. Hillary is having a get-together tonight."

"She's your friend who lives up on the north end of the beach, right? That should be fun."

Kathryn smiled sadly. "Certainly not as much fun as smoked oysters and beer at Elijah's."

"And dancing," Austin said quickly. "Don't forget the dancing."

She would never forget the dancing. She hoped there would be more. Much more.

KATHRYN AND JANE arrived at Hillary's house a little after eight. There were already a dozen people milling around Hillary's kitchen, munching on crab balls and peel-and-eat shrimp that were dumped in the center of the table atop layers of newspaper. Cocktail and tartar sauces filled bowls on all sides. Hillary roamed the room in a Frostburg State University T-shirt and blue capri pants she still insisted on calling clam diggers because that's what her mother had called them. From behind a scuffed and pock-marked surfboard laid across two sawhorses, Stuart mixed pink squirrels, grasshoppers, and other concoctions that would be unfamiliar to anyone born after 1990.

Kathryn tried to imagine Austin's reaction to the eclectic group. Her thoughts moved on to how his evening with Savannah might be going. Were they having a conversation about the future?

"WE DIDN'T HAVE to come here. I know you don't like it."

"But you do," Savannah said. "I need to think more about things you like."

She had arrived at seven. They were both famished, but she insisted they make the trip to Elijah's. And that they drive her car; she had no interest in riding in Calvin.

From the parking lot, Austin could tell the place was jammed. Even the picnic tables were full. Except one. Austin started toward it, but Savannah held his arm. "The mosquitos are terrible. Let's find a table inside."

She was right. The bugs were thick. Cans of bug repellent were placed on each table, and people used them liberally, spreading a fog of chemicals over everything.

They walked inside, and Austin saw a busboy clearing a table in the center of the room. He grabbed Savannah's hand and pulled her with him to grab it, just edging out a guy in cutoffs and a Peterbilt cap who was trying to claim it too. The guy flipped him off and huffed away.

The server, a girl with a pierced navel and crop top to show it off, took their drink order. Two beers. Light for Savannah. Full-strength for Austin.

"What did you want to talk about?" Savannah asked as she scanned the sweaty crowd.

"It can wait. I can barely hear myself in here. Maybe we can take a walk on the beach later."

"I figured you would want to head straight back to the Sheraton." She ran her tongue across her lips. "We can always talk there. You know... after."

It would have been so easy to just say yes, to let Savannah control the order of events. She knew how capable she was of getting her way with sex. Had he allowed their relationship to reach that point without even realizing it? Was the sex that important? The bigger question was how could Savannah not suspect that his reason for wanting to talk had to do with Kathryn? She had questioned him at length about her the week before.

But that was Savannah. She wasn't one to worry about those kinds of things. She had readily admitted that it was silly to think that Austin might be interested in an older woman.

"I'm sorry for even thinking it could be a thing," she had said as he was leaving Hershey the previous Sunday. Her words, spoken softly and from the heart, had remained with him through the week. Savannah cared deeply about him. And trusted him.

But did she love him? Or did she love the thought of being in love?

And did he love her? It was something he had barely considered since they'd been together.

It was time to find out.

╫╫╫╫╫

KATHRYN TURNED from Stuart's makeshift bar and nearly bumped into the man waiting in line behind her.

"Oh, excuse me," she said, raising her glass to make sure no wine spilled out. "I didn't realize you were—"

"I know you."

He was tall, sandy-haired, and handsome, with a neatly trimmed goatee. His summer-weight oxford fit well even if it was a few years out of date, and his shorts were tan and stitched with tiny blue anchors. He'd arrived with Francie, one of Hillary's work friends.

"Sorry, I don't think you do," Kathryn replied.

"Sure, I do. Not personally, but I've seen you before."

"It's possible, I guess. Bethany Beach isn't very big."

"I don't live in Bethany, so that's not it. Let me think."

Kathryn glanced around the room. Francie was yards away, chatting with Stuart while he mixed her a screwdriver.

"I'm Bill, by the way. As soon as I saw you, I knew that —" He snapped his fingers. "Wait a minute, I know where I saw you. You were at Elijah's. You're the lady who was dancing with the kid."

Kathryn grabbed his arm and brought her fingers to her lips. "Shhh, keep your voice down."

Bill laughed. "It's a party, for crying out loud."

"I mean about me and... and he isn't a kid. He's a young man."

"Yeah. *Really* young."

"It's not like what you think. We went there for dinner."

"Yeah, the food is great, but I saw the way you and that kid — that *young man* — were dancing. It was more than dinner."

"I said keep your voice down. Please?"

He laughed again, louder. Jane looked their way from across the room, her eyebrows raised. Kathryn gave her a thumbs-up.

"Sorry. I've already had more to drink than I should," he said.

"You just got here."

"Yeah, but Francie and me had a couple at her place. So, are you alone tonight? I don't see your young man."

"I came with my friend, Jane. And I would really appreciate you not saying anything about Elijah's."

"Your secret is safe with me, sweetheart. Hillary's weirdo boyfriend said they're going to fire up the stereo later. Maybe we can dance?"

"I don't think so."

He placed his hand on her arm. "I don't mean like you and your young boyfriend. I just meant—"

"Hi, Kathryn," Francie said as she joined them and attached herself to Bill's side. "I see you two have met."

"Yeah," Bill said. "I thought I knew her. She reminded me of somebody I saw dancing at a bar out on the old highway, but I guess not."

"Of course not, silly," Francie giggled. "Kathryn teaches at the college. She would never be caught dead in one of those places where you and your friends hang out."

Bill looked at Kathryn. Leered at her. Then said, "Yeah. Like I said, it was somebody else."

░░░░░

EVERYTHING AT ELIJAH'S seemed off-kilter.

The clam strips weren't as good. The beer wasn't as cold or satisfying. The deejay's song selections missed the mark. And it was hotter and muggier than normal.

The weekend crowd was louder and more raucous than what Austin was used to on his weeknight visits. Kathryn's former student had already tossed out two guys who'd decided it was okay to grope a table of women celebrating a divorce. There was tension in the air—and in Austin's gut. Not being able to have his talk with Savannah only prolonged the inevitable.

It was nine thirty when they paid their bill and returned to the parking lot. The air was still full of humidity and bug spray, but it felt refreshing after the suffocating heat inside.

"Where to now?" Savannah asked.

"How about we sit on the beach in front of your hotel?"

"How about we cuddle up under the sheets in my hotel?"

That was Savannah's way, and she was very good at it. Of course, Austin had never been averse to skipping the beach for the sheets, but he was seeing things as they really were. It still took some effort to push away the thoughts her invitation stirred.

They were pulling out of the parking lot when his phone buzzed. He groaned when he saw who it was. "Hey, Holly. Let me guess. The tenants on Third Street are partying too loudly for the neighbors?"

"Wrong, little brother."

"There's no way it's the people at Sea Turtle Court. They're in their seventies. Is it the place in Fenwick?"

"Why do you think that there's a problem every time I call?"

"Because every time you call, there is a problem."

"Well, not this time. Where are you?"

"Why do you need to know? Are you spying on me?"

"So defensive," Holly said. "I ask because I went by the Windermere and it appears you haven't been staying there, so I thought I would—"

"Wait. You're here?"

"I'm in Bethany Beach. The bigger question is, are you here?"

"I'm out..." Austin paused and glanced at Savannah.

She shook her head and mouthed *no*.

"What did you need to see me about?"

"Nothing really. I just figured you might be lonely. I was going to offer to buy you a drink and catch up."

"Catch up on what?"

"Life. Your summer. I also want to see how the Riley Street property is coming along. I went by earlier and saw there was a lot of work going on, but the house was locked."

There was no way he could ignore his sister. She was too persistent. She probably had already tracked his phone and knew he was some place in the boonies. The only thing he could do was meet her and find out why she was in town. But what to do about Savannah? He hit the mute button on his phone. "Will you go with me to meet Holly? It will only be a couple hours."

She looked at him as if he was nuts. "I didn't drive all the way down here to spend the evening with your sister. Besides, you said you had something you wanted to talk about."

"Baby brother? Are you still there?"

He unmuted the phone and said, "One second, Holly." Then, to Savannah, "I can't ignore her. Please go with us."

"We had plans. You didn't even know she was coming. You *can* ignore her, Austin."

Oh, great. What could he say that would appease both his sister and his girlfriend?

Nothing. There was nothing. Someone was going to be upset.

And that someone had to be Savannah.

"Yeah... uh, where are you staying tonight, Holly?"

"I'm at that nice Sheraton in Rehoboth."

"I'm thirty minutes out of Bethany. How about we meet at that little bar on Garfield Street?"

"The one we used to sneak off to in high school?" Holly giggled. "The one that didn't look too closely at our fake IDs?"

"Yeah, that's the one. Want to meet there?"

"I would love that, but are you forgetting that they close at ten? How about we meet at the north end of the boardwalk? I'll grab something to eat on the way and meet you there."

"Make it ten thirty? I have to drop someone off first."

"And just who might that be?" Holly asked playfully. "Did you meet someone, or is Savannah in town?"

Well, kind of both. "I'll see you at ten thirty."

HILLARY'S little party was going off the rails. Kathryn blamed Stuart. His concoctions were sweet, pretty, and potent. Jane was deep into her third fuzzy navel, swigging them like a kindergartner with an endless supply of juice boxes. They appeared to take the edge off her leg pain, though, so there was that to be happy about. A little before ten, one of Hillary's work friends had the bright idea of filling a Styrofoam cooler with fruit punch and grain alcohol. It quickly became a trough, with people bypassing the dipper and dunking their cups straight into the hooch. Someone found an oldies dance channel on Spotify, and the more adventurous partyers shoved the living room furniture against the walls and attempted to demonstrate they had not lost the moves they claimed to have had in college.

Just as Kathryn was plotting a way to get a very drunk Jane into her car so they could leave, Francie vomited into a potted plant, overpowering the air with the smell of fruit and something akin to spoiled tuna. A few oblivious revelers continued swaying to a Michael Jackson hit. Others opened windows to allow some fresh air. Quick-thinking Stuart grabbed the potted plant and tossed it into the yard. That helped, as did the efforts of another of Hillary's neighbors to mitigate the stench by lighting a joint and passing it around.

"Oh. My. Goodness." Jane slurred her words, and it came out as *Au ma goodneshhhh.* "Is that man smoking mara... mari-ju-wanna?"

Kathryn went to a back bedroom in search of their purses. She picked through a pile until she found them, then turned around and bumped into Francie's boyfriend, Bill. He was close. Too close. And grinning like a lunatic.

"I followed you," he said stupidly.

"Shouldn't you be taking care of Francie?"

"She's passed out. I came to see if we could have that dance."

Bill didn't slur his words. He was drunk, though. And

his type of drunk instilled more bravado than a man who looked and acted like Bill should have.

"Sorry, but my friend and I are leaving."

"Don't leave. I know how much you like to dance."

He just couldn't leave it alone.

"Nope, we're definitely leaving."

She pushed past and headed to the living room. Once they were out with the others, he would cool his jets. He followed close behind, pleading his case. She ignored him until the twerp pinched her backside. Time seemed to slow. Kathryn spun to face him, uncertain what her next move might be. His oily leering smile made the decision for her. She slapped him. *Smack!* She hoped it sounded worse than it really was. The smile remained glued on his face for a moment or two, just enough time for Kathryn to feel things might be okay. Then he dropped as if he'd been decked by Ali himself. His head hit the wall with a thud, and everyone grew quiet except Michael Jackson, who implored Kathryn through the stereo speakers to *just beat it.*

She gulped. Oh, my goodness. Had she killed him?

His eyes rolled back in his head for several beats before he smiled sweetly. Kathryn tried to shake away the sting in her hand, then pushed her way past the gawkers and out the front door. She was reaching for her car keys when she remembered Jane. She couldn't leave Jane. Hillary was in no condition to take her home, and Suzanne had only stayed for an hour before begging off. The others were Hillary's neighbors and work colleagues, people Kathryn didn't know well enough to trust with her friend's safety.

She needed to go back in and get Jane.

But not just yet. Not with grabby Bill still sprawled out on the floor. Let the booze do its job, she thought. Give everyone a few minutes to get back to partying. Let Bill recover. The beach was just three houses away. Maybe a short stroll along the boardwalk would clear her head before retrieving Jane.

▓▓▓▓

AUSTIN WAS SEATED ON A BENCH, staring out at the moonlit ocean, when Holly approached from behind and smacked the back of his head. He jumped up ready to do battle.

"Easy, big boy. Why didn't you just tell me Savannah is in town?"

"How did you know?"

"I saw her in the hotel bar. She didn't look happy."

"I'm not either. What do you want, sis?"

"I needed to get away. Mom and Dad want a status report on the Riley Street project. I get to spend time on the beach. Everyone wins."

"Everyone except me." Austin motioned at the space next to him. "You might as well sit down."

"Let's walk. I didn't get my steps in yet."

"You're one of them?"

"One of who?"

Austin pointed at the fitness watch on her left wrist. "A step counter?"

She laughed. "Who would have ever thunk it? In college, I ate cookies and ice cream every day and never gained a pound. Now..." Holly patted her tummy. "Too much time at the desk. The watch makes me get up and move. I see you don't have that problem. You look skinny."

She was right. Sometimes he became so immersed in his work that Austin forgot to eat. He kicked off his shoes and stowed them under a bench.

"Aren't you worried someone might take those?" Holly asked as they stepped onto the sand.

"Not if they smell them."

Holly removed her sandals and carried them as they approached the water's edge. The ocean temperature was cool, but felt good on Austin's feet and legs. They walked for several minutes before Holly spoke. "So, where are you staying?"

"Not the Windermere."

"C'mon, little brother. You can tell me. Are you and Savannah shacking up at the Sheraton on her daddy's credit card?"

"Only on weekends."

She punched his arm lightly. "You're being evasive. What's up?"

"What makes you think something's up?"

"The vague answers. You haven't been calling home. And when Mom and Dad call you, they get voicemail."

"I talk to Mom and Dad. I keep them updated on how the house is coming along."

"Yeah, and that's another thing. Picket Fence Construction?"

"What about them?"

"I researched Picket Fence Construction. Do you know what I found?"

It didn't matter if he answered or not. Holly was going to tell him.

"There are five companies that call themselves Picket Fence Construction. Two are in Arizona, one's in Nebraska. A fourth is in South Carolina. There was a fifth, in Minnesota, but they filed for bankruptcy after one of the owners was busted for embezzlement."

"That's the guy I hired. He broke out."

Holly laughed. "Sorry, but he's still in prison. I checked."

"Leave it to you to check everything."

Waves lashed the shore, bringing water up to their calves. Was there a storm brewing? The western sky was clear, but there were dark clouds far to the northeast, just above the horizon. The moon had disappeared, leaving them in near darkness. The only illumination came from streetlamps along the streets closest to the beach.

"Should we go back?" Austin asked, hoping to move the conversation toward an end.

"Nah. We'll be fine. And yes, I check everything. And I know that you're not using the company you told Mom and Dad you were using. The only question is, who is doing the renovation?"

"Me."

Holly snapped her fingers. "That's what I thought. When I peeked in the windows, I saw a couple pieces of power equipment that I remembered from Grandpa's shop."

"Do Mom and Dad know?"

"Nope. They're preoccupied with a land acquisition on the Jersey shore. You know it's a matter of time before they figure it out, though, right?"

"If you tell them."

"If they ask, I'll have to tell them."

Austin stopped walking. Holly took several more steps before she realized he wasn't beside her.

"Holly, what happened between us? You used to keep all my secrets. I did the same for you."

"We were kids. That's what kids do. And besides, it wasn't like your secrets were front-page news." She giggled.

"Sneaking out after curfew to play basketball. Driving Brandon Fraley's car when you were fifteen."

"Don't forget the whoopie cushion in ninth grade."

They both laughed at that memory.

"You had two weeks of detention," Holly said. "But Mom never heard it from me."

They grew quiet again, enjoying the memories of a time when a closeness had united them.

"I like construction work, Holly. You know that."

"Yeah, but if you don't pass those classes, Dad and Mom will—"

"I am passing." Austin pulled out his phone and accessed his grades on the school website. "I have an A in Southern Lit and a B-minus in Organizational Theory."

"Wow, that A in Southern Lit is pretty impressive. Who did you bribe?"

"I'm actually doing the work." He told her about reading *Chiefs* and how he was two-thirds through *The Lords of Discipline*. He left out Kathryn and the help she'd given him. "I've really enjoyed that class," he said as he tucked away his phone. "And I still have time to work on the house. It keeps me from being bored."

"I'm impressed. You're growing up this summer. How are things with Savannah?"

"Not as good as Southern Lit."

"Want to tell me?"

Austin decided he did. Not everything. Not the part about Kathryn.

But everything else.

THE BOARDWALK WAS NEARLY DESERTED, and a storm appeared to be brewing to the north. The only people out were a couple of joggers and a young couple walking along the shore a couple hundred yards away. Kathryn sat down on a bench and enjoyed the cool breeze on her face.

What a night.

Hillary's party was unlike the usual sedate affairs of the past. Something had changed, and it wasn't until she thought about it for a few minutes that Kathryn figured it out.

Hillary and Stuart were trying to be fun.

Was it because of the conversation the girls had at Milo's the week before? Had their disbelief that Hillary and Stuart hadn't slept together driven them to become wild and crazy party people? The thought made her giggle. And giggling made her feel better. Better enough that she thought she could go back and get Jane without feeling embarrassed for slapping Bill the butt pincher. After a few months passed, they would all look back at it and laugh. Except for Bill. And maybe Francie.

Kathryn stood and stretched. Weariness was setting in. It was time to go home. The joggers had retreated to their hotel rooms for the night. The only signs of life were the couple walking along the shoreline. Two flashes of lightning over the Atlantic in quick succession illuminated the beach like a strobe light. Kathryn jumped and saw the beachcombing couple do the same.

Get away from the water, she silently admonished them. They seemed to hear her and turned toward the boardwalk. They were still a hundred yards away, but there was no mistaking the guy.

Austin.

He was looking toward the surf, probably considering the odds of getting struck by lightning. He didn't see Kathryn, but the woman did. Their eyes met for a second before Kathryn backed into the shadows of a souvenir shop that was closed for the night. When she dared to peek out from behind a post, the girl wasn't looking at her anymore. Kathryn watched them climb the steps to the boardwalk, then disappear toward the Central Boulevard parking lot. When the coast was clear, she stepped out of the shadows just as the first drops of rain smacked the boardwalk. By the time she reached Hillary's house, the rain was coming down hard and she was drenched. She knocked and was relieved when one of Hillary's sober friends came to the door. She asked her to get Jane, and a few moments later they were on their way home. It was nearly eleven when she dropped her friend off. Jane had fallen asleep on the short drive and Kathryn had to awaken her and help her inside.

Thoughts of Austin consumed her on the drive home.

Who was the woman at the beach? It certainly wasn't Savannah. The beach girl had dark hair and was shorter than Savannah.

Had Austin misled her about his plans?

Was he playing her? Was that what this was all about?

It couldn't be. Austin wasn't that kind of guy.

Was he?

But then, how well did she really know him?

┃┃┃┃┃

HOLLY DROVE Austin to the side street where he'd parked Calvin. "Seriously, Austin? Grandpa's tools and his truck?"

"I needed it for work. And speaking of that..." He paused. "Are you going to tell Mom and Dad?"

Holly stared through the windshield for a few moments as the wipers tried to keep up with the storm. "No," she finally said. "I won't say anything yet. Just don't screw things up, okay, Austin?"

"I promise." He reached for the door handle, then stopped. "What are you doing the rest of the weekend?"

"Tomorrow I'll hang out at the beach until checkout time, then probably head back to Philly. There's a lot of work that needs to get done."

"There's always lots of work," Austin said wearily.

"That's the way our family rolls, little brother. How about you? Will I see you at the Sheraton breakfast bar tomorrow morning?"

Austin shrugged. "Probably not. I had my phone turned down and missed Savannah's texts. The last one had a frowning emoji and said she'll see me tomorrow."

"What about your talk?"

"I guess we'll have it tomorrow."

"Where will you stay?"

"At the house on Riley Street. That's where I've been staying."

She squeezed his hand. "You're really growing up, you know? Oh, I nearly forgot." She reached into the back seat and grabbed a plastic grocery sack. "Here's your mail. Mom asked me to bring it. Your LSAT scores are in there."

Austin's stomach dropped. He'd taken the law school entrance exam last spring and given it little thought since. "Did you open it?"

"Of course not. Don't you know how you did?"

"Nope."

"But you can find out online three weeks after the test."

"I guess I forgot."

Holly shook her head as if dealing with a child. "Will I see you tomorrow?"

"Maybe. Do you want to see the progress I've made on the house?"

"I would rather see myself on the beach. There's no need for me to check up on the work you're doing. I know how good you are at that stuff. I'll tell Mom and Dad that it's coming along great."

Austin leaned across the seat and kissed her forehead. "Thanks, sis. I love you."

"I love you too, little brother. Let's catch up tomorrow."

SIXTEEN

saturday, june 18

AUSTIN SHIFTED the box of Sandy Pony doughnuts from his right hand to his left and softly knocked on the door of Room 315.

No response.

He knocked again, louder.

Several moments passed, but again, no response.

As he pulled his phone from the pocket of his shorts, the doughnut box tipped and fell to the floor. He bent over and snatched it on the bounce, but not before two Charlie Browns landed on the carpet.

Charlie Browns were Savannah's favorites.

Austin scooped them up and returned them to the box. He texted Savannah. *Where are you?*

He leaned against the wall and waited for her reply. She was probably still angry at him. He had it coming. She had driven down from Hershey to see him, and he'd dropped the ball.

And there was still the conversation they had to have. Getting a day's reprieve had given him additional time to sort out what he would say.

He cared for her very much.

Truth.

The time they spent together was important to him.

Truth.

He wasn't ready to commit long term.

Truth, but that one would hurt.

They should continue seeing each other but be open to pursuing other relationships.

That was where the crap would hit the fan.

He had also considered how she might respond.

If it was tears and heartbreak, he would hold her and tell her it was for the best.

If she was afraid of being alone, he would explain, patiently of course, that they could still text and call. Then he would hold her and tell her it was for the best.

If it was anger, he would allow her to get it out, then hold her and tell her it was for the best.

When it was over, when everything was out in the open, he would suggest a walk on the beach. Time to reminisce about the past and consider the future. He would encourage Savannah to see other guys but gently advise her to be careful because some guys could be jerks. They would plan a time to meet up in a few weeks. Maybe when he was in Philly to see his parents or visiting Grandpa. And then they would say farewell. Not forever. Who knew if the future might bring them back together?

He would walk Savannah back to her car, hold her for a few moments, then send her on her way.

But first he had to find her.

His phone buzzed with a text.

I wasn't sure if you were coming.

Before Austin could reply, another arrived.

I went for a drive. I'll be back at the hotel in a half hour if you want to come over.

Austin texted back, *I'm at the hotel now.*

Savannah replied with a smiley emoji and, *I hope you're hungry. I stopped by Sandy Pony and got a dozen doughnuts.*

Austin lifted the lid of his dozen. They looked like they'd been in a car wreck. Vanilla icing from one doughnut had glommed onto the chocolate of another. A cow tail had rainbow sprinkles on it from a pony party. The box was a mess, albeit a delicious mess. He sat down on the floor, pulled out a blue moon, and took a bite.

KATHRYN RINSED out her cereal bowl and returned it to the cabinet, then picked up her phone and typed out a text.

Good morning. I hope you are well.

She deleted it. Too formal.

Good morning. How did your talk with Savannah go?

Too forward. She deleted that one too.

Good morning. Who was the girl I saw you with at the beach last night?

That one made her sound like a stalker.

Good morning. I'm here if you want to talk.

That wasn't bad, but what if Savannah saw it? What if Savannah saw it just as he was telling her he needed some space?

And what if he needed that space to spend more time with the dark-haired girl from the beach?

It all made Kathryn's stomach hurt, so she deleted the message and sat down to work on the week's lessons.

"WHAT DID you want to talk about?"

Austin was barely into his second doughnut, a strawberry stallion, when Savannah asked. He wiped strawberry glaze from his lips and placed the doughnut back in the box that was between them on the bed.

"I was..." Austin's mind raced as he tried to remember what he planned to say. A half hour before, the words had come easily. Now? Gibberish. "I care for you very much."

She smiled and reached for his hand. "Same," she said.

"And... the time we spend together is... very..." What the heck had he planned to say about the time they spent together? "The time we spend is..."

"Fun?" she asked.

"Yeah."

"And special?"

How did she know he was going to say special?

"Yeah. Special too."

"We always have fun," she said. "Except when you stand me up like you did last night."

He hadn't seen that coming. Savannah had expressed her displeasure before he had left to meet Holly the night before.

"I'm sorry. I didn't know that Holly was... I was worried Mom and Dad sent her to spy on me."

"You're forgiven. What else did you want to say?"

Austin cleared his throat and wished he had gotten something to drink when he picked up the doughnuts. "It's... about us, Savannah... about you... and about..."

Savannah took a sharp breath, almost like a gasp. There was fear in her eyes.

215

The last thing Austin wanted to do was hurt her, but there was simply no way around it. "Over the past couple weeks, I discovered that–discovered isn't the right word. I... decided that you and I are—"

"He told you, didn't he?" Savannah cut in.

"I decided that you and I are—wait. What? Who told me?"

"Derek. You talked to Derek, didn't you? Damn him. I knew he couldn't keep it to himself."

Derek? His college roommate, Derek?

"Well... I need to hear from you too."

Savannah flinched. Color rose in her cheeks. Derek and Austin had been roommates since sophomore year, first in the dorm, then later in the loft Derek's parents purchased for him a few blocks from campus. He was awkwardly shy and brilliant. A science major who used words Austin would never comprehend. He was set to graduate a semester early, and from the correspondence he had left strewn across their kitchen table, was already in demand. Big jobs with big companies. And big paychecks.

Derek was going to be wealthy. Sooner, not later.

And he had always had a thing for Savannah. She, on the other hand, had never given him the time of day. He was Austin's nerdy roommate. The pest who never would leave when they wanted the loft to themselves. The wonky science guy who begged her to fix him up with her friends.

It turned out that things had changed.

And Austin never saw it coming.

KATHRYN WAS CLOSING her laptop when she heard a car door slam.

Austin?

She jumped up and scurried to the front door. Hopefully he had a good explanation about the girl from the beach.

She pulled back a corner of a living room shade. It wasn't Calvin in her driveway. It was a red sports car.

And it wasn't Austin climbing her steps.

It was Savannah.

Kathryn dropped the curtain and stepped back from the window. Was Savannah there because Austin had dumped her? Was she there to have it out? To win back her boyfriend?

Savannah knocked on the door. Not loudly. Not with enough force to break the door down. Just a gentle tap. Kathryn took a deep breath and counted to five, then considered retreating deeper into the house where she could hide until Savannah gave up.

But she couldn't do that. She took another deep breath and opened the door. "Savannah?"

"May I come in, Kathryn?"

Kathryn stepped aside and held the door open. She started to ask if everything was okay, but Savannah's face said clearly that it wasn't. Instead, she offered her a glass of water. Savannah accepted. She was seated on the sofa when Kathryn returned. Kathryn sat in the chair on her left. That allowed a bit more space and reaction time if Savannah turned out to be a crazy psychopath.

Was she a crazy psychopath?

Oh, God, she hoped not! Savannah was younger and in much better shape. She had taut arms and legs that came from working out. She was probably quick, too. If Savannah lunged at her, Kathryn would jump from the chair and run for the bathroom. It was small, but the lock was good. And there was a window that faced the house next door. She could yell for help.

"What can I do for you, Savannah?"

Savannah took a sip of water, then placed the glass on a coaster on the coffee table. She licked her lips, blinked several times, then said, "I need to talk, and you seem like someone I can trust."

Kathryn felt dizzy. Her mouth fell open despite her best effort to appear cool. She wished she had gotten herself a glass of water, too. Or maybe something stronger. "Savannah, are you okay?"

Savannah relaxed slightly. "I don't know anyone else here, and I'm worried about Austin."

"What? Are you... did something happen?"

She took another sip of water. Several drops dribbled down her chin. She used the back of her hand to catch them and suddenly looked very young and vulnerable. She dried her hand on her shorts. "I knew there was something he wanted to talk about. What I didn't know was that he had found out about Derek."

"Who is Derek?"

"Austin's roommate at Penn. They've been friends for a long time."

Kathryn's throat went dry. Had something bad happened to Austin's friend? A wreck? Was he in the hospital? Worse?

"What happened to Derek, Savannah?"

"I guess..." Savannah looked away. "I guess *I* happened to Derek."

Savannah told the story of how she and Derek had progressed from strangers to friends to lovers. She appeared remorseful as she admitted that their relationship had begun during the previous year's Christmas break.

"It was easy to keep from Austin," she said as she daubed her tears. "He was busy with his fraternity and intramural sports. It seemed he was always at the gym or the frat house. And it was just a fling at first. Until this summer. Then, with Austin spending all his time down here..." Savannah paused as if choosing her words. "Things became serious."

Kathryn heard Savannah's words, but her mind was on Austin. Even though he'd planned to tell Savannah he needed some distance, it still had to hurt. "How did he take it when you told him?" she asked when Savannah stopped to take a breath.

"He already knew. He had said we needed to talk, so I put two and two together. Derek had already told a couple of his buddies in Philadelphia, so I kind of expected Austin would find out. I have to admit, though, that he seemed surprised.

"Surprised?"

"Yeah, but it was probably just shock. I tried to get him to open up, but he didn't want to." Savannah took a breath. "That's why I came here, Kathryn. You and Austin have become friends. Maybe you can be there for him if he needs support."

"Me? Why?"

"Well, you're older. And more experienced... I guess. You've probably been dumped before. Maybe you can help him see that things will get better."

Oh, sure. The old maid schoolteacher has probably been dumped a time or two. She had, but it was pretty brassy of Savannah to assume it.

"What makes you think I've been dumped?" Kathryn replied coolly.

"I'm sorry. I just meant that you're single and, like... older and everything. I assumed you probably..."

Were married?

In a long-term relationship?

Had been dumped a time or two?

Kathryn had experienced all three, but that wasn't Savannah's business. And as far as being dumped, well, Savannah had narrowly avoided being on the receiving end herself.

As Savannah droned on, Kathryn wished she would hurry and leave so she could check on Austin. And much to her relief, she finally did. Kathryn walked her to the door, a little faster than the situation called for, perhaps, but she had grown weary of listening to Savannah rationalize how her fooling around with Austin's roommate was ultimately for the best. Every time she opened her mouth she proved she was more a kid than an adult. Smart and beautiful, but still a kid.

And it wasn't a kid that Austin needed.

As they said their goodbyes, Savannah hugged her. "Thanks for listening. And for being there for Austin."

She didn't provide a phone number or email address. If she was so concerned about his wellbeing, shouldn't she have left those?

Nope. Sweet, pretty Savannah was all about Savannah.

"I have one question," Kathryn said when they were outside. "Do you think Austin might see someone else?"

Savannah's forehead wrinkled as she pushed a lock of blonde hair away from her face. "I hadn't thought about it, but I guess anything's possible. Why do you ask?"

Kathryn pretended to be clueless. "I was at a friend's house last night and I—"

"The guy from the beach?"

"Excuse me?"

Savannah grinned. "Were you with the guy Austin and I saw you with? He was kind of hunky for an older guy."

"No. Not him. Anyway, I stepped outside for some fresh air and could have sworn I saw Austin walking on the beach with someone."

Savannah's eyes grew large for a second, but then she smiled. "Dark hair? Shorter than me?"

"Maybe. It was hard to see."

"It probably was Austin. His sister came down. He ditched me to spend time with her."

"And you're sure it was her?"

"Very sure. I saw her this morning when I went out for doughnuts. She's staying at the same hotel I'm at."

Had Savannah moved in for another hug, Kathryn would have happily accepted. She might be immature and prone to cheating on her boyfriend, but she had unknowingly allayed those fears that there was someone else. Kathryn practically pushed Savannah toward her car.

After all, she had someplace to be.

⛣

HOLLY LIFTED her head from the beach towel and squinted into the sun. "You seem antsy, Austin. Do you have someplace you need to be?"

Yes, he did. He wanted to see Kathryn. He wanted to tell her everything. How Savannah had been seeing Derek. How they'd been sneaking around behind his back. How she'd been spending Friday nights at his loft in Philadelphia before coming to Bethany Beach on Saturdays.

How she had chosen Derek because he had his future mapped out.

And how things had become more serious the last few weeks, while Austin was away.

And how she had planned to tell him, but was waiting for the right moment.

And then he wanted Kathryn to know how much he appreciated her friendship.

And how he hoped it could become more.

"Austin?"

"No. No place to be."

"I figured that when I saw Savannah loading her stuff in her car this morning. What happened?"

Austin stared at the surf. "She had to get back home."

"Spill it, little brother. She barely spoke to me this morning."

"Like I told you yesterday. We're giving each other some space."

"Who decided? You? Or her?"

"Both."

"Is there someone else? Because I know you would never have made this decision otherwise."

Ouch. Why did Holly have to be so perceptive? Austin lay back and used his arms to prop himself up. She was right, at least partially. But there was more to it. "She's been seeing Derek."

Holly sat up so quickly that Austin wondered for a moment if she'd spotted a bug or a sand crab. "Holy crap, Austin. Derek? Your roommate?"

Austin nodded.

"Skinny, nerdy Derek?"

Austin nodded.

"With the glasses and the acne? That Derek?"

"He got contacts last year. And he hasn't had acne since he started going to the dermatologist."

"Wow!" Holly patted his shoulder. "How are you doing?"

He shrugged. Holly wasn't the person he wanted to be talking to, but he couldn't just blow her off, either. "I was going to tell her I needed space, but she told me about Derek first."

Holly shook her head as she tried to understand. "Okay. But why do you suddenly need space? Is there someone else? Some little side squeeze here at the beach?"

"Don't say side squeeze, Holly. It sounds dumb."

"You're avoiding my question."

Austin got up and shook the sand off his shorts. "I guess I have stuff to do." He bent over and kissed her cheek. "Good to see you, sis."

KATHRYN NEEDED TO SEE HIM, if only to make sure he was okay. Minutes after Savannah pulled away, she was speeding across town toward Riley Street. She was two blocks away when her phone rang.

It was Jane.

Kathryn answered. "Hey, Jane. How are you feeling?"

"Not good."

"Hungover? It would be understandable after all those pretty cocktails you had."

"It's not that, Kathryn. Can you help me?"

There was something in her voice. Something wasn't right. "Of course I can help you. Do you need something from the pharmacy?"

"I think I need to go to the hospital."

Kathryn jammed on the brakes and turned around. "Oh, my goodness. What's wrong?"

"I'm not sure. I probably should call an ambulance, but I don't want to. I need a friend with me."

<hr />

AUSTIN KNOCKED on the front door, but Kathryn didn't come. He peeked in a window. Everything appeared in place. He called, but it went to voicemail.

Was she at school? She went there sometimes on Sundays.

Maybe with her friends? They met at Milo's, but that usually happened on Saturday, didn't it?

He tried the door, just in case something had happened to her inside. It was locked. He considered jimmying a window. It wouldn't be hard. The windows were as old as the house. Getting one open would be a breeze. But he didn't. He pulled out his phone and texted, *Are you home?*

No reply.

He texted again. *Call me when you have time.*

Then he headed to Riley Street. No use waiting around when there was work to be done. He just hoped she replied soon.

SEVENTEEN

sunday, june 19

JANE OPENED HER EYES, groaned, then immediately closed them. She brought her right hand to her face and whimpered. "I just thought I was sick from drinking too much."

Kathryn reached over the bed and flipped off the light. "You did drink too much, but that didn't cause your appendix to burst."

"How long do I have to stay here?"

"Your doctor is coming by in a few minutes. He said last night that you'll probably go home tomorrow morning."

When Jane opened her eyes again, she was able to keep them open. "What time is it?"

"Six-forty-five. And you're doing fine, kiddo." She patted Jane's arm. "Hillary is coming in a bit later to sit with you. I have to run home and do some schoolwork."

Jane tried to sit up, but quickly gave up and sank back into the bed. "I feel like a truck ran over me."

"That's the anesthesia. Just let it run its course. Do you want something to drink?"

Kathryn was pouring a cup of water when Jane's doctor

225

stepped in. She set the cup nearby and gave Jane a hug. "I'll see you soon."

†††††

AUSTIN SET his phone aside when he saw Kathryn's car coming up the street. It was seven fifteen. He had been sitting on her front porch since six, worried after not hearing from her all night. She looked tired and disheveled. She flashed a weary smile as she gathered her things and opened the door.

"Boy, am I glad to see you," he said.

Kathryn wrapped her arms around him and pulled herself close. He hugged her back. "I probably left eight hundred messages for you."

"My phone died last night. I've been with Jane at the hospital. Come in so we can talk. Are you hungry? Because I am."

"Starved. What happened to Jane? Is she okay?"

"Appendicitis. She'll be fine in a day or two. Let me clean up really quick. Then I'll make us something."

"You get cleaned up and I'll go get breakfast. What do you like?"

"Something filling. And greasy. Do you like hash browns?"

Austin laughed. "I love hash browns, and I know just the place. I'll see you in a few minutes."

†††††

THE SHOWER SPRAY struck Kathryn like a thousand pinpricks, pushing aside the weariness and returning some sense of normalcy. Jane's ailments were multiplying faster than they should for someone who had yet to reach her sixtieth birthday, and Kathryn worried things would get worse. The doctor had commented that the extra pounds she carried had already led to high blood pressure and the trouble she was experiencing with her legs. Kathryn vowed to get her friend off the couch and into a regular regimen of walking and bicycling. No more riding one day and skipping the next five.

It touched her to find Austin waiting for her. It had been inconsiderate to let her phone die without checking in, but her thoughts had been focused on Jane. She anticipated his return as she dried off and slipped into her fluffy white robe. She was eager to learn about his conversation with Savannah.

She left the bathroom intending to pick out a flattering summer outfit, but her bed lured her with promises of a few moments of blissful rest before breakfast, so she laid down and turned onto her side, luxuriating in the comfort of the soft mattress. She had no plans for the day and hoped Austin didn't either. The thought of being with him, just the two of them, was sweet and exciting.

▓▓▓▓

AUSTIN LET himself in the back door.

"Kate?"

The house was silent. No shower running. No music or TV. He placed the hash browns on the counter and carried two Styrofoam coffee cups to the bottom of the stairs.

"Kate?"

When she didn't answer, he climbed the steps. Her bedroom door was open and there was a trace of steam in the air.

"Kate?"

He stepped into her bedroom. Bright sunshine brought a luminescence to the yellow walls. A queen-size bed filled the center of the room. Kathryn was asleep, her face burrowed into a soft pillow, her legs drawn up slightly. Her white robe parted below the neck, allowing him a glimpse of the rise of her breasts. His eyes lingered for a moment before shifting away. Her hair was damp and hung against her cheek and neck. One arm was tucked under her, her left hand resting on the pillow just below her face.

She was lovely. More lovely than any woman he had ever seen. Certainly more beautiful and sexier than any of the women in those beauty magazines Savannah liked so much. Austin approached and set the coffee cups on the bedside table, then walked around the bed so he was behind her. He removed his shirt and laid it over the end of the bed, then slid in and nuzzled against her back and neck. She stirred, then allowed herself to be pulled into his embrace. She smelled of soap and shampoo. Her skin, though not as smooth and clear as Savannah's, was soft and welcoming. He buried his face in the back of her neck, breathed in, and realized he was hopelessly in love.

††††††

HIS ARMS WERE AROUND HER, holding her close. He was shirtless, and she could feel his body heat against her back. She breathed deeply and allowed herself to melt into him. His breath was moist against her cheek, the scent of peppermint tickling her nose. It was intoxicatingly sexy and seemed almost like a dream.

When she came fully awake, the dream remained.

She shuddered at the reality. Her mind cleared and her

first thought was one of alarm. Then she remembered—
Austin had been at her house when she came home from
the hospital. He'd gone out for breakfast. She had showered, then lay down for a moment. It was now five minutes
before noon. She had slept for several hours.

And now Austin was there, holding her, snoring gently,
rhythmically. His body swathed her with contentment and
security. When was the last time she had felt like that?
With Troy? Before things turned bad? And even then, had it
felt so perfect?

She couldn't remember.

Her ability to think, to recall, was short-circuited by
Austin's presence. She needed to turn and face him, to press
her face into his neck and chest. To kiss his neck. His ears.
His lips. But she didn't want to move. Not yet. He was
sleeping soundly, contentedly. And his arms around her
seemed as much a part of her as her own flesh. She glanced
down at herself and saw that the folds of her robe had separated. She wondered if it had been like that when he came
in. A warmth began in her chest and radiated out. She
started to pull the robe together but didn't, choosing
instead to stay where she was and as she was until he
awakened. And what might happen after that was anyone's
guess.

iiiiii

A SOUND FROM OUTSIDE, a car motor or maybe
a lawnmower, woke him. He had hardly moved. His arms
were still around her. She had nuzzled closer. Their bodies
touched from shoulder to leg. He tried to remain still, to
prolong the moment and the feelings. But she moved first, a
slight twist of her head, just enough for their eyes to make

229

contact. Nothing was said. He kissed her cheek. She turned a bit more and kissed him back. She was beautiful and warm and close. And he wanted her very much.

KATHRYN SAT up on the side of the bed and started to pull the sheet around herself before reconsidering. She stood and moved into the hallway, excited by the notion that he was watching her. Did he like what he saw? It had certainly seemed that way. The previous two hours had passed with much passion and few words as they explored one another. They hadn't broached the subject of his discussion with Savannah, and that was just fine. There would be plenty of time for that. Kathryn suspected there would be plenty of time for lots of things. She stepped into the hallway bathroom, closed the door behind her, and leaned against the wall, happy, fulfilled, and a little light-headed.

And a whole lot in love.

She looked in the full-length mirror on the back of the door and gasped at her reflection. She had done nothing to her hair before lying down, and it hung like a mop that had been put away wet. Her face was without makeup. As for the rest of her? She looked like a mature thirty-something woman. Not a twenty-year-old. Not Savannah.

Had he noticed the difference?

And if he had, would he still be in the bedroom when she returned?

She turned and tried to glimpse her rear. What had he seen, exactly?

"Oh, my goodness," she whispered. "What have I done?"

She was digging through the closet for a towel to wrap around herself when he tapped softly on the door.

"Kate?"

"Just a..." Her voice was hoarse. "I'm looking for something in the closet. I'll be..."

He opened the door and peeked in. She saw only a sliver of him, still unclothed. It was enough. She pulled open the door and stepped into his arms. He embraced her, then picked her up and carried her back to her bedroom. Then everything began again.

monday, june 20

"WHEN'S OUR next field trip, Dr. Shea?"

"Yeah, Dr. Shea, the trip to Cape Henlopen was bussin'."

"Bussin'? What's that, Garrett? Is it good?"

They laughed at Kathryn's response, a clear sign that bussin' was quite good.

They weren't even supposed to be in class. That was the deal. Show up at Cape Henlopen and get a three-day break. Eleven of her students showed up anyway, knowing that she would be there for the two students who'd foolishly opted to skip the field trip.

And they came enthused. And happy. It might have been the most amazing transformation she'd ever seen. Their happiness fueled hers.

Well, that and the otherworldly Sunday she'd just spent with Austin.

She'd awakened at six-fifteen that morning, relaxed, sated, and strangely excited about school. Those three feelings had been in short supply in recent years.

"I love the idea of another trip," she said to the students

clustered around her in the front of the classroom. "But where do we go?"

Their ideas were inspired, ranging from a nearby zoo to an all-inclusive Mexican resort. Perhaps the last one was a joke, but the discussion was rowdy and invigorating. In the end, Kathryn promised to give it some thought.

One student, a petite redhead who rarely uttered a word in class, stuck around after the others were gone. Worry filled the girl's eyes as she spoke. "Dr. Shea, I'm Ava Hawthorne."

Because of Ava's shy nature, Kathryn had yet to put her face and name together, but there was no need for Ava to know that. "Of course, Ava. What can I do for you?"

It was all the young woman could do to make fleeting eye contact. She started to speak, then smiled slightly, probably from embarrassment. Her teeth were not the usual straight and white of most students. Did that contribute to her shyness?

"I grew up near Laurel. We—our family—never had vacations." She drew a deep breath and searched for what she intended to say. "I'm hoping to become a nurse, but I have to get into college first."

"I understand, Ava. And you need this course for acceptance?"

She nodded. "Yeah–yes, ma'am. I didn't do well in high school. It's not that I'm dumb, but..."

"Of course you're not dumb."

"My brothers and me have to work on our farm before and after school, and we..." She took another heavy breath. "We don't have money for field trips, Dr. Shea. Just the gas to Cape Henlopen blew my budget for a week. If we take longer trips, I'll have to drop the class."

⯼⯼⯼⯼⯼

THE RILEY STREET house teemed with subcontractors. The roofer who had been scheduled for the previous week finally showed up without explanation or apology. A plumbing contractor was in the basement crawl-space, replacing old cast-iron pipes with PVC. Austin had expected they might find lead pipes, but the age of the house avoided that costly problem, so all was good. Pricey but good. Austin was still contemplating the addition of a back porch, but getting it done within his budget and deadline was making it increasingly unlikely, so he concentrated instead on reconfiguring the master bedroom to squeeze in a second bath.

He also thought about Kathryn.

She'd still been asleep when he left at five-twenty. The sun wasn't up, but the twilight sky promised a bright and warm Delaware day that seemed at odds with the muddled thoughts running through his mind. Whether it was unease over so quickly moving from one relationship to another or the same kinds of concerns that had plagued him when he and Savannah had started sleeping together, he couldn't say. He had been gratified by the way Kathryn focused on his needs, even asking if what she did pleased him. He had felt the way Kathryn clung to him after they'd made love. No rolling over and grabbing her phone. She remained in the moment, which kept him in the moment. She aroused and stimulated him physically and emotionally. And he appreciated how smart she was and how she made him think more about his own place in the world.

So, with all that, why did his stomach ache?

"Hey, Austin, you got skunks."

Austin jumped. He hadn't heard the plumber enter the upstairs bedroom. "Skunks?"

"Yeah." The plumber pulled out a handkerchief and wiped sweat from his face. He was grimy from working under the house. "They ain't sprayed yet, but if we keep banging around under there, they will."

"Skunks, huh? How do I get rid of them, Juan?"

"You can do it yourself. Some people use hot sauce. Others coat mothballs with peanut butter. One old boy over in Dorchester County crawled under his house with a shotgun and started blasting. That didn't go very good, though."

"What would you do?"

"I would call a professional. I know a guy in Georgetown who can get them out for you."

"How much?"

Austin's breath caught at the estimate.

"It's a dirty job, man. Nobody wants to hunt skunks."

"I'll think about it. Can you work around them?"

"Sorry, man, but my boys and I aren't going back under there until the skunks are gone. Once they spray you, that smell is hard to get off."

"Give me your friend's number, then."

Austin headed back to his bedroom and took another run at his figures. He muttered a few choice words when the calculator displayed a number that was ten percent higher than what he'd expected to spend so far.

What to do?

His phone buzzed with a text from Kathryn.

Dinner tonight?

Sorry, too much to do, he responded.

Her reply was a sad emoji followed by, *I understand.*

Why had he been so quick to turn her down? It had to be all those things he was feeling about the previous day.

But weren't those good things?

Satisfaction?

Gratification?

Stimulation?

I need to not work so hard, he texted. *I would love dinner if the offer is still open.*

Her answer was immediate.

Yes! Yes!! Yes!!!

She followed with, *I'm going to spend a couple hours with Jane first. I'll pick you up at seven thirty!*

Austin smiled at the enthusiasm she squeezed into her texts. And how she cared so much for her friend. He was still smiling when the roofer came into the room.

"Austin, my guys had to get up in the attic to check for leaks."

Austin said a silent prayer. "Please tell me you didn't find any, Walt."

Walt flashed a thumbs-up. "That old roof has held up pretty good. No leaks, but..."

"No leaks, but what?"

"Bats. The attic is full of 'em."

▓▓▓▓▓

THE ADDRESS WAS one Kathryn wasn't familiar with. It took a couple of wrong turns before she pulled up in front of an old brick building. The sign out front said Windermere Apartments. She parked in a loading zone and turned on the flashers, then double-checked the address Austin had texted.

Yep, right place.

She watched as two men approached the building and tried to open the front door. It appeared to be locked, but after one of the two, a swarthy guy in a smock bearing the logo of a beach confectionery, shook the door for several moments, it opened. The two laughed as they went inside.

Austin came out a couple moments later. "Sorry to drag you out here," he said as he crawled into the front seat. Kathryn leaned over in anticipation of a kiss, but his attention was on a ragged-looking couple crossing the street in front of them. The woman waved at Austin and blew a kiss. He didn't wave back.

"Friend of yours?"

"Charlene. She lives here. We share a bathroom."

"Whoa."

Austin nodded. "It's pretty grim. I haven't been here since I moved my stuff to the house, but the water is off over there, and I needed a shower."

"Lucky for you that Charlene was out."

Austin looked at her curiously for a beat, then laughed. Kathryn's stab at humor seemed to relax him. He leaned over to give her a peck on the cheek, but she turned her head so their lips met. It was head-spinningly magnificent.

And it would be only the beginning.

░░░░

"SKUNKS? AND BATS?"

Austin nodded. "Talk about bad luck. Fortunately, the same guy who gets the skunks out takes care of bats too. They cost a lot more, though."

The restaurant was Pickford's in Rehoboth Beach. Kathryn had made reservations. In any other town, there would have been a dress code that was three levels above Austin's plaid button-down and blue shorts. But as they sat at a table overlooking the beach, Austin realized he was dressed better than most every guy in the place.

And Kathryn was stunning. Her light green dress was incredibly sexy. Austin couldn't take his eyes off her. And she certainly knew her way around a wine list. Their server was effusive in his praise of how her selection complemented his coconut shrimp and her bay scallops.

She listened intently as he poured out the details of his day.

"The subcontractors are costing more than I expected. I hoped to do some of their work myself, but I keep running into things I didn't count on."

"It sounds like you need another set of hands," Kathryn offered.

"Are you volunteering?"

She laughed as she spoke. "If you think you're over budget now, just wait until I start breaking stuff. By the way, I was disappointed to wake up and find you gone this morning."

The conversation was put on hold as their food arrived. The server's presentation was reminiscent of the celebratory dinners Austin's parents used to insist on after successful business ventures. He watched with a level of fascination that was both sincere and a way to buy time and avoid answering her question.

But then, after the server was gone, she brought it up again.

"Don't you dare ever sneak out again without letting me know."

She was joking, but he knew he needed to reply. "I

didn't want to wake you. And I'm worried about falling behind. I need every hour I can get."

†††††

KATHRYN WATCHED him closely as he spoke. Something was wrong.

I'm worried about falling behind.

He didn't seem like the worrying type. He lived in the back bedroom of a house in the middle of renovation. He drove a decades-old truck that was lucky to make it through the day. It was evident that he came from a family of achievers, but Austin appeared to be as comfortable in his skin as anyone she knew.

I need every hour I can get.

Then why had he taken time to drive to Cape Henlopen several times the week before, on the outside chance she was there? Why was he willing to knock off work to join her for dinner, even when there were a couple more hours of daylight?

Kathryn knew people who were driven by the clock. Her father had been one of them. She winced as she recalled the missed school events and family vacations that ended early.

Yet, after all that, she had married Troy, whose plan for a quick ascension to the top reduced their marriage to quick suppers at a neighborhood bistro followed by a few brief minutes of joyless sex.

Nope. That wasn't Austin. There was something else at work. And she was going to find out what.

"Tell me why you really left the house so early."

Austin barked out a laugh as he shook his head. "I told you."

"No, you didn't. You gave some reasons, but they aren't really why you left."

Austin focused on his shrimp. He picked one up and took a bite. Kathryn watched and wondered if this was an instance of their age difference coming into play. If so, it was something they would have to overcome together. She wasn't interested in playing games to get at the truth, but it might be what Austin was used to with Savannah. From what she'd seen, Kathryn suspected that Savannah rarely bothered to dig deep into what was going on in his mind. And come to think of it, toward the end of their marriage, Kathryn had become that way with Troy.

Would Austin speak up if given time? It was a critical step if their relationship was going to develop. She wouldn't push though. "If it's something you want to talk about, I'm willing to listen," she said quietly, patting his hand.

It was on her second forkful of scallops that he spoke again. "Do I stimulate you, Kate?"

She set her fork aside and looked at him. His full attention was on her. "A question like that can be taken a lot of ways, Austin. Maybe you had better elaborate."

He glanced at the neighboring tables to make sure no one was listening in. "You're a college professor. Your friends are professionals. Mature people who have jobs and lives. I'm..." He used his napkin to dab his chin. "I'm a young guy who's close to flunking out of college. I work for my parents and take orders from my sister. About as opposite from you as a guy can be."

Kathryn caught herself before offering the usual responses.

Don't sell yourself short.

You have many good qualities.

You're still finding your way, but I know you will.

Those things were true. But they were also a lot of mumble-jumble that put the person saying them in a position of perceived superiority. She had felt a lot of things during the short time she and Austin had been together. None of them involved superiority.

"Do you remember when you asked me about my date with Scott?" she asked.

"Sure. The night you came by the Riley Street house."

"Do you remember my response?"

Austin thought about it for a moment. "You said you had a good time, and that Scott was a nice guy."

"All true, but what I didn't mention was that I told Scott I wouldn't go out with him again."

Austin's eyes narrowed. "But after you... why?"

"You were about to say after I slept with him."

"No." Austin answered quickly. Then, after a slight hesitation, "Maybe."

"It's okay," Kathryn laughed. "I did sleep with him. And maybe if I tell you the rest, you can understand why I did."

Wow, things were getting deeper than she had anticipated. Fortunately, the people seated around them were deep into their own conversations or sitting quietly across from one another while they studied their cellphones. "Scott is smart and successful. And he was very kind to me." She giggled, then said, "He told me I was spontaneous."

"That's a nice compliment."

"I'm not spontaneous at all, Austin. That's just it. My entire life is centered on routine. Teach, prepare lessons, meet my friends every Saturday morning. I'm thirty-seven going on seventy-seven. I never thought much about it until I met you."

Austin set aside his fork and leaned in. "What did I do?"

"You took me dumpster shopping."

He laughed. "You wanted to go."

"You bet I did. And you took me to Elijah's. And we danced to loud country music. It was the most fun I've had in forever."

"It was fun," he agreed. "I went back to Elijah's with Savannah last week. It wasn't the same."

"And I went to the beach with Scott. We had pizza from the same place and sat on the same bench. And you're right. It wasn't the same." Kathryn grabbed his hand. "So if you want to know if you stimulate me, the answer is hell yes you stimulate me. I feel more alive than I have in years. My students noticed the change, and I'm sure my friends are starting to notice too."

"But with all that going on, why did you sleep with Scott?"

Kathryn groaned. "I regretted it immediately, because it wasn't him I wanted to be with. I just... you know?"

Austin tipped his head to one side, and it reminded Kathryn of how her grandfather's cocker spaniel used to do the same thing when you asked if he wanted to go for a walk.

"When we ran into you and Savannah at the beach, all I could think was that I wished it was me with you instead of her. Savannah had the guy I wanted. Everything I did with Scott—ice cream, Skee-Ball, walking on the beach—were things I imagined you and I doing."

Kathryn took a sip of water. "It was you I wanted to be with that night, Austin. Not Scott. You. It was always you."

HOW DIFFERENT IT ALL WAS. Kathryn seemed to perceive what he was thinking. What she couldn't pick up through intuition she learned by asking questions. She didn't turn the conversation back to herself unless it was to make a point about how she felt.

Amazing.

I wished it was me with you.

The things I did with Scott were things I imagined you and I doing.

It was you I wanted to be with that night.

Holy freaking smokes. This was really going someplace.

And as they finished dinner and dug into dessert—shared, of course—Austin experienced a range of feelings that were very new. With Savannah, his feelings had largely centered on fun. And lust.

But with Kate? So much more.

He wanted her to know.

But when he opened his mouth to tell her, she beat him to the punch.

"How about you, Austin?" she asked.

"I love you."

Wow. There it was. Talk about laying it out there. No pretense. No beating around the bush. And it felt good to say it, so he said it again.

"I love you."

She dipped her chin when she smiled. A fifty-something couple at a nearby table had overheard him. The husband was grinning, but the woman's expression was more guarded, and when Austin made eye contact, she looked away.

"She doesn't like it," Kathryn whispered, nodding at the woman.

"You don't know that," Austin said.

"A woman can tell. It's our age difference. She thinks it's scandalous that I'm with you. She's probably thinking of *The Graduate*."

"What graduate?"

Kathryn giggled. "It's a movie from the late sixties. Dustin Hoffman and Anne Bancroft."

"I know him. *Meet the Fockers*, right?"

Kathryn nodded. "Same guy. He was a young college graduate dating an older woman."

"And I'm Dustin Hoffman?" Austin grinned.

"Yes, but no. It ends terribly for them."

"Oh."

"Austin, I'm fifteen years older than you."

"I don't care."

Kathryn shook her head. "But you may care someday. Like when you're forty-five and I'm sixty."

"Or when you're a hundred and I'm eighty-five? No, it won't matter."

Her serious expression offered the hint of a smile. "How about this? We take things one day at a time. No rush, no promises other than to enjoy each other's company, however and whenever we can."

Austin shrugged. "I guess so, but I have no desire to see anyone except you, Kate."

Her eyes welled up. "I feel the same."

▥

IT WAS after ten when they pulled up in front of the Riley Street house.

"Can I come in and see your progress?"

"I don't know, Kate. It's late and you have class in the—"

"I have time if you do."

He guided her through a battlefield of construction waste toward the front door. The windows were closed to protect his grandfather's power equipment, and the place was stifling hot.

"How do you sleep in here?" Kathryn asked, her skin already sweaty.

"It's not usually like this. Most nights I open the upstairs windows after sunset and it cools things down. Let me show you what I'm planning for the master bedroom."

Like before, his love for the work was evident. He lit up as he led her into what would become the master bath.

When they returned to the upstairs hallway, Kathryn was perspiring. "You can't stay here tonight," she said.

"Sure I can."

"I don't want you to. You have no air conditioning and no water."

"I'll get the water turned back on in a few days. I can shower at the Windermere until then."

"What if Charlene barges in?"

"She won't. They have this system, with a coat hanger. If it's on the wall, you don't go in."

"But what if she doesn't want to follow the system?"

Austin's laugh brought some mirth to the hot, dark hallway. "Then I guess she sees more than she bargained for."

"If anyone is going to see more of you than they bargained for, I want it to be me."

"Seriously, Kate, I—"

"Get your stuff. I'll wait for you downstairs."

AUSTIN THOUGHT there might be an uncomfortable point when they arrived at Kathryn's house and worked out the sleeping arrangements. He was prepared to head to the guest room without complaint. It was a small concession to make for what he felt was happening between them.

There was no discomfort. Kathryn led him upstairs and toward her bedroom. "I hope you want this," she said as she snaked her arms around his waist. "Because I do."

Austin did too.

Later, as he lay behind her in the dark, stroking her shoulders and neck, she murmured, "I used to be married, Austin. A long time ago."

He hoped she didn't notice the hitch in his breathing. Or feel his body tense.

She turned to see his face. "I couldn't let another day go by without you knowing."

He caressed her shoulder as he considered the revelation. Surprised? Yeah. He had never considered the possibility that she might have been married. Everything he knew about her, from her circle of friends to the way she lived, suggested a woman firmly rooted in single life.

"Do you want to know more?" she asked, still gazing at him.

Did he?

Yes.

How much, though? Could he be supportive if her marriage had been hurtful or abusive? He'd been there for a couple of frat brothers when their relationships ended, but consoling them usually involved a pitcher of beer and a night of video games. He remembered several years earlier when he was in high school and Holly came home for spring break, distraught at the breakup with her boyfriend of seventeen months. Austin had been in the next room

246

watching television but also eavesdropping on Holly and their mom. He'd been moved at how understanding Mom had been as Holly poured out her pain. He needed to pull on that experience. Or maybe just listen. Holly's hurt had been fresh. Kathryn's was in the past.

But how far in the past? "I want to hear whatever you feel comfortable telling me."

She took a deep breath, turned her face away, and snuggled closer.

"Where to start?" she mused. "His name was Troy. We met in college, dated for two years, then got married four months after we graduated. He's an architect. We lived in Virginia and were married for three years before it ended."

Austin did the math. Married after graduation, three years... that meant Kathryn was... twenty-five? Over ten years ago. Little wonder she was so accustomed to being on her own.

Ten years ago he'd been in junior high school.

Why did that come to mind? Did it matter?

No, he decided. It didn't. "Was it a hard time?" he asked.

"It was kind of sad, really. Not like you see in some movies. Troy's job consumed him, and I was deep into my studies. I don't know if he was cheating on me. I prefer to think not, and that his only mistress was work."

She relaxed in his arms as she described the end of her marriage. Austin could tell that time and distance had healed the emotional scars. "A friend of mine at the time said she saw him in town with another woman, but there were never any signs that I picked up on. I think we just..." She paused. "We drifted apart. Our fate was sealed when he got a partnership offer from a firm in Louisville. I was entrenched in my coursework and Troy had to accept the job right away."

He felt her shift in front of him, and he moved away just enough to allow her to turn onto her back. The only light came from an ancient clock radio, but it was enough for Austin to see her gazing at the ceiling. "He wasn't willing to concede, and neither was I. We tried living apart for a few months, but nothing changed. He filed the papers in Kentucky. I didn't even have to show up."

"Kate?"

She turned her gaze to meet his.

"Did you love him?"

She smiled faintly. "I've asked myself that question many times. I think so, though it was never as intense as I thought genuine love could be. When he traveled for work, I didn't sit at home and pine for him or anything. But I would say yes, I loved Troy. In the beginning. And I very much loved the idea of being married and having babies." Her smile widened. "After a few years in my career, of course. Three babies in quick succession. Maybe take off until they started school. Join a mothers' group. Have play-dates. It sounded wonderful at the time."

Austin traced his fingers on her arm and felt her shudder. He leaned in to kiss her, then asked, "And now?"

"Kids?"

"Um-hmm."

"I'm thirty-seven, Austin. And single. Some women are awesome single moms, but I want help."

Her words, honest and heartfelt, touched him. It surprised him to find that, on at least some level, he could relate to what she once had with Troy. It wasn't unlike what he had with Savannah. Love on some level, perhaps, but not the kind that would make him want to sacrifice everything. Nothing like that.

Kathryn raised up and kissed him sweetly on the lips.

She wrapped her arms around his neck and trembled as she hugged him.

"I like this very much," she whispered.

Austin didn't reply. There was no need. He just held her. She sighed, and that sigh let him know how contented she was.

Just like him.

friday, june 24

DR. ROSA CUELLAR had been the college's president for six years. She was that rare individual whose smile could make you feel great for a week. Everyone loved her, from the college's board of directors to the night custodians. And when she stepped into Kathryn's classroom, several students greeted her.

Amazingly, she acknowledged each by name before turning to Kathryn. "Dr. Shea? May I have a word with you after class?"

"Of course. Want me to come to your office?"

"I don't want to trouble you after a busy morning of teaching. I'll come to you."

That was another of her endearing traits. President Cuellar was a wanderer. She was as likely to be in the student union or the science building as in her office. Informality was her trademark, and most every employee of the college called her Rosa.

Kathryn's second class gathered in small groups, conducting personal interviews that would become mini biographies. Unlike in the past, when Kathryn had limited interview topics to a few basic areas, she had given students carte blanche to share stories of struggles or victories from their past. The potential for R-rated romantic conquests or illegal activities was no longer a concern. She trusted her students more with each passing day.

Teaching had become fun again.

As students chatted among themselves, Kathryn tried to guess what Rosa wanted to visit about. It was summer and much of the campus was shut down. Committees didn't meet, and student advisement wouldn't begin until August. It was probably nothing big.

Or was it?

Had she heard about Austin?

And if she had, would it matter?

Austin had spent the past five days at her house, but Kathryn had told no one about their relationship. It wasn't the kind of thing one brought up over breakfast at Milo's, in between discussions about rude tourists and the summer seafood selection at Hocker's Market.

Oh, yeah, girls, I nearly forgot to mention that I'm dating a twenty-two-year-old college senior.

She giggled as she considered their reactions.

"Is something funny, Dr. Shea?" a student called out.

"I'm enjoying watching you all work so well together, Miranda."

What do you and this twenty-two-year-old do? That would be Hillary's question.

A lot more than you and Stuart do, she thought and giggled again.

Are you going to bring him to Milo's Saturday morning? Jane would ask.

Not a chance. Jane didn't like change, and adding

Austin to their ladies' breakfast hour would be plenty of change.

And Suzanne? Practical, to-the-point Suzanne? She wouldn't have a question. She would listen for a few minutes before saying, *Don't let him break your heart, honey. And don't mention a word of this around campus.*

Had President Cuellar somehow found out?

No. There was no way.

Was there?

"LORDS OF DISCIPLINE isn't Conroy at his best." The screen showed her name as Sarah Elise. She was obviously in her childhood bedroom—there were *Kim Possible* posters on the wall. Austin remembered watching *Kim Possible* as a kid, but like a lot of kid things he had outgrown it.

"Could your opinion be biased by your distaste for the military?" Austin replied. It was an understatement. Sarah Elise was always railing against the armed forces, the police, and guns in general.

"I'm more open-minded than that," she snipped. "I don't appreciate you making a snap judgment about me."

A guy named Malcolm spoke from the front seat of a very nice sports car. "Conroy could have written three times as many books if it weren't for his hubris."

Most of the faces on the screen nodded in agreement.

"I'm not even sure what that means," Austin said with a shrug.

He heard their snickers. Word had gotten out that he wasn't a literature major. That made him an outcast.

As if he cared what they thought.

They also viewed Professor Chakraborty as an outcast. There was a small percentage of Penn students who saw themselves as set apart from the dregs of society. Most of his Southern Lit classmates fit that category. Austin enjoyed watching as the happy and unaffected Professor Chakraborty continually put the elites in their place, often without them being aware of it. There had been criticism of his teaching style on the class discussion board early on, but nothing lately. Austin suspected a new board had been set up that included neither him nor the Professor.

That was just fine.

Professor Chakraborty jumped in. "Describe what you mean about Conroy's hubris, Malcolm."

"It should seem very obvious. Conroy preferred the florid prose of writers like Welty." Malcolm spoke slowly, as if he was conversing with a child. "He never adapted to the times like James McBride or Rick Bragg. I find that very off-putting."

"Or even John Grisham," a guy named Braydon interjected. "Not that I read Grisham."

"Braydon, I'm going to have you explain why you don't read Grisham," the Professor said. "But first, Malcolm, what do you know about Conroy's personal struggles?"

It turned out that Malcolm knew nothing of Conroy's personal story. Austin didn't either, but he wasn't the smartass trying to show off for the class. By the time Professor Chakraborty was finished tearing Malcolm's argument apart, Braydon had disappeared from the screen, saving the class from hearing about his haughty dislike for John Grisham.

Class was wrapping up when Austin received a private message from the professor.

Fine job, Austin. Sorry if you felt disrespected by the others.

You have a much better grasp on the material than they do. Tell me about the location you're watching from.

Austin smiled. No one had mentioned the scrap lumber stacked against the wall behind him or the tattered window shade that allowed pinpricks of sunlight to cast a glare whenever he shifted in his seat. They probably thought he was preparing for an exorcism or living in a crack house.

He messaged back, *Thank you, sir. I enjoy the class. I am renovating a house in Delaware this summer and am participating from an unfinished bedroom.* He reread the message, then added, *Feel free to come help!* He added a smiley emoji and hit send.

Professor Chakraborty messaged back, *See you next weekend! Send me the address.*

Wait? What?

The professor was joking. That was his way. For a man who had been in America for just a few years, the professor had absorbed much of the culture. He was probably a genius, but the kind of genius who would be fun to meet for a beer.

Have a great weekend, Professor! Austin messaged before signing off.

"HELLO, KATHRYN!"

President Rosa Cuellar's appearance startled Kathryn, who was perusing the agenda for a literature conference she was considering. Forty minutes had passed since class ended, and she had assumed the president had forgotten or been called away.

"I'm sorry, dear. I didn't mean to sneak up on you."

"No, it's fine. Please come in."

Kathryn had straightened her desk and removed a stack of books from the guest chair. Students never came by on Friday. Not with beaches, boardwalks, and summer jobs waiting. She would usually have been long gone, too.

Rosa took a seat, then got down to business. "I heard you took your students on a field trip, Kathryn."

"Yes. We went to Cape Henlopen."

Rosa crossed her legs and leaned forward, placing her arms on Kathryn's desk. "What did you hope to accomplish?"

Kathryn's mind raced. There were no written learning objectives. No mention of how the trip figured into final grades. Had someone complained? There were a few students who had been less enthusiastic than the others. What academic buzzwords and platitudes could she use to convince the college president that the trip was a good idea?

What would Austin say? He had a way of breaking things down into bite-sized thoughts and ideas. There was no doublespeak there. And that was one thing she loved about him.

One thing of many.

What *would* Austin say?

He would tell the truth and let the chips fall where they may.

So would she.

"Students hate this class, Rosa. And I frankly don't blame them. They come to us after struggling with high school English, yet what do we do? We give them more of the same and hope they can somehow pull a passing grade to be accepted here."

Rosa nodded, but her expression didn't change. Was Kathryn getting through? Maybe the president wasn't as progressive as she had assumed. She took a deep breath and continued. "So we took a field trip. Students swam and fished and played volleyball and disc golf. They hung out with one another and talked. Then I had them write about it. Rather than summarize one of Chaucer's poems or describe how they feel after reading a Shakespearean sonnet, I had them write about what they did at Cape Henlopen. Would you like to see some of their papers?"

"Very much."

Kathryn opened her laptop and clicked on a file of student assignments. She pulled up three that she knew were good and two others that were just okay. She turned the laptop so Rosa could read, then sat back and pretended to immerse herself in the dog-eared copy of *The Scarlet Letter* she kept on her desk.

Five minutes passed. Then ten. Each time she glanced up, Rosa was still staring at the screen.

"The paper submitted by Gavin Chambers," she said after a few more minutes. "What are your thoughts?"

Kathryn shook her head. "It's not very good, really. No depth to the writing. No visualization. More like a laundry list."

Rosa cracked a smile. "Agreed."

"But it was the first assignment Gavin has submitted this semester. He had three zeros before that paper, so I count it as progress."

"Three zeros and a..." she glanced at the screen. "A C+. You really think it was worth a C+, Kathryn?"

"Not at all, but the project he turned in yesterday—a more traditional assignment where he interviewed a class-mate—that one *was* worth a C+. Would you like to see that one?"

"That's not necessary." Rosa stood and smoothed the

front of her gray skirt. "Kathryn, this is wonderful. I commend you for stepping out like this."

Kathryn couldn't contain her smile. Rosa's words were like a warm shower on a chilly morning.

"There's a sad shortage of innovative teaching these days," she continued. "When I heard about your field trip, I wanted to learn more. And from what I've seen, you've reached students who some might believe don't belong in college in the first place." She held out her hand. "Thank you."

Kathryn stood, shook Rosa's hand, then rushed around the desk and hugged her. "I would like to do another field trip, Rosa. The students want to go to Washington, DC."

"I'll provide the bus, but you have to promise something in return."

"Anything."

"Take pictures. And submit an article for the college newsletter. I want everyone to know about our most innovative practices, and this will be our first feature."

Would it be too much to hug her again? Kathryn thought not, but there was one more thing. "Can I ask one more thing, Rosa?"

She sat back down. "Certainly."

Kathryn shared the details of her meeting with Ava, the farm girl from Laurel. And her concerns about the costs of things like field trips. "There are, I suspect, plenty of students like Ava. Her family never went on vacations. They barely get by. I would like to figure a way to make opportunities like this affordable for them."

Rosa pulled her phone from her purse and took a few moments to type something on it. "I would too, Kathryn," she finally said. "I'll give this to some people in my office and see what they can come up with." She put her phone away. "But for now let me cover the cost of this trip. That will include lunch in DC and the cost of admittance to a couple of landmarks."

Kathryn clapped her hands like a kid at Christmas. "That's wonderful. I appreciate you so much."

"You're the hero here, Kathryn. One more question, though? Where did you come up with the idea?"

Oh boy. How to respond?

A student at Penn who is working here this summer?

The guy who fixed my fence?

A local handyman?

A young man named Austin?

"The idea came from the man I'm seeing."

"Oh, Kathryn, I'm happy for you." She sounded less like the college president and more like a delighted friend. "Is it serious?"

Kathryn's cheeks felt warm. She nodded. "Yes. I'm falling kind of hard for him."

"Delightful. I hope I get to meet him someday."

Kathryn smiled as she considered the possibility. Would the two ever meet?

And if they did, what would that meeting be like?

KATHRYN SANG Elton John tunes as she tidied up the house. She had wondered at first if it would be difficult to adapt to having another person in her home, but Austin left barely a trace of his presence. A second towel and a few toiletries in the upstairs bathroom, his laptop on the coffee table, and a drinking glass next to the kitchen sink. He kept his clothes, mostly T-shirts and shorts, in the closet of the guest bedroom, despite her urging him to move them into her closet.

The text message she received as she removed dishes from the dishwasher made her stomach flutter.

The roofer is finishing up. I'll lock up and be home by six.

Home.

Home!

Before, his texts had referred to it as *your house.*

I'm going to run by your house to pick up my phone charger.

Amazon left a package at your house.

He was starting to think of it as home.

She was sweeping a bit of sand into the dustpan when she heard the unique growl of Calvin's motor. She could already pick it out from the sounds of other vehicles that passed by. The feelings it brought with it—joy, a sense of security, and something deeper that she was just beginning to understand —washed over her. She hurried to the kitchen to put away the broom before making her way to the front door to greet Austin. It was reminiscent of those old black-and-white TV shows she had watched as a little girl. The ones where the wife lived to take care of her husband and their home. The shows people scoffed at today, complaining that they set women back a century. Maybe they did, but at that moment, Kathryn couldn't imagine anything she wanted more than to meet her man at the front door, because he was *home.*

AUSTIN COULDN'T CONTAIN his grin when he saw Kathryn's car in the driveway. He grabbed the two sacks of groceries he'd picked up along with some accumulated mail from the Riley Street house. Should he have given her a heads-up that he intended to cook dinner? Maybe, but he wanted it to be a surprise. A celebration of their first week together.

He stuffed his mail into one of the grocery sacks and stepped onto the porch just as she pulled open the door. Her smile did that thing to him it always did. She was lovely in pink shorts and a white blouse. And barefoot. She enjoyed being barefoot. She raised up on tiptoes to kiss him, her perfume now familiar enough for him to have detected it on a woman in front of him at the market.

He was filthy after having given the Riley Street house a good top-to-bottom cleaning. His T-shirt was sweat stained and ripe. Sawdust clung to his shorts and legs. Sweat plastered his hair to the nape of his neck. Earlier in the week, he had balked when she'd approached for a hello kiss. She had pointed her finger at him and given him a good-natured rebuke. "Never turn down a kiss."

He remembered.

And was glad he did. It was a wonderful kiss that became several more.

"What do you have there?" she asked, eyeing the grocery sacks.

"I'm cooking dinner."

"Oooh, what are you making?"

He raised the sacks so she couldn't see what they contained. "It's a surprise, but I have to warn you I know nothing about cooking."

She jumped to get a look, but he turned away. "I'm going to put these in the kitchen and get a quick shower. No peeking, okay?"

Kathryn giggled. "At the food or the shower?"

KATHRYN FOLLOWED him upstairs and waited in the hallway when he went into the main bathroom. He was still shy about shedding his clothes in front of her, an endearing trait, so she didn't push. She listened through the door while he started the shower. When she heard the tinkle of the curtain rings closing and his footfall in the tub, she took a quick peek. The shadow of his beautiful form on the filmy curtain caused her breath to catch. She considered asking him to delay dinner, but he had gone to so much trouble.

"How was your day?" he asked as he washed his hair, unaware of her prying eyes.

"You won't believe what happened," she said, feeling the same rush she'd had during her meeting with President Cuellar. She told him all about it.

"That's fantastic!" he called back. "Where will you go on your next trip?"

"I'm thinking Washington, D.C. There are so many choices there. History, art, pop culture."

"Bars," Austin added as he turned off the water. "Some of your students might choose those."

Kathryn laughed. "If they can work them into the essays they write, I'll be fine with it."

She stepped back into the hallway as Austin pulled the curtain. A few moments later, he came out wrapped in one of her flowery girl towels. He took a step back when he saw her seated cross-legged on the floor, then his eyes softened and she knew he was thinking of other things. The same thoughts she had when he was in the shower.

"So, give me a hint about what you're making for dinner."

He grinned. "Don't get too excited."

"It's hard not to. My man is cooking dinner for me."

She followed him into the spare bedroom where he allowed her only the briefest glimpse of bare skin as he hurriedly pulled on a clean pair of shorts and a Penn t-shirt. He was adorable. Who would have thought he was shy like that?

He led her down the stairs. "Dinner time!" he exclaimed as they entered the kitchen. He went to the grocery sacks and started pulling items out.

"Ground beef," he said as he held it up. "Extra lean, of course."

"Of course," Kathryn echoed.

He reached deeper and removed a bag of pre-made salad. "Caesar. With bacon."

"Ooh, bacon! I like the way you think."

He rooted around and wrapped his large hands around a box. He held it up and exposed the side a little at a time until Kathryn could see what it was.

"Hamburger Helper!" she exclaimed. "My favorite!"

Not really. She couldn't remember the last time she had Hamburger Helper. Probably right after she and Troy had split up and money was tight. The few times she had noticed it on the store shelves it reminded her of lean years and the sadness of divorce. Thanks to Austin she could leave those memories behind.

"Not just Hamburger Helper," he said. "*Bacon Cheeseburger* Hamburger Helper."

"More bacon?" Kathryn fanned herself. "Be still my heart."

"And for dessert..." he opened the second sack and groaned.

"What is it?"

He lifted out an ice cream cake that tilted to one side. "I should have put this in the freezer before getting my shower."

Kathryn threw her hands into the air. "How did you know I prefer my ice cream cake melted? You're amazing." She took the cake from him and placed it on the counter, then turned to kiss him. "I can't wait."

⚏

THEY HAD second helpings of melted ice cream cake. Kathryn tore into hers with delight, just as she had with the salad and main course. Austin loved watching her eat. The formality when they first met was gone. She wasn't the uptight woman he had pegged her for. She was sweet and kind and funny. Attentive and giving. She had gone out of her way to make him feel that her home was his home. And when he received a text from Savannah asking if he was doing okay, it was easy to ignore.

He was doing just fine.

Better than he could ever have imagined.

"I have a favor to ask," she said as she ate her last bite of cake. "I want to go shopping for some new clothes, and I need your advice."

"Kate, really?" Austin said with a laugh. "Look at me. Do I look like a guy with any fashion sense?"

A smile played across her lips. "You know what's in style, Austin. I mean... you know what younger women are wearing."

"You are beautiful," he said, taking her hand. "And you have a closetful of clothes."

"Yeah, but I want to wear things you like. Things that make me look younger."

"I love you as you are. Please know that."

His words made her feel good. And loved. But still... "I've allowed myself to become..." She considered how best to put it. "Dowdy. Frumpy."

Austin shook his head. "I don't think so."

"I do. And I want to change. Will you go with me tomorrow morning?"

"It's Saturday. Don't you have to meet your friends?"

"Jane still isn't up to going out yet, and I would rather spend the entire day with you."

He stroked her hand. "Go have breakfast with them. I can catch up on paperwork, then we can shop." He rose and picked up their plates. "And now, the skilled chef will become the skilled dishwasher."

||||||||

KATHRYN WAS THROWING away the grocery sacks when she noticed the stack of mail Austin had left on the counter.

"You can have your mail forwarded here."

He glanced at the stack. "I don't get much. Mostly junk."

Kathryn picked it up and started flipping through. Credit card solicitations, offers of auto insurance, investment plans, and even a prepaid burial program. She held that one up and said, "I'm throwing this away right now."

"Throw all of it away."

One small envelope caught her attention. The return

address was Pennsylvania, and the envelope had *TEST RESULTS* written on the front.

"What is this?" she asked, holding it up.

Austin looked up from a pan he was scrubbing. "Oh, that's my law school entrance exam scores."

"I didn't know you took it."

"Yeah, last spring. My sister brought that down with some other stuff."

"And you haven't opened it?"

Austin shrugged. "Never got around to it I guess."

"May I?"

"Sure."

Kathryn tore the envelope along the perforations and pulled it apart. She studied it for several moments as she deciphered the contents. When she reached the bottom where Austin's overall score was, she gulped.

"What's wrong?" Austin asked.

Unable to find the words to explain, Kathryn shook her head and pointed to the scores.

Austin smiled. "Pretty bad, huh? I didn't study for it, so I'm not surprised."

"Austin, this is unbelievable."

"Just toss it in the trash. I can take it again."

"No, you don't understand." She held up the results. "You didn't do bad at all. In fact..." She waved her hand at the scores. "You got a 178, Austin. That's in the ninety-eighth percentile."

He shrugged again. "I didn't think it was all that hard, to be honest. I took my time on the parts I was worried about."

She couldn't believe how indifferent he was. Did he not understand? He was in the ninety-eighth percentile on the LSAT. He was a freaking genius. "You can get into pretty much any law school you want. Have you thought about where you want to go?"

"Not really. I'm sure my mom and dad will want me to stay close to home. If Penn turns me down, I can try Temple or Villanova."

She jumped from her seat and hugged him. "You are unbelievable. Do you know that? You have your choice of almost any law school in the country, and you don't really care."

He pulled her close, leaned over, and kissed her. "The only place I want to be is where I am right now."

TWENTY

saturday, june 25

THE HIGHLIGHT of breakfast at Milo's was Jane's triumphant return just seven days after her appendectomy.

She came with Hillary. A half-dozen regulars rushed to greet her. Her face, which had been pasty and haggard the afternoon before, glowed with joy at their reception.

"Should she even be out yet?" Suzanne whispered to Kathryn as they waited at their table for her royal arrival.

"The doctor said it was up to her, but I didn't expect to see her this soon."

"She looks good," Suzanne said. "And you do too, Kathryn. I noticed when you arrived how happy you look. Good week?"

Oh boy, was it ever, but how much of it should she share? Suzanne would enjoy hearing of her meeting with Rosa. She respected their college president as much as Kathryn did. But what would she think about Austin?

Was Kathryn ready to find out?

Jane finally made it to their table. Suzanne stood and hugged her, then pulled out Jane's usual chair. Jane grimaced as she sat down, making Kathryn wonder if it was too much too soon. Oh well, she was probably going stir crazy at home, even with her friends' daily visits.

They spent most of breakfast listening to a painfully descriptive rundown of Jane's recovery. By the time she got around to describing the bland diet she had endured for several days, Kathryn's mind was fast-forwarding to her shopping date with Austin. He had awakened before six, hurriedly dressed, and kissed her on the cheek as he headed out to get some work done.

"See you at noon," he whispered as he left her to snooze for another hour.

"What's everyone have planned for today?" Suzanne asked, jumping in when Jane paused for a sip of milk. Kathryn could tell she had heard all she wanted of Jane's recovery.

"Stuart is coming over later," Hillary said. "We talked about going to see his cousin play softball in Georgetown. He's in a league over there." She paused, and her cheeks reddened. "Or we may just stay in and watch a movie. I invited Stuart to stay the night."

Suzanne smacked the table. "Can it be? The virgin Stuart is going to..." She placed her hand over her mouth in mock disbelief. Jane giggled, then grabbed her stomach.

Hillary's eyes blazed. "I told you a girl doesn't kiss and tell," she snapped.

"You brought it up." Suzanne replied.

"But that doesn't mean that we'll..."

"To any red-blooded man it means exactly that," Harvey Bodenschatz interjected. He had come up behind Hillary to fill her coffee cup.

"If you must know, Harvey, we'll probably just order pizza. If we don't go see Stuart's cousin play softball in Georgetown."

"Sure you will," Harvey said before moving on to the next table.

"How about you, Kathryn?" Suzanne asked. "Papers to grade? Lessons to prepare?"

"I'm going shopping." As soon as the words were out of her mouth, Kathryn wished she could take them back.

Suzanne zeroed in. "Clothes shopping?"

Kathryn tried to remain noncommittal. "Yeah... maybe. I might need some groceries too. And maybe some other stuff."

"Do you want company?"

Suzanne's question was not out of line. Their little group often tagged along with one another if something sounded interesting. And other than the adventures of Hillary and Stuart, which never turned out to be adventurous at all, a day of shopping was often more interesting than cleaning the house or going to the beach alone. Kathryn was expected to say yes.

"Well... I sort of made plans. Someone I met who—"

"Is this someone a man?"

How could Jane be so perceptive given all the meds she was on?

"Yes, he is. Someone I met in my neighborhood."

She hated being so evasive, but she hadn't considered how she would tell them about Austin. There was no telling how they would respond.

"My goodness, Kathryn," Hillary said, still salty from their insinuations about her private life. "You're certainly getting out and about these days. Will you let him spend the night like you did that other guy?"

Jane shook her head. "No, Kathryn. Don't. You don't want to get a reputation for..." She waved her hand in a circle, not wanting to say the words.

Hillary didn't mind, though. "For being *promiscuous*."

"Who's promiscuous?" Harvey said, pausing at their table.

"We're worried about Kathryn," Jane said. "She has been dating a lot lately."

"What the hell's wrong with that?" Harvey barked. "You're a good-looking woman, Kathryn. And still young enough to snag a man. You don't want to spend the rest of your life like—" Harvey stopped, but it was obvious where he'd been going. He hurried off to another table.

"I think we just got insulted by Harvey Bodenschatz," Hillary said haughtily.

"Me too," Jane snipped. "And after all the money we spend here."

"No, girls," Kathryn said, trying to smooth things over. "Harvey wasn't talking about you. He just meant that—"

"Nope," Suzanne said. "He meant us. And he's right. We have gotten stuck in our ways."

"Not me," Hillary protested. "Stuart and I have a wonderful relationship."

"Nine years and you haven't slept with him, Hillary," Suzanne shot back. "That's not a relationship. That's just two old people with nothing better to do." She reached out and squeezed Kathryn's hand. "Take Harvey's advice, dear. Enjoy your shopping date. And if you wind up back at your house for the night, good for you."

Wonderful, sweet Suzanne. Dear, amazing Suzanne. She had come to Kathryn's rescue, and Kathryn loved her for it.

It could have ended right there. It should have ended right there, but for whatever reason Kathryn couldn't explain, she opened her mouth and spoke again. "We've been seeing each other for a few weeks."

Why had she said that? Why?

Mouths froze in mid-bite. Jane dropped her fork. Hillary's eyes looked as if they might pop out of her head. Even Suzanne—unflappable Suzanne—sat with her mouth open. She was the first to recover.

"I knew something was different!"

Jane found her voice. "I didn't. And you were at my house every day this week."

"Who is he?" Hillary asked. "He's the guy from before, isn't he?"

"No."

"Please tell us it's not *RodneySellsRehoboth*," Jane exclaimed.

"His name is Austin, and I want you to meet him."

"Great," Hillary said, pushing back her chair. "Let's go meet him."

"Not now. He's at work. How about next week? Dinner maybe? At my house?"

DAD WAS NEVER one to mince words. His hello was short and to the point before he zeroed in on the reason for his call.

"What's gotten done?"

Austin gave him a rundown.

"So we're ahead of schedule. Good job staying on top of the crew, son."

"Not ahead of schedule, but close." That was all Austin could come up with on the spur of the moment.

"Your inside guys are dragging their feet, aren't they?"

Actually, Dad, my inside guys are one guy. Me. I'm putting in sixty hours a week, but working alone is a lot harder than I thought.

271

"Give me some phone numbers, Austin. I'll call and tell them to get off their asses."

"No, Dad. I got this. Things are fine."

The back door opened, and Kathryn stepped inside. She tossed her purse on the kitchen table and came into the living room. Austin pointed to the phone and mouthed *Dad*.

"Are you sure?" Dad countered. "Do you want me to come down there and straighten some people out?"

"There's no need. You'll be happy with the work they're doing. I'll do what I can to speed them up."

"I'll hold you to that. How are your classes? Are you passing?"

"Yes, sir. I'm keeping up. And I'm keeping an eye on the other properties too. There have been no problems."

"I'm proud of you, son. Your mother is too. We were just talking a couple nights ago about how smoothly things are going in Bethany Beach."

They hung up, and Austin looked up at Kathryn. She'd been watching him since she came in.

"What?" he asked.

Kathryn sat down on the sofa and leaned against him. "You really need more help, don't you?" she asked.

"I'll be fine."

"Will you? It seems like a lot of work for one person."

She was right. "I can do the work, but an extra set of hands makes things go much faster."

"Then hire someone."

"I don't have that kind of money. I already spent more than I budgeted for the subcontractors." Austin took a deep breath. "I'll get by. Once the drywall goes up, it'll get easier." He pulled her close and kissed her, his lips on hers as gentle as silk. "Are you ready to go shopping?"

After that kiss? Shopping was the second or third thing

she wanted to do, but the joy of having him under her roof meant there was always time for... whatever. There was no doubt that he was worried about the renovation, though. He might display a cheerful facade, but it was weighing him down.

"We don't have to shop today. Why don't we go over to the house? I can help you. Maybe hold a board or hand you screwdrivers?"

Austin laughed, but the emotion in his eyes went much deeper. "I love you and how you care for me, but if I don't take a break from that place for a day, I'll go nuts." He stood and gently pulled her with him. "Let's go."

Kathryn followed. She didn't like seeing him worry, but there was little she could do to help with his work. What she could do was help him have a fun and worry-free day. Yep, that she could handle.

Oh, yes, and one more thing. "Are you ready for your next book?"

He brightened. "I am. Dr. Chakraborty wants me to try something more traditional. Something the other students might consider real southern fiction."

"I have just the one." She went to her school bag and pulled out a well-worn copy of *A Confederacy of Dunces*. She handed it to Austin and could tell by the way he looked at it he was skeptical.

"A wonderful story written by a man with a tragic life." Kathryn explained how the book was published after author John Kennedy Toole's suicide at thirty-one. "The characters, particularly Ignatius, are over the top, but I think you'll love it."

Austin scanned the back cover, then looked up. "You're two for two, Kate. I'll start reading this week."

They took her car. He drove. It was becoming a habit,

and Kathryn loved it. If he found her Toyota to be boring or uninspired, he never mentioned it. Didn't young guys like fast cars?

Troy certainly had. They had spent way too much of those early paychecks on cars. A Mercedes something or other for him, a white BMW for her. Both leased. He had insisted that cars were as important to climbing the ladder of success as hard work and the right college.

But the leases lasted longer than the marriage. When Kathryn had finally gotten out from under the Beamer's excessive mileage fees, she'd opted for a three-year-old Toyota. That remained her car-buying strategy. Troy would probably laugh if he knew she was seeing a guy who shuttled from place to place in his grandfather's old work truck. Troy would probably find much of her life in Bethany laughable. Her job at a community college no one had ever heard of. The Toyota. The tiny house. Her peculiar circle of friends.

She studied Austin as he navigated Route 1 traffic. He appeared at peace with the world, despite the tension over the house project. She stroked his hand. He glanced at her and smiled. It was good and right and she was feeling things for him that she had wondered if she would ever feel again.

So why was she hesitant to tell her friends?

It was the age difference. Definitely the age difference.

But that wasn't going away. And she certainly hoped Austin wasn't going away. There would always be fifteen years separating them. She needed to get over what others thought.

Did he worry about it too?

Would he hesitate to tell his parents about her? His sister? His friends?

She glanced at him again and intuitively knew the answer. Austin wasn't worried about any of that stuff. Maybe it was because he was still young and hadn't faced a lot of adversity. Or maybe he just wasn't the kind to let things bother him. Perhaps his parents were open-minded and accepting of whoever their adult children dated.

He parked her car in a spot near the center of the outlet mall. A man getting in the car in front of them spotted Kathryn and waved.

Oh, my goodness. Not him. Please, anyone but him.

"I think that guy is trying to get your attention," Austin said. "A friend?"

"No. I know him from... He's dating a friend of Hillary's."

Bill.

Grabby, butt-pinching Bill.

The last time she'd seen him, he was sprawled out on the floor after she'd slapped him. "His name is Bill. He saw us together at Elijah's."

Austin studied him for a moment. "I remember. He was with some other guys. They were trying to get girls to dance with them. They weren't having any luck, though."

Kathryn sat motionless, hoping Grabby Bill would get the message and just leave. But no. He came to her side of the car.

"Hey, Kathryn! I wasn't sure it was you at first, but—" He took a good look at Austin. "I remember you from Elijah's." When he reached through the window, Kathryn pushed herself back into the seat. The proximity of Bill's arm to her chest gave her the willies, but he was extending his hand to shake with Austin. "I'm Bill."

"Austin. I remember seeing you there."

"I love the place." Bill extracted his arm from the car.

"Especially on nights when the deejay is there. Lots of good-looking women to dance with, you know?" He glanced suddenly at Kathryn, then back at Austin. "Not anymore, though, buddy. Not since Francie and me started going out. I'm a one-woman man, let me tell you."

Perhaps he didn't think Kathryn would see the wink he gave Austin, but he was a bad actor who wanted Austin to know he was still open to playing the field. "I knew you guys were an item," he said, not allowing more than a couple seconds of silence to pass. "I could tell by the way you were dancing. I even told Francie, 'That Kathryn's got herself a young stud for a boyfriend.'" He chuckled. "But Francie said there was no way. 'Not Kathryn. She teaches at the college. There's no way she's going to date a kid, but—'"

"He's not a kid," Kathryn snapped. "And you have a few things to learn about being a gentleman."

Bill's eyes grew wide. He took a step back before recovering. He smiled smugly. "What the hell do I care if you have a boy toy, Kathryn?"

Her heart raced. What had she started? She should never have responded like she had. She'd obviously stung Bill, and now he was trying to get back at her. And what would Austin think?

Austin was laughing. "Did you call me a boy toy?" His tone was free of malice or intimidation.

It caught Bill off guard. "Well, aren't you?"

"That's so eighties," Austin replied good-naturedly. "You should go with cub, like a cougar's cub. Or maybe a boycycle. Those are more today."

Bill blinked several times. Shook his head. Finally he laughed. "Thanks for the advice." He faced Kathryn. "Please accept my apology for the way I acted at Hillary's place."

Kathryn nodded. "Apology accepted."

Bill bowed deeply. "And with that, I'll take my leave. Have a good day, you two."

They watched him get in his car and drive away.

"Should we get started?" Austin asked.

Kathryn shook her head. "Aren't you going to ask what happened at Hillary's party?"

"I wasn't planning to. It sounds like whatever it was is taken care of."

Kathryn raised her hands in frustration. "Don't you even want to know why he felt the need to apologize?"

Austin shrugged.

Always with the shrugs. "Are you sure you're only twenty-two?"

"Yep. Twenty-two." He reached across and put his arm around her. "The perfect age for a boy toy."

Kathryn giggled and playfully slapped his chest. "And you're darn good at it." She grabbed her purse from the floor and put it over her shoulder. "Let's get going. I've got a surprise for you, boy toy."

※※※※※

THEY HELD hands as they window-shopped. It was a fresh experience for Austin. Savannah bought most of her stuff online or on girls-only shopping trips with her friends. The few clothes Austin owned had been birthday or Christmas gifts, supplemented by quick trips into a couple of favorite stores armed with his parents' credit card. The pace was leisurely, but Kathryn knew soon after entering each store if they had anything she liked. He noticed how the things she looked at—shorts, skirts, and a variety of tops — differed from what she usually wore. It was obvious she was going for a younger look. If that was what she wanted, fine, but as far as he was concerned, she would look lovely in anything.

They shopped for two hours, pausing once to share a soft pretzel from a kiosk. He introduced her to the Philadelphia tradition of spreading a bit of mustard on top. She loved it.

After her last purchase, a pair of slip-ons, they paused on the sidewalk while she scanned the surroundings. "I think I've done enough damage to my bank account for one day."

Austin shifted a couple of the half-dozen bags from one hand to the other to balance the load. "I'm impressed."

"Thank you, sir." she teased. "We have one more stop to make, though. Right down there." She pointed to a swimwear shop a few doors away.

"A new bikini?"

She laughed. "I can't go that far... yet. We're getting something for you."

"I don't need anything, Kate. Really."

"Do you own a swimsuit?"

"I just swim in whatever I'm wearing."

"Not anymore."

She led the way.

Austin followed, bags in hand. Even when she offered to take some of the load, he declined. Once inside, they went to the men's section and Kathryn surveyed the selection of suits. She held up one, a tiny thing, and raised her eyebrows. "You like?"

"Never in a million years."

"But it's okay for me to wear a bikini?"

He grinned. "Absolutely."

She moved down the row before coming to a selection

of suits that were somewhere in length between Austin's usual board shorts and the brief she'd held up before. She selected one that was shorter than he might usually wear, but he had noticed similar styles on the beach. He nodded. She held it up in front of him, gauging the size, and the way she did it made Austin think it was one of the most erotic things he had ever experienced. She nodded her approval and headed for the register.

"My gift to you," she said as she handed it to him. Now let's go home.

THEY STOPPED FOR TAKEOUT TACOS, then returned to the house. Kathryn hadn't realized how famished she was until she was downing the last bite of her second chicken taco. Austin had eaten five.

"Okay, it's time for the fashion show," she said, hopeful he wouldn't roll his eyes.

He didn't.

She gathered the bags and headed upstairs. "Follow me. I want your opinion on everything. If something doesn't look right, tell me and I'll return it."

He sprawled out on one side of the bed while she placed the shopping bags on the other. She dug through a couple before pulling out a green floral print dress and heading for the bathroom. When she returned a few moments later, Austin was propped up on one arm. Kathryn spun slowly for him to see. He took a deep breath and nodded. "It's perfect."

"Are you sure? I can always take it back."

"Please don't. It's incredibly sexy."

Kathryn giggled and liked the way it sounded. Like a

younger woman. A woman with no worries. A woman in love. She pulled out another selection and returned to the bathroom.

DID she have any clue how turned on he was?

He watched her retreat to the bathroom. She didn't close the door, but from where he was, he couldn't see her as she changed. He could hear the swish of fabric as she removed one outfit and put on another. He could hear her breathing as she stretched to pull a blouse over her head. He could see her in his mind, and what he saw was more erotic than if she were standing in front of him.

"Are you ready?" she called out from the bathroom. Austin rose and walked to the door just as she was coming out. She was startled to find him there, but smiled and did another pirouette. The outfit, a simple pair of shorts and a sleeveless pastel top, looked great on her. He pulled her to him and let her know. She thanked him, then reached up and kissed him in a way that made him foggy with desire.

"Are you ready for the next outfit?" she purred into his neck.

"Do it out here this time."

She looked up at him, nodded, then stepped back and slowly removed the outfit, watching for his reaction. She never got to the next one.

wednesday, june 29

"AUSTIN, can you stay on after class?"

Texts were undoubtedly flying back and forth among the smug lit majors who had picked up that the kid with sawdust in his hair was Professor Chakraborty's favorite. He had just given several of them a dressing down for trying to substitute posturing and attitude for real work. Austin felt their contempt, but their smirks were long gone.

Professor Chakraborty doled out assignments for the next week, then smiled as he swatted away two condescending questions like flies at a cookout. "That's it, everyone."

The other screens went blank.

"Austin," he said, "It may look like no one is on here, but people lurk." He winked, then said, "This is of a personal nature, so I'll call you."

"Yes, sir."

"Austin?" someone called from outside his makeshift office. Austin closed his laptop and looked up from his plywood desk. It was one of the subs, a pretty good tile guy from Salisbury, who was preparing a bid. "Hey Percy."

"I can squeeze you in next week. I had a job fall through at the last minute."

The euphoria over getting something done early crashed head-on into the anxiety of knowing he wouldn't be close to ready for bathroom tile work. Two men, maybe three, working all week could prep the areas. But Austin, working on his own, had no chance.

His phone rang.

Professor Chakraborty.

Austin glanced at the phone, then turned back to the sub. "Sure, Percy. Put us on your calendar." He answered the phone. "Hello, Professor."

"Austin, how are things down there?"

"I'm bailing like crazy to keep the boat afloat."

The professor laughed, a deep baritone that hinted at the kind heart underneath. "That's why I'm calling. I have no classes Friday and was thinking about coming down."

"You'll love it, Professor. The beaches are some of the nicest on the East Coast."

Again came the booming laugh. "You've seen my complexion, Austin. Do I look like a sun worshipper? My tan comes through heredity, not Coppertone. I'm coming down to help you with your house project."

He was? Austin had assumed the professor was joking. "Professor, that's kind of you, but you shouldn't use your time off to help me. Have you ever rehabbed a house before?"

"I helped my father build our first house in Meerut. Our second and third too. Each time he got a promotion at the university, we built a new house."

The offer sounded better and better. "Well, Professor, to be honest, I need help. If you're willing to swing a hammer and maybe help with some drywall and electrical, I can use you."

"Oh, Austin, I'm delighted I can help. I'm becoming bored sitting around my apartment every weekend. I'll get to meet some other faculty during fall semester, but for now, it's just me."

"No family, Professor?"

"No, but I'm open to offers. If you know any available women at the beach, have them come by your house while I'm there. I figure the sight of a sweaty, hard-working man can set the stage. Then I can win them over with my wit and intelligence."

His candor made Austin laugh. The professor's help wouldn't be enough to get him back on schedule, and he still might have to work day and night to be ready for Percy the tile guy, but at least there was hope. He gave the professor the address, then said, "I'll arrange a room for you at a nearby hotel. I can't pay you a lot, but I'll feed you and take care of your lodging."

"Don't be ridiculous, Austin. I'm excited by the chance to do something with my hands. I'll see you Friday morning."

Austin felt a tug of emotion at the man's kindhearted offer. He tried to speak, but had to wait a couple of beats to get his feelings in check. "Sir, thank you. Now if only tonight can go as well as today."

"Big plans tonight?"

"Yes, sir. The woman I've been seeing for the past few weeks is introducing me to her friends."

"It must be serious, then. You're a lucky guy. In our family, marriages are arranged. We don't have much say in who or when. I left that tradition behind. I spent ten years in the United Kingdom and am here now. Still no Mrs.

Chakraborty. If that doesn't change, I may have to head back to Meerut."

"I hope it works out, sir, because you're one of the best professors I've had."

"Thank you, Austin. Now get ready to put me to work this weekend."

#

DINNER WAS AT SIX THIRTY. Kathryn should have known that Jane and Hillary would arrive early. She offered them wine. Jane had just been released from her doctor's orders not to imbibe and emptied her glass in record time.

"Where is your Austin?" Jane asked as she pushed her empty glass toward the wine bottle in front of Hillary. Hillary shook her head and moved the bottle out of reach.

"Not too fast, honey," she said. "Pace yourself before you do more damage."

"They took my appendix out," Jane snapped. "It's in a specimen jar someplace. How much more can I damage it?"

"There's still your liver to worry about."

"Hillary's right," Kathryn said from the stove where she was stirring pasta sauce. "I don't want a replay of that night at the party. Speaking of which..." She laid aside the spoon and leaned on the island. "I saw Bill at the outlet mall this weekend. He apologized for the way he acted."

"He should," Hillary said quickly. "Francie still doesn't believe he pinched your butt."

Jane sat up straighter. "Wait a minute! When did this happen?"

"You were three sheets to the wind," Hillary answered. "Bill got frisky with Kathryn and she decked him."

"I didn't deck him. I slapped him."

"Oh, my." Jane's eyes were wide. "You're really becoming a different person this summer, Kathryn. Slapping frisky men, dating people you meet on television, and letting them—"

"I met them on dating apps, Jane. Not television."

"Oh, yes, that's right. And letting them sleep over."

Kathryn turned back to her sauce, wondering if Jane's head would explode when she met Austin. She checked her watch, slid two handfuls of pasta into a pot of boiling water, and turned her attention to the salad. Twenty minutes until dinner time.

The spaghetti was about to hit the fan.

AUSTIN DOWNSHIFTED as he turned onto Sea Turtle Court. A tired-looking Kia was parked in the drive. He had hoped to arrive in time to shower and change, but someone had beaten him to the house.

He parked and was getting out of Calvin when a car pulled up behind him. A woman, short-haired and serious looking, was behind the wheel. She looked at him curiously. Wrong address, maybe? She opened the door and stepped out. She was probably his mother's age, and her outfit was like what many retirees in the area wore. Baggy shorts, a white blouse, and Crocs.

"Hello," Austin said, staying a few feet away to save her from having to smell him.

"Can I help you?" she asked, eyeing him skeptically. "Are you needing money?" She reached for her purse.

"No. I don't need money."

"Then why are you here? This is a residential area, you know."

She had to be one of Kathryn's friends. How much had she told them? How much had she left out? "Well, ma'am... I'm sorry, but I don't know your name."

"And you won't."

Austin nodded. She had him pegged as a drifter, one of those who went door to door offering to do odd jobs. He placed his hand on Calvin's tailgate and thought about how easily she might jump to that conclusion. Dirty, smelly guy. Old truck.

"I'm Austin." He wiped his hand on his shorts before holding it out. She stared at his hand, then at him, but didn't speak. "I'm Kate's—Kathryn's... we're seeing each other."

He could tell when it clicked for her. The guardedness slipped away a bit. Not completely, though. She smiled slightly. "I'm sorry that I didn't... I wasn't expecting you to be... I'm Suzanne, Kathryn's friend. We work together at the college. But not really together, because she's in the English department and I'm in economics." Her eyes drifted to Calvin. "Is your car in the repair shop? It would be just like some shops around here to give you a loaner that's... no, I didn't mean that."

"The truck is my grandfather's, but I borrow it. I work in construction, so it comes in handy."

"Yeah, I know... well, not really. I never worked in construction, but I can guess... so you're Austin?"

"I sure am." Austin nodded toward the house. "Shall we go in? I really need to clean up before dinner."

"Uh... sure."

KATHRYN WAS PUTTING the final garnishments on the salad when the front door opened.

"That'll be Suzanne," Hillary announced.

"Or maybe Kathryn's new gentleman," Jane said.

Kathryn grabbed a towel to wipe her hands, then headed to the living room.

Suzanne walked in, looking shellshocked. Austin was behind her, filthy and sexy from a day's work. He winked.

"Well, hello, you two!" she exclaimed. She hadn't planned for them to meet out front. And she'd completely forgotten that Austin would need time to clean up. Oh well, might as well get the show on the road. "I see you already met."

Suzanne fumbled for a moment before saying, "I thought he was a panhandler."

Austin smiled and shrugged. "It was an easy mistake to make."

"Well, come in, both of you." She turned and led the way into the kitchen. "Jane and Hillary, I want to introduce Austin."

Their faces became caricatures. Large unblinking eyes locked on Austin. Mouths forming perfect circles. Austin had likely encountered the same thing with Suzanne.

Fortunately for everyone, Suzanne had recovered. "For crying out loud, girls," she snapped. "Stop gaping at him and say hello."

"Hello," Hillary said.

"Hello," Jane said.

"Hey," Austin said.

"Okay," Kathryn said cheerily as she tried to keep from

laughing at their awkwardness. "Now that we have that out of the way, we have about ten minutes before dinner. Suzanne, Austin, can I get you something to drink?"

"Water," Suzanne said.

"I'm going to shower and change," Austin said, already on his way to the stairs.

They watched him disappear upstairs, then remained quiet for a few moments before Jane said, "Doesn't he need clothes to change into? I didn't see a backpack or—"

"Oh, my goodness." Hillary gasped. "Kathryn, is Austin *living* here?"

"Of course he's living here, Hillary!" Suzanne snapped. "The world isn't like you and Stuart. Not every single person is a virgin."

"We're not virgins!" The words hung in the air before Hillary ventured to clarify. "I mean, I've not been a virgin since Clark–I mean, you do remember that I was married at one time. Years ago."

"I thought your husband's name was Phil," Jane said.

"It was."

"Then who was Clark?"

Hillary tried to hide her red cheeks. "Did I say Clark? I meant Phil. But Stuart isn't a virgin either. I mean, not since—"

"Hillary, stop while you're ahead," Suzanne said. "Or behind. Or wherever you are at the moment." She turned to Kathryn. "Does he make you happy, honey?"

Kathryn beamed. "Very happy. Happier than I've been in a long time."

"Then we will make him feel welcome."

"If you ask me, he already feels pretty welcome," Jane said, casting a reproachful look toward the stairs.

░░░░

KATHRYN WAS SETTING the table when Austin came back downstairs. Suzanne was filling water glasses. "Can I get you anything to drink?" Suzanne asked pleasantly.

"Water's fine, thank you."

He still wasn't sure who was Jane and who was Hillary. One of them, the younger one, was leaning against the refrigerator. The older one was still seated at the kitchen island. She was pale and shaky; she was probably the one who'd had an appendectomy.

Or she could be shaky from the nearly empty wine glass in her hand.

She smiled but didn't make eye contact.

Kathryn patted his arm as she passed. "There's beer in the fridge."

"Is he old enough to drink alcohol?" the woman by the refrigerator asked.

The pale lady at the island snorted.

"Hillary, really?" Suzanne snipped.

That cleared up who was who. "I'm old enough," Austin said. "And thanks, Kate, but I'll stick to water."

"Did he call you Kate?" Jane asked as she struggled to pull herself up and move to the table.

Kathryn nodded. Her smile brought a moment of normalcy to the situation. "He did. I kind of like it, actually."

"Like Kate Hepburn," Suzanne said.

"I loved her in *On Golden Pond*," Hillary said.

"*Guess Who's Coming to Dinner* was on that classic

movie channel last month," Suzanne said. "I had forgotten how good it was."

"It was good," Kate interjected. "So was *The African Queen*."

"Oh, for sure," Suzanne turned to Austin, "Are you a movie fan?"

He shook his head. "I've never been much for movies or TV."

"Well, goodness' sakes, how do you spend your time?" Jane asked.

"College classes. And work. I love working with my hands."

"Lucky for Kathryn," Suzanne quipped. Her comedic timing was perfect. The others laughed.

Even Jane.

<hr />

DINNER CONVERSATION WAS SOMEWHERE between a job interview and a quilting bee. Kathryn did her best to keep the conversation flowing in a direction that included Austin. Suzanne did too, bless her heart.

Still, there were moments when she knew he had to feel left out. Like when Jane droned on about a nasty case of acid reflux her sister was dealing with. Or when Hillary described every collectible on the most recent episode of *Antiques Roadshow*. They were her friends. Her closest friends, but Kathryn couldn't get over how old they seemed.

But Austin? He was taking it in stride, even asking a couple questions about Jane's sister's acid reflux. They were impressed that he was a student at Penn, the closest Ivy

League school to Bethany Beach. At one point, when Austin left the table to refill his water glass, Kathryn thought she saw Hillary sizing him up from the back. She could hardly blame her. It was a pretty good view. Especially compared to Stuart.

While they were eating dessert, a delicious strawberry shortcake Kathryn had picked up from a Rehoboth Beach bakery, she started to think that it might just work out. They were adapting to Austin's presence. He and Hillary even discovered a common acquaintance, a man who had done some work for Austin's family through the years.

Then Jane stated what the others were probably wondering. "What I don't understand is how the two of you wound up together."

Kathryn shared the story of the picket fence and dumpster shopping. She giggled as she told them about dancing at Elijah's.

That should have been enough.

But it wasn't, at least not for Jane.

"But why?" she asked Austin. "I can see why Kathryn would enjoy the company of a younger man, but aren't there more desirable girls out there your own age?"

Was she serious? Or was it the alcohol? Whatever it was, she was looking to Austin for an answer, even after the audible gasps of her friends. Kathryn started to get up. Austin touched her arm, but that wasn't enough to keep her from rising to his defense. "Jane, you can't—"

The doorbell rang. Austin considered jumping up to get it, but his legs wouldn't move.

Kathryn took a deep breath. "Excuse me."

She left the kitchen, and the room was silent. Suzanne and Hillary concentrated on their pasta. Jane took a sip from her water glass and stared into space.

🏛

KATHRYN'S HANDS WERE SHAKING. Jane had always been about Jane, but she usually wasn't rude. She had never encountered a situation like Kathryn and Austin, though. And she was older than the others and probably found it harder to accept. She had insulted Kathryn, though, with her insinuation that she wasn't attractive enough or desirable enough to warrant Austin's attention.

Kathryn's own lingering uncertainties were probably what was really bothering her. Like what she'd felt for a few moments at the outlet mall the previous weekend. Austin had stepped outside of one store to check his messages while Kathryn paid for her purchases. She could see him through the front window as he leaned against a wall and studied his phone. A pretty blonde approached and said something. The conversation was brief, ending when Austin nodded toward the store where Kathryn was finishing up. The girl had glanced her way, then walked on. Kathryn had considered asking about it but didn't. After all, she was the one he was going home with, right?

Even so, the doubts emerged occasionally. And Jane wasn't doing her any favors by bringing them to light.

And she would tell her so as soon as she sent whoever was on the other side of the door on their way. She peered through the peephole and saw an older gray-haired man. A stranger. She opened the door. "Can I help you?"

"Yes." He pulled out a slip of paper. "This is 111 Sea Turtle Court, right?"

"It is."

"I'm looking for Austin McGinnis. There's a sign on the

house he's rehabbing that says he can be found here. And I saw Calvin parked outside."

"He's here. Can I tell him who you are?"

The man grinned. "Tell him it's—"

"Grandpa!" Austin came up beside Kathryn and pulled the man into a hug. "Kate, this is my Grandpa Staley. I don't know what he's doing in Bethany, but I'm happy to see him. Grandpa, why didn't you let me know you were coming?"

"My phone's been dead since Sunday." The old man turned to Kathryn and stuck out his hand. "Charlie Staley."

"Kathryn Shea. Come in, Mr. Staley."

"I don't want to intrude. I just wanted to let my favorite grandson know that I'm in town."

Austin grinned at Kathryn. "I'm his only grandson. Have you eaten yet, Grandpa?"

"I'm just headed out to find something. I'm thinking about a soft crab sandwich from that little place down in Ocean City."

"Nonsense, Mr. Staley," Kathryn said. "We have plenty of pasta and salad."

Austin's grandfather appeared reluctant.

"C'mon and eat with us, Grandpa. We can catch up."

And maybe add to the weirdness, Kathryn thought.

"Well," Mr. Staley glanced back toward the street. "If you're sure you've got plenty, yeah, a home-cooked meal sounds just fine."

<hr/>

"EVERYONE, this is my grandfather, Charlie Staley." Austin introduced Suzanne, Hillary, and Jane. Grandpa graciously nodded and repeated their names to be sure he had them right. Suzanne called him Charlie; Hillary called him Mr. Staley. Jane mumbled something about the evening getting more interesting by the minute. If Grandpa picked up on her indifference, he didn't let it affect him.

He took a seat next to Suzanne while Kathryn grabbed a plate. "Something to drink, Mr. Staley?" she said as she returned to the table.

"How about some of what she's having," he said, pointing to Jane's half-empty glass of wine. "And call me Charlie, all of you." He flashed the same disarming grin that Austin had seen him use on difficult subcontractors. "Except Austin. To you I'll always be Grandpa."

Who would have guessed that Grandpa's appearance would help smooth over the awkwardness? He was one of those few people who seemed to know a little about everything but didn't come across as a know-it-all. When Hillary mentioned a TV series she and Stuart were binging, Grandpa filled in some plot holes. Kathryn's upcoming class trip to Washington, D.C. led to a discussion of everyone's favorite landmarks. Grandpa was a veteran, but not over the top about it, and his recommendation of the Vietnam War Memorial led to each of them sharing accounts of relatives and friends who had served in the military. He not only fit in; he kept the conversation flowing.

For everyone except Jane. Austin couldn't get a feel for her. When Kathryn had spoken of her, it was with a mixture of respect and sympathy. Respect for the way Jane had soldiered on after the death of her husband when they were in their late thirties. She had been a stay-at-home mom until then, but the loss meant she had to return to the elementary school teaching career she had left behind in her twenties. And sympathy for the direction Jane's life was heading. Kathryn felt Jane should not have retired when she did. "Her children live hours away and are wrapped up in their own lives," he remembered her saying. "Without them and her students, we're all she has left. She doesn't exercise or go out much. And she's drinking more than she used to."

As the others became more comfortable and shared stories of past places and events, Jane seemed to withdraw further into herself and her wineglass. Even when Hillary left a bit after nine and Suzanne followed ten minutes later, Jane remained at the table. Austin looked at Kathryn for some idea of what to do. She caught his gaze, then said, "Jane, you're in no condition to drive home, honey. I'm going to take you."

Jane argued she was fine, but she slurred her words.

Even Grandpa appeared worried for her, but said nothing.

"Austin, you enjoy a few minutes with Charlie. I'll be back in a half hour."

After they were gone, Grandpa glanced around the table. "Maybe we should clean up these dishes."

"No, Grandpa. I'll get them."

"Nonsense," he said, getting to his feet and stacking the plates. "That's a nice group of friends you've got there, Austin. I enjoyed dinner very much."

It was time to explain what was going on, but Austin wasn't sure where to begin. How much had Grandpa figured out? For all he knew, Austin had befriended a group of local ladies who cooked dinner for him occasionally.

"Yeah, they're nice. And Kate is an excellent cook, isn't she?"

"She sure is. That pasta sauce was some of the best I've

had." Grandpa placed the stack of plates in the sink, then asked, "How long have the two of you been an item?"

Austin's stomach dropped.

Grandpa winked at him. "I wasn't born yesterday, you know.".

"We—a few weeks."

"Does Savannah know?"

Austin nodded. "We broke things off. She was seeing someone else."

"I see. Sorry to hear about Savannah, but it seems you've bounced back pretty well. You want to wash or dry?"

"What?"

Grandpa pointed to the sink. "The dishes? Wash or dry?"

"Oh, neither. We'll put them in there." Austin shuffled past his grandfather and opened the dishwasher.

Grandpa scraped plates in the sink and handed them to Austin. They worked silently for a few moments before Grandpa spoke again. "Aren't you going to ask why I'm here?"

Given the revelations that had come to light about Austin and Kathryn, he hadn't had time to process what Grandpa was doing in Bethany. "I figured you needed Calvin for something back home. Have you been staying busy?"

"Not busy enough. I finished the inventory at Proctor's lumberyard in four days. The odd jobs along my street kept me busy for a few hours, but I'm bored, so I came down to see what kind of trouble you're getting into." He took a quick look around the kitchen and smiled. "Not quite what I expected to find."

"Grandpa, it's... how did you know?"

"You called her Kate. The ladies called her Kathryn.

Except Jane. She didn't say much of anything. I'm guessing she doesn't approve of the two of you."

"It was the first time we'd met. If you thought that was awkward, you should have seen how things were before you showed up."

They finished loading the dishes just as Kathryn returned. She took a seat at the island and said, "I don't know what I'm going to do with her." To Grandpa she said, "Sorry about that, Charlie."

"Means nothing to me. I enjoyed getting to spend the evening with you folks." He glanced at his watch. "I better find someplace to spend the night if I'm going to get enough sleep to help my grandson in the morning."

"We've—I've got a spare room." Kathryn said.

"Thanks, Kathryn, but I'll get a room at one of those old motels on the edge of town. Austin, how's that little apartment your parents bought for you?"

"It's terrible, Grandpa. There's noise and drinking. And it doesn't have a private bathroom."

"I spent four years in the Marines. I'm used to not having my own latrine. And when it comes to noise," He reached behind an ear and pulled out a hearing aid. "I take these out and a train could run past my bed and I wouldn't know it. How about you give me the key and the address? And give me the keys to Calvin, too. I've missed him. You can use Grandma's Buick." He winked at Kathryn. "Might be more fitting to drive this beautiful young woman around in that instead of Calvin, anyway."

AUSTIN CLOSED the door after seeing Grandpa out, then leaned against it and took a deep breath.

297

"What the hell went on here tonight?" Kathryn moaned as she went to him for a hug.

"Well," Austin said as he looked toward the heavens. "I met your friends, and we had pasta and wine."

"Too much wine for some," Kathryn said.

"My grandfather showed up out of the blue to help me with the house."

"That part is wonderful." Kathryn stretched to kiss his cheek. "How much did you tell him about us?"

"He figured it out. He noticed I called you Kate."

"What did he say?"

"Nothing, really." Austin kissed her on the nose, then the forehead. "Grandpa understands me. Maybe I should say we understand each other. He always marched to his own drum."

"Like you."

"I wish. When it comes to my sister and me, my parents have everything planned out."

Kathryn caught his gaze and held it when he tried to look away. "That doesn't sound like the Austin I know and love."

"You know how I am here, Kate. In Bethany. Doing what I love." His jaw tightened. "Even when things aren't going as well as they should, like now when I'm behind and over budget, I wake up every morning and can't wait to get started."

"You don't think you'll feel that way about law?"

He shook his head. "Since I was a kid, my parents have preached the importance of family. Of continuing the success Grandpa started forty years ago."

"You can do that in ways other than being a lawyer."

"That would crush Mom and Dad."

"How do you know?"

Austin exhaled heavily. "There might have been a time when I could have stepped out and considered something else, but that ship sailed when I enrolled in the pre-law track. I can't imagine how my parents would react if I told them I want to build houses."

Kathryn nodded.

But there was something more. He could see it in the way she pursed her lips. He waited for her to tell him.

She said nothing.

"What?" he asked.

"Nothing." She glanced past him, then let her gaze wander around the room.

"Come on, Kate."

Kathryn's face twisted for a second. "I think I understand why it would be hard for your parents. If I had children and one of them told me they wanted to work in a trade instead of going to college, it would be hard to accept."

"A skilled carpenter makes as much as most college professors." The words were barely out of Austin's mouth before he wanted them back. Kathryn's eyes became wide, and her shoulders drooped. "I'm sorry I said that. I wasn't referring to you, Kate. I don't have any idea how much you make."

"Probably less than a skilled carpenter," she admitted. "This was only supposed to be a brief stop on my climb up the old career ladder."

Austin pushed a strand of hair away from her forehead. "I guess we have something in common, don't we?"

Her puzzled look said she didn't follow.

"We both see ourselves doing something different than what we're doing."

After considering it she nodded slowly. "Yes, but there's

one big difference." She took Austin's hand and led him toward the stairs. "You're still young enough to do something about it."

"Don't do that, Kate. You're not Jane. You're not Suzanne or Hillary, either. You're you. And there's nothing you can't do if you want to."

She kissed him softly. "That's sweet of you to say, Austin."

"I mean it. The more I get to know you, the more I see it. You allowed yourself to get in a rut, maybe, but there's so much more to you than what people see."

Her eyes misted. Had he said something wrong?

But she breathed deeply and said, "No one has encouraged me like that since my mother passed away. And you're right about the rut. I have grown stale."

Austin pulled her into his arms and raised her chin. When their lips met, there was an intensity that wasn't there before. A single sweet kiss became another. She ran her fingers down his arm and across his hip and belly. Austin's breath caught. Then he swept her into his arms and carried her upstairs.

TWENTY-TWO

thursday, june 30

AUSTIN WOULD HAVE PREFERRED to spend the day with Kathryn. Something had changed between them following the dinner party the previous evening. He suspected she'd noticed it too. But with Grandpa at the job site, it wasn't to be.

He couldn't articulate that change, other than that it seemed like one of those shared moments that brought people closer. Sort of like in the movies where situations throw two people together and lead them toward love. He had a feeling that long-term relationships were built on moments like those. Wonderful moments, but probably a few difficult ones too. And a few, like the previous evening, that were just odd.

It certainly would give them something to talk about later.

Austin smiled at the sight of Grandma's Buick. Would it always be Grandma's Buick? It was definitely a way of keeping her memory alive a little longer. Grandpa still hadn't gotten around to giving her clothes away, but healing probably came in its own time and at its own pace.

Yes, he decided, it would be Grandma's Buick for as long as it was around.

When he arrived at Riley Street a little before seven, Calvin was parked in front and the house's windows were open. From inside came the high-pitched percussion of Grandpa's table saw.

The smell of sawdust greeted Austin when he opened the front door.

Grandpa was setting aside a length of wood. He was already covered with sawdust and sweat, and was grinning from ear to ear. "I hope you don't mind," he said, wiping his forehead with a shop rag. "I missed my power tools. I'll have this room trimmed out by noon."

▒▒▒▒▒

THE CLASS ERUPTED in applause when Kathryn shared the news.

Washington, D.C.

An entire week's classes canceled for everyone who went. And if they didn't want to drive, they could ride the charter bus the college was providing.

"Road trip!" one young man shouted.

Kathryn explained the assignment. They had to visit two landmarks that had personal significance, then share their experiences with the class.

A few students already knew where they would go.

The Holocaust Museum because a great grandparent had perished during that dark period.

The National Civil Rights Museum because of stories relatives had told.

One student asked if a Georgetown sports bar counted.

Kathryn counteroffered with the Smithsonian's Museum of Contemporary History.

As they discussed the trip—just ten days away—Kathryn felt their enthusiasm growing. Only a handful had spent more than a few fleeting hours in the nation's capital, and most sightseeing had been limited to the Washington Monument and Lincoln Memorial. Their assignment for the weekend, she said as the hour wound down, was to research the many D.C. landmarks and choose based on their interests.

Students nodded, fist-bumped, and whispered to each other, already planning what they would see.

▓▓▓▓

WHEN AUSTIN CAME DOWNSTAIRS, Grandpa sat on a sawhorse, drinking a Diet Dr. Pepper. "I thought you had class," he said.

"Professor Chakraborty posted our assignment but said class was canceled. That's interesting because he just told me yesterday that—"

"Did someone say my name?"

Professor Chakraborty was larger than Austin expected —at least six-two with broad shoulders and muscular arms. He wore cutoff jean shorts, a Frank Zappa T-shirt, and work boots.

Austin rushed to the door with his hand out. "Professor, I wasn't expecting you until tomorrow."

"I couldn't wait," he said. "It's good to finally meet you in person, Austin." He looked past Austin to where Grandpa was seated. "Hello, sir."

Austin made formal introductions, then offered the

professor a bottle of water. He accepted and downed half of it.

"Grandpa, Professor Chakraborty offered to help us this weekend."

"Wonderful. Know anything about home renovation, Professor?"

"A little. And please call me Vi. You too, Austin. I'm not Professor this weekend, just Vi. Now, tell me where you want me."

⚞⚟

AUSTIN SHUT things down at five thirty. Grandpa and Vi protested until he told them about Elijah's. They insisted on riding together, and despite the thirty-year age difference, Austin could see they were forming a bond based upon their shared love for fine craftsmanship and cold beer, a six-pack of which they had consumed over the course of the afternoon.

Austin recommended several chain hotels, but Vi settled on a budget place near the highway. He and Grandpa agreed to meet there at six thirty and follow Austin and Kathryn to Elijah's. With that out of the way, Austin headed home.

Kathryn was waiting for him. She had never looked more beautiful than when he opened the front door and saw her in an outfit from their shopping trip. The sapphire-blue shorts were cut several inches above her knees, and Austin wondered for a moment if she might feel self-conscious after wearing more modest outfits in the past. He hoped not, because they and the pale cream top she had chosen were amazing. He couldn't take his eyes off her, and when she kissed him, his heart did funny things.

304

She didn't care that he was sweaty and his clothes were filthy. She actually seemed charmed by it. His mind wandered back to their lovemaking the previous night; how she seemed to always know what he wanted, and how perfectly in sync they were physically and emotionally.

"You look..." He fumbled for how to say the words that beautiful Kate deserved to hear. "You are so incredibly... so... I love you so much."

She buried her face against his shoulder. "You've been such a blessing to me," she murmured. "And I love you. And everything about you."

They remained there for a time. Holding one another. Cherishing the moment.

Austin had no desire, no inclination, to move from that spot, to break the embrace of the woman who was changing his life day by sweet day.

CARS WERE PARKED along both sides of the narrow road leading into Elijah's gravel lot. Austin wedged Kathryn's Toyota into a space between a motorcycle and a pickup truck that was jacked so high they could see its underside. The Professor pulled up next to them in his Volkswagen bug. Grandpa rolled down the window and called out, "Vi feels lucky. We're going to look for a spot up close. Want to hop in?"

"No thanks," Austin said. He took Kathryn's hand. "We'll walk."

Dusk was settling in and stars were making their appearance. Kathryn figured they were a quarter mile from Elijah's, but she could still hear the faint melody of an old country song she recognized. Austin put his arm around her as they walked.

"We should have invited your friends," he said.

The thought of Jane at Elijah's made her laugh. "What will Charlie think of it?"

"I think he'll enjoy it. He and Grandma used to go dancing at the American Legion in Coatesville."

"Maybe I'll get him out on the dance floor," Kathryn said as they rounded a bend and Elijah's came into view.

They arrived at the maze of picnic tables and began searching for Charlie and the Vi. All around them, people washed down heaping plates of seafood with longnecks and frosty mugs. A few people were dancing between tables, and farther away, on the edge of the woods, a couple was making out against a tree.

"Either they're inside or they got lost in the woods," Austin said as he surveyed the craziness. The door was open, but all Kathryn could see in the gloomy interior were bodies mashed together. It reminded her of a subway ride she'd taken during a trip to New York City years earlier.

"I've never seen it this busy," Austin said. "Let's see if we can find them." He led the way, elbowing and shouldering his way through the crowd. A sweaty tattooed arm bumped against Kathryn's shoulder, then a hand brushed her backside.

"Sorry," the offender, a woman following her man just like Kathryn was, called out.

"There they are!" Austin hollered over a song about guitars and Cadillacs.

She couldn't see past the people surrounding her so she hung on to Austin's arm until they reached a table next to the one where they'd sat last time. She'd been looking forward to meeting Vi, but what would he think of her?

Sure, they were both college professors, but the similarities ended there. She had googled Professor Vihaan Chakraborty and learned he had the kind of international resume that Ivy League schools coveted. He had taught doctoral level classes in European literature and guided dissertation research in Eastern Europe.

She taught remedial English in rural Delaware.

Austin had to shout to be heard. "How did you get in here?" he asked his grandpa.

Grandpa still didn't hear him, but Professor Chakraborty did. "Charlie slipped that guy a twenty!" He pointed toward the bar where Kathryn's onetime student and future Elijah's co-owner waved. "We've already put in our drink order," the Professor said. "Let the server know what you want." He stood and extended his hand to Kathryn. "Hey, I'm Vi."

"Kathryn."

Austin caught the server's attention and raised two fingers. When he brought their beers, he grinned at Kathryn. "Hey! Good to see you back. You look real pretty."

Kathryn demurred as the three men at her table nodded in agreement.

Charlie and Vi appeared fascinated by Elijah's. "Kind of crowded, isn't it?" Kathryn said.

"The best places always are." Charlie sipped his beer. "Beer's damned good, though."

"I grew up in India," Vi said. "Crowds like this are nothing. My three brothers and I shared a bedroom until I was ten." He nodded at Kathryn. "Austin said you teach at the local college. I envy you getting to live and work near the beach. Maybe I need to look into that."

Kathryn giggled. "Yeah, I understand why you would

want to be here. I mean, compared to Lower Delaware Community College, Penn is the minor leagues."

⊞

KATHRYN'S little joke about Penn did the trick. Vi belly-laughed, then leaned in closer to talk. He asked a question that Austin didn't catch, something about the classes she taught. She answered, and they both laughed at her response.

Across the table, Grandpa sipped his beer while he observed everything around him.

"I'm glad you came down, Grandpa," Austin said. "Could you tell I was in over my head?"

"Not at all. The work you've done is very good, but then I expected that." Grandpa chuckled. "After all, I'm the one who taught you."

"Mom and Dad think I hired a local contractor."

"I figured. Are you going to tell them the truth?"

"When I'm done. If I get done."

"Oh, you'll get done. Vi and me will see to that. He plans to come down every weekend for the rest of the summer. And you'll have me every day."

"I can't put in seven days a week, Grandpa. It'll kill me. I need to turn down his offer."

"When I was just getting started in this business, I worked seven days a week, sometimes fifteen hours a day." Grandpa nodded at Kathryn. "I suspect you *could* put in seven days but would rather spend time with that pretty lady. And who can blame you?"

Kathryn and Vi remained immersed in conversation. Something about faculty senates and tenure abatement, whatever that meant. Kathryn glanced his way and winked.

Austin returned his attention to Grandpa and told him the story of how he and Kathryn had met.

"That must be quite a picket fence," Grandpa chuckled.

"You couldn't see it when you came by the other night, but yeah, it's pretty nice. And you won't believe the tools I used." Now they were on familiar turf. Hand tools and woodworking were a language they had shared since Austin was an inquisitive Cub Scout spending time in Grandpa's shop.

Their food arrived, and they were digging in when the Professor blurted out, "What is it they call the two of you in America?"

Austin held his breath.

"It's a Tuesday and Saturday thing? No, it's something different. A reference to time that captures the meaning of a couple where one is older than the other. I cannot remember now."

"May–December," Kathryn said, winking at Austin. "A May–December romance. Like in *Jane Eyre*, except we're in reverse."

Wasn't that the title of the book from her doctoral dissertation? He had only read the first few pages, but Austin was certain it was.

"Exactly!" Vi said. "I haven't read *Jane Eyre* in so long. It might be time to return to it."

"Charlotte Brontë has several wonderful books," Kathryn said, "but have you sampled her poetry?"

Austin and Grandpa looked on silently as Kathryn and Vi discussed the Brontë sisters. After a few moments, Grandpa leaned across the table and whispered, "Do you know these women?"

Austin grinned. "I think they lived a long time ago."

Grandpa shrugged. "Guess I'll have to wait for the movie."

Kathryn overheard and leaned Grandpa's way. "There have already been many movie adaptations of *Jane Eyre*."

"I must have missed them."

"The most famous one starred Charlton Heston," Kathryn said.

"Emma loved Charlton Heston," Grandpa said, his eyes growing dreamy at the mention of Grandma.

"George C. Scott was in another."

"The guy from Patton?" Grandpa asked. "The General?"

Kathryn nodded. "Perhaps we can watch one of them sometime? I have them all."

Vi was all in. Grandpa was noncommittal.

It was obvious how much Kathryn loved the story and its author. Her enthusiasm made him want to read more, and as soon as he finished reading her dissertation, they'd spend a romantic evening discussing the works of this Miss Charlotte Brontë.

But for now, he was content to listen and learn.

"I'm going to take a wild guess and say you haven't told your parents about Kathryn," Grandpa whispered after Kathryn and Vi returned to their conversation.

"What they think of Kate is the least of my worries because I think they're going to lose their shit about everything else. They sent me down here to pass the courses I flunked and watch their properties."

"And you are passing your courses?"

"I have an A in Southern Lit. Vi's a good professor."

The Professor overheard. "You've done excellent work." He looked at Kathryn. "And I'm beginning to understand why."

"Kathryn recommended the books," Austin said.

"But you read them and made them yours. That's more than many of your classmates have done. They're all about getting the grade. You developed feelings for the characters. I can't wait to hear what you think of Ignatius Reilly and *A Confederacy of Dunces*."

The conversation flowed through dinner, muted occasionally by the noise and laughter that filled Elijah's. Snippets of conversation drifted at them from every direction. A discussion of cantaloupe prices at one table, plans for an early morning trip to the beach from another. At the table behind Austin, out of sight but easy to hear, a raspy-voiced woman berated a mostly silent man about a woman named Daphne. Judging by his muted apologies, he was guilty of something.

"I'll work weekends with Vi," Grandpa said to Austin after they'd finished their food. "It's fun to be back in the saddle again, and he's pretty good, so I won't have to worry about his work. You spend the weekends with Kathryn."

"Grandpa, I feel guilty about that. I'm the one who took this on. I should be the one who—"

"If you're going to work in construction, you need to learn how to trust the people who work for you, Austin. Just give me and Vi our marching orders, then go enjoy yourself."

Had he not worried about how it would look, he would have planted a kiss on Grandpa's cheek right then and there. He wouldn't have the chance, though, as Kathryn slid from her seat and came around the table. She tapped Grandpa on the shoulder.

"Let's dance, Charlie."

Grandpa was on his feet before the words were out of her mouth. He stepped around his grandson and held out his hand to Kathryn just as the deejay queued up a Patsy Cline tune.

Austin was about to move closer to Vi, but the professor waved him off. "See her?" Vi said, pointing to a buxom woman with a blonde ponytail. "She's been looking my way all evening. It's time to make my move."

✦

"THAT WAS the most fun I've had in a long time," Kathryn exclaimed as she and Austin stepped into the house. "Charlie is such a gentleman. And a great dancer. And Vi is so *smart*."

"I'm glad you had a great time." Austin's voice contained a tinge of sarcasm. "I spent most of my night alone while you danced your cute backside off."

"Hey, mister, it was your idea."

"I loved seeing you and Grandpa getting along so well. It made me wonder how it will be when you meet my parents and Holly."

Kathryn took his arm and turned so they were facing. "How will that be?"

Austin shrugged. "Okay. I hope. Dad and Mom are pretty cool about stuff when it isn't business related."

Kathryn wasn't as sure. Something Charlie had said during their last dance made her wonder. "You'll find that Austin and me aren't like the rest," he'd said. "My way of life skipped my daughter, and my son-in-law never had it to begin with." He'd paused. "Don't let them get in the way of what's important."

But it was too fun an evening to worry about stuff like that. Especially with the way Austin was looking at her as they headed upstairs.

TWENTY-THREE

saturday, july 2

DESPITE GRANDPA'S and Vi's insistence that he take the weekend off, Austin arrived at seven. He unlocked, opened the windows, and got things ready for their arrival.

The professor showed up first, ashen-faced and shaky on his feet.

"I brought doughnuts," Austin said, motioning to a box on the staircase.

Vi raised his hands as if warding off evil spirits.

Austin tried not to laugh. "Rough night, Professor?"

Vi shook his head. "I haven't drank that much in..." He waved his hand in defeat.

"Are you going to be okay?"

"Oh, yeah. Charlie drove me back to the hotel. I don't get it, Austin. He drank more than I did, but it didn't faze him in the slightest. After you and Kathryn left, he danced with four women and barely broke a sweat." Vi forced a smile that appeared to make his head hurt. "She's a good one, your Kathryn. I can see why you like her so much. And if my comment about your age difference offended you, I apologize."

"Don't worry about it, Vi. I enjoyed listening to you discuss the books she loves. I hope I can do the same someday."

"That's a very kind gesture, Austin." Vi gently lowered himself onto the staircase next to the doughnuts. He peeked in the box before pushing it away. "But please remember that there are plenty of people who can discuss Charlotte Brontë, but only one who has captured Kathryn's heart."

"I don't understand."

Vi used his index finger to lift the lid of the doughnut box again, then reached in and removed a chocolate glazed. "The gleam I saw in Kathryn's eyes last night didn't come from Brontë. Like the Southern authors say, she's fallen head over heels for you."

Austin felt a thickness in his throat. Experiencing what he felt for Kate was one thing, but for someone else to notice was something else entirely.

"And if you don't mind me saying so," Vi continued, "you need to be mindful of her feelings. You're still very young, Austin. People your age sometimes view relationships differently."

Austin went back to cleaning the table saw, if only to give himself something to focus on while he considered Vi's observation. "How do you mean?"

"I'm guessing that Kathryn is in her thirties. We don't get to that stage of life without a certain amount of heartbreak."

Austin nodded but didn't reply.

"We view relationships differently as we mature. The chances of finding love with someone we want to spend our lives with become fewer. What might be just another fling for a twenty-year-old can have much more significance a few years later."

"It's not a fling, Professor, I promise you."

"Austin, I sense what you say is the truth, but as a slightly older man who has had his heart jumped on a few times, I felt I needed to say something."

Vi remained on the staircase. The doughnut was gone, and there was a chocolate smudge on his chin. He looked at that moment less like a successful Ivy League professor and more like a good friend.

✦✦✦✦✦✦

KATHRYN COULDN'T WAIT to tell the girls about her upcoming class trip to Washington, but from the minute she arrived at Milo's, all Hillary wanted to talk about was Austin. She peppered Kathryn with questions. "What do the two of you do?"

"We spend time together. He has paperwork to do some evenings. I have papers to grade and lessons to prepare."

"What do you talk about?"

"We talk about normal stuff. His work. My work. Hey, I wanted to tell you about the field trip that I've—"

"Does he like any of the things you like, or does he play video games all day?"

"I've never seen him play video games. He enjoys his work and is taking a couple of summer courses at Penn."

Suzanne had joined the two of them during Hillary's interrogation but said nothing, her head turning from left to right as if watching a tennis match.

"Where is his family, other than the grandfather?" Hillary asked. "Have you met them?"

"Not yet. They're in Philadelphia."

"Do you think they'll flip out when they find out you're dating their son?"

"I hope not." Kathryn turned to Suzanne. "You won't believe what happened at school this week. I—"

"For the life of me, I can't see what you have in common," Hillary cut in. "I mean, Stuart and I have our TV shows. And we enjoy dominos. But there's only one thing I can imagine a boy that age wanting from you, Kathryn."

"Hillary wants to know if the sex is good," Suzanne interjected.

Hillary gasped. "I would never ask about that."

"What'll it be, ladies?" Harvey said brusquely as he approached with pen and pad in hand. "The usual? And where's Jane?"

"She'll be here any moment," Kathryn said. "Are you in a bad mood, Harvey?"

He glowered toward a group of eight seated nearby. "Fourth of July weekend. The idiots from D.C. and Philly are in town with their bad accents and ridiculous demands." He raised his voice to a mocking falsetto. "I ordered my eggs shirred. This is not shirred!" A matronly brunette glared at Harvey. He glared back. "This is Bethany Beach, lady. We got scrambled and sunny side up. If you'd smile once in a while, we might poach 'em."

"Your menu says eggs cooked any way," she snapped.

"Who the hell ever heard of shirred eggs?" Harvey raised his voice so he could be heard across the entire diner. "Any of you ever ask to have your eggs shirred?"

Locals knew better than to go against Harvey. Most tourists had figured it out too, except for the matronly brunette and the guy seated next to her. He raised his hand, then quickly put it down when someone at an adjoining table whispered, "You're gonna get thrown out."

"I love your eggs, Harvey," a redhead in a halter top said cheekily.

316

"Me too," others added.

Harvey nodded, cast a baleful look at the shirred eggs lady, and stalked off to the kitchen as Jane arrived.

"What did I miss?" she asked as she took her usual seat.

"Shirred eggs," Suzanne answered.

"I love shirred eggs."

"You should order some," Suzanne said. "Harvey loves when people order shirred eggs. Where have you been?"

"I got a late start."

"We were worried," Hillary said. "How are you feeling?"

"Much better," Jane said, smiling. "Much, much better."

"Big plans for today, Jane?" Kathryn asked.

Hillary cut in. "Kathryn's trying to avoid my questions about her new boyfriend."

"Stop it, Hillary," Jane said. "If Kathryn wants to keep her relationship private, who are we to pry?"

The table grew quiet. Jane usually fed into the gossip. Perhaps her recent health scare brought a change of attitude. Whatever it was, Kathryn was happy it deflected the questions about Austin. The girls could learn about him over time. It was better that way.

AUSTIN WAS UPSTAIRS INSTALLING bathroom fixtures when he heard Grandpa arrive, whistling the theme from an old TV show. Austin set aside his tools and headed downstairs to meet him. "The Windermere must seem a lot more comfortable to you than it did to me," Austin said.

"It's fine, son. Just fine." Grandpa looked around the corner to the kitchen where Vi was at work. "How you feeling, Professor? Able to sleep it off?"

"I'm getting better every minute, Charlie."

"Sorry I'm running late. I had a stop to make. Where do you want me, Austin?"

"Can you take over the upstairs bathroom?"

"Sure, as long as you get the heck out of here and enjoy the sunshine. That storm that's been lurking out in the Atlantic turned west overnight. They're saying it might bring us some rough weather later today and into tomorrow. Maybe you should pick up Kathryn and enjoy a morning at the beach."

"We might do that, Grandpa, though it'll be crazy crowded. The Fourth of July holiday started last night."

"I believe that for a fact. The traffic is bumper to bumper. Certainly nothing like Coatesville. Folks around here are going to be mighty disappointed if the weather turns bad."

Austin gathered his stuff but felt guilty for leaving them to work while the rest of Bethany Beach celebrated. "Are you sure you're okay with me getting out of here?"

"We demand that you leave, young man!" Vi called from the kitchen. "Charlie can take over as boss, and I'll do whatever he says. As long as he doesn't say it very loud."

"Thank you both. I was worried that I bit off more than I could chew, but you being here has helped so much."

"You're still a young man," Grandpa said kindly. "You deserve time to do young man things. Now go."

thursday, july 7

AS HE HAD ALL WEEK, Austin unlocked the house, opened the windows, and waited for Grandpa. The amount of work they had completed since his arrival was incredible. The project was coming together, and if they continued at their present pace, everything should be buttoned up by Labor Day.

It was twenty past eight when Grandpa showed up. "What are you doing here?" he asked Austin. "I thought you and Kathryn would be on your way to Washington by now."

"We're leaving from the college at ten. I didn't want to leave without seeing you first. You've been rolling in later than expected, Grandpa. Is everything okay at the Windermere?"

"Everything is fine. Don't worry about me. I just don't get around as early as I used to."

"Okay, but promise me you'll not do anything too strenuous while I'm gone."

Grandpa raised his fingers in a Boy Scout salute. "I'll finish installing that bathroom vanity and supervise the painting crew. Are you sure you want to go with that pale yellow on the exterior? It's not too late to change your mind."

"Kathryn said yellow would set the place apart. The other houses on the street are light blue and gray."

"If Kathryn says yellow, then yellow it is. Vi called this morning. He'll be here around lunchtime tomorrow. I'll leave the toilet installation for him."

Austin took a quick look around and marveled at how well things were going. Best of all, the costs were falling into line, closer to his original projections. He had little doubt that with Grandpa and Vi, they would do even better. He felt good about the job. And about Kathryn and what was developing between them. Bethany Beach was feeling more like home too—as long as he didn't let thoughts of August and his return to Penn get in the way.

KATHRYN LAUGHED when they walked into a Washington D.C. Shake Shack and spotted half of her students already eating.

"There are a dozen or more restaurants close by," she said to Austin as they waited their turn at a self-service kiosk. "German food, Thai, Ethiopian, French, but here they are at a burger place."

"Just like us," he laughed. "There's no Shake Shack within a hundred miles of Bethany Beach."

"Good point."

Several students greeted them as they placed their order. The surprise on their faces that morning when they realized she and Austin were a couple had passed by the time the charter bus crossed into Maryland. The mood on the bus had been jovial, and Kathryn couldn't get over how excited they were. Once the bus reached the city, the students quickly went their own ways, bound for destinations across the District and into northern Virginia. Kathryn opted for a visit to the Arlington neighborhood where she was raised, and Austin seemed to enjoy seeing landmarks from her childhood as much as she did.

The restaurant was packed and tables were scarce, but Ava Hawthorne and two of her friends waved them over. Kathryn suspected they were all in the same boat—small-town kids who'd never had the means to spend the night in a D.C. hotel and enjoy the sights.

When Austin brought their order to the table, Ava's friend Hattie, a sweet shy girl who was developing a genuine talent for writing, asked, "So how did you guys get together? Were you a student at the college, Austin?"

Kathryn's ears grew hot, but Austin didn't flinch. "I fixed her fence," he said easily. "She must have liked the job I did because she kept me around."

The girls laughed. Clearly they found him good-looking and funny, and the conversation moved on to how each had spent their afternoon. Hattie and their other friend, Stephanie, went to Ford's Theater. Ava spent the afternoon at the Vietnam Veterans' Memorial. They chatted about what they had seen and how they planned to turn their adventures into class projects.

Their hotel, a Hilton property, was a few blocks from the restaurant. The girls finished their burgers and excused themselves to do some souvenir shopping before heading back. It was after nine when Kathryn and Austin stood up to leave.

"Have you been here after dark?" Kathryn asked as they stepped outside.

"Shake Shack? Yeah. Several times. We have one near campus."

Kathryn punched his arm playfully. "I mean Washington."

"Mostly we came on family day trips."

"In that case, I have a treat for you." She took his hand and led him down the sidewalk. The streets were bustling with sightseers gaping at monuments, and locals headed to their favorite nightspots. After several blocks, the crowds thinned out as they passed under the Eisenhower Freeway and along Wharf Street. They walked hand-in-hand and passed other couples doing the same. Ten minutes later, they entered an area overflowing with trees and greenery.

"We're almost there," Kathryn said. "Let's go this way." Two more turns and the Jefferson Memorial came into view across an expansive body of water.

"This is the Tidal Basin. My favorite view in all of Washington."

✶

IT WAS SPECTACULAR. The Jefferson Memorial was beautifully illuminated, its rippled reflection covering much of the water. Austin leaned against a fence and gazed across the water.

"My grandparents brought me here," Kathryn said. "My grandfather knew all the best places to view the city. Want to sit?"

They seated themselves on a nearby bench. Austin put his arm around her and felt her sigh. He was uncertain how much time passed. The view was mesmerizing, as was the company.

"This trip wouldn't have happened had you not encouraged me," Kathryn finally said. "Cape Henlopen was the key that opened the door. I've enjoyed these summer classes so much since we took that trip. The students have too." When she paused he saw concern in her eyes. "Now if only Casper is happy with the changes."

"There can't be any doubt. Look at how your students have bonded with you and each other. What you have with them is amazing."

Kathryn snuggled closer. "It's turned out to be a wonderful summer. In many ways."

Austin inhaled the clean scent of her hair and skin. "And to think it all started with a fence."

They didn't speak for a few moments as they watched a passing couple pause nearby to enjoy the view. The sky was clear and stars were visible. The summer air was heavy with humidity, but it didn't matter. As far as Austin was concerned, everything was perfect.

"What comes next?"

She'd spoken the words so softly that he barely caught them. She wasn't asking about later that evening or even the next day or week. Fall classes started in five weeks. And the thought of leaving her made him hurt inside.

"Penn isn't that far away," he answered, trying to sound casual. "But I don't want that."

"What do you mean?"

"I feel like I'm doing what I was meant to do, Kate. Watching that house go from the rundown condition it was in a few weeks ago, it's hard to imagine finding the same satisfaction in a courtroom."

"Be true to yourself. If building and remodeling houses is what you love, you need to pursue it."

"Ha," Austin said, chuckling. "If only Mom and Dad felt that way. They spent a lot of money on my education."

"Education is more than preparing for a job, Austin. You've experienced things and learned things that will remain with you for your entire life."

"Like Southern Lit." Austin laughed. "Who knew there were books out there that I would enjoy reading?"

"But more than that. There are your fraternity experiences and the friends you've made. You may not become a lawyer, but there's so much you've learned that would make you a fantastic carpenter."

"Yeah, but could you ever love a carpenter, Kate?"

She hugged him tight and reached up for a kiss. "I already do."

saturday, july 9

KATHRYN ARRIVED home from breakfast with the girls to an empty house. She'd hoped Austin might be there, but it was hard to tear himself away from the job site when Charlie and Vi were in town. The previous two days in Washington had probably set back his schedule, but they had been wondrous for their relationship.

She'd left her phone in her bedroom, so she ran upstairs to see if he had called. He hadn't, but there was a message from a local number she didn't recognize. Kathryn played the message.

"Hello, Dr. Shea. This is Mary from President Cuellar's office. I've been asked to contact you about a matter that has just come up here at the college. I'm sorry for the short notice, but President Cuellar is hoping you are available to attend the board of regents meeting today at eleven. If you can't make it, please call me back as soon as possible. Otherwise, we will see you later this morning."

Kathryn's stomach churned. Rosa wanted to see her on a Saturday? She listened to the message a second time. Her stomach hurt worse. It couldn't have anything to do with

Austin, could it? Perhaps one of her students had mentioned him coming along on the trip to Washington. She had not tried to hide the fact that they were seeing each other.

Should she have?

Her thoughts returned to the biology teacher who had impregnated a student. Well, *she* certainly wasn't pregnant. The thought made her giggle and feel a bit better.

No, she decided, it had to be something different.

But what?

Casper Fillmore? The Professional Improvement Plan?

She felt miserable again. That was it. It had to be. She had pushed that mess to the far reaches of her mind over the last few weeks. Her classes were going well. Rosa had been complimentary. And Casper hadn't returned to her class since that tumultuous first week. Kathryn hadn't even seen him around campus, come to think of it. He hadn't witnessed the transformation taking place in her classes. Could it be he was proceeding with his plan to reassign her summer classes?

Her phone buzzed.

It was Suzanne. "Kathryn, I need a new dress for my niece's church confirmation. Want to tag along?"

"No thanks, Suzanne. There's a meeting that I need to..." Kathryn choked back the tears and tried to continue.

"Kathryn, what's wrong? Is it something with Austin?"

"No, it's not Austin. It's..." She couldn't get any further before letting go. Crying was so unlike her.

Suzanne knew that too. "Stay put. I'll be there in five minutes."

"No, Suzanne. You don't have to—"

Suzanne was already gone.

Kathryn's hands shook as she disconnected. Why was

this happening? What was happening? She didn't break rules. She never even bent them. It was the way she had been raised. Respect authority. Do what's right. Never compromise your integrity.

"Get a grip," she whispered as she called Austin. He would know what to say to calm her.

But Austin didn't answer.

AUSTIN WAS BACKING out of the Riley Street driveway when he spotted Savannah on the sidewalk next to her car. He hit the brakes harder than he meant to and felt the seatbelt lock up. She walked toward him, laughing. "Surprise!"

He opened the door and got out. "Savannah? What are you doing here?"

She opened her arms. Austin glanced toward the house, then hugged her the way a brother might hug his sister. "Wow, is that all I get?" she said as he pulled away.

"I'm sorry. I wasn't expecting to... you didn't call or anything."

"I wanted to surprise you. Is there someplace we can talk?" She nodded toward the house. "Maybe inside?"

"It's a mess, and Grandpa's here. He's helping me out. And one of my Penn professors too. They're—no. We can't talk in there."

"How about we go for brunch?" Savannah licked her lips in that way that she knew he found irresistible. "My treat? That little place out on the highway?"

Austin took a deep breath and checked his watch. He and Kathryn had made no plans other than to spend the day together. Still, she was expecting him back at the house. "I already have—I mean, I'm—"

"Austin, it's important that we talk. If not now, then later. There have been some changes in my life that you need to know about. Changes that affect you."

Was she pregnant? The thought hit him in the gut. What were the odds? She'd been on the pill for as long as he'd known her. But still, the pill wasn't one hundred percent effective, was it? People used it and still got pregnant sometimes, didn't they?

Even if she was pregnant, how could she be sure the baby was his? What about Derek?

"Please, Austin. Let's go someplace and talk. If not brunch, how about the beach?"

Austin rubbed at the sweat on the back of his neck and looked up and down the street. Was there some way he could escape?

But Savannah wouldn't be denied. And he needed to know what brought her to Bethany. He pulled out his phone—he'd missed a call from Kathryn. Maybe he should call her, let her know he would be late getting back. And tell her about Savannah? She needed to know, but not in a text.

I'm going to be late. I'll explain later, he texted Kathryn. He faced Savannah. "The beach will be packed. Let's get something to eat."

⧘⧘⧘

"HELLO, DR. SHEA."

Mary Hewison, the college's long-time executive secretary, greeted Kathryn warmly as she and Suzanne stepped into the waiting area outside the college conference room. She wore a light blue pantsuit that was considerably more formal than her usual weekday attire. Kathryn had hastily changed into a simple coral dress and wished she had given it more thought. The door to the conference room was closed, but there were voices on the other side.

"Hi, Mary. Suzanne came along with me."

While Kathryn felt a bit underdressed, Suzanne in khaki shorts and a Grand Canyon T-shirt looked ready for a round of mini golf. She couldn't have cared less. "What's this about, Mary?" she asked curtly.

"I'm sorry, Dr. Towne, but this meeting is for Dr. Shea. You'll have to wait out here."

"Nope," Suzanne said quickly. "I'm here for my friend. You called Kathryn at the last minute and demanded she come in. She deserves someone in her corner, just as the college has an entire board in theirs."

Mary pursed her lips for a moment before saying, "Dr. Towne, it's not like that."

"You and I have always gotten along fine, Mary, but you need to know that I'm not leaving my friend."

Mary considered both of them for a moment, then smiled.

"Well, Doctor, if you insist."

"We insist," Suzanne shot back.

Mary gestured to the closed door. "The college board of regents is meeting inside. We'll join them."

"We want to know what this is about," Suzanne said.

"I'm not at liberty to tell you. You'll have to hear it from the board."

"What if we don't want to go in?" Kathryn asked.

"I believe you want to go in, Dr. Shea, or you wouldn't have come." She walked to the door and held it open. "Please follow me."

Kathryn had been in the college conference room many

times for department meetings and other special functions, but its setup today was different. Several rows of chairs were placed in front of the conference table for spectators, but only three were occupied.

Rosa and six other people sat around the table. Kathryn recognized a couple of them, but her interactions with the college board had been negligible. The business and governance side of the college was something that had never interested her, other than when she had been striving for tenure. After that had been achieved, she barely paid attention to board minutes or elections. A slightly built woman about Kathryn's age was seated at the center of the table. She nodded and said, "Have a seat in front, please, Dr. Shea."

Her voice was pleasant enough. And was that a smile on her face? Kathryn felt herself relax for just a moment as she took a seat. Suzanne sat down beside her.

"Dr. Shea, I am Marcella Thornton, the chair of the college Board of Regents." She introduced the others. "And of course you know President Cuellar."

"Yes."

"Fine, then we'll get started." Marcella Thornton shifted some papers in front of her. "Do you have any idea why you're here, Dr. Shea?"

A thousand thoughts raced through Kathryn's mind. Her throat was dry, and she felt herself perspiring. "Is this about..." she stammered. "Perhaps you heard—"

"Dr. Shea does *not* know why she is here," Suzanne stood as she spoke. "And she is dismayed that you summoned her in such a perfunctory manner. She's a busy scholar and academician, and the call from Ms. Hewison took her away from some very important work."

"This is Dr. Suzanne Towne," Mary said from her seat off to the side. "She is here to support Dr. Shea."

"I apologize for the last-minute call, Dr. Shea," the chairperson said. "But some things cannot wait." She coughed, took a sip of water, then continued. "Dr. Shea, you currently have a student named Ava Hawthorne in your remedial English class."

Kathryn cleared her throat. "Yes, I know Ava."

"Dr. Shea, Miss Hawthorne did something that came to our attention late last night."

"Don't answer any more questions," Suzanne whispered.

"President Cuellar received word last evening that Miss Hawthorne submitted your name to the selection board for the National Community College Association's Innovative Educator award."

What? This wasn't about Austin? Or Casper Fillmore?

Kathryn looked around the room. The entire board was smiling, but none as brightly as Rosa.

The chairperson continued. "Miss Hawthorne beat the June 28 deadline by a matter of minutes, but according to the head of their selection committee, her description of how you arranged a class field trip to Cape Henlopen to reach your remedial English students impressed the committee members."

What was going on?

Were they upset? Or happy? Did Ava Hawthorne's nomination of her for this award thing derail their plans to get rid of her?

Rosa had said she loved the idea.

So... why was she in front of the college board?

Chairperson Thornton wasn't done yet.

"The selection committee also learned of your plan for an educational field trip to Washington, D.C."

"Yes, ma'am. I spoke to Rosa—President Cuellar—about that."

"They were most impressed that you made sure no students would have to miss out because of the cost." Chairperson Thornton paused for a moment, then added, "Miss Hawthorne described you as a kind and caring teacher. And a role model."

Wow!

It wasn't anything like Kathryn had expected.

They weren't out to get her. Far from it. They were... commending her.

Wow. Wow. Wow!

"The selection committee chair contacted President Cuellar last evening to let her know you are one of six national winners this year."

The board rose as one and applauded.

Kathryn remained seated, her head spinning. She wanted to laugh. She even wanted to cry a little. She had been so scared just a couple minutes before. And now she was winning a big award.

Suzanne grabbed her arm. "Congratulations! Now stand up. And close your mouth. I can see your molars. That won't look good in pictures."

Kathryn hadn't realized anyone was taking pictures. Her legs were still wobbly when Rosa made a beeline for her with arms extended. Their embrace gave Kathryn time to pull herself together.

"You won twenty-five hundred dollars and a trip to the national conference in November," Rosa whispered. "I'm so proud of you, Kathryn!"

"I—what am I supposed to—where is the conference?"

"Well, it's in Knoxville, Tennessee. Last year's was in Las Vegas."

"That's fine. I don't like Las Vegas much."

Rosa laughed. "The head of the selection committee told me she did some research and saw how many students we serve from low-income families. Your efforts to make sure that no students were left out impressed the committee very much."

"It wasn't really a big thing," Kathryn whispered back. "The idea came from—"

"Don't be modest," Rosa said. "You earned this, Kathryn."

"Dr. Shea," the chairperson said as she returned to her seat. "The board wishes to thank you for your service to our students and community. We understand you made a choice to become a longtime member of our faculty, and we appreciate it very much."

"Thank you." Kathryn gathered her thoughts. "If I may, I would like to thank President Cuellar for being a supporter and friend. And also Suzanne." She grabbed her friend's hand. "She's always got my back."

"We could tell!" The chairperson's quip brought a round of laughter.

Kathryn wanted to say more, but getting the words out might make her cry. She took a breath. "While he's not here, I owe so much to Austin McGinnis. He is a very important part of my life and, more than anyone, Austin encouraged me to find ways to help my students. He's my biggest fan."

The chairperson smiled. "I hope we get to meet Mr. McGinnis and thank him on behalf of the college. We have a reception planned in your honor at the beginning of fall semester. But today, we have something else President Cuellar needs to discuss with you. If it's okay with the board, we will take a brief recess to allow you to chat."

SAVANNAH ASKED Austin to drive her car. "Just like old times," she added.

Something inside told him to take his own car, if only to escape if things went off the rails. He didn't, though.

"It's nice that your grandpa came down to help," Savannah said as they crawled through stop-and-go traffic.

"He's making a big difference." Austin told her about how Professor Chakraborty had volunteered as well. It wasn't the kind of stuff Savannah cared about, but it kept the conversation light and steered it away from topics he preferred not to discuss.

"Are you still living in that upstairs bedroom?"

Topics like that one.

"I can't imagine how you could with all that dust and mess."

"It is messy." Austin hoped his evasive answer would end that line of questioning.

"So are you?"

He should have known better. "Savannah, why are you here? What's so important that we need to talk?"

She studied her cuticles. Was she about to cry? Her lower lip was quivering, but she was stronger than that. Was she about to say she was pregnant? Please, not that.

"I had to see you." She dabbed her eyes with her palm. "Can't we wait until we get to the restaurant?"

"Okay." Austin took a deep breath. "When does that civics camp start that you're helping with?"

"I'm not going. It's just too much. Not after everything that happened." She paused. "How is Kathryn?"

"Busy with summer school. Just like I'm busy with the house project." Austin's tone was sharper than he intended. Or maybe not. Savannah's questions were closing in on a discussion he wasn't ready to have.

"Why are you snapping at me? I'm just trying to make conversation."

Austin pulled onto a side street and stopped in front of a row of small cottages. "Savannah," he said as parked the car and turned up the air conditioning. "I'm not going to brunch or anywhere else until you tell me why you're here."

"Let's not do this now, Austin. Please." She looked at the surroundings. "Someone will come out and wonder why we're—"

"Nobody cares. And it's more private than a noisy restaurant."

"Fine, then." She pulled open the glove box, took out a wad of tissue and dabbed at her eyes, careful not to ruin her eye makeup.

"I'm not seeing Derek anymore."

How was he supposed to feel about that? Because he felt nothing, but he should probably try to be supportive. He awkwardly touched her shoulder.

She grabbed his hand and held it in her lap. The back of his hand rested against her thigh, and the sensation caused something to stir inside him. He started to pull his hand away but didn't, though he knew he should. "What happened?"

She rubbed his hand and held on tightly. "It wasn't right. It never was. I knew that down deep. That's why I never broke up with you."

Austin shook his head as if clearing cobwebs from his

brain. He couldn't believe what he was hearing. "So you would have been fine continuing with Derek if I *hadn't* found out?"

"That's not what I meant. I knew it wasn't right and that I needed to end it, but—"

"But what?"

"But I didn't. And I'm ashamed." Savannah's face crumbled. She did nothing to stop the tears and clutched his hand as if it were a lifeline.

Her sudden need of his support, coupled with the touch of her leg against his hand, stirred something he'd forgotten. Even when crying, she was beautiful. Austin leaned closer, ready to tell her things would be okay.

Then, as if a cloud lifted and his thinking cleared, he knew what he needed to do. He pulled his hand away.

She grabbed for it but missed. "What?"

"You hurt me, Savannah. But even if you hadn't hurt me, I would have eventually hurt you."

Savannah shook her head. "You would never hurt me. It's not who you are."

Austin took a deep breath. "What we had wasn't really..." It took a couple moments to find his voice. "We had fun, but it wasn't the kind of... there wasn't a future there."

"How can you say that?" She sat up, ramrod straight. "I assumed we would get married. My mother did too, Austin. We even talked about it a few weeks ago. Remember? We said we would live someplace between Philly and Harrisburg while I work for the governor. Remember?"

He did. "Savannah—"

"You never said anything about not wanting to be together. Is this new, Austin? Is there someone else? Did you meet someone this summer?"

Austin swallowed and felt his stomach turning to mush. "Look, Savannah, I—"

"That's it, isn't it? There's someone else. I should have known when I didn't hear from you."

"I didn't call you because you were sleeping with my roommate," he snapped.

"And I said I was sorry!" Her voice rose. "What can I do to get us back to where we were?"

"It's too late."

Savannah massaged her temples. Was it the onset of one of her migraines? Austin patted her shoulder and she recoiled. "Don't touch me! Just get out of my car!"

Even though Bethany was several miles away, getting out and walking was preferable to riding back with her. He reached into his back pocket for his phone—

He'd left it at the house.

Walking still sounded good.

He got out and looked up and down the street, then started walking east, toward the beach. Toward the house on Riley Street.

He was already halfway down the block when he heard Savannah's car start. A few moments later, she pulled up alongside him and lowered the passenger window. "Get in. I'll take you back."

He shook his head and kept walking.

"Austin! Dammit, get in. I can at least do that much."

If there was a time to keep walking, that was it. But he longed for some type of closure that didn't involve her screaming at him. He got in and closed the door. "Take a left at the next—"

"I know how to get there!"

They rode in silence for a few minutes before she spoke again. Her tone was barely above a whisper.

"I hope she treats you well."

Austin nodded.

"Can you tell me her name?"

"It won't make any difference."

"I'm not sure if I should say this now, but Derek was a slouch in bed."

Austin felt a headache of his own coming on. "You shouldn't say it."

"And the asshole had the audacity to break up with me."

What?

"I thought you ended it. It was Derek?"

"I would have. I planned to, but he's not like you, Austin. He would rather spend his time doing whatever he and his genius-ass friends do."

There was nothing Austin could say to salvage the moment. No kind words. No offers of condolence. No hope for the future. He concentrated on the road.

And thought of Kathryn.

And how twisted, messed-up situations like what was happening between him and Savannah—petty jealousies and worries about who the other person was seeing or doing—would never be a part of his relationship with Kathryn.

He had outgrown that. Savannah had unknowingly helped him understand how important commitment and devotion were. Things between the two of them were ending badly, but the experience was making him a better person for Kate. And for that he would always be grateful.

"VICE PRESIDENT FOR STUDENT OUTREACH?" Suzanne exclaimed as they left the college on their way back to Bethany Beach. "What happened to Oscar Stevens?"

"He submitted his resignation the day before yesterday. He's taking a position at a private school in Ohio."

"That's just as well. He never really did anything. Why didn't you just accept it on the spot? You would be great in that position. It will be a pay increase, plus you won't have to worry about lesson plans and exams and all the crap we do as instructors."

"I want to talk to—" Kathryn stopped before saying Austin's name. It would probably sound ludicrous to Suzanne that she wanted to talk to her twenty-something boyfriend before accepting a position that would be a definite step forward in her career. "I want some time to think it over. There's no need to jump into something."

"I thought the new Kathryn—Kate—was about living in the moment."

"No, it's just that I've been a college instructor for so long that I'm not sure if I'm cut out for administration. Besides, I've really been enjoying the classroom a lot more lately."

"You need to do what's best for you. The board chair seemed like a decent enough person. It was interesting how she brought up that you've dedicated your life to your work." Suzanne giggled. "It made you sound like a nun in a convent."

"I don't want to be nun, Suzanne. It's just the way things played out. Until recently."

"By recently you're referring to him."

"His name is Austin. Can't you say it?"

"Sure, I can say it. Austin. There you go. Is that better?"

Suzanne's tone was stilted, and Kathryn wondered if she had more she wanted to say. They were quiet for a few moments before Suzanne spoke again. "What I don't understand, Kathryn, is why?"

Yep, she had more she wanted to say.

"Why?"

"He's a kid. I mean, not really, but he is. He's still in college. How can a guy that young give you what you need?"

"He's doing a far better job than anyone else ever did. And I thought you supported me, Suzanne. You said as much."

Suzanne slowed as she approached a crosswalk on the outskirts of Bethany. She checked both ways, then proceeded. "I do support you. And I also care about you. I've not said anything in front of Jane and Hillary, but this relationship worries me." She paused and glanced at Kathryn. "*You* worry me."

Was Suzanne kidding? She had been just a few moments before, about how the board chair had made her sound like a nun. Kathryn turned to get a good look at her.

Nope. She wasn't kidding. Her eyes were glued to the road ahead, but her jaw was set.

"Can't you just be happy for me, Suzanne? I might have expected blowback from Hillary or Jane, but you?"

"You aren't thinking this through, Kathryn. I'm certain of it. You've never rushed into anything like you have this relationship. He's a kid."

"He's a man," Kathryn snapped.

"He's weeks removed from spending weekends with his college sweetheart. And suddenly he's sharing your house and your life."

"You don't understand, Suzanne."

"Maybe not, but what would you have said if I showed up at Milo's some Saturday and dropped the bombshell that I had a new guy in my life and he had already moved in... and that he's fifteen years younger than me?"

"I would have said..." The truth was, Kathryn didn't know what she might say. The image of Suzanne and a much younger guy was impossible to conjure up. When she didn't finish what she had been about to say, Suzanne continued.

"What if this is just a physical thing? What young man wouldn't be enthralled by the possibilities of being with an older woman?"

"Seriously, Suzanne?" Kathryn scoffed. "For two years he's dated a girl who's drop-dead gorgeous and slept with him regularly. If it was about sex, do you think he would have left her for me?"

Suzanne raised her hands. "We're talking about a young guy here. With young-guy curiosity and a sex drive like a... I just don't want you to be hurt if he heads back to his little coed. Or finds another one."

What could she say that would convince Suzanne that she wasn't being irrational? Sure, there was a chance she could be hurt, but a person had to take an occasional risk of being hurt, right? And she was discovering how much more she liked herself when she took risks. The thought of returning to a time when Saturday mornings at Milo's were the highlight of her week made her claustrophobic. There was more to life, and she hated that she'd nearly given up searching for it.

Fortunately, she didn't have to continue the discussion. Suzanne hung a right onto Sea Turtle Court.

"I thought Austin would be here," Kathryn said when

Suzanne stopped in front of her house. "I called him a hundred times."

Suzanne was probably thinking something like, *Get used to it. He's a kid.* Fortunately, she didn't say it. "Want me to wait here?"

"No, but thanks. Having you with me this morning meant so much, but I'm fine now. Can I ask a favor, though?"

"Of course."

"Austin and his grandfather are rehabbing a house on Riley Street. It's about two miles from here. Would you drop me off on your way home? I suspect he got involved with the remodel and lost track of time."

A few minutes later, they pulled up in front of the house. Austin's grandpa was on the front steps, chugging a bottle of Gatorade.

"Hello, Charlie!" Kathryn called out.

"Hey, Kathryn." Charlie shielded his eyes from the sun's glare. "Who's that with you?"

"It's me, Charlie. Suzanne." Suzanne waved just as the professor stepped outside to join them.

"Who is that?" Suzanne whispered, nodding at the professor.

"That's Vi. He's the Penn professor I told you about. Want to meet him?"

"I wish I had time, but I really need to get back. But please think about what we talked about, will you?"

The farewell was awkward, and Kathryn was relieved when Suzanne pulled away. She crossed the yard and stepped onto the porch. "Is Austin upstairs?"

"He left a couple hours ago," Charlie said. "I assumed he was picking you up."

"I've been at the college all morning. He couldn't have gone far. Your car is here and Calvin is parked out front."

"That's the darndest thing," Charlie said, following Kathryn's gaze toward the driveway. "I could have sworn I heard a car take off when he left. You want me to take you back to your place, Kathryn?"

"Would it be okay if I wait here?"

Vi hustled back inside and retrieved a lawn chair. "I brought this with me, but Charlie never allows me time to sit." He opened it and set it to one side of the porch, then waved with a flourish. "For you, madam. And you have to tell me all about the lovely lady who dropped you off."

"Why, Vi, if I didn't know better, I would think you might be interested in getting to know my friend Suzanne."

"If she's single, I'm interested," he said with a laugh. "Why were you at work on a Saturday morning? Preparing for the coming week?"

Kathryn filled them in on what had taken place, including the fear she'd felt that she might be in some kind of trouble.

They celebrated her award with bottles of water. "You must be quite the educator," Vi said.

"I don't know about that, but I try." Kathryn felt herself choke up. "Austin has helped me so much. The field trips were his idea." She glanced toward the street. "I wish I knew where he was."

⋔

THE TEMPERATURES HAD FALLEN ten degrees since they had left the house. When they were a block away, the skies opened and it began to pour. Savannah fumbled to get the windshield wipers working.

"Are you heading back to Pennsylvania?" Austin asked. "It's supposed to get bad later today. There's a hurricane out in the Atlantic."

Savannah shuddered, either because of the falling temperature or because of what was happening between them. She flipped off the air conditioner and leaned forward to see better. "Yeah, I'm going back. There's nothing here for me."

Austin was at a loss as to what he could say.

Can we still be friends?

Wasn't that what people said when they were breaking up?

You'll be okay.

True, but Savannah probably didn't want to hear that from him.

I wish you well.

Puh-leeze.

No, it was best to say nothing.

"Maybe we'll run into each other back at Penn," she said as they turned onto Riley Street.

"Yeah. Maybe."

She pulled to the curb, then reconsidered and pulled into the driveway behind Grandma's Buick. "The least I can do is get close to the door so you won't get completely soaked."

<hr>

KATHRYN CALLED Austin's phone three more times with no luck. She pulled the chair inside when the rain started and sat in the gloom as Vi worked upstairs and Charlie hung cabinets in the kitchen.

As she waited, she had time to think. Vi's hammering

and the sound of Charlie's electric drill provided a staccato of white noise that allowed her to lose herself in thought. Thoughts about the summer. And of Austin. And what was happening between them.

Along with those thoughts were concerns. Was Suzanne right about their compatibility? Was the age difference fair to Austin? Fifteen years was a lot, and while the gap seemed less as people aged, it could well rear its head later in life. What if she fell into ill health at seventy? He would be fifty-five. Probably still practicing law or swinging a hammer or doing whatever his future held. How would he feel about having to take care of a sick, elderly woman? And who was to say that some forty-year-old with a good figure and good health might catch his eye?

And what about things like childbirth and menopause? Sure, there was still time for babies, but she had read somewhere that the average age for the onset of menopause was between forty-five and fifty-five. The lower number was only eight years away. That scared her. What if Austin wanted children? What if he wanted children and they struggled to conceive? The clock would always be ticking.

And speaking of kids? What would their children think when they were in junior high and their parents showed up for school events? There would be their father, young and handsome, next to their much older mom. Would she be an embarrassment to her own children?

Maybe *RodneySellsRehoboth* was right all along. Maybe she was destined to be an old maid schoolteacher after all.

"Stop it, Kathryn," she chided herself.

"Did you say something?"

She hadn't seen Charlie enter the room. "Just talking to myself."

"Okay, but if you need anything you know where to find me." He headed back to the kitchen.

Kathryn stood and walked to the front windows. They were covered with sawdust and dirt, and the rain and humidity had steamed them up. She pulled a tissue from her pocket and rubbed a spot so she could look out.

There was a car in the driveway. Its lights were on, and the wipers were working against the steady rain.

Hadn't she seen that car before? Maybe a few weeks earlier—

Savannah!

Kathryn cleared a larger spot in the window and raised a hand to her brow to better see through the filmy mist.

There were two people inside the car.

One was Austin.

†††††

SAVANNAH TURNED TO FACE HIM. Her eyes bored into his as they always did, and Austin could hear the pain in her voice when she asked, "How are these moments supposed to end?"

He understood what she meant. They were parting ways as a couple. And while he had already put that part of his life behind him, she hadn't. "I think it's best that we just say goodbye and I get out."

She glanced away. The breath she took was ragged, as if she might begin crying again. "Is it that easy for you, Austin?"

He had no answer. At least none that would assuage her hurt feelings.

"Does she treat you well?"

His stomach lurched. There was no good way to

respond. At least none that could help Savannah. It was probably best to get it over with. "We're still getting to know one another, but yes. She treats me well, and I hope I do the same for her."

"You do," Savannah said softly. "You've always been wonderful to me. Even when I didn't deserve it."

When he didn't reply, she took a deep breath and said, "Take care, Austin."

The way she spoke the words did something to him. He tried to speak, but the words caught in his throat. Could he get out of the car without crying? "You too, Savannah." He reached for the door handle, ready to break away and end an impossibly hard moment.

She rested her hand on his shoulder. "Can I give you a hug?"

No. It's probably not a good idea.

But he had already hurt her enough. What could one quick hug hurt?

He opened his arms. She leaned into him. It was awkward over the console, but sweet in its own way. She nuzzled her head against his chest and sighed. Not long ago, that would have been enough for him to want to go further. To gently lift her face and kiss her. To let her know he was there for her.

When some of those old familiar feelings surfaced, he knew it was time to let go. He pulled away. She clung for a moment, then turned and looked away.

It was over. He closed the car door and walked slowly, sluggishly toward the porch, making a point not to look back. As he reached the front door, he heard her backing from the driveway. He stepped inside. Only then did he venture a glance over his shoulder.

Savannah was gone.

"Hey, Austin."

Vi's greeting from the top of the stairs made him jump.

"Sorry to scare you," Vi said. "Is everything okay?"

"Yeah. I think everything's okay. I need to go back to Kathryn's house."

"She's here."

Austin's chest tightened. He looked past Vi, but there was no sign of her.

"Maybe she's in the kitchen with Charlie," Vi said. "Charlie?"

"Yeah, Vi? You need help with something?"

"Is Kathryn with you?"

Grandpa stepped out of the kitchen. "No. She was right here looking out the window a few minutes ago." He pointed to a spot where the window had been wiped clean. "She was watching for you, Austin."

She had been watching. What she saw must have hurt terribly. And that made him hurt. And frantic to find her. Austin did a quick walk through the first floor. He reached the back of the house and found the door ajar. He went outside and checked the backyard, but again, no Kathryn.

"Kate?" he yelled.

There was no response. Other than the sound of rain splattering against the house and the hum of traffic in the distance, all was silent.

THE UBER DROPPED Kathryn off at the corner of Pennsylvania Avenue and Second Street, a block west of the Bethany Beach boardwalk. The rain had stopped, but with streets wet and the sky threatening, pedestrians were few. It was perfect for walking. And thinking.

She took off in the direction of the ocean and wished she had a sweater. The storm had chilled the air into the sixties. She considered cutting down Pennsylvania toward Sea Turtle Court, but she needed time to process things.

Damn the thoughts.

And the doubts.

She saw what she saw. That much was certain.

Austin in the car with Savannah.

Talking.

Embracing.

Just like he had embraced her that morning.

There was a reasonable explanation.

Wasn't there?

Kathryn turned south when she reached the boardwalk. The breeze sent a chill down her spine. She passed storefronts but didn't stop to window-shop.

What would he say? How would he explain?

It wasn't like Savannah was around all the time. She wouldn't have come to Bethany without a reason.

And he wouldn't have gotten in the car with her. And hugged her. Without a reason.

Or many reasons... like fifteen.

One for every year that separated them. The college kid and the old maid schoolteacher. The professor who had dedicated her life to students. But really hadn't. That was just an excuse for striking out at love.

Was Suzanne right?

Was Kathryn setting herself up for heartache?

And what about Austin?

Was it fair to him to be saddled in a relationship with someone like her? Someone who was still trying to find herself? Someone who was looking for something more to life, and whose path he just happened to cross at the right time?

Or the wrong time?

Kathryn stepped onto the beach. The sand was hard-packed and wet. And cold. She pulled off her sandals and walked to the edge of the surf. The waves were high, as they usually were when storms were brewing. She stepped close enough to allow those waves to wash over her feet. The water was warmer than she'd expected. Cringeworthy to those used to the warm Gulf currents of Florida, but pleasant to the more weathered souls who claimed Bethany as their own.

"What do I do?" she asked aloud. She considered repeating herself, even screaming into the wind.

She didn't, though. There was no need.

She knew the answer.

She knew what she needed to do.

She needed to do what she hadn't done with Troy. Get things out in the open.

But she also needed to trust Austin. He was younger and perhaps less mature in some ways, but if there was any chance of a long-term relationship, she needed to trust him.

And she also needed to give him the space he needed to grow and mature.

Because whether she wanted to admit it or not, fifteen years was a lot.

It was time to go home.

⊞

KATHRYN'S CAR WAS HOME, but where was she?

Austin called her name as he walked through the house, just to be sure something hadn't happened to her. She had likely seen him arrive at the Riley Street house with Savannah, and if she saw him arrive, she'd also witnessed their farewell. How must that have looked? Without the benefit of knowing what had led to that moment? He knew how he would feel if the situation were reversed; if he saw Kathryn hugging another man, he would be hurt. And mad.

Or would he?

It was hard to say because of the nature of their relationship. The petty jealousies occasionally expressed by Savannah over the past two years didn't seem to exist between him and Kathryn. If he came across her and another man, and they were hugging, he would assume there was a perfectly good reason, right? That was the way Kathryn was. She assumed the best of him, and, by assuming the best, she made him better.

And that was one more reason he loved her so much.

But where was she?

THE RAIN RETURNED with a fury as Kathryn walked home. Three blocks seemed like three miles as she trudged through a cold northwesterly wind with raindrops smacking her cheeks. By the time she reached the front porch, her clothes were wringing wet, and her hair hung down her face and neck.

But Austin's car in the driveway made her happy.

At first.

Until the lingering doubts crept back. She'd decided that her worries dealt less with the sight of Austin and Savannah and more with her own insecurities. Was Austin up to hearing about all of that? He was at an age where fraternity mixers and video games provided escapes from dealing with life's problems. *Well, buddy,* she thought as she fished her keys from her waterlogged purse, *there ain't gonna be no dodging this.*

She didn't get the key in the lock before the door opened. It was him, dry and warm in blue shorts and a Philadelphia Eagles T-shirt. He looked her up and down, then up and down again.

"I got caught in the rain," Kathryn said. "I was at the beach and—"

"Kate, I'm sorry for what you saw at the house. Me and Savannah. I want you to know—"

"Savannah and me," Kathryn said, cutting him off.

She hoped her smile might ease his worry, but other than blinking a few times, he still looked concerned.

"Okay... Savannah and me. But it wasn't like it looked, Kate. We were—"

"I know, Austin. I trust you."

▟▛▟▛

SHE TRUSTED HIM. She knew he wouldn't cheat on her.

But why was she so distant? And her eyes. They were sad.

"I'm so glad to hear that," Austin said as he held out his arms, an invitation to come close.

But she didn't. "Can we talk?" she asked.

His stomach hurt. "Uh, sure. In the living room?"

"Yes, but let me shower and change first."

He watched her head for the stairs.

Instead of following her, he stayed downstairs and wandered from the kitchen to the living room, then back. He heard water running and knew it was the master bath. They had showered together two evenings earlier, a first for him, and an experience that had threatened to short-circuit his senses. Later they had lain in the darkness and talked about whatever came to mind. Kate wanted to know everything about the progress on the Riley Street house. She asked about his classes and gently scolded him when he confessed he was a week behind in Organizational Theory. She made him promise he would catch up, and he had the next morning.

The water stopped running. She would be downstairs in a few minutes, so he took a deep breath and sat down to wait.

HE WAS on the sofa when Kathryn returned. He had seemed nervous earlier, but he looked downright scared now.

She shouldn't have stressed him out like this, but such an intimate conversation would have been impossible while dripping wet. No, it was good she had made them wait. Now, though, where should she sit? It was so tempting to cuddle up against him on the sofa, but that would make it much harder to get the words out.

As if reading her mind, Austin sat up a little straighter and patted the spot next to him.

Kathryn moved to the far end of the sofa, then reconsidered and scooched over. Austin held out his hand, and she took it.

"Are you breaking up with me, Kate?" he asked.

She squeezed his hand. She hadn't noticed he was trembling.

"No, Austin. Not really *breaking up*. More like..." Darn it. She thought she had committed to memory what she wanted to say, but with him seated next to her and hearing the fear and concern in each labored breath, it wasn't like she had rehearsed. Nothing like it at all.

"It's because of Savannah, isn't it?"

"It's not. But seeing the two of you—"

"She came to Bethany to tell me she wanted to get back together, but I said no, so she—"

"Really, Austin, you don't have to tell me. I knew that you and Savannah were—"

He wiped his eye with the back of his hand. "I do have to tell you, Kate, because if you hadn't seen us together, we wouldn't be sitting here about to have a discussion I don't want to have."

Her heart broke a little. "Maybe not now," she said, forcing herself to go on. "But eventually we would be here. It's not just Savannah, Austin. It's us, the difference in our ages."

Austin looked into her eyes. "We've gone over this before. I don't care about that, Kate. What I feel for you has nothing to do with age."

"Remember when we were at the outlet mall and you waited outside while I checked out at the last store? Remember the girl who came over and started talking to you?"

His gaze turned skyward as if searching to recall that moment. "Maybe? Did she have red hair?"

"No. She was a blonde. She asked you something. I don't know what, but you smiled and said something back to her. She put her hand on your arm. Do you remember that?"

He shook his head. "I remember waiting for you while you paid. And thinking about how I had never expected shopping to be fun." He paused. "I remember thinking how incredible you would look in a bikini."

"How about when you came to school to pick me up and go dumpster shopping? Remember that?"

"How could I forget? We had a great day."

"You were waiting for me outside my classroom, and several of my students were checking you out. Brianna, Chloe, and a couple of others. They were ogling your biceps when I came out."

Austin shook his head. "I remember you had on a green dress. Sleeveless. You were beautiful."

Why was he making this so hard? Kathryn took a deep breath. "I'm thirty-seven. In thirteen years, I'll be fifty and you still won't be thirty-seven. Have you taken a good look at any fifty-year-old women, Austin?"

"No, but I never looked at any thirty-seven-year-old women before you."

"I'll be in the middle of menopause and you'll still be at your sexual peak. I'll be starting to droop and you'll be flashing those big muscular arms. It's not fair, Austin. It's not fair to you."

"How about you let me decide what's fair to me?"

She squeezed his hands again, preparing for what she had intended to say all along. "I'm not saying we completely break things off. I just think we should step back and consider where we are."

He shook his head. "I don't know what that means."

"You need to see women your age. And I... need to see men with whom I have things in common." There. She'd said the words, but she wasn't feeling them. Hopefully he wouldn't pick up on that.

"You mean like Scott?"

"No—I mean, yes, like Scott, but not Scott."

"I thought you didn't like Scott."

"I didn't, but I didn't really give him a fair shake either. I just..." What in the heck was she trying to say? That she slept with him and dumped him? That wasn't what she was looking for. Not at all. What she was looking for was sitting right next to her. But he needed a chance to be certain if the same was true for him. It was a chance he wouldn't have unless she did what she was about to do. What she needed to do.

"Austin, I want you to move out. I think you should date other women. I want to continue to see you when we can, but I also think you need to pursue relationships with women your age."

Those muscular shoulders that Brianna and Chloe had drooled over slumped. He shook his head, but no words came.

Somehow he needed to understand that she had his best interests in—

Someone pounded at the door.

Kathryn jumped to her feet, Austin too. Who would hammer on her door like the world was on fire?

It was Vi. His eyes were wide with fear. "Charlie fell. I found him and called the ambulance. He's... he's... I don't know if he's going to make it."

iiiiiii

AUSTIN DIDN'T WAIT for Vi to move his car. He made a U-turn in the yard, nearly backing over the picket fence in his haste to make it to the hospital in Lewes, twenty miles north.

Vi had returned from his lunch run to find Grandpa unconscious in the rain-soaked yard. A toppled extension ladder lay on the ground nearby. The emergency team that responded told Vi that Grandpa was struggling to breathe and that there might be other internal injuries. Falling, even when the ground was saturated with rainwater, could result in catastrophe.

What had Grandpa been doing on the wet roof?

Was he going to be okay?

Austin beat his fists on the steering wheel as he waited for a light to change on the outskirts of Rehoboth Beach. Traffic was heavy, with cars pulling in and out of shops and restaurants. After a near miss with a minivan, he slowed down enough to avoid winding up in the hospital himself.

He was pulling into the emergency room parking lot when Kathryn called. In his haste to leave, he hadn't said goodbye, but the thought of their discussion added to his panic. He let the call go to voicemail.

He asked about Grandpa at the check-in desk and was told to wait. He sat in the corner of the ER waiting area that was overflowing with scrapes, cuts, and other maladies. Five minutes stretched to fifteen before he was called back to the desk.

"Your grandfather was transferred to Penn Presbyterian in Philadelphia," the receptionist said. "They left here a half hour ago."

"Why?" Austin asked. "What was his condition?"

"I don't have that information."

"Who does?"

"The attending physician, Dr. Leftwich."

"Get him for me, please."

"I can't do that. He's in surgery. That's part of the reason your grandfather was transferred. We're experiencing a high volume of emergencies today because of the weather."

Austin clenched his fists and felt the muscles in his neck grow tense. "So you're saying that no one can tell me what happened to my grandfather?"

The receptionist's eyes grew soft. "I understand your worry. I really do, and I know you want answers. If I were you, I would take off for Presbyterian. I'll give Dr. Leftwich your number and have him call you, but by the time he's out of surgery, you might already be there."

Austin tore a sheet of paper from a pad on the counter and jotted down his number.

"Do you need directions to Presbyterian?" the receptionist asked.

"I know where it is." He handed the slip of paper to her. "But thank you."

She squeezed his hand as she took the paper. "I saw your grandfather before he left. I would encourage you to get there as quickly as you can, but be safe, okay?"

Her words brought a glimmer of hope to the moment. Austin turned and started for the exit.

"Young man," the receptionist called to him. He turned. "I'll be praying for your grandfather."

████

KATHRYN TRIED Austin's number again, but again it went to voicemail. The rain was picking up as Vi drove through stop-and-go traffic. She sensed the guilt he was feeling for not being there when Charlie had fallen, but her thoughts were on Austin and how much he was having to deal with. First her, then his grandfather, a man he revered.

There was no sign of Austin's car in the hospital parking lot, and inside was a madhouse. Vi tried to get information from the receptionist at the front desk, but when she learned they were not related to Charlie, she told them she couldn't give out any information.

Frustrated, Vi turned to Kathryn. "What do we do now?"

"Let's go to my house and hope Austin calls us."

The receptionist looked up from her computer. "Austin? Are you friends of the patient's grandson?"

"Yes," Kathryn said quickly. "I'm his... we're close friends."

The woman nodded. "He left here about twenty minutes ago. He's on his way to Philadelphia. Unfortunately I can't tell you any more than that." She reached below her desk and pulled out Austin's phone. "This fell from his pocket when he was waiting for the doctor. Can you see that he gets it?"

OUTSIDE DOVER, Austin pulled into a convenience store parking lot after searching for his phone without success. He got out and checked under the seats and anywhere else it might have dropped. He tried to remember the last time he had it and realized it was while he was waiting to speak to someone at the hospital. That was fifty miles back. He would lose two precious hours if he returned, so that was out of the question. He got back in the car and took off. If traffic was light and the cops weren't running radar, he could make it to Presbyterian in a little over an hour.

BACK IN THE CAR, Kathryn hit the home button on Austin's phone and saw he had several missed messages. She tried to unlock the phone, but her code guesses didn't work.

"Try his birthday," Vi offered as they pulled from the hospital parking lot.

It didn't work.

"Try your birthday."

Again, no luck.

"Try his home address."

"I don't know it."

Vi pointed the car toward Bethany. "I need to lock up the house," he said. "Do you want me to drop you off at home?"

"I'll go with you. Maybe we'll hear from Austin."

▥

PRESBYTERIAN HOSPITAL WAS SPREAD out over a large swath of real estate northeast of the Penn campus. Austin was familiar with the area, but had no idea which building was which. He drove to the center of the complex, lucked into a parking spot, and took off on a dead run for the closest building.

The first person he found had no idea where the trauma unit might be located, but the second pointed out a building not far away. Inside, the attendant told him Grandpa was in the intensive care unit. He gave Austin directions, but it still took two wrong turns before he found the ICU.

The entrance was closed, and a sign said to pick up a nearby phone for assistance. When he told them who he was, someone buzzed him in, and he continued down the hallway until he found room 571. It had been exactly two hours since he left Lewes when he walked into Grandpa's room.

What he saw took his breath away.

Grandpa was in the room's only bed, a sheet spread haphazardly over his legs and right side. A tube filled with blood came from his left side just below his ribs. His breathing was ragged, his eyes were closed, and his skin had a bluish pallor. Beeping monitors flashed a steady stream of numbers across a screen.

Austin moved closer and was about to speak when a man in scrubs who was not much older than him came up behind him. "Are you a relative?" the man asked.

Austin choked up as he spoke. "He's my grandpa."

"I'm Montel, his nurse for today. Do you have questions?"

Austin shook his head and fought to keep from breaking down. "Is he going to be okay?"

"He's stable. We're watching to see if he needs surgery. We should know within the next couple hours."

"Why does he have the tube in his side?"

"Your grandfather suffered two broken ribs. One punctured his left lung. The tube is draining blood from the area. He's sedated because of the pain and trauma."

Austin looked down at Grandpa as he fought to maintain his composure. If he had been there, Grandpa would never have been on the roof. Austin wouldn't have let him. Allowing him to help on the house had been a huge mistake, one that he hoped didn't result in... No, he didn't want to think about that. He had to believe that Grandpa would pull through. He was tough, the toughest person Austin had ever known.

But Grandpa didn't look so tough at the moment. And Austin got scared all over again.

"You can only stay for a few minutes," Montel said softly. "There's a waiting room down the hall. When I hear anything, I'll let you know."

He didn't want to leave. Someone needed to be there, just in case Grandpa woke. But he needed to allow the doctors and nurses space to do their jobs. He swallowed. Wiped his tears. "Is there a chapel close by?"

There was. A few minutes later, Austin stepped inside the silent room. It was tiny but very churchlike. He hadn't been to church since elementary school when the family moved to the city and drifted away from regular attendance. He took a seat in the empty chapel and looked up at the ceiling, then down at the floor.

And he cried.

VI LOCKED up the Riley Street house and gave the keys to Kathryn.

"Will you see that Austin gets these? I'm going back to Philadelphia. There's no reason for me to stick around."

She took the keys, and the uncertainty of the situation hit hard. Her last words to Austin had been that he should move out. Would she see him again? Had she pushed too hard? Too quickly? Her heart broke for him and for what he was going through. Maybe she should get in her car and follow Vi back to Philadelphia.

But how could she find Austin or Charlie without knowing what hospital they were at?

She put the keys in her pocket. They returned to Vi's car

and he drove her home. They said quiet goodbyes and promised to keep in touch.

︎

A CUSTODIAN POINTED Austin to the hospital cafeteria where he bought a ham sandwich and two bottles of water. He retraced his steps to the ICU and stepped into a cramped waiting area near Grandpa's room. Mom, Dad, and Holly were gathered around a small table. Holly and Mom were busy on their laptops. Dad was immersed in his phone. They didn't see Austin, and for a moment he felt an overwhelming need to flee.

Then Dad looked up. "Austin, where the hell have you been?" His tone was sharp, and he nearly stumbled as he sprang from his seat.

Mom was right behind him. Holly remained seated, but her expression told Austin everything he needed to know. Things weren't good.

"We've been trying to call you for hours!" Mom cried. "Did you know Grandpa was down at the Delaware shore?"

"Of course he didn't, Charla," Dad said. He turned back to Austin. "Grandpa suffered some kind of fall. We're not sure how. We called you, but you didn't answer. They transported him here after they figured out how serious things were."

"They think they'll have to operate," Mom said. Her eyes had that wide, deer-in-the-headlights look. "I talked to him Wednesday, but he never said a thing about taking a trip."

Holly locked eyes with Austin. She was savvy enough to put the puzzle pieces together. And she was waiting for him to acknowledge the truth. The set of her jaw and the way she pursed her lips said that all hell was going to break loose when he spoke.

His earlier inclination to flee had been on the mark, but he wasn't thirteen anymore. It was time to tell them everything, accept responsibility, and clear the air. "I took on the renovation project on Riley Street. Grandpa came down to help."

Mom was speechless.

Dad, not so much. "I don't understand," he said. "You said you had hired a company. What was it called, Charla?"

Mom didn't speak. She lowered herself into her chair as she shook her head sadly.

"Picket Fence Construction," Austin said. "I made it up."

Dad's eyes blazed. "You made it up," he spat. "Let me guess. You either fell behind or screwed up and called Grandpa to come bail you out. Which is it?"

"Neither. Well, I did fall behind, but Grandpa was bored at home and just showed up.

"Where were you when he fell?" He pivoted to Holly. "That's workers' comp, isn't it?"

Holly shrugged.

"He was at the house. For some reason, he climbed up on the roof. It had been raining and I suspect he slipped, but I wasn't there, so I—"

Mom was on her feet again. She came closer. "You let him crawl on the roof alone? Austin, how could you? You knew he fell and hurt himself years ago. That's why he retired."

"Mom, he wasn't alone. I had just left. Vi was there, but we never figured Grandpa would—"

"Who the hell is Vi?" Dad asked.

"He's one of my college professors at Penn. He—"

"A college professor?" Dad said, his tone skeptical. "This

story gets crazier by the second."

"Look, Dad, it's... Mom, Grandpa was working on..." Austin could see in their faces that they were dubious. And angry. And why wouldn't they be? He had been evasive about his activities in Bethany, and Grandpa was injured as a result. Was it too late to turn and run?

"Hold on a minute." Holly's tone was calm. She didn't even stand up as she spoke. "Mom and Dad, come sit down, please. Austin, you too. I think it's best that we start at the beginning."

"Did you know something about this, Holly?" Mom asked as they returned to the table.

"Yes, but hear Austin out."

They reluctantly returned to their seats. Austin started from the beginning. Repairing the fence, the preliminary demo work he did. His love for construction. Borrowing Grandpa's power tools.

"And things were going really well," he explained. "I was falling behind, partially because of trouble getting subs, but also because it was more work than one person could do alone."

He told them about Professor Chakraborty and the relationship they had built. "He's a great professor, but even a better carpenter."

He shared how Grandpa had gotten in touch and about his desire to help, smiling sadly as he described how Vi and Grandpa had become buddies over seafood and beers at Elijah's. "It was a side of Grandpa I haven't seen since Grandma passed," he said. "He was dancing and telling stories. It was the most fun I've had with him in a long time."

Then he shared how he had broken things off with Savannah.

Mom and Dad listened intently but said little. Austin thought he saw a change in Mom's demeanor when he mentioned how much Grandpa was enjoying himself. She even laughed when Austin said, "Grandpa moved into the Windermere and said it wasn't as bad as the army. I think he actually liked it."

Dad didn't laugh. "If Grandpa was at the Windermere, where were you?"

Holly had maintained a poker face throughout, but Dad's question piqued her curiosity. She leaned a little closer.

"I stayed at the Riley Street house for a while. I kept an upstairs bedroom closed up." He'd reached the point where he needed to mention Kathryn. He took a deep breath. "I met a woman this summer."

Dad nodded and waited for him to go on.

Mom blinked. "A *woman*?"

Austin nodded. "Her name is Kathryn."

"A woman?" Mom said again. "Not a girl? A woman?"

"Mom, I'm twenty-two. I'm not a boy anymore."

Dad seemed to accept his answer, but Holly appeared more interested than ever.

But Mom wasn't done. "How old is this woman, Austin?"

"Her name is Kathryn, Mom. Kathryn Shea."

Mom and Dad waited for him to continue.

Holly grabbed her phone and started typing, clearly checking social media for Kathryn Shea. He would have done the same thing for any guy she was dating. It's what siblings did.

"She owns the house on Sea Turtle Court, next to our rental. It was her fence that our tenants trashed. I got to know her while I was repairing it."

"And you moved in?"

"Eventually. Not right away. It was..." Geesh, why did he feel like he was ten years old again and Mom was grilling him about who ate the entire box of Ding Dongs? "It was later. The Riley Street house was hot and full of dust, and she asked me."

"So let me get this straight," Dad interrupted. "There is no Picket Fence Construction? You made that up so you could do the work yourself?"

"Leave that for a minute, Jay," Mom said. "I want to know more about where you've been staying, Austin. And about that woman. What did you say her name was?"

"Kathryn. She teaches at the community college. English and literature."

"You've been shacking up with a college professor?"

Dad frowned. "How close to done are you on the house?"

"Jay, stop. Just stop! Austin, how old is she?"

"Thirty-seven."

Now Dad was interested. "Holy crap, Austin!"

Holly whistled in disbelief.

Mom's eyes couldn't have gotten wider without her eyeballs falling out. "She's *fifteen years* older than you? Isn't that illegal?"

"Austin's twenty-two, Mom," Holly said. "He's an adult."

"I don't care. If she's thirty-seven, then she's too old to—"

"Mrs. McGinnis?"

Mom turned toward the door where a white-coated, gray-haired woman stood framed in the door.

"Dr. Zeller, hello again." Mom nodded at Austin. "This is our son, Austin. He just arrived."

"Yes, we could hear your discussion down the hall. I wanted to tell you we're taking your father back for surgery. He has a massive hemothorax, and his CT scan shows a lung laceration that needs to be repaired."

Mom grew misty eyed. Dad put his arm around her, and she leaned into him. "What are the risks, Dr. Zeller?" he asked. "Is Charlie going to be okay?"

"Mr. Staley's age is a factor. Falls like he experienced can affect the body in ways that we don't know until we operate. Also, the anesthesia is harder on us as we grow older. And we're uncertain what we'll find when we get into the lung area. There are definite concerns."

"How long will surgery take?" Austin asked.

"It depends. A couple hours, maybe more. I'll come see you as soon as we finish."

Dr. Zeller left, and silence filled the room. Mom sank down onto the couch. Dad joined her and held her hand.

Holly glanced at Austin. "I'm going to get something to eat. Anyone want anything?"

Mom didn't answer, and Dad said no.

Holly tipped her head toward the hallway. "Austin, come with me," she said.

They grabbed some snacks and found a table in the crowded cafeteria. "What a mess," Austin said as he pulled open a bag of corn chips.

"Which mess? Grandpa's condition or yours?" She cracked a smile. "Grandpa will probably pull through, but I'm pretty sure that Mom's not done with you yet."

"Yeah," he deadpanned. "You think?"

"Tell me about this..." She formed air quotes with her fingers. "...*woman* you're shacked up with."

She was pulling his chain, which was a relief after the scene in the waiting room. "We're not really shacking up anymore. She was kicking me out when I got word about Grandpa."

"Oh, little brother, I'm sorry." Holly reached out and squeezed his arm. "Want to talk about it? And don't give me that famous Austin shrug."

Austin smiled. "Kathryn says the same thing, that I shrug when I should be speaking."

"Use your words!" Holly scolded good-naturedly. "That's what Mom used to say when you were little. Even then you shrugged."

"Kate thinks that her being older than me will lead to problems, that I'll grow restless and want to find someone closer to my age."

"Like Savannah?"

"Definitely not Savannah. If there's one thing that came out of being with Kate, it's that I know what an adult relationship looks like."

"So, it wasn't just about the sex?"

His cheeks grew hot. "I'm not talking about sex with you, Holly. But, no, it was never about that. It's about how Kate listens to me and wants to know how I feel about things. We talk about books and current events, and I even came up with some ideas to help her with her classes."

"Still, whether you want to acknowledge the age thing or not, it's a legitimate concern. Even a knucklehead like you should have picked up on that. We women worry about the way we look. Guys are part of the problem. You expect us to weigh the same as when you met us, even after you put us through the agony of having babies. We deal with hormones and menopause and sagging boobs and butts, then you expect us to throw on some sexy nightie and seduce you."

"I don't care about all that. I just love being with her."

"You've got it bad, don't you?" Holly said.

He did.

"You're going to need every bit of fortitude you can find by the time Mom and Dad are done with you."

Holly didn't finish her thought, but Austin knew where she was going. Not telling them he had taken on the renovation was one thing. Pulling Grandpa into the mix was another.

And Kathryn? Austin had assumed the age thing wouldn't be an unsurmountable hurdle for his parents. Now he wasn't so sure.

▥

THE DARKNESS WAS alive with the sounds of rain and the occasional clap of thunder. It was after nine, and Kathryn had called seven Philadelphia hospitals to find Charlie. Several said that policies dictated they could not confirm or deny that any patient might be there. The others reported he was not a patient in their facilities.

She was considering a more thorough search of suburban hospitals when Vi texted her. *I found out through a Penn colleague that Charlie is at Presbyterian Med. No visitors other than family, though. I'm going to try to get in tomorrow.*

I'm going with you. Kathryn texted back. *I'll leave here first thing in the morning.*

▥

THERE WAS another family clustered in a corner of the waiting room when Austin and Holly returned. Austin took a deep breath before sitting down with his parents to further explain what had happened in Bethany Beach. The first words were barely out of his mouth before Mom made a slashing motion with her right hand. "Not now," she snapped. "I have enough to worry about with your grandfather. The last thing I want to talk about is some adult woman with designs on my son."

"Mom," Holly said cautiously. "You should listen to Austin. He wants to—"

"Holly! Don't think I've forgotten that you were privy to some of this and neglected to tell me. We're not talking about it now, and that's that."

The force behind Mom's words caught the attention of the family seated across the waiting room. Seeing he wasn't getting anywhere, Austin sank onto one end of the open sofa while Holly took the other.

Things were quiet until a few minutes before eleven when Dr. Zeller appeared. They all stood and waited for her to speak.

She cleared her throat and smiled slightly, the first sign that things might turn out okay. "Mr. Staley is out of surgery. We located and repaired the laceration without having to remove any of his lung. He lost a lot of blood, so he'll be receiving a transfusion, but that shouldn't be an issue. We'll keep him intubated and sedated for the next forty-eight hours so that the lung can heal, but all in all he came through well and I believe he'll be just fine."

There was a collective sigh of relief. Mom smiled through her tears while Dad pulled her into a tight hug. Holly high-fived Austin, then leaned in close and whispered, "One family emergency down, one to go. If it means anything, little brother, I'm on your side."

TWENTY-SIX

sunday, july 10

KATHRYN WAS ALREADY AWAKE when Vi texted her at six thirty.

Weather is miserable here. Flash flooding and high winds along the coast. Probably best to put off the trip.

It was expected, but still she wanted to see Austin and let him know she was there for him. Charlie too since he had been so kind to her.

She turned on the television and chose the same spot on the sofa where she and Austin had sat the day before. She pressed her nose to the back cushion and thought she could detect his cologne.

Was he thinking about her like she was thinking about him?

Fat chance. Not after she'd said they needed more time apart. And with everything he was going through with Charlie, well, he had more on his mind than the spinster schoolteacher in Bethany Beach.

One of the local stations confirmed what Vi said in his text. Gale-force winds, heavy rain, and flooding. The only good news was that the storm was tracking away from land. The Monday forecast was for mostly cloudy skies with a chance of light rain. She'd take off for Philadelphia immediately after class.

She found a number for Presbyterian and called and asked if someone could give her an update on Charlie's condition. Her request was turned down after the person on the line checked her name against their list of family members.

"Is there any chance you can connect me with someone from the family? Austin McGinnis, perhaps?"

"Ma'am, we have no way of knowing if they are here. Perhaps you should contact them personally."

"I would if I could," she said as she disconnected.

Then, a thought. Austin had said his sister was the person she'd spoken to when she'd called Cornerstone Properties. She called the number. It went straight to voicemail, which was understandable because Charlie was Holly's grandpa too. She was probably at the hospital.

Kathryn left a message for Austin to call her.

AUSTIN WOKE A LITTLE BEFORE NINE, feeling as if he hadn't even been to sleep. He had spent the night in his childhood bedroom. His baseball and soccer trophies were still on the dresser, dusted weekly by whatever cleaning service Mom was using these days.

More than anything he wanted to call Kathryn. What would he say though? She felt strongly that they needed some space, whatever that meant. At the very least, he could tell her that Grandpa was out of the woods. She would want to know.

The only problem was, he needed a phone.

He threw on the clothes he'd worn the day before and

went to see if Holly was up. They'd driven home together after leaving the hospital a little after midnight. Mom and Dad had remained.

The smell of bacon greeted Austin as he went downstairs. Holly sat at the kitchen table, nibbling on a plate of bacon and scrambled eggs. "Get ready," she said. "Mom and Dad are on their way home, and judging from the way they sounded on the phone, you're going to catch hell."

"Can I use your phone, sis?"

She pointed to where it lay on the counter. "Help yourself."

Austin picked it up.

"Dang it, I don't have the number memorized. Do you know of any way to find it?"

"Cellphone?" Holly asked.

"Yeah."

"Start with Google."

Austin entered Kathryn's name.

The only number that came back was from the college. A lot of good that would do on a Sunday. He scrolled through several pages and tried a couple variations of her name. Still nothing.

"Any luck?" Holly asked as she scooped up the last of her eggs.

"Nope, but there are a bunch of ads that will sell the number to me."

"Are you looking for *her* number?"

"She has a name. Kathryn."

"Sorry, little brother. I didn't mean to offend you. Mom and Dad will probably do enough of that. But about the number. Since she's single, she probably had her name removed from most of those databases. That's what I did."

They heard the garage door going up.

"Put your search on hold," Holly said, taking her plate to the sink. "Can I give you some advice?"

"Please do."

"Stand your ground, Austin. Don't let Mom and Dad dictate your life to you."

"You mean like they dictated yours?"

Holly flinched but didn't look away. Still, he could see that his question struck a nerve. "I'm sorry, sis, I just meant that—"

"Don't apologize. I love what I do. I just wish I would have had some time to know there wasn't something better out there first. You have that opportunity. Take it."

The kitchen door opened, and their parents stepped inside. They appeared haggard. Dad's heavy beard had moved past a five o'clock shadow into something that would take many guys a week to grow.

"How is Grandpa?" Holly asked.

Mom ran her hand through her hair. "Resting. The doctor says they'll take the intubation tube out late this afternoon. They are already cutting back on his sedation. He should be awake and able to communicate by evening." She turned her attention to Austin. "Come into the den. We need to talk. Holly, you come too."

"Mom, seriously," Holly protested. "You guys are exhausted. Get some sleep and let's talk after Grandpa is awake."

"No." Dad snapped. "Now."

RAIN PELTED the side of the house, but each time Kathryn checked, she saw the picket fence standing strong. She watched weather updates and checked her phone for messages through the early part of the morning until a little before ten when her doorbell rang.

It had to be Austin. Who else would be out in such terrible conditions? She jumped up and scampered to the door. "Hey!" she exclaimed as she pulled it open.

But it was Jane, stomping water from her rain boots. Kathryn pulled her inside. "Why are you out in this weather? Is everything okay?"

Jane pulled the hood down on her coat and wiped raindrops from her forehead. "Have you heard from Austin today?"

"No, he left his phone at the hospital and I can't... Jane, I told him we should break things off, then he found out that Charlie—you remember Charlie, don't you? Austin's grandfather?"

"That's why I'm here. We need to talk."

AUSTIN SAT on the sofa with Holly beside him, even though she could have stayed out of firing range. Mom and Dad stood while they told him how disappointed they were. Dad did most of the talking, and he didn't pull any punches. Austin had lied to them. He was responsible for tending to the rentals, keeping them ready as renters came and went. He was responsible for getting his grades up so he could avoid academic probation.

He almost reminded them that the rentals were being tended to and that his grades were up, but that would only make things worse.

To his parents, his most egregious mistake was pulling Grandpa into his plan. Emotion choked Mom's voice. "Austin, he could have been killed."

Tears filled his eyes, and he struggled to hold them back.

"Mom!" Holly slid closer and put her arm around Austin's shoulder.

"Holly, it's the truth," Dad said. "It's time for Austin to take responsibility for his actions."

Mom nodded. "Your dad called the management company we used before. They're covering the rental units through September. Austin, you will stay here for the rest of the summer. I'll monitor your coursework to make sure you get passing grades."

"I'm passing both classes. I have an A in Southern Lit."

Mom's voice rose as she snapped, "Is your college professor girlfriend doing the work for you?"

"No, Mom, I'm doing my own work." His shoulders tensed. The urge to stand and defend himself was strong, but it was probably better that he say what he had to say while sitting. "I've done a good job on the renovation. At a cost that is way below anything you would pay a local contractor."

"And look where that got us," Mom said. "My father nearly fell to his death."

"Mom! That wasn't—" He paused. Getting up and walking out was so tempting, but that wasn't something adults did. "Grandpa asked to help. I didn't reach out to him. He came to me."

"I'm going down to Bethany as soon as your grandfather is out of the woods," Dad said. "I'll find someone to finish the work. It'll probably cost me more now since they'll say they have to tear out some of what you've done, but maybe we can get it ready for next season."

Austin shot to his feet. "My work is good!"

The two remained rooted in place, locked in a faceoff

that Austin was determined not to lose. After a few moments, Dad waved his hand dismissively. "I don't have time for this," he mumbled as he left the room. Austin remained standing until he was gone. There was so much more he wanted to say. He loved his parents and knew they loved him, but they didn't *know* him.

Grandpa knew him. Even Holly knew him. Kathryn certainly knew him. She had taken the time to find out what was important to him. And she supported his dreams. Mom and Dad needed to know him that same way. He had to convince them he wasn't cut out to be a lawyer. He wanted to work with his hands. He wanted to be a carpenter.

And he wanted to be with Kathryn. The woman he loved. The woman who loved him.

But would he get that chance? Could he make her see that age meant nothing to him? That if the situation arose, he would happily stand beside her and take care of her?

All of that would have to wait, because in a few hours the doctors would remove Grandpa's breathing tube and allow him to begin his recovery. Austin had been praying since he first walked into the ICU that Grandpa would be able to return to his beloved workshop and the odd jobs he enjoyed doing for neighbors. He wanted Grandpa to be there when he got married. And to be present in the lives of his great-grandchildren. Even more importantly, he wanted Grandpa to be the vibrant, hearty man Austin had seen at Bethany Beach.

Instead of trying to change his parents' minds, Austin said nothing. There was a time for further confrontation, and that time wasn't now.

But that time would come.

﷽

THEY RETURNED to the hospital as a family, though little of consequence was said during the drive. Grandpa had been moved to a regular room, and when they finally found it and stepped inside, he was sitting up in bed. He looked rough but was awake.

Mom rushed to his side and hugged him. Everyone else was right behind her.

"Can you talk, Dad?" Mom asked.

Grandpa nodded. "A little." His voice was raspy and hard to hear, but the doctor had said that would pass quickly. Grandpa swallowed twice and coughed before asking, "Where's Ja..."

A look of concern flashed between Austin's parents. Holly grabbed Austin's hand.

"Jay is right here, Dad." Mom said, pulling Dad closer.

"Ja...?"

"I'm here, Charlie," Dad said.

Holly squeezed Austin's arm and whispered, "Doesn't he recognize Dad?"

Austin's mother stroked his forehead. "We're all here, Dad. Jay and me. And Holly and Austin too. You took a nasty fall, but you—"

Someone knocked at the door.

Austin opened it.

"Send whoever it is away, Austin," Mom said.

It was Jane. The sight of her made Austin's breath catch. Why was she there? Could that mean that Kathryn was there too?

"Jane!" Grandpa said with more force than he had shown earlier. "Jane!"

Jane rushed into the room and leaned over the bed. Grandpa lifted his head and kissed her cheek. The simple gesture left him spent and breathy, but smiling.

"Mom, Dad, Holly, this is Jane," Austin said, still not sure what the heck was going on. "She's a friend from Bethany Beach."

"Jane!" Grandpa said as he reached for her hand.

"I was so worried about you, Charlie."

Grandpa took several deep breaths, still getting used to breathing on his own. His brow was sweaty, but his smile showed everyone how delighted he was to see Jane. He lifted his hand and made a sweeping gesture. "Out," he rasped. "Just Jane."

||||||||

"DOES someone want to tell me what the hell just happened?" Dad said as the door closed behind them.

Mom's voice was loud enough to turn heads. "Why does Dad want to see her alone? What do you know about her, Austin?"

"Just that she's a retired schoolteacher that Grandpa met a couple weeks ago. Beyond that, not much."

"I will not stand for this," Mom said. "I'm going back and—"

"Folks, you're going to have to lower your voices and clear the hallway," a nurse chided from the nurses' station three doors away.

"We belong in there," Mom said, pointing to Grandpa's door.

"Only if the patient wants you in there," the nurse countered. "Until he does, I must ask you to move to the waiting area at the end of the hallway."

"But, he's... he's my..." Mom glanced at Austin, then at Holly, looking, it appeared, for support. Austin hadn't seen her that way before. She was usually in control of any situation. Holly picked up on it, too. She approached and took her arm. Mom allowed herself to be led away. Austin followed, wanting to let her know that things would be okay. He wanted to see her strong side return, even if it was directed at him.

"Mom, Holly and I will—"

He froze.

Was that... at the far end of the hall? Was that Kathryn?

His heart started to race.

Had she come to Philly?

Was it really her?

Her back was turned, and he couldn't be sure. He nearly yelled her name, but knew he shouldn't.

Then she turned.

It was her!

She smiled at him and made him want to run the length of the hall to be with her. To pull her into his arms and tell her he needed her.

And loved her.

But she had said that things needed to change. What if she still believed that? What if he ran to her and she stopped him? What if she had come to make sure Grandpa was okay, but also to tell him she still wanted to cool their relationship?

The possibility made his stomach roil.

So, he walked.

"Hello," he said when they were a few feet apart.

"I brought you this," Kathryn said, holding out his phone. "I came with Jane. Did you have any idea about what was going on between them?"

He smiled. And ached for her. "That they were seeing each other? No idea at all."

"More than seeing each other," Kathryn laughed. "Charlie has been staying there."

"That explains why he never complained about the Windermere," Austin said. "And why he's been showing up for work later and later."

"Austin?"

He turned.

Holly stood at the other end of the hallway, making sure he was okay.

"I'm good, sis." He turned back to Kathryn. "Care to take a walk?"

░░░░░

AUSTIN UPDATED her on Charlie's condition as they passed through the labyrinth of hallways that led to the hospital's main exit. Kathryn listened, but there was so much she wanted Austin to know—her feelings for him, how he had infused her life with love and excitement, and how much she regretted her boneheaded suggestion that they spend some time apart. If there was one thing she had learned from her ride to Philadelphia—other than that Jane was a badass driver in terrible weather—it was that love could mold itself to fit any situation. While not as unlikely a pair as she and Austin, Jane and Charlie came from much different backgrounds and interests, yet in just a couple weeks they had found a love that rivaled what she felt for Austin.

Sharing those thoughts was impossible in the bustling hospital hallway, though. Nor in the pelting rain they encountered when they stepped outside. Fortunately,

Austin was thinking ahead and grabbed a loaner umbrella from a box near the exit. He opened it and pulled her close. "Can I take you someplace?" he asked.

"Any place."

After a short walk, they came to a beautiful nineteenth century cathedral. The door was open, so they stepped inside and found seats in an area off to one side. "I don't know how long we'll be here before someone kicks us out," Austin said. "So I'll say what I have to say."

Kathryn's insides tensed, but she took a seat and tried to control her trembling.

"Yesterday you said you wanted to give me space to see other women. You did it because you're concerned about our age difference."

All Kathryn could do was nod.

"I don't accept that, Kate."

Her breath caught. What did he mean?

"I love you. I've known it for a long time, and there's nothing you can do to change it. Now, if you're sure you want us to see other people, I'll go along with it, but you need to know that there is no one else who can make me feel like you do."

"Austin, you need to think this through. When you're thirty, I'll be—"

"You'll be Kate. You'll be Kate when you're fifty and sixty and a hundred and ten."

"But it's not fair for you to—"

"Let *me* decide what is fair to me, Kate. My parents have tried to decide things for me in the past. I listened, and look at where I am. I'm almost finished with a degree I don't want in a field I hate. I have three more years of law school and then I go into practice. It sounds terrible, and I'm finally going to tell them it's not what I want." He paused and leaned his forehead against hers. "I'm making my own decisions, Kate, and the first is that I want you in my life."

Kathryn threw her arms around his neck. The tears came quickly.

"I want you so much." She smiled through her tears. "And I'm never letting you get away again."

TWENTY-SEVEN

monday, july 11

MOM AND DAD entered Grandpa's hospital room and looked about uncertainly. Jane was seated in a chair on Grandpa's left. Holly stood behind her. Austin and Kathryn were on Grandpa's right. And Vi stood at the end of the bed.

"Good morning," Grandpa said, his voice stronger than the day before.

"Dad," Mom said, "what's happening? You told us not to get here until ten thirty. Is everything all right?"

"We're having a meeting," Grandpa answered. "Let me introduce you to my friend, Vi. He has a much longer name, but my old brain can never remember it."

The professor stepped forward and offered his hand. "Vihaan Chakraborty. I'm one of Austin's professors at Penn."

Mom accepted the professor's hand, but she was definitely off her game. "Hello."

"Your son is the best student in my Southern Literature class, Mr. and Mrs. McGinnis. He has won the respect and admiration of his classmates for the way he delves into the material. If I knew he would be amenable, I would push him toward a career in the humanities."

Dad's laugh was harsh. "Austin's going to be a lawyer, but thanks anyway, Professor."

"Austin introduced Vi and me this summer," Grandpa continued. "We share a love of carpentry and a mutual admiration of my grandson." He turned to where Austin and Kathryn were standing. "This pretty thing—I know I'm not supposed to say things like that, but when I say it, I mean she's pretty inside and out—this is Kathryn."

Mom's uncertainty dissolved into something darker. Her eyes bored into Kathryn's, and she began to speak but held back, instead turning to Grandpa. "Dad, what is going on? Last night we honored your wishes to give you time with your new... friend, Jane, but we came here this morning expecting to have some time with you alone. And you need time to rest and recover."

"I'm much better, Charla. It was my decision to bring everyone together. I've made some decisions, and I wanted to get things sorted out before I told you."

Mom's eyes darted around the room. "Okay, but why don't we do this one-on-one rather than with a roomful of strangers? Just you and me? And Jay, of course."

"These aren't strangers, Charla. They're my friends. But if it will make it easier for you, I'll ask them to step out. Not Austin and Holly, though. They're family."

Mom glanced at Dad. He nodded.

Vi moved toward the door. Jane got to her feet with Holly's help. Austin squeezed Kathryn's hand, then she followed.

Things were going exactly as planned.

So far.

But Austin's stomach still hurt. Being at odds with his

parents wasn't something he was used to. But it was now or never.

"Sit down," Grandpa said to Mom, pointing to the chair Jane had vacated. Mom slid into the seat and started to speak, but Grandpa motioned for her to wait. "First things first," he said. "Stop blaming Austin for my accident."

"Dad, you should never have been on that roof. Austin knew better than to—"

"Dammit, Charla, I'm old, but I still make my own decisions. Even dumb ones like crawling up on a roof in a rainstorm. It was a mistake I won't make again, but even if I do, the blame lies with me."

"The fact remains," Dad jumped in, "that Austin lied to us about the renovation."

"He did, sort of." Grandpa countered. "But what would you have said if he had asked for permission?"

"That wasn't why we sent him down to Bethany Beach," Mom answered. "He had to work on his grades and take care of the properties."

"You heard what Vi said about his performance in class." Grandpa looked up at Holly. "Sweetheart, have you received any complaints from tenants or neighbors?"

"Only when Kathryn's fence got knocked down, and Austin took care of that."

Grandpa nodded. "So, there you are. Good grades, properties maintained. And the work he's done on that renovation has been as good as anything I did in my prime. He uses quality materials. He thinks things through. We're going to have ourselves a nice rental property when the work is done, and it won't cost us near what we would have paid to hire it out."

Grandpa's logic appeared to take the wind out of Mom's sails. Austin noticed how his father had eased into the background. He had never been one to argue with Grandpa. Part of that was because Dad derived his livelihood from the company his father-in-law had started. Even though he and Mom had taken it to new heights, Dad never forgot that it was Grandpa who laid the foundation.

And just like they had discussed before his parents' arrival, they were at the point where Austin would pick up the conversation. He straightened his shoulders and cleared his throat. "Mom, Dad, I'm not going to be a lawyer. I want to build houses."

"Austin, no," Mom said. "You're capable of so much more than carpentry." She quickly realized her gaffe. "Dad," she blurted. "I don't mean to disparage what you do. It's just that—"

"Mom, I'll be miserable as the company lawyer."

"But your test scores, Austin," Dad said. "Your SAT scores were even higher than Holly's."

"The family dummy," Holly said cheekily, getting laughs from everyone and providing a much-needed bit of comedy relief.

"That stuff always was easy for me, but I don't want to look back when I'm your age or Grandpa's age and wish I had taken a different road."

"Austin, we don't want you to drop out of college," Mom said. "What if you change your mind later and want to become a lawyer? Or something else?"

"I won't drop out. I'll just approach it a different way. Vi said he would help me get the coursework I need to graduate. Most of it can be done online. It might take me an extra year, but I'll get my degree. I owe that to you for all the love and support you've given me."

Mom and Dad eyed one another across the room. Was that the trace of a smile that crossed Dad's lips? Even if it was, Austin still knew that it was Mom he had to win over. And when she looked back at him, he saw it in her eyes. Things were going to work out. They were good people. Maybe a bit too deep into their work to see what was going on around them sometimes, but there was never any doubt they loved him.

"I'm going to need time to sort this all out," Mom said. She turned to Austin's dad. "Jay?"

Dad rubbed the back of his neck and sighed. "Are you going to join one of our crews? I can get that set up for you if it's what you want."

"We have a plan, Jay," Grandpa said. "It's something I've been working on since I started helping Austin, and when I shared it with him this morning, he asked to be included."

Holly pulled a file from her bag. She handed it to Grandpa, who opened it and spread papers across the bed in front of him. "Lean in so you can see," Grandpa said to Mom and Dad. "I think you'll agree that it's a pretty good plan."

friday,
september 2

THE GUY from planning and zoning was shaking his head as he came up the sidewalk. Fortunately for Austin and Grandpa, he was also smiling.

"Mr. Staley," he said, nodding at the catering truck in the driveway. "If I didn't know better, I would think that either you're trying to bribe me with food or you're celebrating an occupancy permit that I haven't granted yet."

"Mr. McCloud, I would never try to sway your decision," Grandpa said amiably. "And when you look around inside, pay no attention to the celebration we're planning for the moment you leave."

McCloud patted Grandpa on the arm, said a quick hello to Austin, and pulled a clipboard from his bag. "1705 Riley Street, correct?"

"Yes, sir," Austin said.

He glanced over the paperwork before stepping back to get a good look at the exterior.

"Is that lead paint on those windows?" he asked.

"Nope," Grandpa said. "None of that."

McCloud smiled again. He and Grandpa had developed a friendly rapport over the past several weeks, a relationship that Austin hoped would continue for many years.

"Who chose the exterior color?" McCloud asked.

Grandpa winked at Austin. "A nice lady professor at the community college. She thought pale yellow would fit in real well on this block."

McCloud nodded. "Now, about that new HVAC. Did you test it?"

"I did," Austin said. "Temperature readings are on target downstairs, and within three degrees on the second floor."

"Not bad," McCloud said. "These older houses always lose some efficiency upstairs, but there's not much you can do about it. Smoke detectors?"

"Yes, sir. In every room. I can show you."

"Not necessary." He paused again and gazed at the catering truck. "Yeah, maybe you should show me. The smoke detectors, I mean."

Grandpa opened the front door and waved McCloud in ahead of him.

"Folks," McCloud greeted the six people in the kitchen. He moved past folding tables loaded down with brisket, fried chicken, and a half-dozen side dishes, then reached up and pushed the button on a smoke detector. It screeched. He was satisfied.

The next several minutes stretched interminably as McCloud checked off boxes and made notes. Everyone waited for the okay to cut loose. Kathryn joined Austin at the island; Grandpa winked at Jane, who was getting around much better; Mom, Dad, and the Professor sat at the kitchen table; and Holly leaned against the fridge.

McCloud returned to the kitchen, sniffed the air, and

said, "That fried chicken certainly smells good. It reminds me of the chicken my mother used to make."

"There are sweet potato biscuits too," Jane said. "Can I fix you a plate?"

"That won't be necessary. I really shouldn't." He glanced at his clipboard, signed the bottom of the top page, and handed it to Austin. "There you go, young man. You are free to occupy the premises."

Vi rose and applauded as if they had just reached the end of a famous opera. The others joined in.

McCloud seemed embarrassed by the attention, but recovered quickly. "Now," he said, "I need to conduct a closer inspection of the chicken and biscuits."

The party was on. Holly opened the fridge and pulled out beer and homemade lemonade. Conversations picked up and laughter overflowed as everyone filled their plates.

Austin and Kathryn leaned against the counter to eat. McCloud stood beside them. "Have you got renters lined up?"

"The first ones arrive next week." Austin nodded at Holly, who was devouring a pulled pork sandwich. "My sister is handling that. Grandpa and I have two more houses we're starting on."

"You did fine work on this place, young man," McCloud said through a mouthful of chicken. "Did I hear you made an offer on that old bungalow on East Second Street?"

"We did. And I think we'll get it."

"It's in rough shape," McCloud said.

"We'll probably do a complete teardown and rebuild. By the way, Mr. McCloud, do you know a Walt Mickens?"

"Sure, I know Walt."

"He caught me at the hardware store day before yesterday. He has a commercial property on the edge of Bethany that needs rehabbing. I just wanted to make sure he's on the up and up."

"Walt grew up here. Now that place of his isn't much to look at. He runs the garage and keeps that up, but I'm guessing he's wanting to open the restaurant again."

"He thinks he might have a tenant for it."

"Getting that place up to code is going to be a big job. The last time the restaurant was open for business was pretty near twenty years ago. You make sure you get a good look before you bid it, son."

WATCHING the way Austin interacted with the inspector filled Kathryn's heart. He was taking to his new role with seriousness and enthusiasm. She loved the name he had bestowed on the new company. Picket Fence Construction and Renovation. A forever reminder about what brought them together. And Charlie being there to help and support the new venture, especially with Charla and Jay still lukewarm toward the changes in their son's life, was the cherry on the sundae.

At least they were cordial toward her. She understood their reticence. Learning that their only son was living with a woman they had never met was a lot to grasp, particularly on the heels of what had nearly become a family tragedy. They would come around in time though. Jay had asked a few questions about her background, a sure sign the frostiness was melting, but it looked like it might take longer for Charla.

Inspector McCloud finished his plate and prepared to go. "Anything else you need from me before I leave?"

"You like fishing, Mr. McCloud?" Charlie asked.

393

"Depends. I get sick as a dog out on the ocean, but I enjoy dropping a hook in calmer waters now and then. Why do you ask?"

"I just purchased a little place out on Vines Creek. The folks out there called yesterday to let me know we can close next week."

"Dad, what?" Charla said quickly.

"Grandpa?" Holly exclaimed. "I had no idea."

Kathryn grabbed Austin's arm. "Did you know about this?" she whispered.

He shook his head. "He never said a word."

"Charlie," Jay said. "Why? I thought you planned to just keep—" His face turned red, and everyone knew what he had been about to say.

"You figured I would just keep shacking up with Jane? Is that where you were going, Jay?"

"Uh, I meant..."

Charlie laughed and said, "It's okay, son. I decided to make Jane an honest woman. A preacher she knows is going to marry us out there week after next. The folks selling that place already have it cleaned out. We'll take possession Saturday the eighteenth and have our own little ceremony that afternoon in the backyard." As he spoke, he moved to a spot behind Jane's chair and rubbed her shoulders. "Jane's still a young thing, but at my age there's no need to delay."

AUSTIN HADN'T SEEN it coming. But he hadn't given Grandpa's budding romance a lot of thought, consumed as he was in his own. It made sense though. Grandpa and Jane had come of age in an era when people married first, then moved in together. They had certainly been inseparable since his accident.

It didn't just make sense, it was perfect. Grandpa was happier than he'd been since Grandma's passing. He seemed a decade younger than he had the day he'd loaned Austin his power tools. Austin raised his bottle in the air. "To Grandpa and Jane!"

The others followed his lead. Vi, Holly, and Kathryn hugged the prospective groom and his bride. Dad slapped Grandpa on the back. Inspector McCloud shook his hand, then grabbed another piece of chicken. Mom was smiling, but her eyes said she was still trying to sort everything out.

That was fine. There was plenty of time for sorting things out.

Besides, Austin had a surprise of his own, but it would be for Kathryn only.

🖌

KATHRYN GIGGLED when Austin pulled up in Calvin. She sprang from her seat on the porch and scurried to the street. Nightfall had arrived, and while tired from the busy day they'd had, she was excited about the evening ahead.

"You really have my curiosity piqued," she said as she got in. She kissed him on the cheek. "We haven't been on a date in Calvin since we went dumpster shopping."

"I wanted tonight to be special," Austin said. He pointed to the bag she had with her. "You remembered a jacket, right?"

"Of course. It's starting to feel like fall. Don't you love that feeling?"

"Yes. And I especially love how small Bethany Beach feels when the summer tourism season is over."

Kathryn scooted over and sat next to him. "So, tell me where we're going. I'm dying to know."

"You'll have to wait a little longer."

***

AUSTIN FOLLOWED Coastal Highway to an area a couple miles north of Bethany. He pulled onto a side road that led to a cluster of homes along the beach.

"Why are we—"

He raised a finger to his lips, and Kathryn smiled and stopped speaking. They pulled up to a security gate, and he punched a code that gave them access. The houses were amazing. Large and modern, with windows that allowed views in all directions. Austin steered Calvin off the road and onto a wide strip of patchy grass between two homes.

"Are we going to get arrested for—"

Again with the finger to the lips. He pulled Calvin down onto the sand and turned so the back of the truck faced the ocean.

"Stay here," he said. "And don't look."

Kathryn did as she was told.

Austin left the motor running and the radio tuned to an oldies station she liked. Other than the occasional creak or rattle from the bed of the truck, she heard little until he returned and opened her door. "Will you join me?"

"With pleasure," she said, taking his hand and allowing him to help her from the truck.

The air was fresh with the smell of salt water. The uncharacteristically calm ocean kissed the sand a few yards away. And just beyond Calvin's tailgate, Austin had placed two beach chairs in front of a small firepit. Between the chairs were two glasses and a bottle of champagne.

"Oh, my goodness. Austin? What are you—"

Was he about to...?

It couldn't be that. Sure, they had discussed getting married someday, but hadn't they agreed to wait a bit? Seeing how over the moon Charlie and Jane were had made her think maybe they should do that sooner instead of later.

But this soon?

"I brought you here to talk about something, Kate. Something that is very special to you."

The way he said it made it clear that there was something else. But what?

"I've been doing some reading the past few weeks."

"I haven't seen any books," Kathryn said.

"It's kind of a surprise. I wanted to read something that meant a lot to you." He reached for the canvas messenger bag she had bought him to celebrate passing his summer courses. After digging around, he pulled out a dog-eared paperback and held it up.

Kathryn laughed when she saw the title. "You read *Jane Eyre*?"

"I wanted to. Since that night at Elijah's when you and Vi were talking about Charlotte Brontë, I want to be part of discussions like that. And I know how much Brontë and this book mean to you."

She took the book from him and flipped through it absently. "But other than that night, I've never mentioned Charlotte Brontë. How did you—"

Austin placed a large bound book in her lap. "I read this."

When Kathryn turned it over and saw the title, tears

flooded her eyes. She looked from the book to Austin, then back again. "How did you find this?"

"I borrowed it through a lending service, but I enjoyed it so much I bought my own copy."

"And you actually read it?"

"Yes."

"The whole thing?"

"The whole thing."

She wiped her eyes with the back of her hand. "Austin, dear, nobody reads dissertations."

He pulled his chair closer and wrapped his arm around her shoulders. And the world felt more perfect than Kathryn had ever known it to feel.

"Someone read this one." He took the book from her lap and held it up in the firelight. "And now, Dr. Kathryn Shea, author of the wonderful doctoral thesis 'Charlotte Bronte— Her Life in Her Writing,' will you please allow me the pleasure of discussing your research and Miss Brontë's wonderful book?"

Kathryn leaned in and kissed him. "I can't think of anything I would enjoy more, Mr. McGinnis."

***

NINETY MINUTES SWEPT by as Kathryn delved into aspects of Jane Eyre that Austin had never considered. How her childhood affected her life as an adult and how Jane Eyre's life reflected the author's. Kathryn spoke with animation and affection, and Austin understood that her deep passion for literature was the same as he felt about his handiwork. They were from different worlds but were finding that those worlds could coexist without either getting lost.

"Why didn't you tell Vi that this was your dissertation subject?"

Kathryn pushed a lock of hair behind her ear. "We had just met, and to be honest I was intimidated. He's an Ivy League professor of literature, and here's little old me in lower Delaware. Now I realize it wouldn't matter."

They held hands while gazing at the fire and the ocean beyond. Whereas Austin used to be concerned that too much silence might be a bad thing, he now understood how people in love could enjoy quiet moments of introspection. The breeze picked up and caused the fire to bob and dance as a crescent moon hid and reemerged from the clouds.

"What are you thinking about, Kate?"

"Lots of things," she said with a sigh. "The end of summer. The beginning of school in a few days." She paused before adding, "Us."

Austin took a deep breath and relaxed into his chair. "We're thinking about the same things. Are you ready for the first day of school?"

"Don't rush it, mister," she teased. "I still have this weekend and Labor Day, but yeah, I'm ready. And excited."

"Vice President for Student Outreach." Austin drew out the words that still sounded strange to her after so many years in her previous position.

"I've already got a lot of stuff done," she said. "We're identifying students who might need additional support. Suzanne has agreed to chair a committee that clears obstacles for kids who are struggling. It's so exciting."

"How did Casper Fillmore react to your decision to keep teaching summer classes?"

Kathryn laughed. "He didn't like it at first, but with Rosa in my corner he didn't have much choice. Working down the hall from her is going to be amazing. And I don't think I would have accepted the position had they not let me continue teaching part-time." Kathryn turned so they were facing. "You helped me remember why I teach. Every good thing in my life right now is because of you."

It was getting chilly, and their comfy bed at home was tempting, but Kathryn was in no hurry to bring such a perfect evening to a close.

"You know what I thought you were about to do?" she asked as they watched the fire burn down.

"Ask you to marry me?"

"Yep."

"You know we're going to get married."

"I want that more than anything," she said. "But I also want it to be right for everyone."

"My parents?"

"Um-hmm. We're getting there."

Austin didn't need to say anything. There had been a lot of change in his life over the course of the summer. Mom and Dad deserved a chance to catch up. And they would. Soon enough.

She clutched his hand to her cheek and luxuriated in its warmth. "We've come so far, Austin. And I love you so much."

His face lit up. "I love you. And we have come far. Remember when fifteen years seemed like such a big deal?"

"Not for you," she said. "You seemed to know from the beginning. And you were right all along." Kathryn sighed.

"Fifteen years means nothing when there's love."

afterword

People sometimes ask if there is any truth behind the events, places, and people in our writing. In a word, yes! It would be impossible to write without including a little bit of ourselves and our lives and experiences.

Bethany Beach is the setting for *Drifting Together*. It's a wonderful community on the Delaware coast. Unlike **Rehoboth Beach** to the north and **Ocean City, Maryland** to the south, Bethany is smaller and more laid-back. Some streets in this book are real. We made others up. **Milo's**, where **Harvey Bodenschatz** yells at you if you order shirred eggs, is purely fictional.

Austin and Kathryn spend time in Rehoboth Beach, enjoying pizza on the boardwalk. This is a favorite pastime of ours, too, though we sometimes substitute **Thrasher's french fries** for pizza. **The bandstand** where Kathryn meets Scott is a well-known Rehoboth landmark. Other Delaware communities mentioned include **Georgetown**, **Laurel**, **Milford**, **Cape Henlopen**, and **Frederica**. You can see them all in an afternoon. Let us know if you do.

Near the end of the book Grandpa Staley buys a home

on **Vines Creek**. The creek is real, but good luck finding Grandpa Staley.

Elijah's sounds fun, doesn't it? A local joint where the music is loud and the beer is cold enough to give you a headache. An off-the-beaten-path destination that serves seafood fresh off the boat. There are plenty of great local dives on the Delmarva Peninsula. Unfortunately, Elijah's isn't one of them. If you try to follow the route Austin takes to get there, you'll wind up lost. Fortunately, the people of those parts are very friendly, so there will probably be someone nearby to help you find your way back to wherever you came from.

We love crab cakes! We especially like **Miss Eleanor's crab cakes**. If you read our short novel, **Connecting Flights**, you are already familiar with Miss Eleanor's famous crab cakes. Yep, they're the real deal. Unfortunately, you have to know somebody who knows somebody if you want to experience them. Miss Eleanor is Paul's mom. She's been making her crab cakes for decades, and they are the best. *The best.*

If you can't have Miss Eleanor's crab cakes, you can at least sample **Dogfish Head Beer**, a local favorite. Alison and her cousins, Erin and Wesley, give it rave reviews.

Calvin... ah, Calvin. Grandpa's trusted **1963 International pickup**. Paul learned to drive a stick in a truck exactly like Calvin. His grandfather traded it off twice, then bought it back both times. It's long gone now, but lives on in these pages.

Southern Delaware Community College doesn't exist. We mention **Delaware State University**, **Salisbury University**, and even **Frostburg State**. They're all real.

There are lots of other places mentioned, too. We don't

have enough space to go through all of them, so you'll just have to visit the Delaware beaches and find out for yourself.

And the books! We don't need to make those up. There are so many great ones. The three that Kathryn loans to Austin—*Chiefs* by Stuart Woods, *Lords of Discipline* by Pat Conroy, and *A Confederacy of Dunces* by John Kennedy Toole are three of Paul's favorites. If you want recommendations, you can email him at paul@robinpaulromance.com.

Everything comes back to Kathryn and Austin. They sure were fun to create. Two kind souls in search of the perfect mate. They are better together, we think. We hope you do, too.

Warm wishes,

Robin, Paul, and Alison

acknowledgments

Special thanks go to Paul's long-ago college roommate, Tom Moak, for sharing his knowledge of hand tools. Tom is an attorney in beautiful Eastern Kentucky these days, but does a lot of woodworking on the side. We had no idea what a brace-and-bit was until Tom enlightened us.

We appreciate our editor, Sally Bradley, and our cover designer, Berni Stevens. They do good stuff.

And to our Romance Review Crew, we appreciate your support. Keep doing what you do so well! A special thanks goes to Review Crew member Gloria Knipp.

And of course, to our readers. Thank you, thank you, thank you!

about robin paul

Robin Paul is the pen name of **Robin and Paul Wootten**. *Drifting Together* is their second novel. They live on Florida's Gulf Coast and in Kansas City.

These Three Publishing is a family affair. Daughter **Alison Correnti** joins Robin and Paul to handle social media and marketing. She lives in New Jersey.

We want to get to know you. Please check out our website at www.robinpaulromance.com. We have freebies, special offers, and news about upcoming events. You can also follow us on Facebook and Instagram.

Would you be kind enough to leave a review of *Drifting Together* on Amazon? It's quick and easy, and really helps us build our brand.

And finally, get ready for our next holiday book, **Christmas Carl**, which debuts this fall.

Made in the USA
Coppell, TX
08 July 2022

79715026R00226